EVERYMAN,

I WILL GO WITH THEE,

AND BE THY GUIDE,

IN THY MOST NEED

TO GO BY THY SIDE

EVERYMAN'S POCKET CLASSICS

LOVE
STORIES

EDITED BY DIANA SECKER TESDELL

EVERYMAN'S POCKET CLASSICS

Alfred A. Knopf New York London Toronto

THIS IS A BORZOI BOOK
PUBLISHED BY ALFRED A. KNOPF

This selection by Diana Secker Tesdell first published in
Everyman's Library, 2009

US website: www.randomhouse.com/everymans

ISBN: 978-0-307-27087-0 (US)
978-1-84159-602-0 (UK)

A CIP catalogue reference for this book is available from the
British Library

Typography by Peter B. Willberg

Typeset in the UK by AccComputing, North Barrow, Somerset

Printed and bound in Germany by GGP Media GmbH, Pössneck

LOVE
STORIES

Contents

GUY DE MAUPASSANT

CLAIR DE LUNE

ABBÉ MARIGNAN'S MARTIAL name suited him well. He was a tall, thin priest, fanatic, excitable, yet upright. All his beliefs were fixed, never varying. He believed sincerely that he knew his God, understood His plans, desires and intentions.

When he walked with long strides along the garden walk of his little country parsonage, he would sometimes ask himself the question: 'Why has God done this?' And he would dwell on this continually, putting himself in the place of God, and he almost invariably found an answer. He would never have cried out in an outburst of pious humility: 'Thy ways, O Lord, are past finding out.'

He said to himself: 'I am the servant of God; it is right for me to know the reason of His deeds, or to guess it if I do not know it.'

Everything in nature seemed to him to have been created in accordance with an admirable and absolute logic. The 'whys' and 'becauses' always balanced. Dawn was given to make our awakening pleasant, the days to ripen the harvest, the rains to moisten it, the evenings for preparation for slumber, and the dark nights for sleep.

The four seasons corresponded perfectly to the needs of agriculture, and no suspicion had ever come to the priest of the fact that nature has no intentions; that, on the contrary, everything which exists must conform to the hard demands of seasons, climates and matter.

But he hated woman – hated her unconsciously, and

despised her by instinct. He often repeated the words of Christ: 'Woman, what have I to do with thee?' and he would add: 'It seems as though God, Himself, were dissatisfied with this work of His.' She was the tempter who led the first man astray, and who since then had ever been busy with her work of damnation, the feeble creature, dangerous and mysteriously affecting one. And even more than their sinful bodies, he hated their loving hearts.

He had often felt their tenderness directed towards himself, and though he knew that he was invulnerable, he grew angry at this need of love that is always vibrating in them.

According to his belief, God had created woman for the sole purpose of tempting and testing man. One must not approach her without defensive precautions and fear of possible snares. She was, indeed, just like a snare, with her lips open and her arms stretched out to man.

He had no indulgence except for nuns, whom their vows had rendered inoffensive; but he was stern with them, nevertheless, because he felt that at the bottom of their fettered and humble hearts the everlasting tenderness was burning brightly – that tenderness which was shown even to him, a priest.

He felt this cursed tenderness, even in their docility, in the low tones of their voices when speaking to him, in their lowered eyes, and in their resigned tears when he reproved them roughly. And he would shake his cassock on leaving the convent doors, and walk off, lengthening his stride as though flying from danger.

He had a niece who lived with her mother in a little house near him. He was bent upon making a sister of charity of her.

She was a pretty, brainless madcap. When the abbé preached she laughed, and when he was angry with her she would give him a hug, drawing him to her heart, while he sought unconsciously to release himself from this embrace which nevertheless filled him with a sweet pleasure, giving him the sensation of paternity which slumbers in every man.

Often, when walking by her side, along the country road, he would speak to her of God, of his God. She never listened to him, but looked about her at the sky, the grass and flowers, and one could see the joy of life sparkling in her eyes. Sometimes she would dart forward to catch some flying creature, crying out as she brought it back: 'Look, uncle, how pretty it is! I want to hug it!' And this desire to 'hug' flies or lilac blossoms disquieted, angered, and roused the priest, who saw, even in this, the ineradicable tenderness that is always budding in women's hearts.

Then there came a day when the sexton's wife, who kept house for Abbé Marignan, told him, with caution, that his niece had a lover.

Almost suffocated by the fearful emotion this news roused in him, he stood there, his face covered with soap, for he was in the act of shaving.

When he had sufficiently recovered to think and speak he cried: 'It is not true; you lie, Mélanie!'

But the peasant woman put her hand on her heart, saying: 'May our Lord judge me if I lie, Monsieur le Curé! I tell you, she goes there every night when your sister has gone to bed. They meet by the river side; you have only to go there and see, between ten o'clock and midnight.'

He ceased scraping his chin, and began to walk up and down impetuously, as he always did when he was in deep thought. When he began shaving again he cut himself three times from his nose to his ear.

All day long he was silent, full of anger and indignation. To his priestly hatred of this invincible love was added the exasperation of her spiritual father, of her guardian and pastor, deceived and tricked by a child, and the selfish emotion shown by parents when their daughter announces that she has chosen a husband without them, and in spite of them.

After dinner he tried to read a little, but could not, growing more and more angry. When ten o'clock struck he seized his cane, a formidable oak stick, which he was accustomed to carry in his nocturnal walks when visiting the sick. And he smiled at the enormous club which he twirled in a threatening manner in his strong, country fist. Then he raised it suddenly and, gritting his teeth, brought it down on a chair, the broken back of which fell over on the floor.

He opened the door to go out, but stopped on the sill, surprised by the splendid moonlight, of such brilliance as is seldom seen.

And, as he was gifted with an emotional nature, one such as had all those poetic dreamers, the Fathers of the Church, he felt suddenly distracted and moved by all the grand and serene beauty of this pale night.

In his little garden, all bathed in soft light, his fruit trees in a row cast on the ground the shadow of their slender branches, scarcely in full leaf, while the giant honeysuckle, clinging to the wall of his house, exhaled a delicious sweetness, filling the warm moonlit atmosphere with a kind of perfumed soul.

He began to take long breaths, drinking in the air as drunkards drink wine, and he walked along slowly, delighted, marvelling, almost forgetting his niece.

As soon as he was outside the garden, he stopped to gaze upon the plain all flooded with the caressing light, bathed in that tender, languishing charm of serene nights. At each moment was heard the short, metallic note of the cricket, and distant nightingales shook out their scattered notes – their light, vibrant music that sets one dreaming, without thinking, a music made for kisses, for the seduction of moonlight.

The abbé walked on again, his heart failing, though he knew not why. He seemed weakened, suddenly exhausted; he wanted to sit down, to rest there, to think, to admire God in His works.

Down yonder, following the undulations of the little river, a great line of poplars wound in and out. A fine mist, a white haze through which the moonbeams passed, silvering it and making it gleam, hung around and above the mountains, covering all the tortuous course of the water with a kind of light and transparent cotton.

The priest stopped once again, his soul filled with a growing and irresistible tenderness.

And a doubt, a vague feeling of disquiet came over him; he was asking one of those questions that he sometimes put to himself.

'Why did God make this? Since the night is destined for sleep, unconsciousness, repose, forgetfulness of everything, why make it more charming than day, softer than dawn or evening? And why does this seductive planet, more poetic than the sun, that seems destined, so discreet is it, to illuminate things too delicate and mysterious for the light of day, make the darkness so transparent?

'Why does not the greatest of feathered songsters sleep like the others? Why does it pour forth its voice in the mysterious night?

'Why this half-veil cast over the world? Why these tremblings of the heart, this emotion of the spirit, this enervation of the body? Why this display of enchantments that human beings do not see, since they are lying in their beds? For whom is destined this sublime spectacle, this abundance of poetry cast from heaven to earth?'

And the abbé could not understand.

But see, out there, on the edge of the meadow, under the arch of trees bathed in a shining mist, two figures are walking side by side.

The man was the taller, and held his arm about his sweetheart's neck and kissed her brow every little while. They imparted life, all at once, to the placid landscape in which they were framed as by a heavenly hand. The two seemed but a single being, the being for whom was destined this calm and silent night, and they came towards the priest as a living answer, the response his Master sent to his questionings.

He stood still, his heart beating, all upset; and it seemed to him that he saw before him some biblical scene, like the love of Ruth and Boaz, the accomplishment of the will of the Lord, in some of those glorious stories of which the sacred books tell. The verses of the Song of Songs began to ring in his ears, the appeal of passion, all the poetry of this poem replete with tenderness.

And he said unto himself: 'Perhaps God has made such nights as these to idealize the love of men.'

He shrank back from the two who still advanced with arms intertwined. Yet it was his niece. But he asked himself now if he would not be disobeying God. And does not God permit love, since He surrounds it with such visible splendour?

And he went back musing, almost ashamed, as if he had intruded into a temple where he had no right to enter.

ITALO CALVINO

BLOOD, SEA

Translated by William Weaver

THE CONDITIONS THAT obtained when life had not yet emerged from the oceans have not subsequently changed a great deal for the cells of the human body, bathed by the primordial wave which continues to flow in the arteries. Our blood in fact has a chemical composition analogous to that of the sea of our origins, from which the first living cells and the first multicellular beings derived the oxygen and the other elements necessary to life. With the evolution of more complex organisms, the problem of maintaining a maximum number of cells in contact with the liquid environment could not be solved simply by the expansion of the exterior surface: those organisms endowed with hollow structures, into which the sea water could flow, found themselves at an advantage. But it was only with the ramification of these cavities into a system of blood circulation that distribution of oxygen was guaranteed to the complex of cells, thus making terrestrial life possible. The sea where living creatures were at one time immersed is now enclosed within their bodies.

Basically not much has changed: I swim, I continue swimming in the same warm sea, – *Qfwfq said*, – or rather, the inside isn't changed, what was formerly the outside, where I used to swim under the sun, and where I now swim in darkness, is inside; what's changed is the outside, the present outside, which was the inside before, that's changed all right; however, it doesn't matter very much. I say it doesn't matter very much and you promptly reply: What do you mean, the outside doesn't matter much? What I mean is that if you look at it more closely, from the point of view of the old outside, that is from the present inside, what is the present outside? It's simply where it's dry, where there is no flux or reflux, and as far as mattering goes, of course, that matters too, inasmuch as it's the outside, since it's been on the outside, since that outside has been outside, and people believe it's more deserving of consideration than the inside. When all is said and done, however, even when it was inside it mattered, though in a more restricted range or so it seemed then. This is what I mean: less deserving of consideration. Well, let's start talking right now about the others, those who are not I, our neighbor: we know our neighbor exists because he's outside, agreed? Outside like the present outside. But before, when the outside was what we swam in, the very dense and very warm ocean, even then there were the others, slippery things, in that old outside, which is like the present inside, and so it is now when I've changed places and given the wheel to Signor Cècere, at the Codogno service station, and in front, next to him, Jenny Fumagalli has taken the passenger's seat, and I've moved in back with Zylphia: the outside, what is the outside? A dry environment, lacking in meaning, a bit crammed (there are four of us in a Volkswagen), where all is indifferent and interchangeable, Jenny Fumagalli, Codogno, Signor Cècere, the service station, and as far as Zylphia is concerned, at the moment when I placed my hand on her knee, at perhaps 15 kilometers from Casalpusterlengo, or else she was the one who started touching me, I don't remember, since outside events tend to be confused, what I felt, I mean the sensation that came from outside, was really a weak business compared to what went through my blood and to what I have felt ever since then, since the time when we were swimming together in the same torrid, blazing ocean, Zylphia and I.

The underwater depths were red like the color we see now only inside our eyelids, and the sun's rays penetrated to brighten them in flashes or else in sprays. We undulated with no sense of direction, drawn by an obscure current so light that it seemed downright impalpable and yet strong enough to drag us up in very high waves and down in their troughs. Zylphia would plunge headlong beneath me in a violet, almost black whirlpool, then soar over me rising toward the more scarlet stripes that ran beneath the luminous vault. We felt all this through the layers of our former surface dilated to maintain the most extended possible contact with that nourishing sea, because at every up and down of the waves there was stuff that passed from outside of us to our inside, all sustenance of every sort, even iron, healthful stuff, in short, and in fact I've never been so well as I was then. Or, to be more precise: I was well since in dilating my surface I increased the possibilities of contact between me and this outside of me that was so precious, but as the zones of my body soaked in marine solution were extended, my volume also increased at the same time, and a more and more voluminous zone within me became unreachable by the element outside, it became arid, dull, and the weight of this dry and torpid thickness I carried within me was the only shadow on my happiness, our happiness, Zylphia's and mine, because the more she splendidly took up space in the sea, the more the inert and opaque thickness grew in her too, unlaved and unlavable, lost to the vital flux, not reached by the messages I transmitted to her through the vibration of the waves. So perhaps I could say I'm better off now than I was then, now that the layers of our former surface, then stretched on the outside, have been turned inside out like a

21

glove, now that all the outside has been turned inward and has entered and pervaded us through filiform ramifications, yes, I could really say this, were it not for the fact that the dull arid zone has been projected outward, has expanded to the extent of the distance between my tweed suit and the fleeting landscape of the Lodi plain, and it surrounds me, swollen with undesired presences such as Signor Cècere's, with all the thickness that Signor Cècere, formerly, would have enclosed within himself – in his foolish manner of dilating uniformly like a ball – now unfolded before me in a surface unsuitably irregular and detailed, especially in his pudgy neck dotted with pimples, taut in his half-starched collar at this moment when he is saying: 'Oh, you two on the back seat!' and he has slightly shifted the rear-view mirror and has certainly glimpsed what our hands are doing, mine and Zylphia's, our diminutive outside hands, our diminutively sensitive hands that pursue the memory of ourselves swimming, or rather our swimming memory, or rather the presence of what in me and Zylphia continues swimming or being swum, together, as then.

This is a distinction I might bring up to give a clearer idea of before and now: before, we swam, and now we are swum. But on sober reflection I prefer not to go into this, because in reality even when the sea was outside I swam in it the same way I do now, without any intervention of my will, that is to say I was swum even then, no more nor less than now, there was a current that enfolded me and carried me this way and that, a gentle and soft fluid, in which Zylphia and I wallowed, turning on ourselves, hovering over abysses of ruby-colored transparence, hiding among turquoise-coloured filaments that wriggled up from the depths; but these sensations of movement – wait and I'll explain it to you – were due only to what? They were due to a kind of general pulsation, no, I don't want to confuse things with the way they are now, because since we've been keeping the sea closed inside us it's natural that in moving it should make this piston effect, but in those days you certainly couldn't have talked about pistons, because you would have had to imagine a piston without walls, a combustion chamber of infinite volume as the sea appeared infinite to us, or rather the ocean, in which we were immersed, whereas now everything is pulsation and beating and rumble and crackling, inside the arteries and outside, the sea within the arteries that accelerates its course as soon as I feel Zylphia's hand seeking mine, or rather, as soon as I feel the acceleration in the course of Zylphia's arteries as she feels my hand seeking hers (the two flows which are still the same flow of a same sea and which are joined beyond the contact of the thirsty fingertips); and also outside, the opaque thirsty outside that seeks dully to imitate the beat and rumble and crackling of inside, and vibrates in the accelerator under Signor Cècere's foot, and all the line of cars stopped at the exit from the superhighway tries to repeat the pulsing of the ocean now buried inside us, of the red ocean that was once without shores, under the sun.

It is a false sense of movement that this now-motionless line of cars transmits, crackling; then it moves and it's as if it were still, the movement is false, it merely repeats signs and white stripes and roadbeds; and the whole journey has been nothing but false movement in the immobility and indifference of everything that is outside. Only the sea moved and moves, outside or inside, only in that movement did Zylphia and I become aware of each other's presence, even if then we didn't so much as graze each other, even if I was undulating in this direction and she in that, but the sea had only to quicken its rhythm and I became aware of

Zylphia's presence, her presence which was different, for example, from Signor Cècere, who was however also around even then and I could sense him as I felt an acceleration of the same sort as that other one but with a negative charge, that is the acceleration of the sea (and now of the blood) with regard to Zylphia was (is) like swimming toward each other, or else like swimming and chasing each other in play, while the acceleration (of the sea and now of the blood) with regard to Signor Cècere was (is) like a swimming away to avoid him, or else like swimming toward him to make him go away, all of this involving no change in the relationship of our respective distances.

Now it is Signor Cècere who accelerates (the words used are the same but the meanings change) and passes an Alfa Romeo in a curve, and it is with regard to Zylphia that he accelerates, to distract her with a risky maneuver, a false risky maneuver, from the swimming that unites her and me: false, I say, as a maneuver, not as a risk because the risk may well be real, that is to our inside which in a crash could spurt outside; whereas the maneuver in itself changes nothing at all, the distances between Alfa, curve, Volkswagen can assume different values and relationships but nothing essential happens, as nothing essential happens in Zylphia, who doesn't care a bit about Signor Cècere's driving, at most it is Jenny Fumagalli who exults: 'My, isn't this car fast?' and her exultation, in the presumption that Signor Cècere's bold driving is for her benefit, is doubly unjustified, first because her inside transmits nothing to her that justifies exultation, and secondly because she is mistaken about Signor Cècere's intentions as he in turn is mistaken, believing he is achieving God knows what with his showing off, just as she, Jenny Fumagalli, was mistaken before about my intentions, when I was at the wheel and she at my side, and there in back

24

next to Zylphia Signor Cècere, too, was mistaken, both concentrating – he and Jenny – on the reverse arrangement of dry layers of surface, unaware – dilated into balls as they were – that the only real things that happen are those that happen in the swimming of our immersed parts; and so this silly business of passing Alfas meaning nothing, like a passing of fixed, immobile, nailed-down objects which continues to be superimposed on the story of our free and real swimming, continues to seek meaning by interfering with it, in the only silly way it knows, risk of blood, a false return to a sea of blood which would no longer be blood or sea.

Here I must hasten to make clear – before by another idiotic passing of a trailer truck Signor Cècere makes all clarification pointless – the way that the common blood-sea of the past was common and at the same time individual to each of us and how we can continue swimming in it as such and how we can't: I don't know if I can make this sort of explanation in a hurry because, as always, when this general substance is discussed, the talk can't be in general terms but has to vary according to the relationship between one individual and the others, so it amounts practically to beginning all over again at the beginning. Now then: this business of having the vital element in common was a beautiful thing inasmuch as the separation between me and Zylphia was so to speak overcome and we could feel ourselves at the same time two distinct individuals and a single whole, which always has its advantages, but when you realize that this single whole also included absolutely insipid presences such as Jenny Fumagalli, or worse, unbearable ones such as Signor Cècere, then thanks all the same, the thing loses much of its interest. This is the point where the reproductive instinct comes into play: we had a great desire, Zylphia and I, or at least I had a great desire, and I think she must have had it too, since she was willing, to multiply our presence in the sea-blood so that there would be more and more of us to profit from it and less and less of Signor Cècere, and as we had our reproductive cells all ready for that very purpose, we fell to fertilizing with a will, that is to say I fertilized everything of hers that was fertilizable, so that our presence would increase in both absolute number and in percentage, and Signor Cècere – though he too made feverish clumsy efforts at reproducing himself – would remain in a minority – this was the dream, the virtual obsession that gripped me – a minority that would become smaller and smaller, insignificant, zero point zero zero etc. per cent, until he vanished into the dense cloud of our progeny as in a school of rapid and ravenous anchovies who would devour him bit by bit, burying him inside our dry inner layers, bit by bit, where the sea's flow would never reach him again, and then the sea-blood would have become one with us, that is, all blood would finally be our blood.

This is in fact the secret desire I feel, looking at the stiff collar of Signor Cècere up front: make him disappear, eat him up, I mean: not eat him up myself, because he turns my stomach slightly (in view of the pimples), but emit, project, outside myself (outside the Zylphia-me unit), a school of ravenous anchovies (of me-sardines, of Zylphia-sardines) to devour Signor Cècere, deprive him of the use of a circulatory system (as well as of a combustion engine, as well as the illusory use of an engine foolishly combustive), and while we're at it, devour also that pain in the neck Fumagalli, who because of the simple fact that I sat next to her before has got it into her head that I flirted with her somehow, when I wasn't paying the slightest attention to her, and now she says in that whiny little voice of hers:

'Watch out, Zylphia' (just to cause trouble), 'I know that gentleman back there . . .' just to suggest I behaved with her before as I'm behaving now with Zylphia, but what can la Fumagalli know about what is really happening between me and Zylphia, about how Zylphia and I are continuing our ancient swim through the scarlet depths?

I'll go back to what I was saying earlier, because I have the impression things have become a bit confused: to devour Signor Cècere, to ingurgitate him was the best way to separate him from the blood-sea when the blood was in fact the sea, when our present inside was outside and our outside, inside; but now, in reality, my secret desire is to make Signor Cècere become pure outside, deprive him of the inside he illicitly enjoys, make him expel the lost sea within his pleonastic person; in short, my dream is to eject against him not so much a swarm of me-anchovies as a hail of me-projectiles, rat-tat-tat to riddle him from head to foot, making him spurt his black blood to the last drop, and this idea is linked also to the idea of reproducing myself with Zylphia, of multiplying with her our blood circulation in a platoon or battalion of vindictive descendants armed with automatic rifles to riddle Signor Cècere, this in fact now prompts my sanguinary instinct (in all secrecy, given my constant mien as a civil, polite person just like the rest of you), the sanguinary instinct connected to the meaning of blood as 'our blood' which I bear in me just as you do, civilly and politely.

Thus far everything may seem clear: however, you must bear in mind that to make it clear I have so simplified things that I'm not sure whether the step forward I've made is really a step forward. Because from the moment when blood becomes 'our blood', the relationship between us and blood changes, that is, what counts is the blood insofar as it is 'ours', and all the rest, us included, counts less. So there was in my impulse toward Zylphia, not only the drive to have all the ocean for us, but also the drive to lose it, the ocean, to annihilate ourselves in the ocean, to destroy ourselves, to torment ourselves, or rather – as a beginning – to torment her, Zylphia my beloved, to tear her to pieces, to eat her up. And with her it's the same: what she wanted was to torment me, devour me, swallow me, nothing but that. The orange stain of the sun seen from the water's depths swayed like a medusa, and Zylphia darted among the luminous filaments devoured by the desire to devour me, and I writhed in the tangles of darkness that rose from the depths like long strands of seaweed beringed with indigo glints, raving and longing to bite her. And finally there on the back seat of the Volkswagen in an abrupt swerve I fell on her and I sank my teeth into her skin just where the 'American cut' of her sleeves left her shoulder bare, and she dug her sharp nails between the buttons of my shirt, and this is the same impulse as before, the impulse that tended to remove her (or remove me) from marine citizenship and now instead tends to remove the sea from her, from me, in any case to achieve the passage from the blazing element of life to the pale and opaque element which is our absence from the ocean and the absence of the ocean from us.

The same impulse acts then with amorous obstinacy between her and me and with hostile obstinacy against Signor Cècere: for each of us there is no other way of entering into a relationship with the others; I mean, it's always this impulse that nourishes our own relationship with the others in the most different and unrecognizable forms, as when Signor Cècere passes cars of greater horse-power than his, even a Porsche, through intentions of mastery toward these superior cars and through ill-advised amorous intentions toward Zylphia and also vindictive ones toward me and also self-destructive ones toward himself. So, through risk, the insignificance of the outside manages to interfere with the essential element, the sea where Zylphia and I continue our nuptial flights of fertilization and destruction: since the risk aims directly at the blood, at our blood, for if it were a matter only of the blood of Signor Cècere (a driver, after all, heedless of the traffic laws) we should hope that at the very least he would run off the road, but in effect it's a question of all of us, of the risk of a possible return of our blood from darkness to the sun, from the separate to the mixed, a false return, as all of us in our ambiguous game pretend to forget, because our present inside once it is poured out becomes our present outside and it can no longer return to being the outside of the old days.

So Zylphia and I in falling upon each other in the curves play at provoking vibrations in the blood, that is, at permitting the false thrills of the insipid outside to be added to those that vibrated from the depths of the millennia and of the marine abysses, and then Signor Cècere said: 'Let's have a nice plate of spaghetti at the truck drivers' café,' masking as generous love of life his constant torpid violence, and Jenny Fumagalli, acting clever, spoke up: 'But you have to get to the spaghetti first, before the truck drivers, otherwise they won't leave you any,' clever and always working in the service of the blackest destruction, and the black truck with the license Udine 38 96 21 was there ahead, roaring at its forty m.p.h. along the road that was nothing but curves, and Signor Cècere thought (and perhaps said): 'I'll make it,' and he swung out to the left, and we all thought (and didn't say): 'You can't make it,' and in fact, from the curve the Jaguar was already arriving full tilt, and to avoid it the Volkswagen scraped the wall and bounced back to scrape its side against the curved chrome bumper and, bouncing, it struck the plane tree, then went spinning down into the precipice, and the sea of common blood which floods over the crumpled metal isn't the blood-sea of our origin but only an infinitesimal detail of the outside, of the insignificant and arid outside, a number in the statistics of accidents over the weekend.

T. CORAGHESSAN BOYLE

SWEPT AWAY

from *The New Yorker*

PEOPLE CAN TALK, they can gossip and cavil and run down this one or the other, and certainly we all have our faults, our black funks and suicides and wives running off with the first man who'll have them and a winter's night that stretches on through the days and weeks like a fore-taste of the grave, but in the end the only real story here is the wind. The puff and blow of it. The ceaselessness. The squelched keening of air in movement, running with its currents like a new sea clamped atop the old, winnowing, harrowing, pinching everything down to nothing. It rakes the islands day and night, without respect to season, though if you polled the denizens of Yell, Funzie, and Papa Stour, to a man, woman, lamb, and pony they would account winter the worst for the bite of it and the sheer frenzy of its coming. One January within living memory, the wind blew at gale force for twenty-nine days without remit, and on New Year's Eve back in '92 the gusts were estimated at two hundred and one m.p.h. at the Muckle Flugga light-house here on the northernmost tip of the Isle of Unst. But that was only an estimate: the weather service's wind gauge was torn from its moorings and launched into eternity that day, along with a host of other things, stony and animate alike.

Junie Ooley should have known better. She was an Amer-ican woman – 'the American ornithological woman' is the way people around town came to refer to her, or sometimes just 'the bird woman' – and she hadn't just barely alighted from the ferry when she was blindsided by Robbie Baikie's old one-eyed tom, which had been trying to inveigle itself across the roof tiles of the kirk after an imaginary pigeon. Or perhaps the pigeon wasn't imaginary, but by the time the cat blinked his eyes whatever he had seen was gone with the wind. At any rate, Junie Ooley, who was at this juncture a stranger to us all, came banking up the high street in a store-bought tartan skirt and a pair of black tights, with a rucksack flailing at the small of her back and both hands clamped firmly to her knit hat, and she never saw the cat coming, for all her visual acuity and the fine-ground photographic lenses she trucked with her everywhere. The cat – his name was Tiger and he must have carried a good ten or twelve pounds of pigeon-fed flesh on his bones – caught a gust and flew off the kirk tiles like a heat-seeking missile locked in on Junie Ooley's hunched and flapping form.

The impact was dramatic, as you would have had reason to testify had you been meditating over a pint of bitter at the rattling window of Magnuson's Pub as we were that day, and the bird woman, before she'd had a chance even to discover the whereabouts of her lodgings or offer up a 'Good day' or 'How do you do?' to a single soul, was laid out flat on the flagstones, her lips quivering unconsciously over the lyrics to a tune by the Artist Formerly Known as Prince. At least, that was what Robbie claimed afterward, and he's always been dead keen on the Artist, ever since he came by the CD of *Purple Rain* in the used-disc bin of a record shop in Aberdeen and got it for less than half of what it would have cost new. We had to take his word for it. He was the first one out the door and come to her aid.

There she was, flung down on the stones like a wilted flower amid the crumpled stalks of her limbs, the rucksack

34

stuffed full of spare black tights and bird-watching paraphernalia, her kit and dental floss and all the rest, and Tiger just pulling himself up into a ball to blink his eyes and lick at his spanned paws in a distracted way, when Duncan Stout, ninety-two years on this planet and in possession of the first Morris automobile ever manufactured, came down the street in that very vehicle at twice his normal speed of five and a half miles per hour, and if he discerned Junie Ooley lying there was anybody's guess. Robbie Baikie flailed his arms to head off Duncan's car, but Duncan was the last man in these islands to be expecting anything unexpected out there in the middle of the high street designed and reserved exclusively for the traffic of automobiles and lorries and the occasional dithering bicycle. He kept coming. His jaw was set, his cap pulled down to the orbits of his milk-white eyes. Robbie Baikie was not known for thinking on his feet – like many of us, he was a deliberative type – and before he thought to scoop Junie Ooley up in his arms the car was on them. Or just about.

People were shouting from the open door of the pub. Magnus Magnuson himself was in the street now, windmilling his arms and flinging out his feet in alarm, the bar rag still clutched in one hand like a flag of surrender. The car came on. Robbie stood there. Hopeless was the way it looked. But then we hadn't taken the wind into account, and how could any of us have forgotten its caprices, even for a minute? At that crucial instant, a gust came up the canyon of the high street and bowled Robbie Baikie over atop the bird woman even as it lifted the front end of Duncan's car and flung it into the nearby street lamp.

The wind skreeled off down the street, carrying bits of paper, cans, bottles, old bones, rags, and other refuse along with it. The bird woman's eyes blinked open. Robbie Baikie, all fifteen stone of him, lay pressed atop her in a defensive posture, anticipating the impact of the car, and he hadn't even thought to prop himself on his elbows to take some of the crush off her. Junie Ooley smelled the beer on him and the dulcet smoke of his pipe tobacco and the sweetness of the peat fire at Magnuson's and maybe even something of the sheep he kept, and she couldn't begin to imagine who this man was or what he was doing on top of her in the middle of the public street. 'Get off me,' she said in a voice so flat and calm Robbie wasn't sure he'd heard it at all, and because she was an American woman and didn't commonly make use of the term 'clod', she added, 'you big doof'.

Robbie was shy with women – we all were, except for the women themselves, and they were shy with the men, at least for the first five years after the wedding – and he was still fumbling with the notion of what had happened to him and to her and to Duncan Stout's automobile and couldn't have said one word even if he'd wanted to.

'Get off,' she repeated, and she'd begun to add physical emphasis to the imperative, writhing beneath him and bracing her upturned palms against the great unmoving slabs of his shoulders.

Robbie went to one knee, then pushed himself up even as the bird woman rolled out from under him. In the next moment, she was on her feet, angrily shifting the straps of her rucksack where they bit into the flesh, cursing him softly but emphatically and with a kind of fluid improvisatory genius that made his face light up in wonder. Twenty paces away, Duncan was trying to extricate himself from his car, but the wind wouldn't let him. Howith Clarke, the greengrocer, was out in the street now, surveying the damage with a sour face, and Magnus was right there in the middle of things, his voice gone hoarse with excitement. He was inquiring after Junie Ooley's condition – 'Are you all right, lass?' – when a gust lifted all four of them off their feet and sent them tumbling like ninepins. That was enough for Robbie. He picked himself up, took hold of the bird woman's arm, and frog-marched her into the pub.

In they came, and the wind with them, packets of crisps and beer coasters sailing across the polished surface of the bar, and all of us instinctively grabbing for our hats. Robbie's head was bowed and his hair blown straight up off his crown as if it had been done up by some mad cosmetologist, and Junie Ooley heaving and thrashing against him till he released her to spin away from him and down the length of the bar. No one could see how pretty she was at first, her face all deformed with surprise and rage and the petulant crease stamped between her eyes. She didn't so much as look in our direction, but just threw herself back at Robbie and gave him a shove as if they were children at war on the playground.

'What the hell do you think you're doing?' she demanded, her voice piping high with her agitation. And then, glancing round at the rest of us: 'Did you see what this, this big *idiot* did to me out there?'

No one said a word. The smoke of the peat fire hung round us like a thin curtain. Tim Maconochie's Airedale lifted his head from the floor and laid it back down again. The bird woman clenched her teeth, set her shoulders. 'Well, isn't anybody going to do anything?'

Magnus was the one to break the silence. He'd slipped back in behind the bar, unmindful of the chaff and bits of this and that that the wind had deposited in his hair. 'The man saved your life, that's about all.'

Robbie ducked his head out of modesty. His ears went crimson.

'Saved –?' A species of comprehension settled into her eyes. 'I was . . . something hit me, something the wind blew. . . .'

Tim Maconochie, though he wasn't any less tightfisted than the rest of us, cleared his throat and offered to buy the girl a drop of whiskey to clear her head, and her face opened up then like the sun coming through the clouds so that we all had a good look at the beauty of her, and it was a beauty that made us glad to be alive in that moment to witness it. Whiskeys went round. A blast of wind rattled the panes till we thought they would burst. Someone led Duncan in and sat him down in the corner with his pipe and a pint of ale. And then there was another round, and another, and all the while Junie Ooley was perched on a stool at the bar talking Robbie Baikie's big glowing ears right off him.

That was the beginning of a romance that stood the whole island on its head. Nobody had seen anything like it, at least since the two maundering teens from Cullivoe had drowned themselves in a suicide pact in the Ness of Houlland, and it was the more surprising because no one had ever suspected such depths of passion in a poor slug like Robbie Baikie. Robbie wasn't past thirty, but it was lassitude and the brick wall of introspection that made him sit at the bar till he carried the weight of a man twice his age, and none of us could remember seeing him in the company of a woman, not since his mother died, anyway. He was the sort to let his sheep feed on the blighted tops of the heather and the wrack that blew up out of the sea, and he kept his heart closed up like a lockbox. And now, all of a sudden, right before our eyes, he was a man transformed. That first night, he led Junie Ooley up the street to her lodgings like a gallant out of the picture films, the two of them holding hands and leaning into the wind while cats and flowerpots and small children flew past them, and it seemed that he was never away from her for five minutes consecutive after that.

He drove her all the wind-blasted way out to the bird sanctuary at Herma Ness and helped her set up her equipment in an abandoned crofter's cottage of such ancient provenance that not even Duncan Stout could say who the landlord might once have been. The cottage had a thatched roof, and though it was rotted through in half a dozen places and perfervid with the little lives of crawling things and rodents, she didn't seem particular. It was in the right place, on a broad barren moor that fell off into the sea among the cliffs where the birds made their nests, and that was all that mattered.

There was no fuss about Junie Ooley. She was her own woman, and no doubt about it. She'd come to see and study the flocks that gathered there in the spring – the kittiwakes, puffins, terns, and northern fulmars nesting the high ledges and spreading wide their wings to cruise out over the sea – and she had her array of cameras and telephoto lenses to take photographs for the pricey high-grade magazines. If she had to rough it, she was prepared. There were the cynical among us who thought she was just making use of Robbie Baikie for the convenience of his Toyota minivan and the all-purpose, wraparound warmth of him, and there was no end to the gossip of the biddies and the potboilers and the kind who wouldn't know a good thing if it fell down out of Heaven and conked them on the head, but there were also those who saw it for what it was: love, pure and simple.

If Robbie had never much bothered about the moorits and Cheviots his poor dead and buried father had bred up over the years, now he positively neglected them. If he lost six blackface ewes stranded by the tide or a Leicester tup caught on a bit of wire in his own yard, he never knew it. He was too busy elsewhere. The two of them – he and the bird woman – would be gone for a week at a time, scrabbling over the rock faces that dropped down to the sea, she with her cameras, he with the rucksack and lenses and the black bottles of stout and smoke-tongue sandwiches, and when we did see them in town they were either having tea at the hotel or holding hands in the back nook of the pub. They scandalized Mrs Dunwoodie, who let the rooms over the butcher's shop to Junie Ooley on a monthly basis, because she'd seen Robbie coming down the stairs with the girl on more than one occasion and once in the night had heard what could only have been the chirps and muffled cries of coital transport drifting down from above. And a Haroldswick man – we won't name him here, for decency's sake – even claims that he saw the two of them cavorting in the altogether outside the cottage at Herma Ness.

One night when the wind was up, they lingered in Magnuson's past the dinner hour, murmuring to one another in a soft indistinguishable fusion of voices, and Robbie drinking steadily, pints and whiskeys both. We watched him rise for another round, then weave his way back to the table, a pint clutched in each of his big red hands. 'You know what we say this time of year when the kittiwakes first return to us?' he asked her, his voice booming out suddenly and his face aflame with the drink and the very joy of her presence.

Conversations died. People looked up. He handed her the beer and she gave him a sweet, inquisitive smile and we all wished the smile were for us and maybe we begrudged him it just the smallest bit. He spread his arms and recited a little poem for her, a poem we all knew as well as we knew our own names, the heart stirrings of an anonymous bird-lover lost now to the architecture of time:

Peerie mootie! Peerie mootie!

O, du love, du joy, du Beauty!

Whaar is du came frae? Whaar is du been?

Wi di swittlin feet and di glitterin een?

It was startling to hear these sentiments from Robbie Baikie, a man's man who was hard even where he was soft, a man not given to maundering, and we all knew then just how far overboard he'd gone. Love was one thing – a rose blooming atop a prickly stem risen up out of the poor soil of these windswept islands, and it was a necessary thing, to be nourished surely – but this was something else altogether. This was a kind of fealty, a slavery, a doom – he'd given her *our* poem, and in public, no less – and we all shuddered to look on it.

'Robbie,' Magnus cried out in a desperation that spoke for us all, 'Robbie, let me stand you a drop of whiskey, lad,' but if Robbie heard him he gave no sign of it. He took the bird woman's hand, a little bunch of chapped and wind-blistered knuckles, and brought it to his lips. 'That's the way I feel about you,' he said, and we all heard it.

It would be useless to deny that we were just waiting for the other shoe to drop. There was something inhuman in a passion as intense as that – it was a rabbity love, a tup's love, and it was bound to come crashing down to earth, just as the Artist lamented so memorably in 'When Doves Cry'. There were some of us who wondered if Robbie even listened to his own CDs anymore. Or heeded them.

And then, on a gloomy grey dour day with the wind sitting in the north and the temperatures threatening to take us all the way back to the doorstep of winter again, Robbie came thundering through the front door of the pub in a hurricane of flailing leaves, thistles, matchbooks, and fish-and-chips papers and went straight to the bar for a double whiskey. It was the first time since the ornithological woman had appeared among us that anyone had seen him alone, and if that wasn't sign enough there were those who could divine by the way he held himself and the particular roseate hue of his ears that the end had come. He drank steadily for an hour or two, deflecting any and all comments – even the most innocuous observations about the weather – with a grunt or even a snarl. We gave him his space and sat at the window to watch the world tumble by.

Late in the day, the light of the weltering sun slanted through the glass, picking out the shadow of the mullions, and for a moment it laid the glowing Cross of our Saviour in the precise spot where Robbie's shoulder blades conjoined. He heaved a sigh then – a roaring, single-malt, tobacco-inflected groan it was, actually – and finally those massive shoulders began to quake and heave. The barmaid (Rose Ellen MacGooch, Donal MacGooch's youngest) laid a hand on his forearm and asked him what the matter was, though we all knew. People made their voices heard so he wouldn't think we were holding our breath; Magnus made a show of lighting his pipe at the far end of the bar; Tim Maconochie's dog let out an audible fart. A calm settled over the pub, and Robbie Baikie exhaled and delivered up the news in a voice that was like a scouring pad.

He'd asked her to marry him. Up there, in the crofter's hut, the wind keening and the kittiwakes sailing through the air like great overblown flakes of snow. They'd been out all morning, scaling the cliffs with numb hands, fighting the wind, and now they were sharing a sandwich and a bottle of stout over a turf fire. Robbie had kissed her, a long, lingering lover's kiss, and then, overcome by the emotion of the moment, he'd popped the question. Junie Ooley had drawn herself up, the eyes shining in her heaven-sent face, and told him that she was flattered by the proposal, flattered and moved, deeply moved, but that she just wasn't ready to commit to something like that, like marriage, that is, what with him being a Shetland sheepman and she an American woman with a college degree, and a rover at that. Would he come with her to Patagonia to photograph the chimango and the nandu? Or to the Okefenokee Swamp in search of the elusive ivorybill? To Singapore? São Paulo? Even Edinburgh? He said he would. She called him a liar. And then they were shouting and she was out in the wind, her knit cap torn from her head in a blink and her hair beating mad at her green eyes, and he tried to pull her to him, to snatch her arm and hold her, but she was already at the brink of the cliff, already edging her way down amid the fecal reek and the raucous avian cries. 'Junie!' he shouted. 'Junie, take my hand, you'll lose your balance in this wind, you know you will! Take my hand!'

And what did she say then? 'I don't need any man to cling to.' That was it. All she said and all she wrote. And he stood in the blast, watching her work her way from one handhold to another out over the yawning sea as the birds careened around her and her hair strangled her face, and then he strode back to the minivan, fired up the engine, and drove back into town.

That night, the wind soughed and keened and rattled like a set of pipes through the canyon of the high street on till midnight or so, and then it came at us with a new sound, a sound people hadn't heard in these parts since '92. It was blowing a gale. Shingles fled before the gusts, shrubs gave up their grip on the earth, the sheep in the fields were snatched up and flung across the countryside like so many puffs of lint. Garages collapsed, bicycles raced down the street with no more than a ghost at the pedals. Robbie was unconscious in the sitting room of his cottage at the time, sad victim of drink and sorrow. He'd come home from the pub before the wind rose up in its fury, boiled himself a plate of liver muggies, then conked out in front of the telly before he could so much as lift a fork to them.

It was something striking the side of the house that brought him to his senses. He woke to darkness, the electric gone with the first furious gusts, and at first he didn't know where he was. Then the house shuddered again and the startled bellow of the Ayrshire cow he kept for her milk and butter roused him up out of the easy chair and he went to the door and stuck his head out into that wild night. Immediately the door was torn from his grasp, straining back on its hinges with a shriek even as the pale form of the cow shot past and rose up like a cloud over the shingles of the roof. He had one thought then, and one thought only: *Junie. Junie needs me.*

It was his luck that he carried five hundred pounds of coal in the back of his minivan as ballast, as so many of us do, because without it he'd never have kept the thing to the road. As it was, he had to dodge the hurtling sheep, rabbits that flew out of the shadows like nightjars, posts torn from their moorings, the odd roof or wall, even a boat or two lashed up out of the heaving seas. He could barely see the road for the blowing trash, the wind slammed at him like a fist, and he had to fight the wheel to keep the car from flipping end over end. If he was half looped when he climbed into the car, now he was as sober as a foud, all the alcohol in his veins burned away with the terrible anxiety that drove him. He put his foot to the floor. He could only pray that he wouldn't be too late.

Then he was there, fighting his way out of the car, and he had to hold to the door to keep from being blown away himself. The moor was as black as the hide of an Angus bull. The wind shrieked in every passage, scouring the heather till it lay flat and cried out its agony. He could hear the sea battering the cliffs below. It was then that the door of the minivan gave way, and in the next instant he was coasting out over the scrub like a tobogganer hurtling down Burra-firth Hill, and there'll be men to tell you that it was a tree that saved him from going over, but what tree could grow on an island as stingy as this? It was a thornbush is what it was, a toughened black unforgiving snarl of woody pith combed down to the ground with fifty years of buffeting, but it was enough. The shining white door of the minivan ran out to sea as if it would run forever, an awkward big plate of steel that might as well have been a Frisbee sailing out over the waves, but Robbie Baikie was saved, though the thorns dug into his hands and the wind took the hair off his head and flailed the beard from his cheeks. He squinted against the airborne dirt and the darkness, and there it was, two hundred yards away and off behind him to the left: the crofter's cottage, and with her in it. 'Junie!' he cried, but the wind beat at the sound of his voice and carried it away till it was no voice at all. 'Junie!'

As for her, the bird woman, the American girl with the legs that took the breath out of you and the face and figure that were as near perfection as any man here had ever dreamed of on the best night of his life, she never knew that

45

Robbie had come for her. What she did know was that the wind was very bad. Very bad. She must have struggled against it and realized how futile it was to do anything more than succumb to it, huddle and cling and wait it out. Where were the birds? she wondered. How would they weather this – on their wings? Out at sea? She was cold, shivering, the fire long since consumed by the gusts that tore at the chimney. And then the chimney went, with a sound of claws raking at a windowpane. There was a crack, and the roof beams gave way, and then it was the night staring down at her from above. She clung to the andirons, but the andirons blew away, and then she clung to the stones of the hearth, but the stones were swept away as if they were nothing more than motes of dust, and what was she supposed to cling to then?

We never found her. Nobody did. There are some who'll say she was swept all the way to the coast of Norway and came ashore speaking Norse like a native, or that a ship's captain, battened down in a storm sea, found her curled round the pocked safety glass of the bridge like a living figurehead, but no one really believes it. Robbie Baikie survived the night and he survived the mourning of her, too. He sits even now over his pint and his drop of whiskey in the back nook at Magnuson's, and if anybody should ask him about the only love of his life, the bird woman from America, he'll tell you he's heard her voice in the cries of the kittiwakes that swarm the skies in spring, and seen her face there, too, hanging over the black crashing sea on the stiff white wings of a bird. Poor Robbie.

ELIZABETH BOWEN

DEAD MABELLE

THE SUDDEN AND horrible end of Mabelle Pacey gave her a publicity with the European press worth millions to J. and Z. Gohigh of Gohigh Films Inc., Cal., USA. Her personality flashed like a fused wire. Three-year-old films of Mabelle – with scimitar-curves of hair waxed forward against the cheeks, in the quaint creations of 1924 – were recalled by the lesser London and greater provincial cinemas. *The Merry Magdalene* – Mabelle with no hair to speak of, in a dinner jacket – was retained for weeks by the 'Acropolis' and the 'Albany', wide-porticoed palaces of the West End; managers of the next order negotiated for it recklessly and thousands had to be turned away during its briefer appearances in Edinburgh, Dublin and Manchester. The release of her last, *Purblind*, was awaited breathlessly. Her last, when brimming with delighted horror, horrified delight, with a sense of foreknowledge as though time were being unwound from the reel backwards, one would see all Mabelle's unconsciousness under the descending claw of horror. Nothing she had ever mimicked could approach the end that had overtaken her. It was to be, this film, a feast for the epicure in sensation; one would watch the lips smile, the gestures ripple out from brain to finger-tips. It was on her return from the studio at the end of the making of this very picture that she had perished so appallingly.

The management of the Bijou Picturedrome at Pamsleigh considered themselves fortunate in having secured *The*

White Rider, a 1923 production. Since dusk, on a framework erected above the façade of the Picturedrome, green electricity scrawled 'Mabelle' in the rainy sky. She was with them for three nights only; the habitués streamed in; uncertain patrons, pausing under her superscription, thumbed the edge of a florin, looked up and down the street, and when the metal ticket finally clicked out, dived still two-thirds reluctant into the stifling tunnel of tobacco fumes and plush. From half-past five, for half an hour before the first showing, the entrance curtain never settled down into stillness; at half-past eight another rush began.

William Stickford's afternoon at the Bank went by distractedly. He was intelligent, solitary, self-educated, self-suspicious; he had read, without system, enough to trouble him endlessly; text-books picked up at random, popular translations, fortnightly publications (scientific and so on) complete in so many parts, potted history and philosophy – philosophy all the time. On walks alone or lying awake in the dark he would speculate as to the nature of reality. 'What am I – but *am* I? If I am, what else is? If I'm not, is anything else? *Is* anything...' He would start awake, sweating, from a nightmare of something that felt like an empty barrel rolling over the ups and downs in his brain and bumping into craters that were the craters of the moon, or of going round to the house where he lived to pay a surprise call on himself and being sent away with a head-shake, told point-blank he had never been heard of here. Sometimes – an idle but anguishing sport of the mind – he told himself he was the victim of some practical joke on the scale of the universe of which everybody and everything, from the stars and the Manager to the pipe-cleaners, tooth-soap and bootlaces fringing his existence, were linked in furtive enjoyment.

He never 'went with a girl'; his landlady deplored this; to do so, she said, would make him more natural-like. She liked a young fellow to *be* a young fellow, and William apparently wasn't. His Manager, a kind unperceptive old man who believed in the personal touch, asked him up for a musical evening to meet his nieces, but William achieved being shy and aggressive, looked askance round the side of his glasses, snubbed the nieces and couldn't relax with the Manager. The girls discouraged their uncle from asking him home again. A fellow at the Bank called Jim Bartlett succeeded in knowing him up to a point; *he* couldn't get Jim quite into focus but he supposed he liked him all right. Jim would force his way in of an evening, paw his books with a snigger of admiration and sit with his feet on the fender and the soles of his boots steaming till twelve o'clock, till one's brain went stiff and dry. Theoretically, William needn't have listened, but he did listen; other existences tugged at him with their awful never-dismissable, never-disposable of possibility, probability even. Sometimes Jim forced him out. William was cinema-shy, he resisted the cinema till a man with important-looking initials mentioned it in a weekly review as an 'art-form'; then he went there with Jim and saw Mabelle. 'I can't think,' Jim had said, that first evening, impatiently gathering up his change at the box-office, 'how a lot of this girl's stuff ever gets past the censor.' William expected Mabelle's appeal to be erotic and went in armoured with intellectuality, but it was not erotic – that *he* could see.

The film had begun; with a startled feeling he had walked down the tilted gangway towards Mabelle's face and the dark-and-light glittering leaves behind. A caption: 'Can't you believe me?' then a close-up: Mabelle's face jumped forward at him, he stepped back on to Jim's toe and stared at a moon-shaped white light in an eye, expecting to see himself reflected. He stood for a moment, feeling embraced in her vision. 'Confound you!' said Jim and pushed him sharp to the left. They waded through to their places; William sat down, shaken, and put up a hand to his eyes. 'It's beastly jumpy,' he said, 'I always heard they were jumpy.'

'You get used to them – Gosh, what a lovely girl, isn't she? Look at that, old man, look at that for a figure!'

It had been all very abstract, he recognized in it some hinterland of his brain. He understood that passion and purity, courage, deception and lust were being depicted and sat there without curiosity, watching Mabelle. That was some five months ago, before her death; she had long been known to the connoisseur, but her real vogue was only then beginning. She had an unusual way with her, qualities overlapped strangely; in that black-and-white world of abstractions she alone moved in a blur. Each movement, in unexpected relation to movements preceding it, outraged a preconception. William sat with an angry, disordered feeling as though she were a rising flood and his mind bulrushes. She had a slow, almost diffident precision of movement; she got up, sat down, put out a hand, smiled, with a sparklingly mournful air of finality, as though she were committing herself, and every time William wanted to rise in his seat and say 'Don't, don't – not before all these people!' Her under lids were straight, she would lean back her head and look over them. Her upper lids arched to a point, she had three-cornered eyes; when her face went into repose the lids came down slowly, hiding her eyes for moments together. When she looked up again that dark, dancing, direct look came out as it were from hiding, taking one unawares. It was as though she leaned forward and touched one.

William, who suffered throughout from a feeling of being

detained where he had no business, was glad when the film was over. He said on the way home, 'She's awfully different from what I expected, I must say.' Jim Bartlett responded 'Aha?' He kept saying 'Aha!' with an infinite archness and refusing to volunteer much about Mabelle himself. 'She's got temperament,' was the most William got out of him. 'You know what I *mean*; temperament. Jolly rare thing. She ought to play Irish Storm in *The Green Hat.*' That night it was William who wanted to bring Jim in and keep him talking. Not that Jim's ineptitudes were any more tolerable, but he had a feeling of someone at home in him, in possession, very assured in the darkness, mutely and sardonically waiting till he was alone.

A week or so later he saw in the local paper that *The Fall*, featuring Mabelle, was showing at Belton, ten miles off. Eluding Jim, he bicycled that same evening over to Belton. He pedalled furiously, mounting the steep sleek high-road over the ridge, his brain a cold clamour of self-curiosity. Enlightened shamefully, burning, he bicycled home in the teeth of an icy wind. Next morning, cornered by Jim's too pressing inquiries, he lied as to where he had been. It had been Jim's fault, he shouldn't have asked him.

Thought, as he understood thought, became pale and meaningless, reading scarcely more than a titillation of the eye-balls. Lapses appeared in his work. He was submerged by uneasiness, alternately, as it were, straining after a footfall and slamming a door.

There was this thing about Mabelle: the way she made love. She was tired, oh fearfully tired. Her forehead dropped down on the man's shoulder, her body went slack; there seemed no more hope for her than for a tree in a hurricane. When her head fell back in despair, while the man devoured her face horribly, one watched her forgotten

53

arm hang down over his shoulder: the tips of the fingers twitched. What was she thinking about, what did women think about – *then*?

One night Jim Bartlett, routing about among William's possessions, pulled out the *Picturegoer* from between some books and the wall. On the cover Mabelle, full length, stood looking sideways, surprised and ironical, elegantly choked by a hunting-stock, hair ruffled up as though she had just pulled a hat off, hand holding bunched-up gauntlets propped on a hip. Jim, shocked into impassivity, stared at the photograph. His pipe sticking out at an angle from his expressionless face reminded William of a pipe stuck into a snowman.

'Pretty photograph, isn't it?' said William aggressively, to shatter the bulging silence.

Jim removed his pipe thoughtfully. 'Upon my word,' he began, 'upon my *word*! You really *are* you know. I mean really, old man –'

'I got it for you, as a matter of fact. If you hadn't gone messing about I'd have –'

'Oo-hoo,' said Jim, 'we don't think. No, *don't* think –'

'Then don't think. And damn you, get out!'

They were always very polite to each other at the Bank; there was little coarse talk or swearing. Jim Bartlett was very much shocked and went home. Next morning William apologized. 'Say nothing more about it, old man,' said Jim nicely. 'I quite understand. Beg yours, I'm sure. If I'd had any idea you were going to take it like that –' Good-feeling made him perfectly goggle-eyed. He came round punctually that same evening to hear all about it. William was out; he remained out till half-past eleven. He did this three evenings successively, avoiding Jim at the Bank, and after that Jim didn't come any more.

If William had been open and manly about the business, as pal to pal, Jim Bartlett would have been discretion itself. As it was, in the course of events, he told all the other fellows. They told the Manager's nieces, who told the Manager: the Manager soon had occasion to speak to William seriously about work and excessive cinema-going. This concentration of interest upon him, of derision, hardened him outwardly, heightened his sensibility. He avoided the 'Bijou' at Pamsleigh, the 'Electra' at Belton, but took excursion tickets to London and saw Mabelle there. Expeditions to the remoter suburbs were often necessary, he would sup or take tea dazedly in gas-lit pastry-cooks' and wander between showings of the film through anonymous vacant streets. Life all these months rushed by him while he stood still.

William never looked at his newspaper before lunchtime; others did. One morning, coming to the Bank he was aware of a tension, of a scared shy greediness in the others' faces, of being glanced at and glanced across. Jim Bartlett came up once or twice, looked strangely, flinched off, cleared his throat and kept on beginning – 'I say . . .'

'What's up?' snapped out William, exasperated by what seemed a new form of persecution.

'Nothing much – seen the paper?'

'No.'

Jim Bartlett, driven and urgent, fidgeted round in a semicircle under the blank and intense glare of William's glasses. 'There's something – look, come home to dinner.'

'Oh, thanks, I don't think so,' said William in the consequential sleek little voice he'd assumed. Jim tugged at the lobe of a crimson ear helplessly, shrugged a 'So be it, then', and went off.

In his sitting-room, the *Daily Mail* was propped against William's water-jug. Mabelle's name blazed out over the

centre column, with 'Fearful Death'. With a sudden stillness, with a feeling of awful, extended leisure, William put
out his hand for the paper. While he read he kept putting
his hand up and touching his throat. Each time he did
this he started as though he had touched someone else, or
someone else had touched him. He read carefully down to
the end of the column, looked over the top of the paper
and saw his chop slowly congealing behind it. He ran from
the room and was violently sick. When this was over he
took up the paper again, but he couldn't read well, the lines
bulged and dipped. He waited a little to see if he was going
to be sick any more, then went out and bought all the other
papers. Coming out of the newsagent's he met the wind
tearing down the street. He stood on the kerbstone, not
knowing which way to go; the wind got into the papers and
rattled and sang in them; they gave out an inconceivable
volume of sound to which he believed the whole town must
turn round and listen. He looked this way and that, then
pressing the papers against him ran across the street and
went into the church. Here he read all the other versions.
Physical detail abounded. He sat for a long time crushed up
to a wall in the gloom of a pew, then went back to the Bank.

Five weeks later, *The White Rider* featuring Mabelle Pacey
came to Pamsleigh. 'Going?' said Jim to William, who
seemed to have 'got over things' wonderfully well. 'Oh, I
dunno,' said William, 'I've some work on at home' (he was
doing one of those correspondence courses), 'I don't know
that I've got time.'

On Monday and Tuesday he did not go to the Picturedrome; he disappeared utterly, no one knew where he had
gone. The last day of Mabelle was Wednesday; Wednesday came.

The afternoon at the Bank went by, then, distractedly. Rain fell past the tall windows blurring the outlook, the trickle and stutter of drops racked the nerves. With dread, William looked up at the clock again and again, uneager as never before for release, half hoping by some resolution, some obduracy, to staunch the bleeding-away of the minutes. The door to the back passage was open for some minutes; William kept looking away from it, and while he was looking away Mabelle stood there, leaning a shoulder against the lintel, smiling and swinging a gauntlet. She was confident he would be there tonight. He faced round to the empty doorway. Mightn't she as well be *there* who wasn't anywhere? Who was not. She was incapable now of confidence, of a smile, of pressure against a lintel. He had faced for these last weeks her absolute dissolution. At that reiteration, in his mind and the doorway, of emptiness, he must have made some movement or sound, for the others looked up from their ledgers. William coughed and showed himself as in some agony of calculation; the faces dropped. The afternoon dwindled out, the office shrank in the dusk and began to be crowded with shadows. Somebody climbed on a chair with a taper; the gas coughed alight and the rain sliding and streaming down the window-panes scintillated against the thickening night. Woven securely into the room's industrious pattern William rested, but now the pattern was torn up violently into shreds of clamour and movement. They all went home. William lingered over his ledger a long time, but was finally drawn out after them.

At ten past eight he was pushing against the 'Bijou's' interior curtain. Its voluminousness, a world of plush, for some moments quenched and smothered him; a prickly contact to hands and face, exhaling a warm dankness. The attendant fought him out of it, taking away his ticket.

'Standing room only! –' he grudged her her little triumph, he had been told that outside. He chose a place along the transverse gangway and gripped with hands still pricking from the plush a cold brass rail behind the expensive seats.

He looked down a long perspective, a flickering arcade of shadow. For twenty seconds or so there was no one – the trees' fretful movements, the dazzlingly white breaking-through of the sky. The orchestra wound off their tune with a flourish and sharply, more noticeably, were silent down in their red-lighted pit. The flutter and click of machinery streamed out across the theatre, like the terrified wings of a bird imprisoned between two window-panes – it gave him the same stretched sensation of horror and helplessness. A foreign whiteness, a figure, more than a figure, appeared; a white-coated girl on a white horse drawn sideways across the distant end of the drive. She listened, all tense, to that same urgent flutter and clicking, then wheeled the horse round and dashed forward into the audience, shadows streaming over her. William recoiled from the horse's great hammer-head, the hoofs dangerous as bells, the flick of the eyeballs. He looked up with a wrench at his being; advancing enormously, grinning a little at the moment's intensity, Mabelle looked down. They encountered. Visibly thunder-ing, horse and rider darkened the screen.

Gripping the bar tight, William leaned back to look up at the bright, broadening shaft from the engine-room directed forward above him. Along this, fluid with her personality, Mabelle (who was now nothing) streamed out from reel to screen, thence rebounded to his perception. It was all, her intense aliveness, some quivering motes which a hand put out with intention would be able to intercept. The picture changed focus, receded; Mabelle, in better perspective, slipped from her horse and stood panting and listening;

the horse turned its head, listened too. Their sympathy, their physical fineness, sent a quiver across the audience. In protest, a burst of assertion, the music began again. '*Tum* – tirumti *tum* – turum ti *too*, rum ti *too* –' Mabelle tied her horse to a tree and turned off cautiously into the forest.

The man was there, in a glade, that man she generally acted with, whom one had a dozen times watched her make herself over to, her recurring lover. He stood with his back to a tree, with a grin as of certainty, waiting for her. However much he might repel at the outset, however craven, false or overtly lustful he might show himself, he had her ultimately, he had to have her, every film. She liked her men fallible (evidently); unsympathetic to audiences, subject to un-timely spasms of passion. It brought out all her coolness, her lovely desperation, her debonair fatedness. Her producer kept this well in mind. With unavailing wariness she now came stepping with her white-breeched legs, the light glanc-ing off her riding-boots, high over the fallen trees, low under the overhanging branches. Shadow struck off her head again and again. The man smiled, threw his cigarette away, stepped round his tree and closed with her ... A poignant leap-back, one was shown the white horse standing, tor-mented by intuition, tossing its head uneasily, twitching its ears.

William had come late, the end was sooner than he expected. Mabelle in a black straight dress, in meekness and solitude, stood by a high stone mantel looking into a fire. The preceding caption was red, the light now tinged with a realistic redness. Flames, in leisurely anticipation of their triumph, spurted and leapt at her feet; the firelight fingered its way up her, crept round her arms' fine moulding, her throat, her chin, with curbed greed, assurance, affection almost. She stood there – to the eyes of that four-years later audience – dedicated. It was as though the fire knew... A log crashed in, she started, looked with appalled eyes away from the fire. She was waiting.

Oh, *Mabelle*... She was too real, standing there, while more and more of her came travelling down the air. She seemed perpetual, untouchable. You couldn't break that stillness by the fire; it could shatter time. You might destroy the film, destroy the screen, destroy her body; this endured. She was beyond the compass of one's mind; one's being seemed a fragment and a shadow. Perished, dissolved in an agony too fearful to contemplate (yet he had contemplated it, sucked meaning out till fact had nothing more to give), she returned to this, to this imperishable quietness. Oh, *Mabelle*...

Somewhere a door opening, light that lanced the darkness. Movement went through her like the swerve of a flame. She held her arms out, the illusion shattered, she was subject once again to destiny. William sharply turned with tight-shut eyes. He groped his way along the guiding bar, was at fault a moment, collided with the attendant looping back the curtain for the exodus. He went out slowly, into the glaring vestibule, down the three steps into the lit-up, falling rain. Rain brushed his face, drops here and there came through to the roots of his hair. He put his hat on; heard the drops, defeated, pattering on the brim.

The street, unreal as that projected scene, was wide; he hesitated half way across it, then slowly turned to the left. Behind, inside the open doors, he heard as it were a wave break, a crash of freed movement, a rasping sigh. The band played the National Anthem. Feasted with her they all came streaming out, and she, released from their attention, dismissed, dispelled now – where was she?

His way home was at an angle from the High Street, up

a by-path. Water in the steep gutters hissed and gurgled. There were spaces of inky darkness, here and there some lamplight dimly caught a patch of humid wall. He looked back, once, towards the town and the Picturedrome. One moment 'Mabelle' was blazing emerald over the white façade; the next the lights were out, 'Mabelle', the doors beneath, had disappeared. So she went. In another month or so, when her horror faded and her vogue had died, her films would be recalled – boiled down, they said. He had heard old films were used for patent leather; that which was Mabelle would be a shoe, a bag, a belt round some woman's middle. These sloughed off, what of her? 'You're here,' he said, and put out a hand in the darkness. '*You* know *I* know you're here, you proud thing! Standing and looking. Do you see me? . . . You're more here than I . . .'

Going blindly, he passed within inches of a pair of lovers, plastered together speechlessly under the wall. A too urgent pressure had betrayed them by the creak of a mackintosh. Love! His exaltation shuddered at the thought of such a contact. Then for a moment under the blight of that dismal embrace, he had lost her. Mabelle . . . *Mabelle*? Ah, here . . .

Here, by him, burning into him with her actuality all the time. Burdening him with her realness. He paused again where a bicycle with lighted lamp had been leant up against some palings. The murky dark-yellow light streamed across the rain; some ghostly chrysanthemums drained of their pinks and yellows raised up their heads in a clump in it, petals dishevelled and sodden. As he watched, one stem with its burden detached itself and swayed forward, dipped through the lamplight and vanished. He listened and heard the stem snap. How – why – while the other stems stood up erect and unmoving, sustaining their burden? *Who* had –?

Oh no, not that! He began to be terrified. 'Don't press

me too hard, I can't stand it. I love you too much. Mabelle, look here – don't!' He looked beyond the chrysanthemums, left and right, everywhere. She was there, left, right, everywhere, printed on darkness.

William, at home in his sitting-room, walked about in a state of suspension, looking, without connection of thought, at his books and pictures. A clock struck twelve, it was already tomorrow. *This* morning he'd be at the Bank, back again in the everyday, no one the wiser. Now he could sleep a short time, then life, that abstraction behind the business of living, was due to begin again. *He* was alive, enclosed in a body, in the needs of the body; tethered to functions. In the gaslight it looked rather shabby, this business of living. Greasy stains on the tablecloth where he'd slopped his dinner over the edge of his plate, greasy rim round the inside of his hat where he'd sweated. This was how one impressed oneself on the material. And on the immaterial? – Nothing. Comfortless, perilous, more perishable than the brains in his skull even, showed his structure of thought. He had no power of being.

Of feeling? Only that life was worth nothing because of Mabelle who was dead. And by death, had he hope that he wouldn't quench himself utterly while Mabelle, who impinged herself everywhere, brightly burned on?

The right-hand top drawer of his bureau was empty of what such a drawer should contain: the means to the only fit gesture that he could have offered her. He had jerked the drawer open with an unconscious parade of decision, an imitation, more piteously faithful than he was aware, of something which, witnessed again and again under the spell of that constant effusion from Mabelle, had seemed conclusively splendid. The hand slipped, unfaltering into the back of the drawer, the gesture of pistol to temple, the trail of smoke fugitive over an empty screen . . .

He was denied this exit. Under the stare, vaguely mocking, of three-cornered eyes he bent down to study the notebooks, the bitten pencil-stump, match-ends, attempt at a sonnet, a tie, crumpled up and forgotten, that littered the drawer.

F. SCOTT FITZGERALD

WINTER DREAMS

I

SOME OF THE caddies were poor as sin and lived in one-room houses with a neurasthenic cow in the front yard, but Dexter Green's father owned the second best grocery-store in Black Bear – the best one was 'The Hub', patronized by the wealthy people from Sherry Island – and Dexter caddied only for pocket-money.

In the fall when the days became crisp and grey, and the long Minnesota winter shut down like the white lid of a box, Dexter's skis moved over the snow that hid the fairways of the golf course. At these times the country gave him a feeling of profound melancholy – it offended him that the links should lie in enforced fallowness, haunted by ragged sparrows for the long season. It was dreary, too, that on the tees where the gay colors fluttered in summer there were now only the desolate sand-boxes knee-deep in crusted ice. When he crossed the hills the wind blew cold as misery, and if the sun was out he tramped with his eyes squinted up against the hard dimensionless glare.

In April the winter ceased abruptly. The snow ran down into Black Bear Lake scarcely tarrying for the early golfers to brave the season with red and black balls. Without elation, without an interval of moist glory, the cold was gone.

Dexter knew that there was something dismal about this Northern spring, just as he knew there was something gorgeous about the fall. Fall made him clinch his hands and tremble and repeat idiotic sentences to himself, and make brisk abrupt gestures of command to imaginary audiences and armies. October filled him with hope which November raised to a sort of ecstatic triumph, and in this mood the fleeting brilliant impressions of the summer at Sherry Island were ready grist to his mill. He became a golf champion and defeated Mr T. A. Hedrick in a marvellous match played a hundred times over the fairways of his imagination, a match each detail of which he changed about untiringly – sometimes he won with almost laughable ease, sometimes he came up magnificently from behind. Again, stepping from a Pierce-Arrow automobile, like Mr Mortimer Jones, he strolled frigidly into the lounge of the Sherry Island Golf Club – or perhaps, surrounded by an admiring crowd, he gave an exhibition of fancy diving from the springboard of the club raft. . . . Among those who watched him in open-mouthed wonder was Mr Mortimer Jones.

And one day it came to pass that Mr Jones – himself and not his ghost – came up to Dexter with tears in his eyes and said that Dexter was the — best caddy in the club, and wouldn't he decide not to quit if Mr Jones made it worth his while, because every other — caddy in the club lost one ball a hole for him – regularly—

'No, sir,' said Dexter decisively, 'I don't want to caddy any more.' Then, after a pause: 'I'm too old.'

'You're not more than fourteen. Why the devil did you decide just this morning that you wanted to quit? You promised that next week you'd go over to the State tournament with me.'

'I decided I was too old.'

Dexter handed in his 'A Class' badge, collected what money was due him from the caddy-master, and walked home to Black Bear Village.

'The best — caddy I ever saw,' shouted Mr Mortimer Jones over a drink that afternoon. 'Never lost a ball! Willing! Intelligent! Quiet! Honest! Grateful!'

The little girl who had done this was eleven – beautifully ugly as little girls are apt to be who are destined after a few years to be inexpressibly lovely and bring no end of misery to a great number of men. The spark, however, was perceptible. There was a general ungodliness in the way her lips twisted down at the corners when she smiled, and in the – Heaven help us! – in the almost passionate quality of her eyes. Vitality is born early in such women. It was utterly in evidence now, shining through her thin frame in a sort of glow.

She had come eagerly out on to the course at nine o'clock with a white linen nurse and five small new golf-clubs in a white canvas bag which the nurse was carrying. When Dexter first saw her she was standing by the caddy house, rather ill at ease and trying to conceal the fact by engaging her nurse in an obviously unnatural conversation graced by startling and irrelevant grimaces from herself.

'Well, it's certainly a nice day, Hilda,' Dexter heard her say. She drew down the corners of her mouth, smiled, and glanced furtively around, her eyes in transit falling for an instant on Dexter.

Then to the nurse:

'Well, I guess there aren't very many people out here this morning, are there?'

The smile again – radiant, blatantly artificial – convincing.

'I don't know what we're supposed to do now,' said the nurse, looking nowhere in particular.

'Oh, that's all right. I'll fix it up.'

Dexter stood perfectly still, his mouth slightly ajar. He knew that if he moved forward a step his stare would be in her line of vision – if he moved backward he would lose his full view of her face. For a moment he had not realized how young she was. Now he remembered having seen her several times the year before – in bloomers.

Suddenly, involuntarily, he laughed, a short abrupt laugh – then, startled by himself, he turned and began to walk quickly away.

'Boy!'

Dexter stopped.

'Boy—'

Beyond question he was addressed. Not only that, but he was treated to that absurd smile, that preposterous smile – the memory of which at least a dozen men were to carry into middle age.

'Boy, do you know where the golf teacher is?'

'He's giving a lesson.'

'Well, do you know where the caddy-master is?'

'He isn't here yet this morning.'

'Oh.' For a moment this baffled her. She stood alternately on her right and left foot.

'We'd like to get a caddy,' said the nurse. 'Mrs Mortimer Jones sent us out to play golf, and we don't know how without we get a caddy.'

Here she was stopped by an ominous glance from Miss Jones, followed immediately by the smile.

'There aren't any caddies here except me,' said Dexter to the nurse, 'and I got to stay here in charge until the caddy-master gets here.'

'Oh.'

Miss Jones and her retinue now withdrew, and at a proper distance from Dexter became involved in a heated conversation, which was concluded by Miss Jones taking one of the clubs and hitting it on the ground with violence. For further emphasis she raised it again and was about to bring it down smartly upon the nurse's bosom, when the nurse seized the club and twisted it from her hands.

'You damn little mean old *thing!*' cried Miss Jones wildly.

Another argument ensued. Realizing that the elements of the comedy were implied in the scene, Dexter several times began to laugh, but each time restrained the laugh before it reached audibility. He could not resist the monstrous conviction that the little girl was justified in beating the nurse.

The situation was resolved by the fortuitous appearance of the caddy-master, who was appealed to immediately by the nurse.

'Miss Jones is to have a little caddy, and this one says he can't go.'

'Mr McKenna said I was to wait here till you came,' said Dexter quickly.

'Well, he's here now.' Miss Jones smiled cheerfully at the caddy-master. Then she dropped her bag and set off at a haughty mince toward the first tee.

'Well?' The caddy-master turned to Dexter. 'What you standing there like a dummy for? Go pick up the young lady's clubs.'

'I don't think I'll go out today,' said Dexter.

'You don't—'

'I think I'll quit.'

The enormity of his decision frightened him. He was a favourite caddy, and the thirty dollars a month he earned through the summer were not to be made elsewhere around the lake. But he had received a strong emotional shock, and his perturbation required a violent and immediate outlet.

It is not so simple as that, either. As so frequently would be the case in the future, Dexter was unconsciously dictated to by his winter dreams.

II

Now, of course, the quality and the seasonability of these winter dreams varied, but the stuff of them remained. They persuaded Dexter several years later to pass up a business course at the State university – his father, prospering now, would have paid his way – for the precarious advantage of attending an older and more famous university in the East, where he was bothered by his scanty funds. But do not get the impression, because his winter dreams happened to be concerned at first with musings on the rich, that there was anything merely snobbish in the boy. He wanted not association with glittering things and glittering people – he wanted the glittering things themselves. Often he reached out for the best without knowing why he wanted it – and sometimes he ran up against the mysterious denials and prohibitions in which life indulges. It is with one of those denials and not with his career as a whole that this story deals.

He made money. It was rather amazing. After college he went to the city from which Black Bear Lake draws its wealthy patrons. When he was only twenty-three and had been there not quite two years, there were already people who liked to say: 'Now *there's* a boy –' All about him rich men's sons were peddling bonds precariously, or investing patrimonies precariously, or plodding through the two dozen volumes of the 'George Washington Commercial Course', but Dexter borrowed a thousand dollars on his college degree and his confident mouth, and bought a partnership in a laundry.

It was a small laundry when he went into it but Dexter made a specialty of learning how the English washed fine woollen golf-stockings without shrinking them, and within a year he was catering to the trade that wore knickerbockers.

Men were insisting that their Shetland hose and sweaters go to his laundry just as they had insisted on a caddy who could find golf-balls. A little later he was doing their wives' lingerie as well – and running five branches in different parts of the city. Before he was twenty-seven he owned the largest string of laundries in his section of the country. It was then that he sold out and went to New York. But the part of his story that concerns us goes back to the days when he was making his first big success.

When he was twenty-three Mr Hart – one of the grey-haired men who like to say 'Now there's a boy' – gave him a guest card to the Sherry Island Golf Club for a week-end. So he signed his name one day on the register, and that afternoon played golf in a foursome with Mr Hart and Mr Sandwood and Mr T. A. Hedrick. He did not consider it necessary to remark that he had once carried Mr Hart's bag over this same links, and that he knew every trap and gully with his eyes shut – but he found himself glancing at the four caddies who trailed them, trying to catch a gleam or gesture that would remind him of himself, that would lessen the gap which lay between his present and his past.

It was a curious day, slashed abruptly with fleeting, familiar impressions. One minute he had the sense of being a trespasser – in the next he was impressed by the tremendous superiority he felt toward Mr T. A. Hedrick, who was a bore and not even a good golfer any more.

Then, because of a ball Mr Hart lost near the fifteenth green, an enormous thing happened. While they were searching the stiff grasses of the rough there was a clear call of 'Fore!' from behind a hill in their rear. And as they all turned abruptly from their search a bright new ball sliced abruptly over the hill and caught Mr T. A. Hedrick in the abdomen.

'By Gad!' cried Mr T. A. Hedrick, 'they ought to put some of these crazy women off the course. It's getting to be outrageous.'

A head and a voice came up together over the hill:

'Do you mind if we go through?'

'You hit me in the stomach!' declared Mr Hedrick wildly.

'Did I?' The girl approached the group of men. 'I'm sorry. I yelled "Fore!"'

Her glance fell casually on each of the men – then scanned the fairway for her ball.

'Did I bounce into the rough?'

It was impossible to determine whether this question was ingenuous or malicious. In a moment, however, she left no doubt, for as her partner came up over the hill she called cheerfully:

'Here I am! I'd have gone on the green except that I hit something.'

As she took her stance for a short mashie shot, Dexter looked at her closely. She wore a blue gingham dress, rimmed at throat and shoulders with a white edging that accentuated her tan. The quality of exaggeration, of thinness, which had made her passionate eyes and down-turning mouth absurd at eleven, was gone now. She was arrestingly beautiful. The color in her cheeks was centered like the color in a picture – it was not a 'high' color, but a sort of fluctuating and feverish warmth, so shaded that it seemed at any moment it would recede and disappear. This color and the mobility of her mouth gave a continual impression of flux, of intense life, of passionate vitality – balanced only partially by the sad luxury of her eyes.

She swung her mashie impatiently and without interest, pitching the ball into a sand-pit on the other side of the green. With a quick, insincere smile and a careless 'Thank you!' she went on after it.

'That Judy Jones!' remarked Mr Hedrick on the next tee, as they waited – some moments – for her to play on ahead. 'All she needs is to be turned up and spanked for six months and then to be married off to an old-fashioned cavalry captain.'

'My God, she's good-looking!' said Mr Sandwood, who was just over thirty.

'Good-looking!' cried Mr Hedrick contemptuously, 'she always looks as if she wanted to be kissed! Turning those big cow-eyes on every calf in town!'

It was doubtful if Mr Hedrick intended a reference to the maternal instinct.

'She'd play pretty good golf if she'd try,' said Mr Sandwood.

'She has no form,' said Mr Hedrick solemnly.

'She has a nice figure,' said Mr Sandwood.

'Better thank the Lord she doesn't drive a swifter ball,' said Mr Hart, winking at Dexter.

Later in the afternoon the sun went down with a riotous swirl of gold and varying blues and scarlets, and left the dry, rustling night of Western summer. Dexter watched from the veranda of the Golf Club, watched the even overlap of the waters in the little wind, silver molasses under the harvest-moon. Then the moon held a finger to her lips and the lake became a clear pool, pale and quiet. Dexter put on his bathing-suit and swam out to the farthest raft, where he stretched dripping on the wet canvas of the springboard.

There was a fish jumping and a star shining and the lights around the lake were gleaming. Over on a dark peninsula a piano was playing the songs of last summer and of summers before that – songs from 'Chin-Chin' and 'The Count of

Luxemburg' and 'The Chocolate Soldier' – and because the sound of a piano over a stretch of water had always seemed beautiful to Dexter he lay perfectly quiet and listened.

The tune the piano was playing at that moment had been gay and new five years before when Dexter was a sophomore at college. They had played it at a prom once when he could not afford the luxury of proms, and he had stood outside the gymnasium and listened. The sound of the tune precipitated in him a sort of ecstasy and it was with that ecstasy he viewed what happened to him now. It was a mood of intense appreciation, a sense that, for once, he was magnificently attuned to life and that everything about him was radiating a brightness and a glamour he might never know again.

A low, pale oblong detached itself suddenly from the darkness of the Island, spitting forth the reverberate sound of a racing motor-boat. Two white streamers of cleft water rolled themselves out behind it and almost immediately the boat was beside him, drowning out the hot tinkle of the piano in the drone of its spray. Dexter raising himself on his arms was aware of a figure standing at the wheel, of two dark eyes regarding him over the lengthening space of water – then the boat had gone by and was sweeping in an immense and purposeless circle of spray round and round in the middle of the lake. With equal eccentricity one of the circles flattened out and headed back toward the raft.

'Who's that?' she called, shutting off her motor. She was so near now that Dexter could see her bathing-suit, which consisted apparently of pink rompers.

The nose of the boat bumped the raft, and as the latter tilted rakishly he was precipitated toward her. With different degrees of interest they recognized each other.

'Aren't you one of those men we played through this afternoon?' she demanded.

He was.

'Well, do you know how to drive a motor-boat? Because if you do I wish you'd drive this one so I can ride on the surf-board behind. My name is Judy Jones' – she favoured him with an absurd smirk – rather, what tried to be a smirk, for, twist her mouth as she might, it was not grotesque, it was merely beautiful – 'and I live in a house over there on the Island, and in that house there is a man waiting for me. When he drove up at the door I drove out of the dock because he says I'm his ideal.'

There was a fish jumping and a star shining and the lights around the lake were gleaming. Dexter sat beside Judy Jones and she explained how her boat was driven. Then she was in the water, swimming to the floating surf-board with a sinuous crawl. Watching her was without effort to the eye, watching a branch waving or a sea-gull flying. Her arms, burned to butternut, moved sinuously among the dull platinum ripples, elbow appearing first, casting the forearm back with a cadence of falling water, then reaching out and down, stabbing a path ahead.

They moved out into the lake; turning, Dexter saw that she was kneeling on the low rear of the now uptilted surf-board.

'Go faster,' she called, 'fast as it'll go.'

Obediently he jammed the lever forward and the white spray mounted at the bow. When he looked around again the girl was standing up on the rushing board, her arms spread wide, her eyes lifted toward the moon.

'It's awful cold,' she shouted. 'What's your name?'

He told her.

'Well, why don't you come to dinner tomorrow night?'

His heart turned over like the fly-wheel of the boat, and, for the second time, her casual whim gave a new direction to his life.

III

Next evening while he waited for her to come downstairs, Dexter peopled the soft deep summer room and the sun-porch that opened from it with the men who had already loved Judy Jones. He knew the sort of men they were – the men who when he first went to college had entered from the great prep schools with graceful clothes and the deep tan of healthy summers. He had seen that, in one sense, he was better than these men. He was newer and stronger. Yet in acknowledging to himself that he wished his children to be like them he was admitting that he was but the rough, strong stuff from which they eternally sprang.

When the time had come for him to wear good clothes, he had known who were the best tailors in America, and the best tailors in America had made him the suit he wore this evening. He had acquired that particular reserve peculiar to his university, that set it off from other universities. He recognized the value to him of such a mannerism and he had adopted it; he knew that to be careless in dress and manner required more confidence than to be careful. But carelessness was for his children. His mother's name had been Krimslich. She was a Bohemian of the peasant class and she had talked broken English to the end of her days. Her son must keep to the set patterns.

At a little after seven Judy Jones came downstairs. She wore a blue silk afternoon dress, and he was disappointed at first that she had not put on something more elaborate. This feeling was accentuated when, after a brief greeting, she went to the door of a butler's pantry and pushing it open called: 'You can serve dinner, Martha.' He had rather expected that a butler would announce dinner, that there would be a cocktail. Then he put these thoughts behind him as they sat down side by side on a lounge and looked at each other.

'Father and mother won't be here,' she said thoughtfully.

He remembered the last time he had seen her father, and he was glad the parents were not to be here tonight – they might wonder who he was. He had been born in Keeble, a Minnesota village fifty miles farther north, and he always gave Keeble as his home instead of Black Bear Village. Country towns were well enough to come from if they weren't inconveniently in sight and used as footstools by fashionable lakes.

They talked of his university, which she had visited frequently during the past two years, and of the nearby city which supplied Sherry Island with its patrons, and whither Dexter would return next day to his prospering laundries.

During dinner she slipped into a moody depression which gave Dexter a feeling of uneasiness. Whatever petulance she uttered in her throaty voice worried him. Whatever she smiled at – at him, at a chicken liver, at nothing – it disturbed him that her smile could have no root in mirth, or even in amusement. When the scarlet corners of her lips curved down, it was less a smile than an invitation to a kiss.

Then, after dinner, she led him out on the dark sunporch and deliberately changed the atmosphere.

'Do you mind if I weep a little?' she said.

'I'm afraid I'm boring you,' he responded quickly.

'You're not. I like you. But I've just had a terrible afternoon. There was a man I cared about, and this afternoon he told me out of a clear sky that he was poor as a churchmouse. He'd never even hinted it before. Does this sound horribly mundane?'

'Perhaps he was afraid to tell you.'

'Suppose he was,' she answered. 'He didn't start right. You see, if I'd thought of him as poor – well, I've been mad about loads of poor men, and fully intended to marry them all. But in this case, I hadn't thought of him that way, and my interest in him wasn't strong enough to survive the shock. As if a girl calmly informed her fiancé that she was a widow. He might not object to widows, but—'

'Let's start right,' she interrupted herself suddenly. 'Who are you, anyhow?'

For a moment Dexter hesitated. Then:

'I'm nobody,' he announced. 'My career is largely a matter of futures.'

'Are you poor?'

'No,' he said frankly, 'I'm probably making more money than any man my age in the Northwest. I know that's an obnoxious remark, but you advised me to start right.'

There was a pause. Then she smiled and the corners of her mouth drooped and an almost imperceptible sway brought her closer to him, looking up into his eyes. A lump rose in Dexter's throat, and he waited breathless for the experiment, facing the unpredictable compound that would form mysteriously from the elements of their lips. Then he saw – she communicated her excitement to him, lavishly, deeply, with kisses that were not a promise but a fulfillment. They aroused in him not hunger demanding renewal but surfeit that would demand more surfeit . . . kisses that were like charity, creating want by holding back nothing at all.

It did not take him many hours to decide that he had wanted Judy Jones ever since he was a proud, desirous little boy.

IV

It began like that – and continued, with varying shades of intensity, on such a note right up to the dénouement. Dexter surrendered a part of himself to the most direct and unprincipled personality with which he had ever come in contact. Whatever Judy wanted, she went after with the full pressure of her charm. There was no divergence of method, no jockeying for position or premeditation of effects – there was a very little mental side to any of her affairs. She simply made men conscious to the highest degree of her physical loveliness. Dexter had no desire to change her. Her deficiencies were knit up with a passionate energy that transcended and justified them.

When, as Judy's head lay against his shoulder that first night, she whispered, 'I don't know what's the matter with me. Last night I thought I was in love with a man and tonight I think I'm in love with you—' – it seemed to him a beautiful and romantic thing to say. It was the exquisite excitability that for the moment he controlled and owned. But a week later he was compelled to view this same quality in a different light. She took him in her roadster to a picnic supper, and after supper she disappeared, likewise in her roadster, with another man. Dexter became enormously upset and was scarcely able to be decently civil to the other people present. When she assured him that she had not kissed the other man, he knew she was lying – yet he was glad that she had taken the trouble to lie to him.

He was, as he found before the summer ended, one of a varying dozen who circulated about her. Each of them had at one time been favoured above all others – about half of them still basked in the solace of occasional sentimental revivals. Whenever one showed signs of dropping out through long neglect, she granted him a brief honeyed hour, which encouraged him to tag along for a year or so longer. Judy made these forays upon the helpless and defeated without malice, indeed half unconscious that there was anything mischievous in what she did.

When a new man came to town every one dropped out – dates were automatically cancelled.

The helpless part of trying to do anything about it was that she did it all herself. She was not a girl who could be 'won' in the kinetic sense – she was proof against cleverness, she was proof against charm; if any of these assailed her too strongly she would immediately resolve the affair to a physical basis, and under the magic of her physical splendour the strong as well as the brilliant played her game and not their own. She was entertained only by the gratification of her desires and by the direct exercise of her own charm. Perhaps from so much youthful love, so many youthful lovers, she had come, in self-defense, to nourish herself wholly from within.

Succeeding Dexter's first exhilaration came restlessness and dissatisfaction. The helpless ecstasy of losing himself in her was opiate rather than tonic. It was fortunate for his work during the winter that those moments of ecstasy came infrequently. Early in their acquaintance it had seemed for a while that there was a deep and spontaneous mutual attraction – that first August, for example – three days of long evenings on her dusky veranda, of strange wan kisses through the late afternoon, in shadowy alcoves or behind the protecting trellises of the garden arbors, of mornings when she was fresh as a dream and almost shy at meeting him in the clarity of the rising day. There was all the ecstasy of an engagement about it, sharpened by his realization that there was no engagement. It was during those three days that, for the first time, he had asked her to marry him. She said 'maybe some day,' she said 'kiss me,' she said 'I'd like to marry you,' she said 'I love you' – she said – nothing.

The three days were interrupted by the arrival of a New York man who visited at her house for half September. To Dexter's agony, rumor engaged them. The man was the son of the president of a great trust company. But at the end of a month it was reported that Judy was yawning. At a dance one night she sat all evening in a motor-boat with a local beau, while the New Yorker searched the club for her frantically. She told the local beau that she was bored with her visitor, and two days later he left. She was seen with him at the station, and it was reported that he looked very mournful indeed.

On this note the summer ended. Dexter was twenty-four, and he found himself increasingly in a position to do as he wished. He joined two clubs in the city and lived at one of them. Though he was by no means an integral part of the stag-lines at these clubs, he managed to be on hand at dances where Judy Jones was likely to appear. He could have gone out socially as much as he liked – he was an eligible young man, now, and popular with down-town fathers. His confessed devotion to Judy Jones had rather solidified his position. But he had no social aspirations and rather despised the dancing men who were always on tap for the Thursday or Saturday parties and who filled in at dinners with the younger married set. Already he was playing with the idea of going East to New York. He wanted to take Judy Jones with him. No disillusion as to the world in which she had grown up could cure his illusion as to her desirability.

Remember that – for only in the light of it can what he did for her be understood.

Eighteen months after he first met Judy Jones he became

engaged to another girl. Her name was Irene Scheerer, and her father was one of the men who had always believed in Dexter. Irene was light-haired and sweet and honourable, and a little stout, and she had two suitors whom she pleasantly relinquished when Dexter formally asked her to marry him.

Summer, fall, winter, spring, another summer, another fall – so much he had given of his active life to the incorrigible lips of Judy Jones. She had treated him with interest, with encouragement, with malice, with indifference, with contempt. She had inflicted on him the innumerable little slights and indignities possible in such a case – as if in revenge for having ever cared for him at all. She had beckoned him and yawned at him and beckoned him again and he had responded often with bitterness and narrowed eyes. She had brought him ecstatic happiness and intolerable agony of spirit. She had caused him untold inconvenience and not a little trouble. She had insulted him, and she had ridden over him, and she had played his interest in her against his interest in his work – for fun. She had done everything to him except to criticize him – this she had not done – it seemed to him only because it might have sullied the utter indifference she manifested and sincerely felt toward him.

When autumn had come and gone again it occurred to him that he could not have Judy Jones. He had to beat this into his mind but he convinced himself at last. He lay awake at night for a while and argued it over. He told himself the trouble and the pain she had caused him, he enumerated her glaring deficiencies as a wife. Then he said to himself that he loved her, and after a while he fell asleep. For a week, lest he imagine her husky voice over the telephone or her eyes opposite him at lunch, he worked hard and late, and at night he went to his office and plotted out his years.

At the end of a week he went to a dance and cut in on her once. For almost the first time since they had met he did not ask her to sit out with him or tell her that she was lovely. It hurt him that she did not miss these things – that was all. He was not jealous when he saw that there was a new man tonight. He had been hardened against jealousy long before.

He stayed late at the dance. He sat for an hour with Irene Scheerer and talked about books and about music. He knew very little about either. But he was beginning to be master of his own time now, and he had a rather priggish notion that he – the young and already fabulously successful Dexter Green – should know more about such things.

That was in October, when he was twenty-five. In January, Dexter and Irene became engaged. It was to be announced in June, and they were to be married three months later.

The Minnesota winter prolonged itself interminably, and it was almost May when the winds came soft and the snow ran down into Black Bear Lake at last. For the first time in over a year Dexter was enjoying a certain tranquility of spirit. Judy Jones had been in Florida, and afterward in Hot Springs, and somewhere she had been engaged, and somewhere she had broken it off. At first, when Dexter had definitely given her up, it had made him sad that people still linked them together and asked for news of her, but when he began to be placed at dinner next to Irene Scheerer people didn't ask him about her any more – they told him about her. He ceased to be an authority on her.

May at last. Dexter walked the streets at night when the darkness was damp as rain, wondering that so soon, with so little done, so much of ecstasy had gone from him. May one year back had been marked by Judy's poignant, unforgivable, yet forgiven turbulence – it had been one of those rare times when he fancied she had grown to care for him. That old penny's worth of happiness he had spent for this bushel of content. He knew that Irene would be no more than a curtain spread behind him, a hand moving among gleaming tea-cups, a voice calling to children . . . fire and loveliness were gone, the magic of nights and the wonder of the varying hours and seasons . . . slender lips, down-turning, dropping to his lips and bearing him up into a heaven of eyes. . . . The thing was deep in him. He was too strong and alive for it to die lightly.

In the middle of May when the weather balanced for a few days on the thin bridge that led to deep summer he turned in one night at Irene's house. Their engagement was to be announced in a week now – no one would be surprised at it. And tonight they would sit together on the lounge at the University Club and look on for an hour at the dancers. It gave him a sense of solidity to go with her – she was so sturdily popular, so intensely 'great'.

He mounted the steps of the brownstone house and stepped inside.

'Irene,' he called.

Mrs Scheerer came out of the living-room to meet him.

'Dexter,' she said, 'Irene's gone upstairs with a splitting headache. She wanted to go with you but I made her go to bed.'

'Nothing serious, I—'

'Oh, no. She's going to play golf with you in the morning. You can spare her for just one night, can't you, Dexter?'

Her smile was kind. She and Dexter liked each other. In the living-room he talked for a moment before he said goodnight.

Returning to the University Club, where he had rooms, he stood in the doorway for a moment and watched the dancers. He leaned against the door-post, nodded at a man or two – yawned.

'Hello, darling.'

The familiar voice at his elbow startled him. Judy Jones had left a man and crossed the room to him – Judy Jones, a slender enamelled doll in cloth of gold: gold in a band at her head, gold in two slipper points at her dress's hem. The fragile glow of her face seemed to blossom as she smiled at him. A breeze of warmth and light blew through the room. His hands in the pockets of his dinner-jacket tightened spasmodically. He was filled with a sudden excitement.

'When did you get back?' he asked casually.

'Come here and I'll tell you about it.'

She turned and he followed her. She had been away – he could have wept at the wonder of her return. She had passed through enchanted streets, doing things that were like provocative music. All mysterious happenings, all fresh and quickening hopes, had gone away with her, come back with her now.

She turned in the doorway.

'Have you a car here? If you haven't, I have.'

'I have a coupé.'

In then, with a rustle of golden cloth. He slammed the door. Into so many cars she had stepped – like this – like that – her back against the leather, so – her elbow resting on the door – waiting. She would have been soiled long since had there been anything to soil her – except herself – but this was her own self outpouring.

With an effort he forced himself to start the car and back into the street. This was nothing, he must remember. She had done this before, and he had put her behind him, as he would have crossed a bad account from his books.

He drove slowly down-town and, affecting abstraction,

traversed the deserted streets of the business section, peopled here and there where a movie was giving out its crowd or where consumptive or pugilistic youth lounged in front of pool halls. The clink of glasses and the slap of hands on the bars issued from saloons, cloisters of glazed glass and dirty yellow light.

She was watching him closely and the silence was embarrassing, yet in this crisis he could find no casual word with which to profane the hour. At a convenient turning he began to zigzag back toward the University Club.

'Have you missed me?' she asked suddenly.

'Everybody missed you.'

He wondered if she knew of Irene Scheerer. She had been back only a day – her absence had been almost contemporaneous with his engagement.

'What a remark!' Judy laughed sadly – without sadness. She looked at him searchingly. He became absorbed in the dashboard.

'You're handsomer than you used to be,' she said thoughtfully. 'Dexter, you have the most rememberable eyes.'

He could have laughed at this, but he did not laugh. It was the sort of thing that was said to sophomores. Yet it stabbed at him.

'I'm awfully tired of everything, darling.' She called every one darling, endowing the endearment with careless, individual comraderie. 'I wish you'd marry me.'

The directness of this confused him. He should have told her now that he was going to marry another girl, but he could not tell her. He could as easily have sworn that he had never loved her.

'I think we'd get along,' she continued, on the same note, 'unless probably you've forgotten me and fallen in love with another girl.'

Her confidence was obviously enormous. She had said, in effect, that she found such a thing impossible to believe, that if it were true he had merely committed a childish indiscretion – and probably to show off. She would forgive him, because it was not a matter of any moment but rather something to be brushed aside lightly.

'Of course you could never love anybody but me,' she continued. 'I like the way you love me. Oh, Dexter, have you forgotten last year?'

'No, I haven't forgotten.'

'Neither have I!'

Was she sincerely moved – or was she carried along by the wave of her own acting?

'I wish we could be like that again,' she said, and he forced himself to answer:

'I don't think we can.'

'I suppose not.... I hear you're giving Irene Scheerer a violent rush.'

There was not the faintest emphasis on the name, yet Dexter was suddenly ashamed.

'Oh, take me home,' cried Judy suddenly; 'I don't want to go back to that idiotic dance – with those children.'

Then, as he turned up the street that led to the residence district, Judy began to cry quietly to herself. He had never seen her cry before.

The dark street lightened, the dwellings of the rich loomed up around them, he stopped his coupé in front of the great white bulk of the Mortimer Joneses' house, somnolent, gorgeous, drenched with the splendour of the damp moonlight. Its solidity startled him. The strong walls, the steel of the girders, the breadth and beam and pomp of it were there only to bring out the contrast with the young beauty beside him. It was sturdy to accentuate her slightness

– as if to show what a breeze could be generated by a butter-fly's wing.

He sat perfectly quiet, his nerves in wild clamour, afraid that if he moved he would find her irresistibly in his arms. Two tears had rolled down her wet face and trembled on her upper lip.

'I'm more beautiful than anybody else,' she said bro-kenly, 'why can't I be happy?' Her moist eyes tore at his stability – her mouth turned slowly downward with an exquisite sadness: 'I'd like to marry you if you'll have me, Dexter. I suppose you think I'm not worth having, but I'll be so beautiful for you, Dexter.'

A million phrases of anger, pride, passion, hatred, tender-ness fought on his lips. Then a perfect wave of emotion washed over him, carrying off with it a sediment of wisdom, of convention, of doubt, of honour. This was his girl who was speaking, his own, his beautiful, his pride.

'Won't you come in?' He heard her draw in her breath sharply.

Waiting.

'All right,' his voice was trembling, 'I'll come in.'

V

It was strange that neither when it was over nor a long time afterward did he regret that night. Looking at it from the perspective of ten years, the fact that Judy's flare for him endured just one month seemed of little importance. Nor did it matter that by his yielding he subjected himself to a deeper agony in the end and gave serious hurt to Irene Scheerer and to Irene's parents, who had befriended him. There was nothing sufficiently pictorial about Irene's grief to stamp itself on his mind.

Dexter was at bottom hard-minded. The attitude of the city on his action was of no importance to him, not because he was going to leave the city, but because any outside attitude on the situation seemed superficial. He was completely indifferent to popular opinion. Nor, when he had seen that it was no use, that he did not possess in himself the power to move fundamentally or to hold Judy Jones, did he bear any malice toward her. He loved her, and he would love her until the day he was too old for loving – but he could not have her. So he tasted the deep pain that is reserved only for the strong, just as he had tasted for a little while the deep happiness.

Even the ultimate falsity of the grounds upon which Judy terminated the engagement, that she did not want to 'take him away' from Irene – Judy, who had wanted nothing else – did not revolt him. He was beyond any revulsion or any amusement.

He went East in February with the intention of selling out his laundries and settling in New York – but the war came to America in March and changed his plans. He returned to the West, handed over the management of the business to his partner, and went into the first officers' training-camp in late April. He was one of those young thousands who greeted the war with a certain amount of relief, welcoming the liberation from webs of tangled emotion.

VI

This story is not his biography, remember, although things creep into it which have nothing to do with those dreams he had when he was young. We are almost done with them and with him now. There is only one more incident to be related here, and it happens seven years farther on.

It took place in New York, where he had done well – so well that there were no barriers too high for him. He was thirty-two years old, and, except for one flying trip immediately after the war, he had not been West in seven years. A man named Devlin from Detroit came into his office to see him in a business way, and then and there this incident occurred, and closed out, so to speak, this particular side of his life.

'So you're from the Middle West,' said the man Devlin with careless curiosity. 'That's funny – I thought men like you were probably born and raised on Wall Street. You know – wife of one of my best friends in Detroit came from your city. I was an usher at the wedding.'

Dexter waited with no apprehension of what was coming.

'Judy Simms,' said Devlin with no particular interest; 'Judy Jones she was once.'

'Yes, I knew her.' A dull impatience spread over him. He had heard, of course, that she was married – perhaps deliberately he had heard no more.

'Awfully nice girl,' brooded Devlin meaninglessly, 'I'm sort of sorry for her.'

'Why?' Something in Dexter was alert, receptive, at once.

'Oh, Lud Simms has gone to pieces in a way. I don't mean he ill-uses her, but he drinks and runs around—'

'Doesn't she run around?'

'No. Stays at home with her kids.'

'Oh.'

'She's a little too old for him,' said Devlin.

'Too old!' cried Dexter. 'Why, man, she's only twenty-seven.'

He was possessed with a wild notion of rushing out into the streets and taking a train to Detroit. He rose to his feet spasmodically.

'I guess you're busy,' Devlin apologized quickly. 'I didn't realize—'

'No, I'm not busy,' said Dexter, steadying his voice. 'I'm not busy at all. Not busy at all. Did you say she was – twenty-seven? No, I said she was twenty-seven.'

'Yes, you did,' agreed Devlin dryly.

'Go on, then. Go on.'

'What do you mean?'

'About Judy Jones.'

Devlin looked at him helplessly.

'Well, that's – I told you all there is to it. He treats her like the devil. Oh, they're not going to get divorced or anything. When he's particularly outrageous she forgives him. In fact, I'm inclined to think she loves him. She was a pretty girl when she first came to Detroit.'

A pretty girl! The phrase struck Dexter as ludicrous.

'Isn't she – a pretty girl, any more?'

'Oh, she's all right.'

'Look here,' said Dexter, sitting down suddenly, 'I don't understand. You say she was a "pretty girl" and now you say she's "all right". I don't understand what you mean – Judy Jones wasn't a pretty girl, at all. She was a great beauty. Why, I knew her, I knew her. She was—'

Devlin laughed pleasantly.

'I'm not trying to start a row,' he said. 'I think Judy's a nice girl and I like her. I can't understand how a man like Lud Simms could fall madly in love with her, but he did.' Then he added: 'Most of the women like her.'

Dexter looked closely at Devlin, thinking wildly that there must be a reason for this, some insensitivity in the man or some private malice.

'Lots of women fade just like *that*,' Devlin snapped his fingers. 'You must have seen it happen. Perhaps I've forgotten how pretty she was at her wedding. I've seen her so much since then, you see. She has nice eyes.'

A sort of dulness settled down upon Dexter. For the first time in his life he felt like getting very drunk. He knew that he was laughing loudly at something Devlin had said, but he did not know what it was or why it was funny. When, in a few minutes, Devlin went he lay down on his lounge and looked out the window at the New York sky-line into which the sun was sinking in dull lovely shades of pink and gold.

He had thought that having nothing else to lose he was invulnerable at last – but he knew that he had just lost something more, as surely as if he had married Judy Jones and seen her fade away before his eyes.

The dream was gone. Something had been taken from him. In a sort of panic he pushed the palms of his hands into his eyes and tried to bring up a picture of the waters lapping on Sherry Island and the moonlit veranda, and ging-ham on the golf-links and the dry sun and the gold color of her neck's soft down. And her mouth damp to his kisses and her eyes plaintive with melancholy and her freshness like new fine linen in the morning. Why, these things were no longer in the world! They had existed and they existed no longer.

For the first time in years the tears were streaming down his face. But they were for himself now. He did not care about mouth and eyes and moving hands. He wanted to care, and he could not care. For he had gone away and he could never go back any more. The gates were closed, the sun was gone down, and there was no beauty but the grey beauty of steel that withstands all time. Even the grief he could have borne was left behind in the country of illusion, of youth, of the richness of life, where his winter dreams had flourished.

'Long ago,' he said, 'long ago, there was something in me, but now that thing is gone. Now that thing is gone, that thing is gone. I cannot cry. I cannot care. That thing will come back no more.'

COLETTE

ARMANDE

Translated by Antonia White

'THAT GIRL? But, good heavens, she adores you! What's more, she's never done anything else for ten whole years. All the time you were on active service, she kept finding excuses for dropping in at the pharmacy and asking if I'd had a letter.'

'Did she?'

'She wouldn't leave the shop until she'd managed to slip in her "How's your brother?" She used to wait. And while she was waiting, she'd buy aspirin, cough lozenges, tubes of lanolin, toilet water, tincture of iodine.'

'So naturally, you saw to it she was kept waiting?'

'Well, after all, why not? When I finally did tell her I'd news of you, off she went. But never till I had. You know what she's like.'

'Yes . . . No, to be honest, I *don't* know what she's like.'

'What do you expect, my poor pet? You made everything so complicated for yourself, you're wearing yourself out with all these absurd scruples. Armande is a very well-educated girl, we all know that. She takes her position as a comfortably rich orphan a shade too seriously. I grant you it's none too easy a one in a subprefecture like this. But just because of that, to let her put it over on you to that extent, *you*, Maxime, of all people! Look out, this is the new pavement. At least one can walk without getting one's feet wet now.'

The September sky, black and moonless, glittered with stars that twinkled large in the damp air. The invisible river lapped against the single arch of the bridge. Maxime stopped and leaned on the parapet.

'The parapet's new too,' he said.

'Yes. It was put up by the local tradesmen, with the consent of the Town Council. You know they did tremendously well here out of food and clothing, what with all the troops going through and the exodus.'

'Out of food, clothes, footwear, medical supplies, and everything else. I also know that people talk about "the exodus" as they do about "the agricultural show" and "the gala horse show and gymkhana".'

'Anyway, they wanted to make a great sacrifice.'

Madame Debove heard Maxime laugh under his breath at the word 'sacrifice' and she prudently left her sentence unfinished to revert to Armande Fauconnier.

'In any case, she didn't let you down too badly during the war; she wrote to you, didn't she?'

'Postcards.'

'She sent you food parcels and a marvellous pullover.'

'To hell with her food parcels and her woollies,' said Maxime Degouthe violently, '*and* her postcards! I've never begged charity from her, as far as I know.'

'Good gracious, what a savage character you are . . . Don't spoil your last evening here, Maxime! Admit it was a charming party tonight. Armande is a very good hostess. All the Fauconniers have always been good hosts. Armande knows how to efface herself. There was no chance of the conversation getting on to that children's clinic that Armande supports entirely out of her own money.'

'Who hasn't organized something in the way of a children's clinic during the war?' growled Maxime.

'Why, heaps of people, I assure you! In the first place, you've got to have the means. *She* really has got the means.'

Maxime made no reply. He hated it when his sister talked of Armande's 'means'.

'The river's low,' he said, after a moment or two.

'You've got good eyes!'

'It's not a question of eyes, it's a question of smell. When the water's low, it always smells of musk here. It's the mud, probably.'

He suddenly remembered that, last year, he had said the very same words, on the very same spot, to Armande. She had wrinkled her nose in disgust and made an ugly grimace with her mouth. 'As if *she* knew what mud was . . . Mud, that pearl-grey clay, so soft to the bare toes, so mysteriously musky, *she* imagines it's the same as excrement. She never misses an occasion of shrinking away from anything that can be tasted or touched or smelled.'

Dancing owlet moths almost obscured the luminous globes at either end of the bridge. Maxime heard his sister yawn.

'Come on, let's go. What on earth are we doing here?'

'I'm asking *you*!' sighed Madame Debove. 'Do you hear? Eleven o'clock! Hector's sure to have gone to bed without waiting up for me.'

'Let him sleep. There's no need for us to hurry.'

'Oh, yes, there is, old thing! I'm sleepy, I am.'

He took his sister's arm under his own, as he used to in the old days when they were students, sharing the same illusions, in that halcyon period when a brother and sister believe, quite genuinely, that they are perfectly content with being a chaste imitation of a pair of lovers. 'Then a big, ginger-headed youth comes along and the devoted little sister goes off with him, for the pleasure and the advantages of marrying the Grand Central Pharmacy. After all, she did the right thing.'

A passer-by stepped off the pavement to make room for them and bowed to Jeanne.

'Good evening, Merle. Stopped having those pains of yours?'

'It's as if he'd said, Madame Debove. Good evening, Madame Debove.'

'He's a customer,' explained Jeanne.

'Good Lord, I might have guessed that,' said her brother ironically. 'When you put on your professional chemist's wife voice.'

'What about you when you put on your professional quack's voice? Just listen, am I exaggerating one bit? "Above all, dear lady, endeavour as far as possible to control your nerves. The improvement is noticeable, I will even go so far as to say remarkable, but for the time being, we must continue to be very firm about avoiding all forms of meat," and I preach to you and instruct you and I drench you with awful warnings.'

Maxime laughed wholeheartedly, the imitation of his slightly pontifical manner was so true to life.

'All women are monkeys, they're only interested in our absurdities and our love affairs and our illnesses. The other one can't be so very different from this one.'

He could see her, the other one, as she had looked when he left her just now, standing at the top flight of steps that led up to the Fauconniers' house. The lighted chandelier in the hall behind her gave her a nimbus of blue glass convolvulus flowers and chromium hoops. 'Goodbye, Armande.' She had answered only with a nod. 'You might call her a miser with words! If I had her in my arms, one day, between four walls or in the corner of a wood, I'd make her scream, and for good reason!' But he had never met Armande in the corner of a wood. As to his aggressive instincts, he lost all hope of gratifying them the moment he was in Armande's presence.

Eleven o'clock struck from the hospital, then from a small low church jostled by new buildings, last of all, in shrill, crystalline strokes from a dark ground-floor room whose window was open. As they crossed the Place d'Armes, Maxime sat down on one of the benches.

'Just for one minute, Jeanne! Let me relax my nerves. It's nice out of doors.'

Jeanne Debove consented sulkily.

'You ought to have worked them off on Armande, those nerves of yours. But you haven't got the guts!'

He did not protest and she burst into a malicious laugh. He wondered why sexual shyness, which excites dissolute women, arouses the contempt of decent ones.

'She overawes you, that's it. Yes, she overawes you. I simply can't get over it!'

She elaborated her inability to get over it by inundating him with various scoffing remarks, accompanied now by a neighing laugh, now by a spurt of giggles.

'After all, you're not in your very, *very* first youth. You're not a greenhorn. Or a neurotic. Nor, thank heaven, physically deformed.'

She enumerated all the things her brother was not and he was glad she omitted to mention the one quite simple thing he was – a man who had been in love for a very long time.

Maxime Degouthe's long-persisting love, though it preserved him from debauchery, turned into mere habit when he was away from Armande for a few months. When he was away from her, a kind of conjugal fidelity allowed him to amuse himself as much as he liked and even to forget her for a spell. So much so that, when he had finished his medical studies, he had been paralysed to find himself faced with a grown-up Armande Fauconnier when the Armande he remembered was a gawky, sharp-shouldered, overgrown adolescent, at once clumsy and noble like a bony filly full of promise.

Every time he saw her again, she completely took possession of him. His feeling for her was violent and suppressed, like a gardener's son's for the 'young lady up at the big house'. He would have liked to be rather brutal to this beautiful tall girl whom he admired from head to foot, who was just sufficiently dark, just sufficiently white, and as smooth as a pear. 'But I shouldn't dare. No, I daren't,' he fumed to himself, every time he left.

'The back of the seat is all wet,' said Madame Debove. 'I'm going home. What are your plans for tomorrow? Are you going in to say goodbye to Armande? She's expecting you to, you know.'

'She hasn't invited me.'

'You mean you daren't go on your own? You may as well admit it, that girl's thoroughly got you down!'

'I do admit it,' said Maxime, so mildly that his sister stopped cruelly teasing him.

They walked in silence till they reached the Grand Central Pharmacy.

'You'll lunch with us tomorrow, of course. Hector would have a fit if you didn't have your last meal with him. Your parcel of ampoules will be all ready. No one can say when we'll be able to get those particular serums again. Well, shall I ring up Armande and say you'll be coming over to say goodbye to her? But I needn't say definitely you're not coming?'

She was fumbling endlessly with a bunch of keys. Maxime lent her the aid of his flashlight and its beam fell full on Jeanne Debove's mischievous face and its expression of mixed satisfaction and disapproval.

'She wants me to marry Armande. She's thinking of the money, of the fine, rich house, of "the excellent effect", of my career, as she says. But she'd also like me to marry Armande without being over-enthusiastic about her. Everything's perfectly normal. Everything except myself, because I can't endure the idea that *she*, Armande, could marry me without being in love with me.'

He hurried back to his hotel. The town was asleep but the hotel, close by the station, resounded with all the noises that are hostile to sleep and blazed with lights that aggravate human tiredness. Hobnailed boots, shuddering ceiling lights, uncarpeted floors, the gates of the elevator, the whinnyings of hydraulic pressure, the rhythmic clatter of plates flung into a sink in the basement, the intermittent trilling of a bell never stopped outraging the need for silence that had driven Maxime to his bedroom. Unable to stand any more, he added his own contribution to the selfish human concert, dropped his shoes on the wooden floor, carried them out into the corridor, and shut his door with a loud slam.

He drenched himself with cold water, dried himself carelessly, and got into bed quite naked, after having studied himself in the looking glass. 'Big bones, big muscles, and four complete limbs, after all, that's not too bad, in these days. A large nose, large eyes, a cap of hair as thick as a motorcyclist's helmet, girls who weren't Mademoiselle Fauconnier have found all that very much to their taste. I don't see Mademoiselle Fauconnier sleeping with this naked, black-haired chap . . .'

On the contrary, he saw her only too well. Irritated by fretful desire, he waited for the hotel to become quiet. When – save for a sound of barking, a garage door, the departure of a motorcar – silence was at last established, a breeze sprang up, swept away the last insults inflicted by man on the night, and came in through the open window like a reward.

'Tomorrow,' Maxime vowed to himself. It was a muddled vow that concerned the conquest of Armande quite as much as the return to professional life and the daily, necessary triumph of forced activity over fundamental listlessness.

He reiterated 'Tomorrow', flung away his pillow, rolled over on his stomach, and fell asleep with his head between his folded arms in the same attitude as a small intimidated boy of long ago who used to dream of an Armande with long black curls. Later on, another Maxime had slept like that, the adolescent who had plucked up courage to invite 'those Fauconnier ladies', as they were coming out from High Mass, to have lemon ices at Peyrol's. 'Really, Maxime, one doesn't eat lemon ices at quarter to twelve in the morning!' Armande had said. In that one word 'really' what a number of reproofs she could convey! 'Really, Maxime, you needn't *always* stand right in front of the window, you shut out the daylight. Maxime, really! You've gone and returned a ball *again* when it was "out".'

But when a particular period was over, there had been no more 'reallys' and no more reproaches showered on his head. Still not properly asleep, Maxime Degouthe groped around a memory, around a moment that had restored a little confidence to his twenty-five-year-old self and had marked the end of Armande's gracious condescension. That day, he had arrived with Jeanne at the foot of the steps, just as Armande was opening the silvered wrought-iron door to go out. They had not seen each other for a very long time – 'Hullo, fancy seeing! – Yes, my sister insisted on bringing me with her, perhaps you'd rather I hadn't come. – Now, really, you're joking. – A friend of mine in Paris gave me a lift in his car and dropped me here this morning. – How awfully nice! Are you going to be here for some time? – No, the same friend's picking me up tomorrow after lunch and driving me back. – Well, that *is* a short stay.' In fact, such trivialities as to make either of them blush had either of them paid any attention to what they were saying. From the height of five or six steps, a wide, startled, offended gaze fell on Maxime. He also caught, at the level of his knees, the brush of a skirt hem and a handbag which Armande had dropped and which he retrieved.

After a gloomy game of ping-pong, a tea composed entirely of sugary things, a handshake – a strong, swift, but promptly withdrawn hand had clasped his own – he had left Armande once again, and on the way back, Jeanne had given her cynical opinion of the situation: 'You know, you could have the fair Armande as easy as pie. And I know what I'm talking about.' She added: 'You don't know the right way to go about it.' But those had been the remarks of a twenty-year-old, the infallibility of one girl judging another girl.

He thought he was only half asleep and fell into deep but restless dreams. A nightmare tortured him with the shaming illusion that he was dressing old Queny's incurable foot on the steps leading up to the Fauconniers' house and that Armande was enthroned, impassive, at the top of them. Didn't she owe part of her prestige to those eight broad steps, almost like a series of terraces, that were famous throughout the town? 'The Fauconniers' flight of front steps is so impressive. Without these front steps, the Fauconniers' house wouldn't have nearly such a grand air...' As if insulted, the sleeper sat up with a start. 'Grand air, indeed! That cube! That block with its cast-iron balconies and bands of tiles!' He woke up completely and once again the Fauconnier home inspired him with the old awed respect.

The Fauconnier heliotropes, the Fauconnier polygonums, the Fauconnier lobelias recovered their status of flowers adorning the altar where he worshipped. So, to send himself to sleep again, Maxime soberly envisaged the duties that awaited him the next day, the day after, and all the rest of his life, in the guise of the faces of old Queny, of the elder Madame Cauvain, of her father Monsieur Enfert, of 'young' Mademoiselle Philippon, the one who was only seventy-two . . . For old people do not die off in wartime. He swallowed half his bottle of mineral water at one gulp and fell heavily asleep again, insensible to the mosquitoes coming up from the shrunken river and the noises of the pale dawn.

'My last day of idle luxury.' He had his breakfast in bed, feeling slightly ashamed, and ordered a bath, for which he had to wait a considerable time. 'My last bath . . . I'm not going to get up till I've had my bath! I'm not leaving without my bath!' As a matter of fact, he preferred a very stiff shower or the chance plunges he had taken, straight into rivers and canals, these last months between April and August.

With some caution he made use of a toilet water invented by his brother-in-law, the red-haired chemist. 'Hector's perfumes, when they don't smell of squashed ants, smell of bad cognac.' He chose his bluest shirt and his spotted foulard tie. 'I wish I were handsome. And all I am is just so-so. Ah, how I wish I were handsome!' he kept thinking over and over again as he plastered down his brilliantined hair. But it was coarse, intractable, wavy hair, a vigorous bush that preferred standing up to lying down. When Maxime laughed, he wrinkled his nose, crinkled up his yellow-brown eyes, and revealed his 'lucky teeth', healthy and close-set except for a gap between the two upper front ones. Coatless and buckled into his best belt, he had, at nearly thirty, the free and easy charm and slightly plebeian elegance of many an errand boy you see darting through the crowd on his bicycle, nimble as a bird in a bush. 'But, in a jacket, I just look common,' Maxime decided, as he straightened the lapels of the hand-me-down jacket. 'It's also the fault of the coat.' He threw his reflection an angry glance. 'Nevertheless, beautiful Armande, more than ten others have been quite satisfied with all that and have even said "Thank you."' He sighed, and turned humble again. 'But seeing that it's to no one but Armande I'm appealing when I conjure up my poor little girlfriends, what on earth does it matter whether they thanked me or even asked for more? It's not of them I'm thinking.'

He packed his suitcase with the care and dexterity of a man accustomed to use his hands for manipulating living substance, stopping the flow of blood, applying and pinning bandages. The September morning, with its flies and its warm yellow light, came in fresh through the open window; at the end of a narrow street a dancing shimmer showed where the river lay. 'I shan't go and say goodbye to Armande,' Maxime Degouthe decided. 'For one thing, lunch is always late at Jeanne's; for another, I've got my case of medical supplies to fill up at the last moment, and if I'm to have time to get a bite of food before the train goes, it'll be impossible, yes, physically impossible.'

At four o'clock, he opened the front gate, marched up the gravel path of the Fauconniers' garden, climbed the flight of steps, and rang the bell. A second time, he pressed his finger long and vainly on the bell button, sunk in a rosette of white marble. No one came and the blood rushed up into Maxime's ears. 'She's probably gone out. But where are her two lazy sluts of servants and the gardener who looks like a drunk?' He rang again, restraining himself with difficulty from giving the door a kick. At last he heard steps in the garden and saw Armande running towards him. She stopped in front of him, exclaiming 'Ah!' and he smiled at seeing her wearing a big blue apron with a bib that completely enveloped her. She swiftly untied the apron and flung it on a rosebush.

'But it suited you very well,' said Maxime.

Armande blushed and he blushed himself, thinking that perhaps he had hurt her feelings. 'She would take it the wrong way, naturally. She's impossible, impossible! Pretty, those flecks of white soap in her black hair. I'd never noticed that the skin at the edge of her forehead, just under the hair, is slightly blue.'

'I was at the end of the garden, in the washhouse,' said Armande. 'It's laundry day today, so . . . Léonie and Maria didn't even hear the bell.'

'I shan't keep you from your work, I only looked in for a couple of minutes. As I'm leaving tomorrow morning.'

He had followed her to the top of the steps, and Maxime waited for her to indicate which of the wicker chairs he should sit in. But she said: 'From four to seven the sun just beats down on you here,' and she ushered him into the drawing room, where they sat down opposite each other. Maxime seated himself in one of the armchairs tapestried with La Fontaine's fables – his was 'The Cat, the Weasel, and the Little Rabbit' – and stared at the rest of the furniture. The baby-grand piano, the Revolution clock, the plants in pots, he gazed at them all with hostile reverence.

'It's nice in here, isn't it?' said Armande. 'I keep the blinds down because it faces south. Jeanne wasn't able to come?'

'Goodness, is she frightened of me?' He was on the point of feeling flattered. But he looked at Armande and saw her sitting stiffly upright on 'The Fox and the Stork', one elbow on the hard arm of the chair, the other on her lap, with her hands clasped together. In the dusk of the lowered blinds, her cheeks and her neck took on the colour of very pale terra-cotta, and she was looking straight at him with the steady gaze of a well-brought-up girl who knows she must not blink or look sidelong, or pretend to be shy so as to show off the length of her lashes. 'What the hell am I doing here?' thought Maxime furiously. 'This is where I've got to, where we've both got to, after ten, fifteen years of what's called childhood friendship. This girl is made of wood. Or else she's choked with pride. You won't catch me again in the Fauconnier drawing room.' Nevertheless, he replied to Armande's questions, he talked to her about his 'practice' and the 'inevitable difficulties' of this postwar period.

Nor did he fail to remark: 'But you know better than anyone what these various difficulties are. Look at you, loaded with responsibilities, and all alone in the world!'

Armande's immobility was shattered by an unexpected movement; she unclasped her fingers and clutched the arms of her chair with both hands as if she were afraid of slipping off it.

'Oh, I'm used to it. You know my mother brought me up in a rather special way. At my age, one's no longer a child.'

The sentence, begun with assurance, broke off on a child-ish note that belied the last words. She mastered herself and said, in a different voice: 'Won't you have a glass of port? Or would you prefer orangeade?'

Maxime saw there was a loaded tray within easy reach of her hand and frowned.

'You're expecting guests? Then I'll be off!'

He had stood up; she remained seated and laid her hand on Maxime's arm.

'I never invite anyone on washing day. I assure you I don't.

As you'd told me you were going away again tomorrow, I thought you might possibly...'

She broke off, with a little grimace that displeased Maxime. 'Ah, no! She's not to ruin that mouth for me! That outline of the lips, clear-cut, so full; those corners of the mouth that are so ... so ... What's the matter with her today? You'd think she'd just buried the devil for good and all!'

He realized he was staring at her with unpardonable severity and forced himself to be gay.

'So you're heavily occupied in domestic chores? What a lovely laundress you make! And all those children at your clinic, do you manage to keep them in order?'

He was laughing only with his lips. He knew very well that, when he was with Armande, love made him gloomy, jealous, self-consciously unable to break down an obstacle between the two of them that perhaps did not exist. Armande took a deep breath, squared her shoulders and commanded her whole face to be nothing but the calm regular countenance of a beautiful brunette. But three shadowy dimples, two at the corners of the mouth, one in the chin, appeared when she smiled and quivered at every hint of emotion.

'I've got twenty-eight children over at the clinic, did you know that?'

'Twenty-eight children? Don't you think that's a lot for a young unmarried girl?'

'I'm not frightened of children,' said Armande seriously.

'Children. She loves children. She'd be magnificent, pregnant. Tall as she is, she would broaden at the hips without looking squat, like short women who are carrying babies. She'd take up an enormous amount of space in the garden, in bed, in my arms. At last she'd have trusting eyes, the lovely, dark-ringed eyes of a pregnant woman. But for that to happen, Mademoiselle has got to tolerate someone coming close to her, and a little closer than offering her a ball at arm's length on a tennis racket. She doesn't look as if the idea had ever occurred to her, that girl doesn't! In any case, *I'm* giving up all thought of it!'

He stood up, resolutely.

'This time, Armande, it's serious.'

'What is?' she said, very low.

'Why, the fact that it's five o'clock, that I've two or three urgent things to do, a big parcel of medical supplies to get ready. My little village is right out of everything in the way of serums and pills.'

'I know,' said Armande at once.

'You know?'

'Oh, I just accidentally heard them say so, at your brother-in-law's.'

He had leaned towards her a little; she drew away with such a fierce movement that she knocked her elbow against a monumental lamp-stand.

'Have you hurt yourself?' said Maxime coldly.

'No,' she said, equally coldly. 'Not in the least.'

She passed in front of him to open the front door, with its wrought-iron lacework. It resisted her efforts.

'The woodwork's warped. I keep telling Charost to fix it.'

'Haven't I always known it to stick like that? Don't destroy my childhood memories!'

Pursing her lips tight, she shook the door with a stubborn violence that made its panes rattle. There was a loud crash of glass and metal behind her, and turning around, she saw Maxime staggering among the splintered cups and chromium hoops of the chandelier that had just fallen from the ceiling. Then his knees went limp and he fell over on his side. Prone on the floor, he made an attempt to raise his hand to his ear, could not finish the gesture, and lay perfectly still.

Armande, with her back against the front door she had not had time to open, stared at the man lying at her feet on his bed of broken glass. She said in a strangled, incredulous voice: 'No!' The sight of a trickle of blood running down behind Maxime's left ear and stopping for a moment on the collar of the blue shirt, which it soaked, restored Armande's power of speech and movement. She squatted down, straightened up swiftly, opened the door that was half obstructed by the injured body, and screamed shrill summonses out into the garden.

'Maria! Léonie! Maria! Maria!'

The screams reached Maxime in the place where he reposed, unconscious. Along with the screams, he began to hear the buzzing of hives of bees and the clanging of hammers, and he half opened his eyes. But unconsciousness promptly swallowed him up again and he fell back among the swarms of bees and the hammering to some place where pain, in its turn, tracked him down. 'The top of my head hurts. It hurts behind my ear and on my shoulder.'

Once again, the loud screams disturbed him. 'Léonie! Maria!' He came to, very unwillingly, opened his eyes, and received a sunbeam full in his face. The sunbeam appeared to be red; then it was cut off by a double moving shadow. All at once, he realized that Armande's two legs were passing to and fro across the light; he recognized Armande's feet, the white linen shoes trimmed with black leather. The feet were moving about in all directions on the carpet quite close to his head, sometimes open in a V and staggering, sometimes close together, and crushing bits of broken glass. He felt an urge to untie one of the white shoelaces for a joke, but at that very moment, he was shot through with agonizing pain, and without knowing it, he moaned.

'My darling, my darling,' said a shaking voice.

'Her darling? What darling?' he asked himself. He raised his cheek, which was lying heavily on fragments of pale blue glass and the butt ends of electric light bulbs. The blood spread out in a pool and his cheek was sticky with it. At the pathetic sight of the precious red spilled all about him, he woke up completely and understood all. He took advantage of the fact that the two feet had turned their heels to him and were running towards the terrace to feel his aching head and bruised shoulder and to discover that the source of the blood was behind his ear. 'Good, a big cut. Nothing broken. I might have had my ear sliced off. It's a good thing to have hair like mine. Lord, how my head does ache!'

'Maria! Léonie!'

The black-and-white shoes returned; two knees sheathed in silk went down on the splintered glass. 'She'll cut herself!' He made a slight movement to raise himself, then decided instead to lie low and keep quiet, only turning his head over so as to show Armande where his wound was.

'Oh heavens, he's bleeding,' said Armande's voice. 'Maria! Léonie!'

There was no reply.

'Oh, the bitches,' the same voice said violently.

Sheer astonishment made Maxime give a start.

'Speak to me, Maxime! Maxime, can you hear me? My darling, my darling...'

Sabots were heard running in the garden, then climbing the steps.

'Ah, there you are, Charost! Yes, the chandelier fell down. A person could die in this place without anyone's hearing! Where *are* those two wretched girls?'

'In the paddock, Mademoiselle, spreading out the sheets. Ah, the poor unfortunate young man! He had a hundred years of life ahead of him!'

'I'm quite sure he still has! Run around to Dr Pommier, tell him...If he's not in, Dr Tuloup. If *he's* not in, the chemist, yes, the ginger-haired one, Madame Jeanne's husband. Charost, go and get the towels from my bathroom, the little hand towel from the cloakroom, you can *see* I can't leave him. And the brown box in the cupboard! Hurry up, will you! Get someone to tell those two idiots to leave their washing, don't go yourself, send someone!'

The sabots clattered away.

'My darling, my darling,' said the low, sweet voice.

'It really was me, the darling,' Maxime told himself. Two hot hands feverishly massaged one of his, interrogating it. 'There, there, my pulse is excellent! Don't get in a state! How beautiful she must be at this moment ...' He groaned on purpose and slid the thread of a glance at Armande between his eyelids. She was ugly, with huge, terrified eyes and her mouth gaping stupidly. He closed his lids again, enraptured.

The hands pressed a wet towel over his wound, pushed away the hair. 'That's not right, my pet, that's not right. Isn't there any iodine in the place, then? She'll make me bleed unnecessarily, but what the hell does that matter as long as she keeps busy on me?' The ferruginous smell of iodine rose in his nostrils, he was aware of the wholesome burning pain, and relaxed, content. 'Well done! But when it comes to putting on an efficient bandage, my girl, I'm streets ahead of you. That one won't ever hold. You ought to have shaved off a bit of my hair.' He heard the girl clucking her tongue against her teeth, 'tst tst'; then she became despairing.

'Oh, I'm too stupid! A bloody fool, in fact!'

He very nearly laughed but turned it into a vague, pitiful mumbling.

'Maxime, Maxime!' she implored.

She untied his tie, opened his shirt, and, trying to find his heart, brushed the masculine nipple that swelled with pride. For a moment, the two of them were equally and completely motionless. As the hand withdrew, after receiving its reassuring answer from the heart, it slowly went over the same ground on its way back. 'Oh, to take that hand that's stroking me in this startled way, to get up, to hug that grand, beautiful girl I love, to turn *her* into a wounded, moaning creature, and then to comfort her, to nurse her in my arms. It's so long I've waited for that. But suppose she defends herself?' He decided to go on with his ruse, stirred feebly, opened his arms, and fell back into pretended unconsciousness.

'Ah!' cried Armande, 'he's fainted! Why don't those imbeciles come!'

She leaped to her feet and ran off to fetch a fibre cushion, which she tried to insert between Maxime's head and the splinters of glass. In doing so, the makeshift bandage came off. Maxime could hear Armande stamping her feet, walking away, and slapping her thighs with a forceful plebeian despair. She returned to him, sat down right in the litter of broken glass and the pool of bloodstained water, and half lay down against the wounded man. With exquisite pleasure he could feel she had lost her head and was crying. He squeezed his eyelids together so as not to look at her. But he could not shut out the smell of black hair and hot skin, the sandalwood smell that healthy brunettes exude. She raised one of his eyelids with her finger and he rolled up his eyeball as if in ecstasy or a swoon. With her sleeve, she wiped his forehead and his mouth; furtively, she opened his lips and bent over him to look at the white teeth with the gap between the front ones. 'Another minute of this sort of thing and . . . and I shall devour her!' She bent a little lower, put her mouth against Maxime's, then drew back at once, frightened at the sound of hurried footsteps and breathless voices. But her whole body remained close to him, tamed and alert, and there was still time for her to whisper the hackneyed words girls new to love stammer out before the man has taught them others or they invent more beautiful, more secret ones: 'Darling... My beloved boy. My very own Maxime.'

When the rescue party arrived, she was still sitting on the ground in her soaked skirt and her torn stockings. Maxime was able to wake up, to complete his deception by a few, incoherent words, to smile in a bewildered way at Armande, and to protest at all the fuss going on around him. The Grand Central Pharmacy had provided its stretcher and its pharmacist, who constructed a turban of bandages on Maxime's head. Then the stretcher and its escort set forth like a procession incensed by a choir of voices.

'Open the other half of the door. Watch out, it won't go through. I tell you it will go through if you bear a bit to the right. There... just a bare millimetre to spare. You've got eight steps to go down.'

At the top of the terrace, Armande remained alone, use-less, and as if forgotten. But at the bottom of the steps, Maxime summoned her with a gesture and a look: 'Come... I know you now. I've got you. Come, we'll finish that timid little kiss you began. Stay with me. Acknowledge me...' She walked down the steps and gave him her hand. Then she adapted her step to that of the stretcher-bearers and walked meekly beside him, all stained and dishevelled, as if she had come straight from the hands of love.

D. H. LAWRENCE

THE HORSE DEALER'S DAUGHTER

'WELL, MABEL, AND what are you going to do with yourself?' asked Joe, with foolish flippancy. He felt quite safe himself. Without listening for an answer, he turned aside, worked a grain of tobacco to the tip of his tongue, and spat it out. He did not care about anything, since he felt safe himself.

The three brothers and the sister sat round the desolate breakfast table, attempting some sort of desultory consultation. The morning's post had given the final tap to the family fortunes, and all was over. The dreary dining-room itself, with its heavy mahogany furniture, looked as if it were waiting to be done away with.

But the consultation amounted to nothing. There was a strange air of ineffectuality about the three men, as they sprawled at table, smoking and reflecting vaguely on their own condition. The girl was alone, a rather short, sullen-looking young woman of twenty-seven. She did not share the same life as her brothers. She would have been good-looking, save for the impassive fixity of her face, 'bull-dog', as her brothers called it.

There was a confused tramping of horses' feet outside. The three men all sprawled round in their chairs to watch. Beyond the dark holly-bushes that separated the strip of lawn from the highroad, they could see a cavalcade of shire horses swinging out of their own yard, being taken for exercise. This was the last time. These were the last horses that would go through their hands. The young men watched with critical, callous look. They were all frightened at the collapse of their lives, and the sense of disaster in which they were involved left them no inner freedom.

Yet they were three fine, well-set fellows enough. Joe, the eldest, was a man of thirty-three, broad and handsome in a hot, flushed way. His face was red, he twisted his black moustache over a thick finger, his eyes were shallow and restless. He had a sensual way of uncovering his teeth when he laughed, and his bearing was stupid. Now he watched the horses with a glazed look of helplessness in his eyes, a certain stupor of downfall.

The great draught-horses swung past. They were tied head to tail, four of them, and they heaved along to where a lane branched off from the highroad, planting their great hoofs floutingly in the fine black mud, swinging their great rounded haunches sumptuously, and trotting a few sudden steps as they were led into the lane, round the corner. Every movement showed a massive, slumbrous strength, and a stupidity which held them in subjection. The groom at the head looked back, jerking the leading rope. And the cavalcade moved out of sight up the lane, the tail of the last horse, bobbed up tight and stiff, held out taut from the swinging great haunches as they rocked behind the hedges in a motion-like sleep.

Joe watched with glazed hopeless eyes. The horses were almost like his own body to him. He felt he was done for now. Luckily he was engaged to a woman as old as himself, and therefore her father, who was steward of a neighbouring estate, would provide him with a job. He would marry and go into harness. His life was over, he would be a subject animal now.

He turned uneasily aside, the retreating steps of the horses echoing in his ears. Then, with foolish restlessness, he reached for the scraps of bacon-rind from the plates, and making a faint whistling sound, flung them to the terrier that lay against the fender. He watched the dog swallow them, and waited till the creature looked into his eyes. Then a faint grin came on his face, and in a high, foolish voice he said:

'You won't get much more bacon, shall you, you little b—?'

The dog faintly and dismally wagged its tail, then lowered its haunches, circled round, and lay down again.

There was another helpless silence at the table. Joe sprawled uneasily in his seat, not willing to go till the family conclave was dissolved. Fred Henry, the second brother, was erect, clean-limbed, alert. He had watched the passing of the horses with more *sang-froid*. If he was an animal, like Joe, he was an animal which controls, not one which is controlled. He was master of any horse, and he carried himself with a well-tempered air of mastery. But he was not master of the situations of life. He pushed his coarse brown moustache upwards, off his lip, and glanced irritably at his sister, who sat impassive and inscrutable.

'You'll go and stop with Lucy for a bit, shan't you?' he asked. The girl did not answer.

'I don't see what else you can do,' persisted Fred Henry.

'Go as a skivvy,' Joe interpolated laconically.

The girl did not move a muscle.

'If I was her, I should go in for training for a nurse,' said Malcolm, the youngest of them all. He was the baby of the family, a young man of twenty-two, with a fresh, jaunty *museau*.

But Mabel did not take any notice of him. They had talked at her and round her for so many years, that she hardly heard them at all.

The marble clock on the mantelpiece softly chimed the half-hour, the dog rose uneasily from the hearthrug and looked at the party at the breakfast table. But still they sat on in ineffectual conclave.

'Oh, all right,' said Joe suddenly, *à propos* of nothing. 'I'll get a move on.'

He pushed back his chair, straddled his knees with a downward jerk, to get them free, in horsey fashion, and went to the fire. Still he did not go out of the room; he was curious to know what the others would do or say. He began to charge his pipe, looking down at the dog and saying, in a high, affected voice:

'Going wi' me? Going wi' me are ter? Tha'rt goin' further than the counts on just now, dost hear?'

The dog faintly wagged its tail, the man stuck out his jaw and covered his pipe with his hands, and puffed intently, losing himself in the tobacco, looking down all the while at the dog with an absent brown eye. The dog looked up at him in mournful distrust. Joe stood with his knees stuck out, in real horsey fashion.

'Have you had a letter from Lucy?' Fred Henry asked of his sister.

'Last week,' came the neutral reply.

'And what does she say?'

There was no answer.

'Does she *ask* you to go and stop there?' persisted Fred Henry.

'She says I can if I like.'

'Well, then, you'd better. Tell her you'll come on Monday.'

This was received in silence.

'That's what you'll do then, is it?' said Fred Henry, in some exasperation.

But she made no answer. There was a silence of futility and irritation in the room. Malcolm grinned fatuously.

'You'll have to make up your mind between now and next Wednesday,' said Joe loudly, 'or else find yourself lodgings on the kerbstone.'

The face of the young woman darkened, but she sat on immutable.

'Here's Jack Fergusson!' exclaimed Malcolm, who was looking aimlessly out of the window.

'Where?' exclaimed Joe, loudly.

'Just gone past.'

'Coming in?'

Malcolm craned his neck to see the gate.

'Yes,' he said.

There was a silence. Mabel sat on like one condemned, at the head of the table. Then a whistle was heard from the kitchen. The dog got up and barked sharply. Joe opened the door and shouted:

'Come on.'

After a moment a young man entered. He was muffled up in overcoat and a purple woollen scarf, and his tweed cap, which he did not remove, was pulled down on his head. He was of medium height, his face was rather long and pale, his eyes looked tired.

'Hello, Jack! Well, Jack!' exclaimed Malcolm and Joe. Fred Henry merely said, 'Jack.'

'What's doing?' asked the newcomer, evidently addressing Fred Henry.

'Same. We've got to be out by Wednesday. – Got a cold?'

'I have – got it bad, too.'

'Why don't you stop in?'

'*Me* stop in? When I can't stand on my legs, perhaps I

shall have a chance.' The young man spoke huskily. He had a slight Scotch accent.

'It's a knock-out, isn't it,' said Joe, boisterously, 'if a doctor goes round croaking with a cold. Looks bad for the patients, doesn't it?'

The young doctor looked at him slowly.

'Anything the matter with *you*, then?' he asked sarcastically.

'Not as I know of. Damn your eyes, I hope not. Why?'

'I thought you were very concerned about the patients, wondered if you might be one yourself.'

'Damn it, no, I've never been patient to no flaming doctor, and hope I never shall be,' returned Joe.

At this point Mabel rose from the table, and they all seemed to become aware of her existence. She began putting the dishes together. The young doctor looked at her, but did not address her. He had not greeted her. She went out of the room with the tray, her face impassive and unchanged.

'When are you off then, all of you?' asked the doctor.

'I'm catching the eleven-forty,' replied Malcolm. 'Are you goin' down wi' th' trap, Joe?'

'Yes, I've told you I'm going down wi' th' trap, haven't I?'

'We'd better be getting her in then. – So long, Jack, if I don't see you before I go,' said Malcolm, shaking hands.

He went out, followed by Joe, who seemed to have his tail between his legs.

'Well, this is the devil's own,' exclaimed the doctor, when he was left alone with Fred Henry. 'Going before Wednesday, are you?'

'That's the orders,' replied the other.

'Where, to Northampton?'

'That's it.'

'The devil!' exclaimed Fergusson, with quiet chagrin.

And there was silence between the two.

'All settled up, are you?' asked Fergusson.

'About.'

There was another pause.

'Well, I shall miss yer, Freddy, boy,' said the young doctor.

'And I shall miss thee, Jack,' returned the other.

'Miss you like hell,' mused the doctor.

Fred Henry turned aside. There was nothing to say. Mabel came in again, to finish clearing the table.

'What are *you* going to do, then, Miss Pervin?' asked Fergusson. 'Going to your sister's, are you?'

Mabel looked at him with her steady, dangerous eyes, that always made him uncomfortable, unsettling his superficial ease.

'No,' she said.

'Well, what in the name of fortune *are* you going to do? Say what you mean to do,' cried Fred Henry, with futile intensity.

But she only averted her head, and continued her work. She folded the white table-cloth, and put on the chenille cloth.

'The sulkiest bitch that ever trod!' muttered her brother.

But she finished her task with perfectly impassive face, the young doctor watching her interestedly all the while. Then she went out.

Fred Henry stared after her, clenching his lips, his blue eyes fixing in sharp antagonism, as he made a grimace of sour exasperation.

'You could bray her into bits, and that's all you'd get out of her,' he said, in a small, narrowed tone.

The doctor smiled faintly.

'What's she *going* to do, then?' he asked.

'Strike me if *I* know!' returned the other.

There was a pause. Then the doctor stirred.

'I'll be seeing you tonight, shall I?' he said to his friend.

'Ay – where's it to be? Are we going over to Jessdale?'

'I don't know. I've got such a cold on me. I'll come round to the Moon and Stars, anyway.'

'Let Lizzie and May miss their night for once, eh?'

'That's it – if I feel as I do now.'

'All's one –'

The two young men went through the passage and down to the back door together. The house was large, but it was servantless now, and desolate. At the back was a small bricked house-yard, and beyond that a big square, gravelled fine and red, and having stables on two sides. Sloping, dank, winter-dark fields stretched away on the open sides.

But the stables were empty. Joseph Pervin, the father of the family, had been a man of no education, who had become a fairly large horse dealer. The stables had been full of horses, there was a great turmoil and come-and-go of horses and of dealers and grooms. Then the kitchen was full of servants. But of late things had declined. The old man had married a second time, to retrieve his fortunes. Now he was dead and everything was gone to the dogs, there was nothing but debt and threatening.

For months, Mabel had been servantless in the big house, keeping the home together in penury for her ineffectual brothers. She had kept house for ten years. But previously, it was with unstinted means. Then, however brutal and coarse everything was, the sense of money had kept her proud, confident. The men might be foul-mouthed, the women in the kitchen might have bad reputations, her brothers might have illegitimate children. But so long as there was money, the girl felt herself established, and brutally proud, reserved.

No company came to the house, save dealers and coarse

men. Mabel had no associates of her own sex, after her sister went away. But she did not mind. She went regularly to church, she attended to her father. And she lived in the memory of her mother, who had died when she was fourteen, and whom she had loved. She had loved her father, too, in a different way, depending upon him, and feeling secure in him, until at the age of fifty-four he married again. And then she had set hard against him. Now he had died and left them all hopelessly in debt.

She had suffered badly during the period of poverty. Nothing, however, could shake the curious sullen, animal pride that dominated each member of the family. Now, for Mabel, the end had come. Still she would not cast about her. She would follow her own way just the same. She would always hold the keys of her own situation. Mindless and persistent, she endured from day to day. Why should she think? Why should she answer anybody? It was enough that this was the end, and there was no way out. She need not pass any more darkly along the main street of the small town, avoiding every eye. She need not demean herself any more, going into the shops and buying the cheapest food. This was at an end. She thought of nobody, not even of herself. Mindless and persistent, she seemed in a sort of ecstasy to be coming nearer to her fulfilment, her own glorification, approaching her dead mother, who was glorified.

In the afternoon she took a little bag, with shears and sponge and a small scrubbing brush, and went out. It was a grey, wintry day, with saddened, dark-green fields and an atmosphere blackened by the smoke of foundries not far off. She went quickly, darkly along the causeway, heeding nobody, through the town to the churchyard.

There she always felt secure, as if no one could see her, although as a matter of fact she was exposed to the stare of everyone who passed along under the churchyard wall. Nevertheless, once under the shadow of the great looming church, among the graves, she felt immune from the world, reserved within the thick churchyard wall as in another country.

Carefully she clipped the grass from the grave, and arranged the pinky-white, small chrysanthemums in the tin cross. When this was done, she took an empty jar from a neighbouring grave, brought water, and carefully, most scrupulously sponged the marble headstone and the coping-stone.

It gave her sincere satisfaction to do this. She felt in immediate contact with the world of her mother. She took minute pains, went through the park in a state bordering on pure happiness, as if in performing this task she came into a subtle, intimate connection with her mother. For the life she followed here in the world was far less real than the world of death she inherited from her mother.

The doctor's house was just by the church. Fergusson, being a mere hired assistant, was slave to the countryside. As he hurried now to attend to the outpatients in the surgery, glancing across the graveyard with his quick eye, he saw the girl at her task at the grave. She seemed so intent and remote, it was like looking into another world. Some mystical element was touched in him. He slowed down as he walked, watching her as if spell-bound.

She lifted her eyes, feeling him looking. Their eyes met. And each looked again at once, each feeling, in some way, found out by the other. He lifted his cap and passed on down the road. There remained distinct in his consciousness, like a vision, the memory of her face, lifted from the tombstone in the churchyard, and looking at him with slow, large, portentous eyes. It *was* portentous, her face. It seemed to mesmerize him. There was a heavy power in her eyes which laid hold of his whole being, as if he had drunk some powerful drug. He had been feeling weak and done before. Now the life came back into him, he felt delivered from his own fretted, daily self.

He finished his duties at the surgery as quickly as might be, hastily filling up the bottles of the waiting people with cheap drugs. Then, in perpetual haste, he set off again to visit several cases in another part of his round, before tea-time. At all times he preferred to walk, if he could, but particularly when he was not well. He fancied the motion restored him.

The afternoon was falling. It was grey, deadened, and wintry, with a slow, moist, heavy coldness sinking in and deadening all the faculties. But why should he think or notice? He hastily climbed the hill and turned across the dark-green fields, following the black cinder-track. In the distance, across a shallow dip in the country, the small town was clustered like smouldering ash, a tower, a spire, a heap of low, raw, extinct houses. And on the nearest fringe of the town, sloping into the dip, was Oldmeadow, the Pervins' house. He could see the stables and the outbuildings distinctly, as they lay towards him on the slope. Well, he would not go there many more times! Another resource would be lost to him, another place gone: the only company he cared for in the alien, ugly little town he was losing. Nothing but work, drudgery, constant hastening from dwelling to dwelling among the colliers and the iron-workers. It wore him out, but at the same time he had a craving for it. It was a stimulant to him to be in the homes of the working people, moving as it were through the innermost body of their life. His nerves were excited and gratified. He could come so near, into the very lives of the rough, inarticulate, powerfully emotional men and women. He grumbled, he said he hated the hellish hole. But as a matter of fact it excited him, the contact with the rough, strongly-feeling people was a stimulant applied direct to his nerves.

Below Oldmeadow, in the green, shallow, soddened hollow of fields, lay a square, deep pond. Roving across the landscape, the doctor's quick eye detected a figure in black passing through the gate of the field, down towards the pond. He looked again. It would be Mabel Pervin. His mind suddenly became alive and attentive.

Why was she going down there? He pulled up on the path on the slope above, and stood staring. He could just make sure of the small black figure moving in the hollow of the failing day. He seemed to see her in the midst of such obscurity, that he was like a clairvoyant, seeing rather with the mind's eye than with ordinary sight. Yet he could see her positively enough, whilst he kept his eye attentive. He felt, if he looked away from her, in the thick, ugly falling dusk, he would lose her altogether.

He followed her minutely as she moved, direct and intent, like something transmitted rather than stirring in voluntary activity, straight down the field towards the pond. There she stood on the bank for a moment. She never raised her head. Then she waded slowly into the water.

He stood motionless as the small black figure walked slowly and deliberately towards the centre of the pond, very slowly, gradually moving deeper into the motionless water, and still moving forward as the water got up to her breast. Then he could see her no more in the dusk of the dead afternoon.

'There!' he exclaimed. 'Would you believe it?'

And he hastened straight down, running over the wet, soddened fields, pushing through the hedges, down into the depression of callous wintry obscurity. It took him several minutes to come to the pond. He stood on the bank, breathing heavily. He could see nothing. His eyes seemed to penetrate the dead water. Yes, perhaps that was the dark shadow of her black clothing beneath the surface of the water.

He slowly ventured into the pond. The bottom was deep, soft clay, he sank in, and the water clasped dead cold round his legs. As he stirred he could smell the cold, rotten clay that fouled up into the water. It was objectionable in his lungs. Still, repelled and yet not heeding, he moved deeper into the pond. The cold water rose over his thighs, over his loins, upon his abdomen. The lower part of his body was all sunk in the hideous cold element. And the bottom was so deeply soft and uncertain, he was afraid of pitching with his mouth underneath. He could not swim, and was afraid.

He crouched a little, spreading his hands under the water and moving them round, trying to feel for her. The dead cold pond swayed upon his chest. He moved again, a little deeper, and again, with his hands underneath, he felt all around under the water. And he touched her clothing. But it evaded his fingers. He made a desperate effort to grasp it.

And so doing he lost his balance and went under, horribly, suffocating in the foul earthy water, struggling madly for a few moments. At last, after what seemed an eternity, he got his footing, rose again into the air and looked around. He gasped, and knew he was in the world. Then he looked at the water. She had risen near him. He grasped her clothing, and drawing her nearer, turned to take his way to land again.

He went very slowly, carefully, absorbed in the slow progress. He rose higher, climbing out of the pond. The water was now only about his legs; he was thankful, full of relief to be out of the clutches of the pond. He lifted her and staggered on to the bank, out of the horror of wet, grey clay.

He laid her down on the bank. She was quite unconscious and running with water. He made the water come from her mouth, he worked to restore her. He did not have to work very long before he could feel the breathing begin again in her; she was breathing naturally. He worked a little longer. He could feel her live beneath his hands; she was coming back. He wiped her face, wrapped her in his overcoat, looked round into the dim, dark-grey world, then lifted her and staggered down the bank and across the fields.

It seemed an unthinkably long way, and his burden so heavy he felt he would never get to the house. But at last he was in the stable-yard, and then in the house-yard. He opened the door and went into the house. In the kitchen he laid her down on the hearthrug, and called. The house was empty. But the fire was burning in the grate.

Then again he kneeled to attend to her. She was breathing regularly, her eyes were wide open and as if conscious, but there seemed something missing in her look. She was conscious in herself, but unconscious of her surroundings.

He ran upstairs, took blankets from a bed, and put them before the fire to warm. Then he removed her saturated, earthy-smelling clothing, rubbed her dry with a towel, and wrapped her naked in the blankets. Then he went into the dining-room, to look for spirits. There was a little whisky. He drank a gulp himself, and put some into her mouth.

The effect was instantaneous. She looked full into his face, as if she had been seeing him for some time, and yet had only just become conscious of him.

'Dr Fergusson?' she said.

'What?' he answered.

He was divesting himself of his coat, intending to find some dry clothing upstairs. He could not bear the smell of the dead, clayey water, and he was mortally afraid for his own health.

'What did I do?' she asked.

'Walked into the pond,' he replied. He had begun to shudder like one sick, and could hardly attend to her. Her eyes remained full on him, he seemed to be going dark in his mind, looking back at her helplessly. The shuddering became quieter in him, his life came back in him, dark and unknowing, but strong again.

'Was I out of my mind?' she asked, while her eyes were fixed on him all the time.

'Maybe, for the moment,' he replied. He felt quiet, because his strength had come back. The strange fretful strain had left him.

'Am I out of my mind now?' she asked.

'Are you?' he reflected a moment. 'No,' he answered truthfully, 'I don't see that you are.' He turned his face aside. He was afraid now, because he felt dazed, and felt dimly that her power was stronger than his, in this issue. And she continued to look at him fixedly all the time. 'Can you tell me where I shall find some dry things to put on?' he asked.

'Did you dive into the pond for me?' she asked.

'No,' he answered. 'I walked in. But I went in overhead as well.'

There was silence for a moment. He hesitated. He very much wanted to go upstairs to get into dry clothing. But there was another desire in him. And she seemed to hold him. His will seemed to have gone to sleep, and left him, standing there slack before her. But he felt warm inside himself. He did not shudder at all, though his clothes were sodden on him.

'Why did you?' she asked.

'Because I didn't want you to do such a foolish thing,' he said.

'It wasn't foolish,' she said, still gazing at him as she lay on the floor, with a sofa cushion under her head. 'It was the right thing to do. *I* knew best, then.'

'I'll go and shift these wet things,' he said. But still he had not the power to move out of her presence, until she sent him. It was as if she had the life of his body in her hands, and he could not extricate himself. Or perhaps he did not want to.

Suddenly she sat up. Then she became aware of her own immediate condition. She felt the blankets about her, she knew her own limbs. For a moment it seemed as if her reason were going. She looked round, with wild eye, as if seeking something. He stood still with fear. She saw her clothing lying scattered.

'Who undressed me?' she asked, her eyes resting full and inevitable on his face.

'I did,' he replied, 'to bring you round.'

For some moments she sat and gazed at him awfully, her lips parted.

'Do you love me then?' she asked.

He only stood and stared at her, fascinated. His soul seemed to melt.

She shuffled forward on her knees, and put her arms round him, round his legs, as he stood there, pressing her breasts against his knees and thighs, clutching him with strange, convulsive certainty, pressing his thighs against her, drawing him to her face, her throat, as she looked up at him with flaring, humble eyes of transfiguration, triumphant in first possession.

'You love me,' she murmured, in strange transport,

yearning and triumphant and confident. 'You love me. I know you love me, I know.'

And she was passionately kissing his knees, through the wet clothing, passionately and indiscriminately kissing his knees, his legs, as if unaware of everything.

He looked down at the tangled wet hair, the wild, bare, animal shoulders. He was amazed, bewildered, and afraid. He had never thought of loving her. He had never wanted to love her. When he rescued her and restored her, he was a doctor, and she was a patient. He had had no single personal thought of her. Nay, this introduction of the personal element was very distasteful to him, a violation of his professional honour. It was horrible to have her there embracing his knees. It was horrible. He revolted from it, violently. And yet – and yet – he had not the power to break away.

She looked at him again, with the same supplication of powerful love, and that same transcendent, frightening light of triumph. In view of the delicate flame which seemed to come from her face like a light, he was powerless. And yet he had never intended to love her. He had never intended. And something stubborn in him could not give way.

'You love me,' she repeated, in a murmur of deep, rhapsodic assurance. 'You love me.'

Her hands were drawing him, drawing him down to her. He was afraid, even a little horrified. For he had, really, no intention of loving her. Yet her hands were drawing him towards her. He put out his hand quickly to steady himself, and grasped her bare shoulder. A flame seemed to burn the hand that grasped her soft shoulder. He had no intention of loving her: his whole will was against his yielding. It was horrible. And yet wonderful was the touch of her shoulders, beautiful the shining of her face. Was she perhaps mad?

He had a horror of yielding to her. Yet something in him ached also.

He had been staring away at the door, away from her. But his hand remained on her shoulder. She had gone suddenly very still. He looked down at her. Her eyes were now wide with fear, with doubt, the light was dying from her face, a shadow of terrible greyness was returning. He could not bear the touch of her eyes' question upon him, and the look of death behind the question.

With an inward groan he gave way, and let his heart yield towards her. A sudden gentle smile came on his face. And her eyes, which never left his face, slowly, slowly filled with tears. He watched the strange water rise in her eyes, like some slow fountain coming up. And his heart seemed to burn and melt away in his breast.

He could not bear to look at her any more. He dropped on his knees and caught her head with his arms and pressed her face against his throat. She was very still. His heart, which seemed to have broken, was burning with a kind of agony in his breast. And he felt her slow, hot tears wetting his throat. But he could not move.

He felt the hot tears wet his neck and the hollows of his neck, and he remained motionless, suspended through one of man's eternities. Only now it had become indispensable to him to have her face pressed close to him; he could never let her go again. He could never let her head go away from the close clutch of his arm. He wanted to remain like that for ever, with his heart hurting him in a pain that was also life to him. Without knowing, he was looking down on her damp, soft brown hair.

Then, as it were suddenly, he smelt the horrid stagnant smell of that water. And at the same moment she drew away from him and looked at him. Her eyes were wistful and unfathomable. He was afraid of them, and he fell to kissing her, not knowing what he was doing. He wanted her eyes not to have that terrible, wistful, unfathomable look.

When she turned her face to him again, a faint delicate flush was glowing, and there was again dawning that terrible shining of joy in her eyes, which really terrified him, and yet which he now wanted to see, because he feared the look of doubt still more.

'You love me?' she said, rather faltering.

'Yes.' The word cost him a painful effort. Not because it wasn't true. But because it was too newly true, the *saying* seemed to tear open again his newly-torn heart. And he hardly wanted it to be true, even now.

She lifted her face to him, and he bent forward and kissed her on the mouth, gently, with the one kiss that is an eternal pledge. And as he kissed her his heart strained again in his breast. He never intended to love her. But now it was over. He had crossed over the gulf to her, and all that he had left behind had shrivelled and become void.

After the kiss, her eyes again slowly filled with tears. She sat still, away from him, with her face drooped aside, and her hands folded in her lap. The tears fell very slowly. There was complete silence. He too sat there motionless and silent on the hearthrug. The strange pain of his heart that was broken seemed to consume him. That he should love her? That this was love! That he should be ripped open in this way! – Him, a doctor! – How they would all jeer if they knew! – It was agony to him to think they might know.

In the curious naked pain of the thought he looked again to her. She was sitting there drooped into a muse. He saw a tear fall, and his heart flared hot. He saw for the first time that one of her shoulders was quite uncovered, one arm bare, he could see one of her small breasts; dimly, because it had become almost dark in the room.

'Why are you crying?' he asked, in an altered voice.

She looked up at him, and behind her tears the consciousness of her situation for the first time brought a dark look of shame to her eyes.

'I'm not crying, really,' she said, watching him half frightened.

He reached his hand, and softly closed it on her bare arm.

'I love you! I love you!' he said in a soft, low vibrating voice, unlike himself.

She shrank, and dropped her head. The soft, penetrating grip of his hand on her arm distressed her. She looked up at him.

'I want to go,' she said. 'I want to go and get you some dry things.'

'Why?' he said. 'I'm all right.'

'But I want to go,' she said. 'And I want you to change your things.'

He released her arm, and she wrapped herself in the blanket, looking at him rather frightened. And still she did not rise.

'Kiss me,' she said wistfully.

He kissed her, but briefly, half in anger.

Then, after a second, she rose nervously, all mixed up in the blanket. He watched her in her confusion, as she tried to extricate herself and wrap herself up so that she could walk. He watched her relentlessly, as she knew. And as she went, the blanket trailing, and as he saw a glimpse of her feet and her white leg, he tried to remember her as she was when he had wrapped her in the blanket. But then he didn't want to remember, because she had been nothing to him then, and his nature revolted from remembering her as she was when she was nothing to him.

A tumbling, muffled noise from within the dark house startled him. Then he heard her voice: – 'There are clothes.' He rose and went to the foot of the stairs, and gathered up the garments she had thrown down. Then he came back to the fire, to rub himself down and dress. He grinned at his own appearance when he had finished.

The fire was sinking, so he put on coal. The house was now quite dark, save for the light of a street-lamp that shone in faintly from beyond the holly trees. He lit the gas with matches he found on the mantelpiece. Then he emptied the pockets of his own clothes, and threw all his wet things in a heap into the scullery. After which he gathered up her sodden clothes, gently, and put them in a separate heap on the copper-top in the scullery.

It was six o'clock on the clock. His own watch had stopped. He ought to go back to the surgery. He waited, and still she did not come down. So he went to the foot of the stairs and called:

'I shall have to go.'

Almost immediately he heard her coming down. She had on her best dress of black voile, and her hair was tidy, but still damp. She looked at him – and in spite of herself, smiled.

'I don't like you in those clothes,' she said.

'Do I look a sight?' he answered.

They were shy of one another.

'I'll make you some tea,' she said.

'No, I must go.'

'Must you?' And she looked at him again with the wide, strained, doubtful eyes. And again, from the pain of his breast, he knew how he loved her. He went and bent to kiss her, gently, passionately, with his heart's painful kiss.

'And my hair smells so horrible,' she murmured in distraction. 'And I'm so awful, I'm so awful! Oh, no, I'm too awful.' And she broke into bitter, heart-broken sobbing. 'You can't want to love me, I'm horrible.'

'Don't be silly, don't be silly,' he said, trying to comfort her, kissing her, holding her in his arms. 'I want you, I want to marry you, we're going to be married, quickly, quickly – tomorrow if I can.'

But she only sobbed terribly, and cried:

'I feel awful. I feel awful. I feel I'm horrible to you.'

'No, I want you, I want you,' was all he answered, blindly, with that terrible intonation which frightened her almost more than her horror lest he should *not* want her.

ROALD DAHL

MR BOTIBOL

MR BOTIBOL PUSHED his way through the revolving doors and emerged into the large foyer of the hotel. He took off his hat, and holding it in front of him with both hands, he advanced nervously a few paces, paused and stood looking around him, searching the faces of the lunchtime crowd. Several people turned and stared at him in mild astonishment, and he heard – or he thought he heard – at least one woman's voice saying, 'My dear, *do* look what's just come in!'

At last he spotted Mr Clements sitting at a small table in the far corner, and he hurried over to him. Clements had seen him coming, and now, as he watched Mr Botibol threading his way cautiously between the tables and the people, walking on his toes in such a meek and self-effacing manner and clutching his hat before him with both hands, he thought how wretched it must be for any man to look as conspicuous and as odd as this Botibol. He resembled, to an extraordinary degree, an asparagus. His long narrow stalk did not appear to have any shoulders at all; it merely tapered upwards, growing gradually narrower and narrower until it came to a kind of point at the top of the small bald head. He was tightly encased in a shiny blue double-breasted suit, and this, for some curious reason, accentuated the illusion of a vegetable to a preposterous degree.

Clements stood up, they shook hands, and then at once, even before they had sat down again, Mr Botibol said, 'I have decided, yes I have decided to accept the offer which you made to me before you left my office last night.'

For some days Clements had been negotiating, on behalf of clients, for the purchase of the firm known as Botibol & Co., of which Mr Botibol was sole owner, and the night before, Clements had made his first offer. This was merely an exploratory, much-too-low bid, a kind of signal to the seller that the buyers were seriously interested. And by God, thought Clements, the poor fool has gone and accepted it. He nodded gravely many times in an effort to hide his astonishment, and he said, 'Good, good. I'm so glad to hear that, Mr Botibol.' Then he signalled a waiter and said, 'Two large martinis.'

'No, please!' Mr Botibol lifted both hands in horrified protest.

'Come on,' Clements said. 'This is an occasion.'

'I drink very little, and never, no never during the middle of the day.'

But Clements was in a gay mood now and he took no notice. He ordered the martinis and when they came along Mr Botibol was forced, by the banter and good-humour of the other, to drink to the deal which had just been concluded. Clements then spoke briefly about the drawing up and signing of documents, and when all that had been arranged, he called for two more cocktails. Again Mr Botibol protested, but not quite so vigorously this time, and Clements ordered the drinks and then he turned and smiled at the other man in a friendly way. 'Well, Mr Botibol,' he said, 'now that it's all over, I suggest we have a pleasant non-business lunch together. What d'you say to that? And it's on me.'

'As you wish, as you wish,' Mr Botibol answered without any enthusiasm. He had a small melancholy voice and a way of pronouncing each word separately and slowly, as though he was explaining something to a child.

When they went into the dining-room Clements ordered a bottle of Lafite 1912 and a couple of plump roast partridges to go with it. He had already calculated in his head the amount of his commission and he was feeling fine. He began to make bright conversation, switching smoothly from one subject to another in the hope of touching on something that might interest his guest. But it was no good. Mr Botibol appeared to be only half listening. Every now and then he inclined his small bald head a little to one side or the other and said, 'Indeed.' When the wine came along Clements tried to have a talk about that.

'I am sure it is excellent,' Mr Botibol said, 'but please give me only a drop.'

Clements told a funny story. When it was over, Mr Botibol regarded him solemnly for a few moments, then he said, 'How amusing.' After that Clements kept his mouth shut and they ate in silence. Mr Botibol was drinking his wine and he didn't seem to object when his host reached over and refilled his glass. By the time they had finished eating, Clements estimated privately that his guest had consumed at least three-quarters of the bottle.

'A cigar, Mr Botibol?'

'Oh no, thank you.'

'A little brandy?'

'No really. I am not accustomed...' Clements noticed that the man's cheeks were slightly flushed and that his eyes had become bright and watery. Might as well get the old boy properly drunk while I'm about it, he thought, and to the waiter he said, 'Two brandies.'

When the brandies arrived, Mr Botibol looked at his large glass suspiciously for a while, then he picked it up, took one quick birdlike sip and put it down again. 'Mr Clements,' he said suddenly, 'how I envy you.'

'Me? But why?'

'I will tell you, Mr Clements, I will tell you, if I may make so bold.' There was a nervous, mouselike quality in his voice which made it seem he was apologizing for everything he said.

'Please tell me,' Clements said.

'It is because to me you appear to have made such a success of your life.'

He's going to get melancholy drunk, Clements thought. He's one of the ones that gets melancholy and I can't stand it. 'Success,' he said, 'I don't see anything especially successful about me.'

'Oh yes, indeed. Your whole life, if I may say so, Mr Clements, appears to be such a pleasant and successful thing.'

'I'm a very ordinary person,' Clements said. He was trying to figure just how drunk the other really was.

'I believe,' said Mr Botibol, speaking slowly, separating each word carefully from the other, 'I believe that the wine has gone a little to my head, but...' He paused, searching for words. '...But I do want to ask you just one question.' He had poured some salt on to the tablecloth and he was shaping it into a little mountain with the tip of one finger.

'Mr Clements,' he said without looking up, 'do you think that it is possible for a man to live to the age of fifty-two without ever during his whole life having experienced one single small success in anything that he has done?'

'My dear Mr Botibol,' Clements laughed, 'everyone has his little successes from time to time, however small they may be.'

'Oh no,' Mr Botibol said gently. 'You are wrong. I, for example, cannot remember having had a single success of any sort during my whole life.'

'Now come!' Clements said, smiling. 'That can't be true. Why only this morning you sold your business for a hundred thousand. I call that one hell of a success.'

'The business was left me by my father. When he died nine years ago, it was worth four times as much. Under my direction it has lost three-quarters of its value. You can hardly call that a success.'

Clements knew this was true. 'Yes, yes, all right,' he said. 'That may be so, but all the same you know as well as I do that every man alive has his quota of little successes. Not big ones maybe. But lots of little ones. I mean, after all, goddammit, even scoring a goal at school was a little success, a little triumph, at the time; or making some runs or learning to swim. One forgets about them, that's all. One just forgets.'

'I never scored a goal,' Mr Botibol said. 'And I never learned to swim.'

Clements threw up his hands and made exasperated noises. 'Yes, yes, I know, but don't you see, don't you see there are thousands, literally thousands of other things like . . . well . . . like catching a good fish, or fixing the motor of the car, or pleasing someone with a present, or growing a decent row of French beans, or winning a little bet or . . . or . . . why hell, one can go on listing them for ever!'

'Perhaps *you* can, Mr Clements, but to the best of my knowledge, I have never done any of those things. That is what I am trying to tell you.'

Clements put down his brandy glass and stared with new interest at the remarkable shoulderless person who sat facing him. He was annoyed and he didn't feel in the least sympathetic. The man didn't inspire sympathy. He was a fool. He must be a fool. A tremendous and absolute fool. Clements had a sudden desire to embarrass the man as much as he

149

could. 'What about women, Mr Botibol?' There was no apology for the question in the tone of his voice.

'Women?'

'Yes women! Every man under the sun, even the most wretched filthy down-and-out tramp has some time or other had some sort of silly little success with . . .'

'Never!' cried Mr Botibol with sudden vigour. 'No sir, never!'

I'm going to hit him, Clements told himself. I can't stand this any longer and if I'm not careful I'm going to jump right up and hit him. 'You mean you don't like them?' he said.

'Oh dear me yes, of course. I like them. As a matter of fact I admire them very much, very much indeed. But I'm afraid . . . oh dear me . . . I do not know how to say it . . . I am afraid that I do not seem to get along with them very well. I never have. Never. You see, Mr Clements, I *look* queer. I know I do. They stare at me, and often I see them laughing at me. I have never been able to get within . . . well, within striking distance of them, as you might say.' The trace of a smile, weak and infinitely sad, flickered around the corners of his mouth.

Clements had had enough. He mumbled something about how he was sure Mr Botibol was exaggerating the situation, then he glanced at his watch, called for the bill, and he said he was sorry but he would have to get back to the office.

They parted in the street outside the hotel and Mr Botibol took a cab back to his house. He opened the front door, went into the living-room and switched on the radio; then he sat down in a large leather chair, leaned back and closed his eyes. He didn't feel exactly giddy, but there was a singing in his ears and his thoughts were coming and going more quickly than usual. That solicitor gave me too much wine, he told himself. I'll stay here for a while and listen to some music and I expect I'll go to sleep and after that I'll feel better.

They were playing a symphony on the radio. Mr Botibol had always been a casual listener to symphony concerts and he knew enough to identify this as one of Beethoven's. But now, as he lay back in his chair listening to the marvellous music, a new thought began to expand slowly within his tipsy mind. It wasn't a dream because he was not asleep. It was a clear conscious thought and it was this: I am the composer of this music. I am a great composer. This is my latest symphony and this is the first performance. The huge hall is packed with people – critics, musicians and music-lovers from all over the country – and I am up there in front of the orchestra, conducting.

Mr Botibol could see the whole thing. He could see himself up on the rostrum dressed in a white tie and tails, and before him was the orchestra, the massed violins on his left, the violas in front, the cellos on his right, and back of them were all the woodwinds and bassoons and drums and cymbals, the players watching every movement of his baton with an intense, almost a fanatical reverence. Behind him, in the half-darkness of the huge hall, was row upon row of white enraptured faces, looking up towards him, listening with growing excitement as yet another new symphony by the greatest composer the world has ever seen unfolded itself majestically before them. Some of the audience were clench-ing their fists and digging their nails into the palms of their hands because the music was so beautiful that they could hardly stand it. Mr Botibol became so carried away by this exciting vision that he began to swing his arms in time with the music in the manner of a conductor. He found it was such fun doing this that he decided to stand up, facing the radio, in order to give himself more freedom of movement.

He stood there in the middle of the room, tall, thin and shoulderless, dressed in his tight blue double-breasted suit, his small bald head jerking from side to side as he waved his arms in the air. He knew the symphony well enough to be able occasionally to anticipate changes in tempo or volume, and when the music became loud and fast he beat the air so vigorously that he nearly knocked himself over, when it was soft and hushed, he leaned forward to quieten the players with gentle movements of his outstretched hands, and all the time he could feel the presence of the huge audience behind him, tense, immobile, listening. When at last the symphony swelled to its tremendous conclusion, Mr Botibol became more frenzied than ever and his face seemed to thrust itself round to one side in an agony of effort as he tried to force more and still more power from his orchestra during those final mighty chords.

Then it was over. The announcer was saying something, but Mr Botibol quickly switched off the radio and collapsed into his chair, blowing heavily.

'Phew!' he said aloud. 'My goodness gracious me, what *have* I been doing!' Small globules of sweat were oozing out all over his face and forehead, trickling down his neck inside his collar. He pulled out a handkerchief and wiped them away, and he lay there for a while, panting, exhausted, but exceedingly exhilarated.

'Well, I must say,' he gasped, still speaking aloud, 'that was fun. I don't know that I have ever had such fun before in all my life. My goodness, it *was* fun, it really *was*!' Almost at once he began to play with the idea of doing it again. But should he? Should he allow himself to do it again? There was no denying that now, in retrospect, he felt a little guilty about the whole business, and soon he began to wonder whether there wasn't something downright immoral about it all. Letting himself go like that! And imagining he was a genius! It was wrong. He was sure other people didn't do it. And what if Mason had come in the middle and seen him at it! That would have been terrible!

He reached for the paper and pretended to read it, but soon he was searching furtively among the radio programmes for the evening. He put his finger under a line which said '8.30 Symphony Concert. Brahms Symphony No. 2'. He stared at it for a long time. The letters in the word 'Brahms' began to blur and recede, and gradually they disappeared altogether and were replaced by letters which spelt 'Botibol'. Botibol's Symphony No. 2. It was printed quite clearly. He was reading it now, this moment. 'Yes, yes,' he whispered. 'First performance. The world is waiting to hear it. Will it be as great, they are asking, will it perhaps be greater than his earlier work? And the composer himself had been persuaded to conduct. He is shy and retiring, hardly ever appears in public, but on this occasion he has been persuaded...'

Mr Botibol leaned forward in his chair and pressed the bell beside the fireplace. Mason, the butler, the only other person in the house, ancient, small and grave, appeared at the door.

'Er... Mason, have we any wine in the house?'

'Wine, sir?'

'Yes, wine.'

'Oh no, sir. We haven't had any wine this fifteen or sixteen years. Your father, sir...'

'I know, Mason, I know, but will you get some please. I want a bottle with my dinner.'

The butler was shaken. 'Very well, sir, and what shall it be?'

'Claret, Mason. The best you can obtain. Get a case. Tell them to send it round at once.'

When he was alone again, he was momentarily appalled by the simple manner in which he had made his decision. Wine for dinner! Just like that! Well, yes, why not? Why ever not now he came to think of it? He was his own master. And anyway it was essential that he have wine. It seemed to have a good effect, a very good effect indeed. He wanted it and he was going to have it and to hell with Mason.

He rested for the remainder of the afternoon, and at seven-thirty Mason announced dinner. The bottle of wine was on the table and he began to drink it. He didn't give a damn about the way Mason watched him as he refilled his glass. Three times he refilled it; then he left the table saying that he was not to be disturbed and returned to the living-room. There was quarter of an hour to wait. He could think of nothing now except the coming concert. He lay back in the chair and allowed his thoughts to wander deliciously towards eight-thirty. He was the great composer waiting impatiently in his dressing-room in the concert-hall. He could hear in the distance the murmur of excitement from the crowd as they settled themselves in their seats. He knew what they were saying to each other. Same sort of thing the newspapers had been saying for months. Botibol is a genius, greater, far greater than Beethoven or Bach or Brahms or Mozart of any of them. Each new work of his is more magnificent than the last. What will the next one be like? We can hardly wait to hear it! Oh yes, he knew what they were saying. He stood up and began to pace the room. It was nearly time now. He seized a pencil from the table to use as a baton, then he switched on the radio. The announcer had just finished the preliminaries and suddenly there was a burst of applause which meant that the conductor was coming on to the platform. The previous concert in the afternoon had been from gramophone records, but this one was the real thing. Mr Botibol turned around, faced the fireplace and bowed graciously from the waist. Then he turned back to the radio and lifted his baton. The clapping stopped. There was a moment's silence. Someone in the audience coughed. Mr Botibol waited. The symphony began.

Once again, as he began to conduct, he could see clearly before him the whole orchestra and the faces of the players and even the expressions on their faces. Three of the violinists had grey hair. One of the cellists was very fat, another wore heavy brown-rimmed glasses, and there was a man in the second row playing a horn who had a twitch on one side of his face. But they were all magnificent. And so was the music. During certain impressive passages Mr Botibol experienced a feeling of exultation so powerful that it made him cry out for joy, and once during the Third Movement, a little shiver of ecstasy radiated spontaneously from his solar plexus and moved downward over the skin of his stomach like needles. But the thunderous applause and the cheering which came at the end of the symphony was the most splendid thing of all. He turned slowly towards the fireplace and bowed. The clapping continued and he went on bowing until at last the noise died away and the announcer's voice jerked him suddenly back into the living-room. He switched off the radio and collapsed into his chair, exhausted but very happy.

As he lay there, smiling with pleasure, wiping his wet face, panting for breath, he was already making plans for his next performance. But why not do it properly? Why not convert one of the rooms into a sort of concert-hall and have a stage and rows of chairs and do the thing properly? And have a gramophone so that one could perform at any time without having to rely on the radio programme. Yes by heavens, he would do it!

The next morning Mr Botibol arranged with a firm of

decorators that the largest room in the house be converted into a miniature concert-hall. There was to be a raised stage at one end and the rest of the floor-space was to be filled with rows of red plush seats. 'I'm going to have some little concerts here,' he told the man from the firm, and the man nodded and said that would be very nice. At the same time he ordered a radio shop to instal an expensive self-changing gramophone with two powerful amplifiers, one on the stage, the other at the back of the auditorium. When he had done this, he went off and bought all of Beethoven's nine symphonies on gramophone records, and from a place which specialized in recorded sound effects he ordered several records of clapping and applauding by enthusiastic audiences. Finally he bought himself a conductor's baton, a slim ivory stick which lay in a case lined with blue silk.

In eight days the room was ready. Everything was perfect; the red chairs, the aisle down the centre and even a little dais on the platform with a brass rail running round it for the conductor. Mr Botibol decided to give the first concert that evening after dinner.

At seven o'clock he went up to his bedroom and changed into white tie and tails. He felt marvellous. When he looked at himself in the mirror, the sight of his own grotesque shoulderless figure didn't worry him in the least. A great composer, he thought, smiling, can look as he damn well pleases. People *expect* him to look peculiar. All the same he wished he had some hair on his head. He would have liked to let it grow rather long. He went downstairs to dinner, ate his food rapidly, drank half a bottle of wine and felt better still. 'Don't worry about me, Mason,' he said. 'I'm not mad. I'm just enjoying myself.'

'Yes, sir.'

'I shan't want you any more. Please see that I'm not

disturbed.' Mr Botibol went from the dining-room into the miniature concert-hall. He took out the records of Beethoven's First Symphony, but before putting them on the gramophone, he placed two other records with them. The one, which was to be played first of all, before the music began, was labelled 'prolonged enthusiastic applause'. The other, which would come at the end of the symphony, was labelled 'Sustained applause, clapping, cheering, shouts of encore'. By a simple mechanical device on the record changer, the gramophone people had arranged that the sound from the first and the last records – the applause – would come only from the loudspeaker in the auditorium. The sound from all the others – the music – would come from the speaker hidden among the chairs of the orchestra. When he had arranged the records in the concert order, he placed them on the machine but he didn't switch on at once. Instead he turned out all the lights in the room except one small one which lit up the conductor's dais and he sat down in the chair up on the stage, closed his eyes and allowed his thoughts to wander into the usual delicious regions; the great composer, nervous, impatient, waiting to present his latest masterpiece, the audience assembling, the murmur of their excited talk, and so on. Having dreamed himself right into the part, he stood up, picked up his baton and switched on the gramophone.

A tremendous wave of clapping filled the room. Mr Botibol walked across the stage, mounted the dais, faced the audience and bowed. In the darkness he could just make out the faint outline of the seats on either side of the centre aisle, but he couldn't see the faces of the people. They were making enough noise. What an ovation! Mr Botibol turned and faced the orchestra. The applause behind him died down. The next record dropped. The symphony began.

This time it was more thrilling than ever, and during the performance he registered any number of prickly sensations around his solar plexus. Once, when it suddenly occurred to him that the music was being broadcast all over the world, a sort of shiver ran right down the length of his spine. But by far the most exciting part was the applause which came at the end. They cheered and clapped and stamped and shouted encore! encore! encore! and he turned towards the darkened auditorium and bowed gravely to the left and right. Then he went off the stage, but they called him back. He bowed several more times and went off again, and again they called him back. The audience had gone mad. They simply wouldn't let him go. It was terrific. It was truly a terrific ovation.

Later, when he was resting in his chair in the other room, he was still enjoying it. He closed his eyes because he didn't want anything to break the spell. He lay there and he felt like he was floating. It was really a most marvellous floating feeling, and when he went upstairs and undressed and got into bed, it was still with him.

The following evening he conducted Beethoven's – or rather Botibol's – Second Symphony, and they were just as mad about that one as the first. The next few nights he played one symphony a night, and at the end of nine evenings he had worked through all nine of Beethoven's symphonies. It got more exciting every time because before each concert the audience kept saying, 'He can't do it again, not another masterpiece. It's not humanly possible.' But he did. They were all of them equally magnificent. The last symphony, the Ninth, was especially exciting because here the composer surprised and delighted everyone by suddenly providing a choral masterpiece. He had to conduct a huge choir as well as the orchestra itself, and Benjamino Gigli had flown over from Italy to take the tenor part. Enrico Pinza sang bass. At the end of it the audience shouted themselves hoarse. The whole musical world was on its feet cheering, and on all sides they were saying how you never could tell what wonderful things to expect next from this amazing person.

The composing, presenting and conducting of nine great symphonies in as many days is a fair achievement for any man, and it was not astonishing that it went a little to Mr Botibol's head. He decided now that he would once again surprise his public. He would compose a mass of marvellous piano music and he himself would give the recitals. So early the next morning he set out for the show room of the people who sold Bechsteins and Steinways. He felt so brisk and fit that he walked all the way, and as he walked he hummed little snatches of new and lovely tunes for the piano. His head was full of them. All the time they kept coming to him and once, suddenly, he had the feeling that thousands of small notes, some white, some black were cascading down a chute into his head through a hole in his head, and that his brain, his amazing musical brain, was receiving them as fast as they could come and unscrambling them and arranging them neatly in a certain order so that they made wondrous melodies. There were Nocturnes, there were Études and there were Waltzes, and soon, he told himself, soon he would give them all to a grateful and admiring world.

When he arrived at the piano-shop, he pushed the door open and walked in with an air almost of confidence. He had changed much in the last few days. Some of his nervousness had left him and he was no longer wholly preoccupied with what others thought of his appearance. 'I want,' he said to the salesman, 'a concert grand, but you must arrange it so that when the notes are struck, no sound is produced.'

The salesman leaned forward and raised his eyebrows.

'Could that be arranged?' Mr Botibol asked.

'Yes, sir, I think so, if you desire it. But might I inquire what you intend to use the instrument for?'

'If you want to know, I'm going to pretend I'm Chopin. I'm going to sit and play while a gramophone makes the music. It gives me a kick.' It came out, just like that, and Mr Botibol didn't know what had made him say it. But it was done now and he had said it and that was that. In a way he felt relieved, because he had proved he didn't mind telling people what he was doing. The man would probably answer what a jolly good idea. Or he might not. He might say well you ought to be locked up.

'So now you know,' Mr Botibol said.

The salesman laughed out loud. 'Ha ha! Ha ha ha! That's very good, sir. Very good indeed. Serves me right for asking silly questions.' He stopped suddenly in the middle of the laugh and looked hard at Mr Botibol. 'Of course, sir, you probably know that we sell a simple noiseless keyboard specially for silent practising.'

'I want a concert grand,' Mr Botibol said. The salesman looked at him again.

Mr Botibol chose his piano and got out of the shop as quickly as possible. He went on to the store that sold gramophone records and there he ordered a quantity of albums containing recordings of all Chopin's Nocturnes, Études and Waltzes, played by Arthur Rubinstein.

'My goodness, you *are* going to have a lovely time!'

Mr Botibol turned and saw standing beside him at the counter a squat, short-legged girl with a face as plain as a pudding.

'Yes,' he answered. 'Oh yes, I am.' Normally he was strict about not speaking to females in public places, but this one had taken him by surprise.

'I love Chopin,' the girl said. She was holding a slim brown paper bag with string handles containing a single record she had just bought. 'I like him better than any of the others.'

It was comforting to hear the voice of this girl after the way the piano salesman had laughed. Mr Botibol wanted to talk to her but he didn't know what to say.

The girl said, 'I like the Nocturnes best, they're so soothing. Which are your favourites?'

Mr Botibol said, 'Well...' The girl looked up at him and she smiled pleasantly, trying to assist with his embarrassment. It was the smile that did it. He suddenly found himself saying, 'Well now, perhaps, would you, I wonder... I mean I was wondering...' She smiled again; she couldn't help it this time. 'What I mean is I would be glad if you would care to come along some time and listen to these records.'

'Why how nice of you.' She paused, wondering whether it was all right. 'You really mean it?'

'Yes, I should be glad.'

She had lived long enough in the city to discover that old men, if they are dirty old men, do not bother about trying to pick up a girl as unattractive as herself. Only twice in her life had she been accosted in public and each time the man had been drunk. But this one wasn't drunk. He was nervous and he was peculiar-looking, but he wasn't drunk. Come to think of it, it was she who had started the conversation in the first place. 'It would be lovely,' she said. 'It really would. When could I come?'

Oh dear, Mr Botibol thought. Oh dear, oh dear, oh dear, oh dear.

'I could come tomorrow,' she went on. 'It's my afternoon off.'

'Well, yes, certainly,' he answered slowly. 'Yes, of course. I'll give you my card. Here it is.'

'A. W. Botibol,' she read aloud. 'What a funny name. Mine's Darlington. Miss L. Darlington. How d'you do, Mr Botibol.' She put out her hand for him to shake. 'Oh I *am* looking forward to this! What time shall I come?'

'Any time,' he said. 'Please come any time.'

'Three o'clock?'

'Yes. Three o'clock.'

'Lovely! I'll be there.'

He watched her walk out of the shop, a squat, stumpy, thick-legged little person and my word, he thought, what have I done! He was amazed at himself. But he was not displeased. Then at once he started to worry about whether or not he should let her see his concert-hall. He worried still more when he realized that it was the only place in the house where there was a gramophone.

That evening he had no concert. Instead he sat in his chair brooding about Miss Darlington and what he should do when she arrived. The next morning they brought the piano, a fine Bechstein in dark mahogany which was carried in minus its legs and later assembled on the platform in the concert-hall. It was an imposing instrument and when Mr Botibol opened it and pressed a note with his finger, it made no sound at all. He had originally intended to astonish the world with a recital of his first piano compositions – a set of Études – as soon as the piano arrived, but it was no good now. He was too worried about Miss Darlington and three o'clock. At lunch-time his trepidation had increased and he couldn't eat. 'Mason,' he said, 'I'm, I'm expecting a young lady to call at three o'clock.'

'A what, sir?' the butler said.

'A young lady, Mason.'

'Very good, sir.'

'Show her into the sitting-room.'

'Yes, sir.'

Precisely at three he heard the bell ring. A few moments later Mason was showing her into the room. She came in, smiling, and Mr Botibol stood up and shook her hand. 'My!' she exclaimed. 'What a lovely house! I didn't know I was calling on a millionaire!'

She settled her small plump body into a large armchair and Mr Botibol sat opposite. He didn't know what to say. He felt terrible. But almost at once she began to talk and she chattered away gaily about this and that for a long time without stopping. Mostly it was about his house and the furniture and the carpets and about how nice it was of him to invite her because she didn't have such an awful lot of excitement in her life. She worked hard all day and she shared a room with two other girls in a boarding-house and he could have no idea how thrilling it was for her to be here. Gradually Mr Botibol began to feel better. He sat there listening to the girl, rather liking her, nodding his bald head slowly up and down, and the more she talked, the more he liked her. She was gay and chatty, but underneath all that any fool could see that she was a lonely tired little thing. Even Mr Botibol could see that. He could see it very clearly indeed. It was at this point that he began to play with a daring and risky idea.

'Miss Darlington,' he said. 'I'd like to show you something.' He led her out of the room straight to the little concert-hall. 'Look,' he said.

She stopped just inside the door. 'My goodness! Just look at that! A theatre! A real little theatre!' Then she saw the piano on the platform and the conductor's dais with the brass rail running round it. 'It's for concerts!' she cried.

'Do you really have concerts here! Oh, Mr Botibol, how exciting!'

'Do you like it?'

'Oh yes!'

'Come back into the other room and I'll tell you about it.' Her enthusiasm had given him confidence and he wanted to get going. 'Come back and listen while I tell you something funny.' And when they were seated in the sitting-room again, he began at once to tell her his story. He told the whole thing, right from the beginning, how one day, listening to a symphony, he had imagined himself to be the composer, how he had stood up and started to conduct, how he had got an immense pleasure out of it, how he had done it again with similar results and how finally he had built himself the concert-hall where already he had conducted nine symphonies. But he cheated a little bit in the telling. He said that the only real reason he did it was in order to obtain the maximum appreciation from the music. There was only one way to listen to music, he told her, only one way to make yourself listen to every single note and chord. You had to do two things at once. You had to imagine that you had composed it, and at the same time you had to imagine that the public were hearing it for the first time. 'Do you think,' he said, 'do you really think that any outsider has ever got half as great a thrill from a symphony as the composer himself when he first heard his work played by a full orchestra?'

'No,' she answered timidly. 'Of course not.'

'Then become the composer! Steal his music! Take it away from him and give it to yourself!' He leaned back in his chair and for the first time she saw him smile. He had only just thought of this new complex explanation of his conduct, but to him it seemed a very good one and he smiled. 'Well, what do you think, Miss Darlington?'

'I must say it's very very interesting.' She was polite and puzzled but she was a long way away from him now.

'Would you like to try?'

'Oh no. Please.'

'I wish you would.'

'I'm afraid I don't think I should be able to feel the same way as you do about it, Mr Botibol. I don't think I have a strong enough imagination.'

She could see from his eyes he was disappointed. 'But I'd love to sit in the audience and listen while you do it,' she added.

Then he leapt up from his chair. 'I've got it!' he cried. 'A piano concerto! You play the piano, I conduct. You the greatest pianist, the greatest in the world. First performance of my Piano Concerto No. 1. You playing, me conducting. The greatest pianist and the greatest composer together for the first time. A tremendous occasion! The audience will go mad! They'll be queueing all night outside the hall to get in. It'll be broadcast around the world. It'll, it'll...' Mr Botibol stopped. He stood behind the chair with both hands resting on the back of the chair and suddenly he looked embarrassed and a trifle sheepish. 'I'm sorry,' he said, 'I get worked up. You see how it is. Even the thought of another performance gets me worked up.' And then plaintively, 'Would you, Miss Darlington, would you play a piano concerto with me?'

'It's like children,' she said, but she smiled.

'No one will know. No one but us will know anything about it.'

'All right,' she said at last. 'I'll do it. I think I'm daft but just the same I'll do it. It'll be a bit of a lark.'

'Good!' Mr Botibol cried. 'When? Tonight?'

'Oh well, I don't...'

'Yes,' he said eagerly. 'Please. Make it tonight. Come back and have dinner here with me and we'll give the concert afterwards.' Mr Botibol was excited again now. 'We must make a few plans. Which is your favourite piano concerto, Miss Darlington?'

'Oh well, I should say Beethoven's Emperor.'

'The Emperor it shall be. You will play it tonight. Come to dinner at seven. Evening dress. You must have evening dress for the concert.'

'I've got a dancing dress but I haven't worn it for years.'

'You shall wear it tonight.' He paused and looked at her in silence for a moment, then quite gently, he said, 'You're not worried, Miss Darlington? Perhaps you would rather not do it. I'm afraid, I'm afraid I've let myself get rather carried away. I seem to have pushed you into this. And I know how stupid it must seem to you.'

That's better, she thought. That's much better. Now I know it's all right. 'Oh no,' she said. 'I'm really looking forward to it. But you frightened me a bit, taking it all so seriously.'

When she had gone, he waited for five minutes, then went out into the town to the gramophone shop and bought the records of the Emperor Concerto, conductor, Toscanini – soloist, Horowitz. He returned at once, told his astonished butler that there would be a guest for dinner, then went upstairs and changed into his tails.

She arrived at seven. She was wearing a long sleeveless dress made of some shiny green material and to Mr Botibol she did not look quite so plump or quite so plain as before. He took her straight in to dinner and in spite of the silent disapproving manner in which Mason prowled around the table, the meal went well. She protested gaily when Mr Botibol gave her a second glass of wine, but she didn't refuse it. She chattered away almost without a stop throughout the three courses and Mr Botibol listened and nodded and kept refilling her glass as soon as it was half empty.

Afterwards, when they were seated in the living-room, Mr Botibol said, 'Now Miss Darlington, now we begin to fall into our parts.' The wine, as usual, had made him happy, and the girl, who was even less used to it than the man, was not feeling so bad either. 'You, Miss Darlington, are the great pianist. What is your first name, Miss Darlington?'

'Lucille,' she said.

'The great pianist Lucille Darlington. I am the composer Botibol. We must talk and act and think as though we are pianist and composer.'

'What is *your* first name, Mr Botibol? What does the A stand for?'

'Angel,' he answered.

'Not Angel.'

'Yes,' he said irritably.

'Angel Botibol,' she murmured and she began to giggle. But she checked herself and said, 'I think it's a most unusual and distinguished name.'

'Are you ready, Miss Darlington?'

'Yes.'

Mr Botibol stood up and began pacing nervously up and down the room. He looked at his watch. 'It's nearly time to go on,' he said. 'They tell me the place is packed. Not an empty seat anywhere. I always get nervous before a concert. Do you get nervous, Miss Darlington?'

'Oh yes, I do, always. Especially playing with you.'

'I think they'll like it. I put everything I've got into this concerto, Miss Darlington. It nearly killed me composing it. I was ill for weeks afterwards.'

'Poor you,' she said.

167

'It's time now,' he said. 'The orchestra are all in their places. Come on.' He led her out and down the passage, then he made her wait outside the door of the concert-hall while he nipped in, arranged the lighting and switched on the gramophone. He came back and fetched her and as they walked on to the stage, the applause broke out. They both stood and bowed towards the darkened auditorium and the applause was vigorous and it went on for a long time. Then Mr Botibol mounted the dais and Miss Darlington took her seat at the piano. The applause died down. Mr Botibol held up his baton. The next record dropped and the Emperor Concerto began.

It was an astonishing affair. The thin stalk-like Mr Botibol, who had no shoulders, standing on the dais in his evening clothes waving his arms about in approximate time to the music; and the plump Miss Darlington in her shiny green dress seated at the keyboard of the enormous piano thumping the silent keys with both hands for all she was worth. She recognized the passages where the piano was meant to be silent, and on these occasions she folded her hands primly on her lap and stared straight ahead with a dreamy and enraptured expression on her face. Watching her, Mr Botibol thought that she was particularly wonderful in the slow solo passages of the Second Movement. She allowed her hands to drift smoothly and gently up and down the keys and she inclined her head first to one side, then to the other, and once she closed her eyes for a long time while she played. During the exciting last movement, Mr Botibol himself lost his balance and would have fallen off the platform had he not saved himself by clutching the brass rail. But in spite of everything, the concerto moved on majestically to its mighty conclusion. Then the real clapping came. Mr Botibol walked over and took Miss Darlington by the hand and led her to the edge of the platform, and there they stood, the two of them, bowing, and bowing, and bowing again as the clapping and the shouting of 'encore' continued. Four times they left the stage and came back, and then, the fifth time, Mr Botibol whispered, 'It's you they want. You take this one alone.' 'No,' she said. 'It's you. Please.' But he pushed her forward and she took her call, and came back and said, 'Now you. They want you. Can't you hear them shouting for you?' So Mr Botibol walked alone on to the stage, bowed gravely to right, left and centre and came off just as the clapping stopped altogether.

He led her straight back to the living-room. He was breathing fast and the sweat was pouring down all over his face. She too was a little breathless, and her cheeks were shining red.

'A tremendous performance, Miss Darlington. Allow me to congratulate you.'

'But what a concerto, Mr Botibol! What a superb concerto!'

'You played it perfectly, Miss Darlington. You have a real feeling for my music.' He was wiping the sweat from his face with a handkerchief. 'And tomorrow we perform my Second Concerto.'

'Tomorrow?'

'Of course. Had you forgotten, Miss Darlington? We are booked to appear together for a whole week.'

'Oh ... oh yes ... I'm afraid I had forgotten that.'

'But it's all right, isn't it?' he asked anxiously. 'After hearing you tonight I could not bear to have anyone else play my music.'

'I think it's all right,' she said. 'Yes, I think that'll be all right.' She looked at the clock on the mantelpiece. 'My heavens, it's late! I must go! I'll never get up in the morning to get to work!'

'To work?' Mr Botibol said. 'To work?' Then slowly, reluctantly, he forced himself back to reality. 'Ah yes, to work. Of course, you have to get to work.'

'I certainly do.'

'Where do you work, Miss Darlington?'

'Me? Well,' and now she hesitated a moment, looking at Mr Botibol. 'As a matter of fact I work at the old Academy.'

'I hope it is pleasant work,' he said. 'What Academy is that?'

'I teach the piano.'

Mr Botibol jumped as though someone had stuck him from behind with a hatpin. His mouth opened very wide.

'It's quite all right,' she said, smiling. 'I've always wanted to be Horowitz. And could I, do you think, could I please be Schnabel tomorrow?'

GABRIEL GARCÍA MÁRQUEZ

THE WOMAN WHO CAME AT SIX O'CLOCK

Translated by Gregory Rabassa

THE SWINGING DOOR opened. At that hour there was nobody in José's restaurant. It had just struck six and the man knew that the regular customers wouldn't begin to arrive until six-thirty. His clientele was so conservative and regular that the clock hadn't finished striking six when a woman entered, as on every day at that hour, and sat down on the stool without saying anything. She had an unlighted cigarette tight between her lips.

'Hello, queen,' José said when he saw her sit down. Then he went to the other end of the counter, wiping the streaked surface with a dry rag. Whenever anyone came into the restaurant José did the same thing. Even with the woman, with whom he'd almost come to acquire a degree of intimacy, the fat and ruddy restaurant owner put on his daily comedy of a hard-working man. He spoke from the other end of the counter.

'What do you want today?' he said.

'First of all I want to teach you how to be a gentleman,' the woman said. She was sitting at the end of the stools, her elbows on the counter, the extinguished cigarette between her lips. When she spoke, she tightened her mouth so that José would notice the unlighted cigarette.

'I didn't notice,' José said.

'You still haven't learned to notice anything,' said the woman.

The man left the cloth on the counter, walked to the dark

cupboards which smelled of tar and dusty wood, and came back immediately with the matches. The woman leaned over to get the light that was burning in the man's rustic, hairy hands. José saw the woman's lush hair, all greased with cheap, thick Vaseline. He saw her uncovered shoulder above the flowered brassiere. He saw the beginning of her twilight breast when the woman raised her head, the lighted butt between her lips now.

'You're beautiful tonight, queen,' José said.

'Stop your nonsense,' the woman said. 'Don't think that's going to help me pay you.'

'That's not what I meant, queen,' José said. 'I'll bet your lunch didn't agree with you today.'

The woman sucked in the first drag of thick smoke, crossed her arms, her elbows still on the counter, and remained looking at the street through the wide restaurant window. She had a melancholy expression. A bored and vulgar melancholy.

'I'll fix you a good steak,' José said.

'I still haven't got any money,' the woman said.

'You haven't had any money for three months and I always fix you something good,' José said.

'Today's different,' said the woman somberly, still looking out at the street.

'Every day's the same,' José said. 'Every day the clock says six, then you come in and say you're hungry as a dog and then I fix you something good. The only difference is this: today you didn't say you were as hungry as a dog but that today is different.'

'And it's true,' the woman said. She turned to look at the man, who was at the other end of the counter checking the refrigerator. She examined him for two or three seconds. Then she looked at the clock over the cupboard. It was three minutes after six. 'It's true, José. Today is different,' she said. She let the smoke out and kept on talking with crisp, impassioned words. 'I didn't come at six today, that's why it's different, José.'

The man looked at the clock.

'I'll cut off my arm if that clock is one minute slow,' he said.

'That's not it, José. I didn't come at six o'clock today,' the woman said.

'It just struck six, queen,' José said. 'When you came in it was just finishing.'

'I've got a quarter of an hour that says I've been here,' the woman said.

José went over to where she was. He put his great puffy face up to the woman while he tugged on one of his eyelids with his index finger.

'Blow on me here,' he said.

The woman threw her head back. She was serious, annoyed, softened, beautified by a cloud of sadness and fatigue.

'Stop your foolishness, José. You know I haven't had a drink for six months.'

'Tell it to somebody else,' he said, 'not to me. I'll bet you've had a pint or two at least.'

'I had a couple of drinks with a friend,' she said.

'Oh, now I understand,' José said.

'There's nothing to understand,' the woman said. 'I've been here for a quarter of an hour.'

The man shrugged his shoulders.

'Well, if that's the way you want it, you've got a quarter of an hour that says you've been here,' he said. 'After all, what difference does it make, ten minutes this way, ten minutes that way?'

'It makes a difference, José,' the woman said. And she

stretched her arms over the glass counter with an air of careless abandon. She said: 'And it isn't that I wanted it that way; it's just that I've been here for a quarter of an hour.' She looked at the clock again and corrected herself: 'What am I saying – it's been twenty minutes.'

'OK, queen,' the man said. 'I'd give you a whole day and the night that goes with it just to see you happy.'

During all this time José had been moving about behind the counter, changing things, taking something from one place and putting it in another. He was playing his role.

'I want to see you happy,' he repeated. He stopped suddenly, turning to where the woman was. 'Do you know that I love you very much?'

The woman looked at him coldly.

'Ye-e-es...? What a discovery, José. Do you think I'd go with you even for a million pesos?'

'I didn't mean that, queen,' José said. 'I repeat, I bet your lunch didn't agree with you.'

'That's not why I said it,' the woman said. And her voice became less indolent. 'No woman could stand a weight like yours, even for a million pesos.'

José blushed. He turned his back to the woman and began to dust the bottles on the shelves. He spoke without turning his head.

'You're unbearable today, queen. I think the best thing is for you to eat your steak and go home to bed.'

'I'm not hungry,' the woman said. She stayed looking out at the street again, watching the passers-by of the dusking city. For an instant there was a murky silence in the restaurant. A peacefulness broken only by José's fiddling about in the cupboard. Suddenly the woman stopped looking out into the street and spoke with a tender, soft, different voice.

'Do you really love me, Pepillo?'

'I do,' José said dryly, not looking at her.

'In spite of what I've said to you?' the woman asked.

'What did you say to me?' José asked, still without any inflection in his voice, still without looking at her.

'That business about a million pesos,' the woman said.

'I'd already forgotten,' José said.

'So do you love me?' the woman asked.

'Yes,' said José.

There was a pause. José kept moving about, his face turned toward the cabinets, still not looking at the woman. She blew out another mouthful of smoke, rested her bust on the counter, and then, cautiously and roguishly, biting her tongue before saying it, as if speaking on tiptoe:

'Even if you didn't go to bed with me?' she asked.

And only then did José turn to look at her.

'I love you so much that I wouldn't go to bed with you,' he said. Then he walked over to where she was. He stood looking into her face, his powerful arms leaning on the counter in front of her, looking into her eyes. He said: 'I love you so much that every night I'd kill the man who goes with you.'

At the first instant the woman seemed perplexed. Then she looked at the man attentively, with a wavering expression of compassion and mockery. Then she had a moment of brief disconcerted silence. And then she laughed noisily.

'You're jealous, José. That's wild, you're jealous!'

José blushed again with frank, almost shameful timidity, as might have happened to a child who'd revealed all his secrets all of a sudden. He said:

'This afternoon you don't seem to understand anything, queen.' And he wiped himself with the rag. He said:

'This bad life is brutalizing you.'

But now the woman had changed her expression.

'So, then,' she said. And she looked into his eyes again, with a strange glow in her look, confused and challenging at the same time.

'So you're not jealous.'

'In a way I am,' José said. 'But it's not the way you think.'

He loosened his collar and continued wiping himself, drying his throat with the cloth.

'So?' the woman asked.

'The fact is I love you so much that I don't like your doing it,' José said.

'What?' the woman asked.

'This business of going with a different man every day,' José said.

'Would you really kill him to stop him from going with me?' the woman asked.

'Not to stop him from going with you, no,' José said. 'I'd kill him because he *went* with you.'

'It's the same thing,' the woman said.

The conversation had reached an exciting density. The woman was speaking in a soft, low, fascinated voice. Her face was almost stuck up against the man's healthy, peaceful face, as he stood motionless, as if bewitched by the vapor of the words.

'That's true,' José said.

'So,' the woman said, and reached out her hand to stroke the man's rough arm. With the other she tossed away her butt. 'So you're capable of killing a man?'

'For what I told you, yes,' José said. And his voice took on an almost dramatic stress.

The woman broke into convulsive laughter, with an obvious mocking intent.

'How awful, José. How awful,' she said, still laughing. 'José killing a man. Who would have known that behind the fat and sanctimonious man who never makes me pay, who cooks me a steak every day and has fun talking to me until I find a man, there lurks a murderer. How awful, José! You scare me!'

José was confused. Maybe he felt a little indignation. Maybe, when the woman started laughing, he felt defrauded.

'You're drunk, silly,' he said. 'Go get some sleep. You don't even feel like eating anything.'

But the woman had stopped laughing now and was serious again, pensive, leaning on the counter. She watched the man go away. She saw him open the refrigerator and close it again without taking anything out. Then she saw him move to the other end of the counter. She watched him polish the shining glass, the same as in the beginning. Then the woman spoke again with the tender and soft tone of when she said: 'Do you really love me, Pepillo?'

'José,' she said.

The man didn't look at her.

'José!'

'Go home and sleep,' José said. 'And take a bath before you go to bed so you can sleep it off.'

'Seriously, José,' the woman said. 'I'm not drunk.'

'Then you've turned stupid,' José said.

'Come here, I've got to talk to you,' the woman said.

The man came over stumbling, halfway between pleasure and mistrust.

'Come closer!'

He stood in front of the woman again. She leaned forward, grabbed him by the hair, but with a gesture of obvious tenderness.

'Tell me again what you said at the start,' she said.

'What do you mean?' José asked. He was trying to look at her with his head turned away, held by the hair.

'That you'd kill a man who went to bed with me,' the woman said.

'I'd kill a man who went to bed with you, queen. That's right,' José said.

The woman let him go.

'In that case you'd defend me if I killed him, right?' she asked affirmatively, pushing José's enormous pig head with a movement of brutal coquettishness. The man didn't answer anything. He smiled.

'Answer me, José,' the woman said. 'Would you defend me if I killed him?'

'That depends,' José said. 'You know it's not as easy as you say.'

'The police wouldn't believe anyone more than you,' the woman said.

José smiled, honoured, satisfied. The woman leaned over toward him again, over the counter.

'It's true, José. I'm willing to bet that you've never told a lie in your life,' she said.

'You won't get anywhere this way,' José said.

'Just the same,' the woman said. 'The police know you and they'll believe anything without asking you twice.'

José began pounding on the counter opposite her, not knowing what to say. The woman looked out at the street again. Then she looked at the clock and modified the tone of her voice, as if she were interested in finishing the conversation before the first customers arrived.

'Would you tell a lie for me, José?' she asked. 'Seriously.'

And then José looked at her again, sharply, deeply, as if a tremendous idea had come pounding up in his head. An idea that had entered through one ear, spun about for a moment, vague, confused, and gone out through the other, leaving behind only a warm vestige of terror.

'What have you got yourself into, queen?' José asked. He leaned forward, his arms folded over the counter again. The woman caught the strong and ammonia-smelling vapour of his breathing, which had become difficult because of the pressure that the counter was exercising on the man's stomach.

'This is really serious, queen. What have you got yourself into?' he asked.

The woman made her head spin in the opposite direction.

'Nothing,' she said. 'I was just talking to amuse myself.'

Then she looked at him again.

'Do you know you may not have to kill anybody?'

'I never thought about killing anybody,' José said, distressed.

'No, man,' the woman said. 'I mean nobody goes to bed with me.'

'Oh!' José said. 'Now you're talking straight out. I always thought you had no need to prowl around. I'll make a bet that if you drop all this I'll give you the biggest steak I've got every day, free.'

'Thank you, José,' the woman said. 'But that's not why. It's because I *can't* go to bed with anyone anymore.'

'You're getting things all confused again,' José said. He was becoming impatient.

'I'm not getting anything confused,' the woman said. She stretched out on the seat and José saw her flat, sad breasts underneath her brassiere.

'Tomorrow I'm going away and I promise you I won't come back and bother you ever again. I promise you I'll never go to bed with anyone.'

'Where'd you pick up that fever?' José asked.

'I decided just a minute ago,' the woman said. 'Just a minute ago I realized it's a dirty business.'

José grabbed the cloth again and started to clean the glass in front of her. He spoke without looking at her.

He said:

'Of course, the way you do it it's a dirty business. You should have known that a long time ago.'

'I was getting to know it a long time ago,' the woman said, 'but I was only convinced of it just a little while ago. Men disgust me.'

José smiled. He raised his head to look at her, still smiling, but he saw her concentrated, perplexed, talking with her shoulders raised, twirling on the stool with a taciturn expression, her face gilded by premature autumnal grain.

'Don't you think they ought to lay off a woman who kills a man because after she's been with him she feels disgust with him and everyone who's been with her?'

'There's no reason to go that far,' José said, moved, a thread of pity in his voice.

'What if the woman tells the man he disgusts her while she watches him get dressed because she remembers that she's been rolling around with him all afternoon and feels that neither soap nor sponge can get his smell off her?'

'That all goes away, queen,' José said, a little indifferent now, polishing the counter. 'There's no reason to kill him. Just let him go.'

But the woman kept on talking, and her voice was a uniform, flowing, passionate current.

'But what if the woman tells him he disgusts her and the man stops getting dressed and runs over to her again, kisses her again, does . . . ?'

'No decent man would ever do that,' José says.

'What if he does?' the woman asks, with exasperating

182

anxiety. 'What if the man isn't decent and does it and then the woman feels that he disgusts her so much that she could die, and she knows that the only way to end it all is to stick a knife in under him?'

'That's terrible,' José said. 'Luckily there's no man who would do what you say.'

'Well,' the woman said, completely exasperated now. 'What if he did? Suppose he did.'

'In any case it's not that bad,' José said. He kept on cleaning the counter without changing position, less intent on the conversation now.

The woman pounded the counter with her knuckles. She became affirmative, emphatic.

'You're a savage, José,' she said. 'You don't understand anything.' She grabbed him firmly by the sleeve. 'Come on, tell me that the woman should kill him.'

'OK,' José said with a conciliatory bias. 'It's all probably just the way you say it is.'

'Isn't that self-defense?' the woman asked, grabbing him by the sleeve.

Then José gave her a lukewarm and pleasant look.

'Almost, almost,' he said. And he winked at her, with an expression that was at the same time a cordial comprehension and a fearful compromise of complicity. But the woman was serious. She let go of him.

'Would you tell a lie to defend a woman who does that?' she asked.

'That depends,' said José.

'Depends on what?' the woman asked.

'Depends on the woman,' said José.

'Suppose it's a woman you love a lot,' the woman said. 'Not to be with her, but like you say, you love her a lot.'

'OK, anything you say, queen,' José said, relaxed, bored.

He'd gone off again. He'd looked at the clock. He'd seen that it was going on half-past six. He'd thought that in a few minutes the restaurant would be filling up with people and maybe that was why he began to polish the glass with greater effort, looking at the street through the window. The woman stayed on her stool, silent, concentrating, watching the man's movements with an air of declining sadness. Watching him as a lamp about to go out might have looked at a man. Suddenly, without reacting, she spoke again with the unctuous voice of servitude.

'José!'

The man looked at her with a thick, sad tenderness, like a maternal ox. He didn't look at her to hear her, just to look at her, to know that she was there, waiting for a look that had no reason to be one of protection or solidarity. Just the look of a plaything.

'I told you I was leaving tomorrow and you didn't say anything,' the woman said.

'Yes,' José said. 'You didn't tell me where.'

'Out there,' the woman said. 'Where there aren't any men who want to sleep with somebody.'

José smiled again.

'Are you really going away?' he asked, as if becoming aware of life, quickly changing the expression on his face.

'That depends on you,' the woman said. 'If you know enough to say what time I got here, I'll go away tomorrow and I'll never get mixed up in this again. Would you like that?'

José gave an affirmative nod, smiling and concrete. The woman leaned over to where he was.

'If I come back here someday I'll get jealous when I find another woman talking to you, at this time and on this same stool.'

'If you come back here you'll have to bring me something,' José said.

'I promise you that I'll look everywhere for the tame bear, bring him to you,' the woman said.

José smiled and waved the cloth through the air that separated him from the woman, as if he were cleaning an invisible pane of glass. The woman smiled too, with an expression of cordiality and coquetry now. Then the man went away, polishing the glass to the other end of the counter.

'What, then?' José said without looking at her.

'Will you really tell anyone who asks you that I got here at a quarter to six?' the woman said.

'What for?' José said, still without looking at her now, as if he had barely heard her.

'That doesn't matter,' the woman said. 'The thing is that you do it.'

José then saw the first customer come in through the swinging door and walk over to a corner table. He looked at the clock. It was six-thirty on the dot.

'OK, queen,' he said distractedly. 'Anything you say. I always do whatever you want.'

'Well,' the woman said. 'Start cooking my steak, then.'

The man went to the refrigerator, took out a plate with a piece of meat on it, and left it on the table. Then he lighted the stove.

'I'm going to cook you a good farewell steak, queen,' he said.

'Thank you, Pepillo,' the woman said.

She remained thoughtful as if suddenly she had become sunken in a strange subworld peopled with muddy, unknown forms. Across the counter she couldn't hear the noise that the raw meat made when it fell into the burning grease. Afterward she didn't hear the dry and bubbling crackle as

José turned the flank over in the frying pan and the succulent smell of the marinated meat by measured moments saturated the air of the restaurant. She remained like that, concentrated, reconcentrated, until she raised her head again, blinking as if she were coming back out of a momentary death. Then she saw the man beside the stove, lighted up by the happy, rising fire.

'Pepillo.'

'What!'

'What are you thinking about?' the woman asked.

'I was wondering whether you could find the little windup bear someplace,' José said.

'Of course I can,' the woman said. 'But what I want is for you to give me everything I asked for as a going-away present.'

José looked at her from the stove.

'How often have I got to tell you?' he said. 'Do you want something besides the best steak I've got?'

'Yes,' the woman said.

'What is it?' José asked.

'I want another quarter of an hour.'

José drew back and looked at the clock. Then he looked at the customer, who was still silent, waiting in the corner, and finally at the meat roasting in the pan. Only then did he speak.

'I really don't understand, queen,' he said.

'Don't be foolish, José,' the woman said. 'Just remember that I've been here since five-thirty.'

YASUNARI KAWABATA

IMMORTALITY

Translated by J. Martin Holman

AN OLD MAN and a young girl were walking together.

There were a number of curious things about them. They nestled close together like lovers, as if they did not feel the sixty years' difference in their ages. The old man was hard of hearing. He could not understand most of what the girl said. The girl wore maroon *hakama* with a purple-and-white kimono in a fine arrow pattern. The sleeves were rather long. The old man was wearing clothes like those a girl would wear to pull weeds from a rice field, except that he wore no leggings. His tight sleeves and trousers gathered at the ankles looked like a woman's. His clothes hung loose at his thin waist.

They walked across a lawn. A tall wire net stood in front of them. The lovers did not seem to notice that they would run into it if they kept walking. They did not stop, but walked right through the net as a spring breeze might blow through it.

After they passed through, the girl noticed the net. 'Oh.' She looked at the man. 'Shintarō, did you pass through the net too?'

The old man did not hear, but he grabbed the wire net. 'You bastard. You bastard,' he said as he shook it. He pulled too hard, and in a moment, the huge net moved away from him. The old man staggered and fell holding on to it.

'Watch out, Shintarō! What happened?' The girl put her arms around him and propped him up.

'Let go of the net...Oh, you've lost so much weight,' the girl said.

The old man finally stood up. He heaved as he spoke. 'Thank you.' He grasped the net again, but this time lightly, with only one hand. Then in the loud voice of a deaf person he said, 'I used to have to pick up balls from behind a net day after day. For seventeen long years.'

'Seventeen years is a long time?...It's short.'

'They just hit the balls as they pleased. They made an awful sound when they struck the wire net. Before I got used to it, I'd flinch. It's because of the sound of those balls that I became deaf.'

It was a metal net to protect the ball boys at a golf driving range. There were wheels on the bottom so they could move forward and back and right and left. The driving range and golf course next to it were separated by some trees. Originally it had been a grove of all kinds of trees, but they had been cut until only an irregular row remained.

The two walked on, the net behind them.

'What pleasant memories it brings back to hear the sound of the ocean.' Wanting the old man to hear these words, the girl put her mouth to his ear. 'I can hear the sound of the ocean.'

'What?' The old man closed his eyes. 'Ah, Misako. It's your sweet breath. Just as it was long ago.'

'Can't you hear the sound of the ocean? Doesn't it bring back fond memories?'

'The ocean...Did you say the ocean? Fond memories? How could the ocean, where you drowned yourself, bring back fond memories?'

'Well, it does. This is the first time I've been back to my hometown in fifty-five years. And you've come back here, too. This brings back memories.' The old man could not

190

hear, but she went on, 'I'm glad I drowned myself. That way I can think about you forever, just as I was doing at the moment I drowned myself. Besides, the only memories and reminiscences I have are those up to the time I was eighteen. You are eternally young to me. And it's the same for you. If I hadn't drowned myself and you came to the village now to see me, I'd be an old woman. How disgusting. I wouldn't want you to see me like that.'

The old man spoke. It was a deaf man's monologue. 'I went to Tokyo and failed. And now, decrepit with age, I've returned to the village. There was a girl who grieved that we were forced to part. She had drowned herself in the ocean, so I asked for a job at a driving range overlooking the ocean. I begged them to give me the job . . . if only out of pity.'

'This area where we are walking is the woods that belonged to your family.'

'I couldn't do anything but pick up balls. I hurt my back from bending over all the time . . . But there was a girl who had killed herself for me. The rock cliffs were right beside me, so I could jump even if I were tottering. That's what I thought.'

'No. You must keep living. If you were to die, there wouldn't be anyone on earth who would remember me. I would die completely.' The girl clung to him. The old man could not hear, but he embraced her.

'That's it. Let's die together. This time . . . You came for me, didn't you?'

'Together? But you must live. Live for my sake, Shintarō.' She gasped as she looked over his shoulder. 'Oh, those big trees are still there. All three . . . just like long ago.' The girl pointed, so the old man turned his eyes toward the trees.

'The golfers are afraid of those trees. They keep telling

us to cut them down. When they hit a ball, they say it curves to the right as though sucked in by the magic of those trees.'

'Those golfers will die in due time – long before those trees. Those trees are already hundreds of years old. Those golfers talk that way, but they don't understand the life span of a man,' the girl said.

'Those are trees my ancestors have looked after for hundreds of years, so I had the buyer promise not to cut the trees when I sold the land to him.'

'Let's go.' The girl tugged at the old man's hand. They tottered toward the great trees.

The girl passed easily through the tree trunk. The old man did the same.

'What?' The girl stared at the old man and marveled. 'Are you dead too, Shintarō? Are you? When did you die?'

He did not answer.

'You *have* died . . . Haven't you? How strange I didn't meet you in the world of the dead. Well, try walking through the tree trunk once more to test whether you're dead or alive. If you are dead we can go inside the tree and stay.'

They disappeared inside the tree. Neither the old man nor the young girl appeared again.

The color of evening began to drift onto the small saplings behind the great trees. The sky beyond turned a faint red where the ocean sounded.

DOROTHY PARKER

HERE WE ARE

THE YOUNG MAN in the new blue suit finished arranging the glistening luggage in tight corners of the Pullman compartment. The train had leaped at curves and bounced along straightaways, rendering balance a praiseworthy achievement and a sporadic one; and the young man had pushed and hoisted and tucked and shifted the bags with concentrated care.

Nevertheless, eight minutes for the settling of two suitcases and a hat-box is a long time.

He sat down, leaning back against bristled green plush, in the seat opposite the girl in beige. She looked as new as a peeled egg. Her hat, her fur, her frock, her gloves were glossy, and stiff with novelty. On the arc of the thin, slippery sole of one beige shoe was gummed a tiny oblong of white paper, printed with the price set and paid for that slipper and its fellow, and the name of the shop that had dispensed them.

She had been staring raptly out of the window, drinking in the big weathered signboards that extolled the phenomena of codfish without bones and screens no rust could corrupt. As the young man sat down, she turned politely from the pane, met his eyes, started a smile and got it about half done, and rested her gaze just above his right shoulder.

'Well!' the young man said.

'Well!' she said.

'Well, here we are,' he said.

'Here we are,' she said. 'Aren't we?'

'I should say we were,' he said. 'Eeyop. Here we are.'

'Well!' she said.

'Well!' he said. 'Well. How does it feel to be an old married lady?'

'Oh, it's too soon to ask me that,' she said. 'At least – I mean. Well, I mean, goodness, we've only been married about three hours, haven't we?'

The young man studied his wrist-watch as if he were just acquiring the knack of reading time.

'We have been married,' he said, 'exactly two hours and twenty-six minutes.'

'My,' she said. 'It seems like longer.'

'No,' he said. 'It isn't hardly half-past six yet.'

'It seems like later,' she said. 'I guess it's because it starts getting dark so early.'

'It does, at that,' he said. 'The nights are going to be pretty long from now on. I mean. I mean – well, it starts getting dark early.'

'I didn't have any idea what time it was,' she said. 'Everything was so mixed up, I sort of don't know where I am, or what it's all about. Getting back from the church, and then all those people, and then changing all my clothes, and then everybody throwing things, and all. Goodness, I don't see how people do it every day.'

'Do what?' he said.

'Get married,' she said. 'When you think of all the people, all over the world, getting married just as if it was nothing. Chinese people and everybody, just as if it wasn't anything.'

'Well, let's not worry about people all over the world,' he said. 'Let's don't think about a lot of Chinese. We've got something better to think about. I mean. I mean – well, what do we care about them?'

'I know,' she said. 'But I just sort of got to thinking of them, all of them, all over everywhere, doing it all the time. At least, I mean – getting married, you know. And it's – well, it's sort of such a big thing to do, it makes you feel queer. You think of them, all of them, all doing it just like it wasn't anything. And how does anybody know what's going to happen next?'

'Let them worry,' he said. 'We don't have to. We know darn well what's going to happen next. I mean. I mean – well, we know it's going to be great. Well, we know we're going to be happy. Don't we?'

'Oh, of course,' she said. 'Only you think of all the people, and you have to sort of keep thinking. It makes you feel funny. An awful lot of people that get married, it doesn't turn out so well. And I guess they all must have thought it was going to be great.'

'Come on, now,' he said. 'This is no way to start a honeymoon, with all this thinking going on. Look at us – all married and everything done. I mean. The wedding all done and all.'

'Ah, it was nice, wasn't it?' she said. 'Did you really like my veil?'

'You looked great,' he said. 'Just great.'

'Oh, I'm terribly glad,' she said. 'Ellie and Louise looked lovely, didn't they? I'm terribly glad they did finally decide on pink. They looked perfectly lovely.'

'Listen,' he said. 'I want to tell you something. When I was standing up there in that old church waiting for you to come up, and I saw those two bridesmaids, I thought to myself, I thought, "Well, I never knew Louise could look like that!" Why, she'd have knocked anybody's eye out.'

'Oh, really?' she said. 'Funny. Of course, everybody thought her dress and hat were lovely, but a lot of people seemed to think she looked sort of tired. People have been saying that a lot, lately. I tell them I think it's awfully mean of them to go around saying that about her. I tell them they've got to remember that Louise isn't so terribly young any more, and they've got to expect her to look like that. Louise can say she's twenty-three all she wants to, but she's a good deal nearer twenty-seven.'

'Well, she was certainly a knock-out at the wedding,' he said. 'Boy!'

'I'm terribly glad you thought so,' she said. 'I'm glad some one did. How did you think Ellie looked?'

'Why, I honestly didn't get a look at her,' he said.

'Oh, really?' she said. 'Well, I certainly think that's too bad. I don't suppose I ought to say it about my own sister, but I never saw anybody look as beautiful as Ellie looked today. And always so sweet and unselfish, too. And you didn't even notice her. But you never pay attention to Ellie, anyway. Don't think I haven't noticed it. It makes me feel just terrible. It makes me feel just awful, that you don't like my own sister.'

'I do so like her!' he said. 'I'm crazy for Ellie. I think she's a great kid.'

'Don't think it makes any difference to Ellie!' she said. 'Ellie's got enough people crazy about her. It isn't anything to her whether you like her or not. Don't flatter yourself she cares! Only, the only thing is, it makes it awfully hard for me you don't like her, that's the only thing. I keep thinking, when we come back and get in the apartment and everything, it's going to be awfully hard for me that you won't want my own sister to come and see me. It's going to make it awfully hard for me that you won't ever want my family around. I know how you feel about my family. Don't think I haven't seen it. Only, if you don't ever want to see them, that's your loss. Not theirs. Don't flatter yourself!'

'Oh, now, come on!' he said. 'What's all this talk about not wanting your family around? Why, you know how I feel about your family. I think your old lady – I think your mother's swell. And Ellie. And your father. What's all this talk?'

'Well, I've seen it,' she said. 'Don't think I haven't. Lots of people they get married, and they think it's going to be great and everything, and then it all goes to pieces because people don't like people's families, or something like that. Don't tell me! I've seen it happen.'

'Honey,' he said, 'what is all this? What are you getting all angry about? Hey, look, this is our honeymoon. What are you trying to start a fight for? Ah, I guess you're just feeling sort of nervous.'

'Me?' she said. 'What have I got to be nervous about? I mean. I mean, goodness, I'm not nervous.'

'You know, lots of times,' he said, 'they say that girls get kind of nervous and yippy on account of thinking about – I mean. I mean – well, it's like you said, things are all so sort of mixed up and everything, right now. But afterwards, it'll be all right. I mean. I mean – well, look, honey, you don't look any too comfortable. Don't you want to take your hat off? And let's don't ever fight, ever. Will we?'

'Ah, I'm sorry I was cross,' she said. 'I guess I did feel a little bit funny. All mixed up, and then thinking of all those people all over everywhere, and then being sort of 'way off here, all alone with you. It's so sort of different. It's sort of such a big thing. You can't blame a person for thinking, can you? Yes, don't let's ever, ever fight. We won't be like a whole lot of them. We won't fight or be nasty or anything. Will we?'

'You bet your life we won't,' he said.

'I guess I will take this darned old hat off,' she said. 'It kind of presses. Just put it up on the rack, will you, dear? Do you like it, sweetheart?'

'Looks good on you,' he said.

'No, but I mean,' she said, 'do you really like it?'

'Well, I'll tell you,' he said. 'I know this is the new style and everything like that, and it's probably great. I don't know anything about things like that. Only I like the kind of a hat like that blue hat you had. Gee, I liked that hat.'

'Oh, really?' she said. 'Well, that's nice. That's lovely. The first thing you say to me, as soon as you get me off on a train away from my family and everything, is that you don't like my hat. The first thing you say to your wife is you think she has terrible taste in hats. That's nice, isn't it?'

'Now, honey,' he said, 'I never said anything like that. I only said—'

'What you don't seem to realize,' she said, 'is this hat cost twenty-two dollars. Twenty-two dollars. And that horrible old blue thing you think you're so crazy about, that cost three ninety-five.'

'I don't give a darn what they cost,' he said. 'I only said – I said I liked that blue hat. I don't know anything about hats. I'll be crazy about this one as soon as I get used to it. Only it's kind of not like your other hats. I don't know about the new styles. What do I know about women's hats?'

'It's too bad,' she said, 'you didn't marry somebody that would get the kind of hats you'd like. Hats that cost three ninety-five. Why didn't you marry Louise? You always think she looks so beautiful. You'd love her taste in hats. Why didn't you marry her?'

'Ah, now, honey,' he said. 'For heaven's sakes!'

'Why didn't you marry her?' she said. 'All you've done,

ever since we got on this train, is talk about her. Here I've sat and sat, and just listened to you saying how wonderful Louise is. I suppose that's nice, getting me all off here alone with you, and then raving about Louise right in front of my face. Why didn't you ask her to marry you? I'm sure she would have jumped at the chance. There aren't so many people asking her to marry them. It's too bad you didn't marry her. I'm sure you'd have been much happier.'

'Listen, baby,' he said, 'while you're talking about things like that, why didn't you marry Joe Brooks? I suppose he could have given you all the twenty-two-dollar hats you wanted, I suppose!'

'Well, I'm not so sure I'm not sorry I didn't,' she said. 'There! Joe Brooks wouldn't have waited until he got me all off alone and then sneered at my taste in clothes. Joe Brooks wouldn't ever hurt my feelings. Joe Brooks has always been fond of me. There!'

'Yeah,' he said. 'He's fond of you. He was so fond of you he didn't even send a wedding present. That's how fond of you he was.'

'I happen to know for a fact,' she said, 'that he was away on business, and as soon as he comes back he's going to give me anything I want, for the apartment.'

'Listen,' he said. 'I don't want anything he gives you in our apartment. Anything he gives you, I'll throw right out the window. That's what I think of your friend Joe Brooks. And how do you know where he is and what he's going to do, anyway? Has he been writing to you?'

'I suppose my friends can correspond with me,' she said. 'I didn't hear there was any law against that.'

'Well, I suppose they can't!' he said. 'And what do you think of that? I'm not going to have my wife getting a lot of letters from cheap traveling salesmen!'

'Joe Brooks is not a cheap traveling salesman!' she said. 'He is not! He gets a wonderful salary.'

'Oh yeah?' he said. 'Where did you hear that?'

'He told me so himself,' she said.

'Oh, he told you so himself,' he said. 'I see. He told you so himself.'

'You've got a lot of right to talk about Joe Brooks,' she said. 'You and your friend Louise. All you ever talk about is Louise.'

'Oh, for heaven's sakes!' he said. 'What do I care about Louise? I just thought she was a friend of yours, that's all. That's why I ever even noticed her.'

'Well, you certainly took an awful lot of notice of her today,' she said. 'On our wedding day! You said yourself when you were standing there in the church you just kept thinking of her. Right up at the altar. Oh, right in the presence of God! And all you thought about was Louise.'

'Listen, honey,' he said, 'I never should have said that. How does anybody know what kind of crazy things come into their heads when they're standing there waiting to get married? I was just telling you that because it was so kind of crazy. I thought it would make you laugh.'

'I know,' she said. 'I've been all sort of mixed up today, too. I told you that. Everything so strange and everything. And me all the time thinking about all those people all over the world, and now us here all alone, and everything. I know you get all mixed up. Only I did think, when you kept talking about how beautiful Louise looked, you did it with malice and forethought.'

'I never did anything with malice and forethought!' he said. 'I just told you that about Louise because I thought it would make you laugh.'

'Well, it didn't,' she said.

'No, I know it didn't,' he said. 'It certainly did not. Ah, baby, and we ought to be laughing, too. Hell, honey lamb, this is our honeymoon. What's the matter?'

'I don't know,' she said. 'We used to squabble a lot when we were going together and then engaged and everything, but I thought everything would be so different as soon as you were married. And now I feel so sort of strange and everything. I feel so sort of alone.'

'Well, you see, sweetheart,' he said, 'we're not really married yet. I mean. I mean – well, things will be different afterwards. Oh, hell. I mean, we haven't been married very long.'

'No,' she said.

'Well, we haven't got much longer to wait now,' he said. 'I mean – well, we'll be in New York in about twenty minutes. Then we can have dinner, and sort of see what we feel like doing. Or I mean. Is there anything special you want to do tonight?'

'What?' she said.

'What I mean to say,' he said, 'would you like to go to a show or something?'

'Why, whatever you like,' she said. 'I sort of didn't think people went to theaters and things on their – I mean, I've got a couple of letters I simply must write. Don't let me forget.'

'Oh,' he said. 'You're going to write letters tonight?'

'Well, you see,' she said. 'I've been perfectly terrible. What with all the excitement and everything. I never did thank poor old Mrs Sprague for her berry spoon, and I never did a thing about those book ends the McMasters sent. It's just too awful of me. I've got to write them this very night.'

'And when you've finished writing your letters,' he said, 'maybe I could get you a magazine or a bag of peanuts.'

'What?' she said.

'I mean,' he said, 'I wouldn't want you to be bored.'

'As if I could be bored with you!' she said. 'Silly! Aren't we married? Bored!'

'What I thought,' he said, 'I thought when we got in, we could go right up to the Biltmore and anyway leave our bags, and maybe have a little dinner in the room, kind of quiet, and then do whatever we wanted. I mean. I mean – well, let's go right up there from the station.'

'Oh, yes, let's,' she said. 'I'm so glad we're going to the Biltmore. I just love it. The twice I've stayed in New York we've always stayed there, Papa and Mamma and Ellie and I, and I was crazy about it. I always sleep so well there. I go right off to sleep the minute I put my head on the pillow.'

'Oh, you do?' he said.

'At least, I mean,' she said. ' 'Way up high it's so quiet.'

'We might go to some show or other tomorrow night instead of tonight,' he said. 'Don't you think that would be better?'

'Yes, I think it might,' she said.

He rose, balanced a moment, crossed over and sat down beside her.

'Do you really have to write those letters tonight?' he said.

'Well,' she said, 'I don't suppose they'd get there any quicker than if I wrote them tomorrow.'

There was a silence with things going on in it.

'And we won't ever fight any more, will we?' he said.

'Oh, no,' she said. 'Not ever! I don't know what made me do like that. It all got so sort of funny, sort of like a night-mare, the way I got thinking of all those people getting married all the time; and so many of them, everything spoils on account of fighting and everything. I got all mixed up thinking about them. Oh, I don't want to be like them. But we won't be, will we?'

'Sure we won't,' he said.

'We won't go all to pieces,' she said. 'We won't fight. It'll all be different, now we're married. It'll all be lovely. Reach me down my hat, will you, sweetheart? It's time I was putting it on. Thanks. Ah, I'm sorry you don't like it.'

'I do so like it!' he said.

'You said you didn't,' she said. 'You said you thought it was perfectly terrible.'

'I never said any such thing,' he said. 'You're crazy.'

'All right, I may be crazy,' she said. 'Thank you very much. But that's what you said. Not that it matters – it's just a little thing. But it makes you feel pretty funny to think you've gone and married somebody that says you have perfectly terrible taste in hats. And then goes and says you're crazy, beside.'

'Now, listen here,' he said. 'Nobody said any such thing. Why, I love that hat. The more I look at it the better I like it. I think it's great.'

'That isn't what you said before,' she said.

'Honey,' he said. 'Stop it, will you? What do you want to start all this for? I love the damned hat. I mean, I love your hat. I love anything you wear. What more do you want me to say?'

'Well, I don't want you to say it like that,' she said.

'I said I think it's great,' he said. 'That's all I said.'

'Do you really?' she said. 'Do you honestly? Ah, I'm so glad. I'd hate you not to like my hat. It would be – I don't know, it would be sort of such a bad start.'

'Well, I'm crazy for it,' he said. 'Now we've got that settled, for heaven's sakes. Ah, baby. Baby lamb. We're not going to have any bad starts. Look at us – we're on our honeymoon. Pretty soon we'll be regular old married people. I mean. I mean, in a few minutes we'll be getting in to

New York, and then we'll be going to the hotel, and then everything will be all right. I mean – well, look at us! Here we are married! Here we are!'

'Yes, here we are,' she said. 'Aren't we?'

KATHERINE MANSFIELD

THE STRANGER

IT SEEMED TO the little crowd on the wharf that she was never going to move again. There she lay, immense, motionless on the grey crinkled water, a loop of smoke above her, an immense flock of gulls screaming and diving after the galley droppings at the stern. You could just see little couples parading – little flies walking up and down the dish on the grey crinkled tablecloth. Other flies clustered and swarmed at the edge. Now there was a gleam of white on the lower deck – the cook's apron or the stewardess perhaps. Now a tiny black spider raced up the ladder on to the bridge.

In the front of the crowd a strong-looking, middle-aged man, dressed very well, very snugly in a grey overcoat, grey silk scarf, thick gloves and dark felt hat, marched up and down, twirling his folded umbrella. He seemed to be the leader of the little crowd on the wharf and at the same time to keep them together. He was something between the sheep-dog and the shepherd.

But what a fool – what a fool he had been not to bring any glasses! There wasn't a pair of glasses between the whole lot of them.

'Curious thing, Mr Scott, that none of us thought of glasses. We might have been able to stir 'em up a bit. We might have managed a little signalling. "Don't hesitate to land. Natives harmless." Or: "A welcome awaits you. All is forgiven." What? Eh?'

Mr Hammond's quick, eager glance, so nervous and yet

209

so friendly and confiding, took in everybody on the wharf, roped in even those old chaps lounging against the gangways. They knew, every man-jack of them, that Mrs Hammond was on that boat, and that he was so tremendously excited it never entered his head not to believe that this marvellous fact meant something to them too. It warmed his heart towards them. They were, he decided, as decent a crowd of people – Those old chaps over by the gangways, too – fine, solid old chaps. What chests – by Jove! And he squared his own, plunged his thick-gloved hands into his pockets, rocked from heel to toe.

'Yes, my wife's been in Europe for the last ten months. On a visit to our eldest girl, who was married last year. I brought her up here, as far as Salisbury, myself. So I thought I'd better come and fetch her back. Yes, yes, yes.' The shrewd grey eyes narrowed again and searched anxiously, quickly, the motionless liner. Again his overcoat was unbuttoned. Out came the thin, butter-yellow watch again, and for the twentieth – fiftieth – hundredth time he made the calculation.

'Let me see now. It was two fifteen when the doctor's launch went off. Two fifteen. It is now exactly twenty-eight minutes past four. That is to say, the doctor's been gone two hours and thirteen minutes. Two hours and thirteen minutes! Whee-ooh!' He gave a queer little half-whistle and snapped his watch to again. 'But I think we should have been told if there was anything up – don't you, Mr Gaven?'

'Oh, yes, Mr Hammond! I don't think there's anything to – anything to worry about,' said Mr Gaven, knocking out his pipe against the heel of his shoe. 'At the same time –'

'Quite so! Quite so!' cried Mr Hammond. 'Dashed annoying!' He paced quickly up and down and came back again to his stand between Mr and Mrs Scott and Mr Gaven.

'It's getting quite dark, too,' and he waved his folded umbrella as though the dusk at least might have had the decency to keep off for a bit. But the dusk came slowly, spreading like a slow stain over the water. Little Jean Scott dragged at her mother's hand.

'I wan' my tea, mammy!' she wailed.

'I expect you do,' said Mr Hammond. 'I expect all these ladies want their tea.' And his kind, flushed, almost pitiful glance roped them all in again. He wondered whether Janey was having a final cup of tea in the saloon out there. He hoped so; he thought not. It would be just like her not to leave the deck. In that case perhaps the deck steward would bring her up a cup. If he'd been there he'd have got it for her – somehow. And for a moment he was on deck, standing over her, watching her little hand fold round the cup in the way she had, while she drank the only cup of tea to be got on board . . . But now he was back here, and the Lord only knew when that cursed Captain would stop hanging about in the stream. He took another turn, up and down, up and down. He walked as far as the cab-stand to make sure his driver hadn't disappeared; back he swerved again to the little flock huddled in the shelter of the banana crates. Little Jean Scott was still wanting her tea. Poor little beggar! He wished he had a bit of chocolate on him.

'Here, Jean!' he said. 'Like a lift up?' And easily, gently, he swung the little girl on to a higher barrel. The movement of holding her, steadying her, relieved him wonderfully, lightened his heart.

'Hold on,' he said, keeping an arm round her.

'Oh, don't worry about Jean, Mr Hammond!' said Mrs Scott.

'That's all right, Mrs Scott. No trouble. It's a pleasure. Jean's a little pal of mine, aren't you, Jean?'

'Yes, Mr Hammond,' said Jean, and she ran her finger down the dent of his felt hat.

But suddenly she caught him by the ear and gave a loud scream. 'Lo-ok, Mr Hammond! She's moving! Look, she's coming in!'

By Jove! So she was. At last! She was slowly, slowly turning round. A bell sounded far over the water and a great spout of steam gushed into the air. The gulls rose; they fluttered away like bits of white paper. And whether that deep throbbing was her engines or his heart Mr Hammond couldn't say. He had to nerve himself to bear it, whatever it was. At that moment old Captain Johnson, the harbour-master, came striding down the wharf, a leather portfolio under his arm.

'Jean'll be all right,' said Mr Scott. 'I'll hold her.' He was just in time. Mr Hammond had forgotten about Jean. He sprang away to greet old Captain Johnson.

'Well, Captain,' the eager, nervous voice rang out again, 'you've taken pity on us at last.'

'It's no good blaming me, Mr Hammond,' wheezed old Captain Johnson, staring at the liner. 'You got Mrs Hammond on board, ain't yer?'

'Yes, yes!' said Hammond, and he kept by the harbour-master's side. 'Mrs Hammond's there. Hul-lo! We shan't be long now!'

With her telephone ring-ringing, the thrum of her screw filling the air, the big liner bore down on them, cutting sharp through the dark water so that big white shavings curled to either side. Hammond and the harbour-master kept in front of the rest. Hammond took off his hat; he raked the decks – they were crammed with passengers; he waved his hat and bawled a loud, strange 'Hul-lo!' across the water; and then turned round and burst out laughing and said something – nothing – to old Captain Johnson.

'Seen her?' asked the harbour-master.

'No, not yet. Steady – wait a bit!' And suddenly, between two great clumsy idiots – 'Get out of the way there!' he signed with his umbrella – he saw a hand raised – a white glove shaking a handkerchief. Another moment, and – thank God, thank God! – there she was. There was Janey. There was Mrs Hammond, yes, yes, yes – standing by the rail and smiling and nodding and waving her handkerchief.

'Well that's first class – first class! Well, well, well!' He positively stamped. Like lightning he drew out his cigar-case and offered it to old Captain Johnson. 'Have a cigar, Captain! They're pretty good. Have a couple! Here' – and he pressed all the cigars in the case on the harbour-master – 'I've a couple of boxes up at the hotel.'

'Thenks, Mr Hammond!' wheezed old Captain Johnson.

Hammond stuffed the cigar-case back. His hands were shaking, but he'd got hold of himself again. He was able to face Janey. There she was, leaning on the rail, talking to some woman and at the same time watching him, ready for him. It struck him, as the gulf of water closed, how small she looked on that huge ship. His heart was wrung with such a spasm that he could have cried out. How little she looked to have come all that long way and back by herself! Just like her, though. Just like Janey. She had the courage of a – And now the crew had come forward and parted the passengers; they had lowered the rails for the gangways.

The voices on shore and the voices on board flew to greet each other.

'All well?'

'All well.'

'How's mother?'

'Much better.'

'Hullo, Jean!'

'Hillo, Aun' Emily!'

'Had a good voyage?'

'Splendid!'

'Shan't be long now!'

'Not long now.'

The engines stopped. Slowly she edged to the wharf-side.

'Make way there – make way – make way!' And the wharf hands brought the heavy gangways along at a sweeping run. Hammond signed to Janey to stay where she was. The old harbour-master stepped forward; he followed. As to 'ladies first', or any rot like that, it never entered his head.

'After you, Captain!' he cried genially. And, treading on the old man's heels, he strode up the gangway on to the deck in a bee-line to Janey, and Janey was clasped in his arms.

'Well, well, well! Yes, yes! Here we are at last!' he stammered. It was all he could say. And Janey emerged, and her cool little voice – the only voice in the world for him – said, 'Well, darling! Have you been waiting long?'

No; not long. Or, at any rate, it didn't matter. It was over now. But the point was, he had a cab waiting at the end of the wharf. Was she ready to go off. Was her luggage ready? In that case they could cut off sharp with her cabin luggage and let the rest go hang until tomorrow. He bent over her and she looked up with her familiar half-smile. She was just the same. Not a day changed. Just as he'd always known her. She laid her small hand on his sleeve.

'How are the children, John?' she asked.

(Hang the children!) 'Perfectly well. Never better in their lives.'

'Haven't they sent me letters?'

'Yes, yes – of course! I've left them at the hotel for you to digest later on.'

'We can't go quite so fast,' said she: 'I've got people to say goodbye to – and then there's the Captain.' As his face fell she gave his arm a small understanding squeeze. 'If the Captain comes off the bridge I want you to thank him for having looked after your wife so beautifully.' Well, he'd got her. If she wanted another ten minutes – As he gave way she was surrounded. The whole first-class seemed to want to say goodbye to Janey.

'Goodbye, dear Mrs Hammond! And next time you're in Sydney I'll expect you.'

'Darling Mrs Hammond! You won't forget to write to me, will you?'

'Well, Mrs Hammond, what this boat would have been without you!'

It was as plain as a pikestaff that she was by far the most popular woman on board. And she took it all – just as usual. Absolutely composed. Just her little self – just Janey all over; standing there with her veil thrown back. Hammond never noticed what his wife had on. It was all the same to him whatever she wore. But today he did notice that she wore a black 'costume' – didn't they call it? – with white frills, trimmings he supposed they were, at the neck and sleeves. All this while Janey handed him round.

'John, dear!' And then: 'I want to introduce you to –'

Finally they did escape, and she led the way to her state-room. To follow Janey down the passage that she knew so well – that was so strange to him; to part the green curtains after her and to step into the cabin that had been hers gave him exquisite happiness. But – confound it! – the stewardess was there on the floor, strapping up the rugs.

'That's the last, Mrs Hammond,' said the stewardess, rising and pulling down her cuffs.

He was introduced again, and then Janey and the stewardess disappeared into the passage. He heard whisperings.

She was getting the tipping business over, he supposed. He sat down on the striped sofa and took his hat off. There were the rugs she had taken with her; they looked good as new. All her luggage looked fresh, perfect. The labels were written in her beautiful little clear hand – 'Mrs John Hammond'.

'Mrs John Hammond!' He gave a long sigh of content and leaned back, crossing his arms. The strain was over. He felt he could have sat there for ever sighing his relief – the relief at being rid of that horrible tug, pull, grip on his heart. The danger was over. That was the feeling. They were on dry land again.

But at that moment Janey's head came round the corner.

'Darling – do you mind? I just want to go and say good-bye to the doctor.'

Hammond started up. 'I'll come with you.'

'No, no!' she said. 'Don't bother. I'd rather not. I'll not be a minute.'

And before he could answer she was gone. He had half a mind to run after her; but instead he sat down again.

Would she really not be long? What was the time now? Out came the watch; he stared at nothing. That was rather queer of Janey, wasn't it? Why couldn't she have told the stewardess to say goodbye for her? Why did she have to go chasing after the ship's doctor? She could have sent a note from the hotel even if the affair had been urgent. Urgent? Did it – could it mean that she had been ill on the voyage – she was keeping something from him? That was it! He seized his hat. He was going off to find that fellow and to wring the truth out of him at all costs. He thought he'd noticed just something. She was just a touch too calm – too steady. From the very first moment –

The curtains rang. Janey was back. He jumped to his feet.

'Janey, have you been ill on this voyage? You have!'

'Ill?' Her airy little voice mocked him. She stepped over the rugs, and came up close, touched his breast, and looked up at him.

'Darling,' she said, 'don't frighten me. Of course I haven't! Whatever makes you think I have? Do I look ill?'

But Hammond didn't see her. He only felt that she was looking at him and that there was no need to worry about anything. She was here to look after things. It was all right. Everything was.

The gentle pressure of her hand was so calming that he put his over hers to hold it there. And she said: 'Stand still. I want to look at you. I haven't seen you yet. You've had your beard beautifully trimmed, and you look – younger, I think, and decidedly thinner! Bachelor life agrees with you.'

'Agrees with me!' He groaned for love and caught her close again. And again, as always, he had the feeling that he was holding something that never was quite his – his. Something too delicate, too precious, that would fly away once he let go.

'For God's sake let's get off to the hotel so that we can be by ourselves!' And he rang the bell hard for someone to look sharp with the luggage.

Walking down the wharf together she took his arm. He had her on his arm again. And the difference it made to get into the cab after Janey – to throw the red-and-yellow striped blanket round them both – to tell the driver to hurry because neither of them had had any tea. No more going without his tea or pouring out his own. She was back. He turned to her, squeezed her hand, and said gently, teasingly, in the 'special' voice he had for her: 'Glad to be home again, dearie?' She smiled; she didn't even bother to answer, but

217

gently she drew his hand away as they came to the brighter streets.

'We've got the best room in the hotel,' he said. 'I wouldn't be put off with another. And I asked the chambermaid to put in a bit of a fire in case you felt chilly. She's a nice, attentive girl. And I thought now we were here we wouldn't bother to go home tomorrow, but spend the day looking round and leave the morning after. Does that suit you? There's no hurry, is there? The children will have you soon enough . . . I thought a day's sight-seeing might make a nice break in your journey – eh, Janey?'

'Have you taken the tickets for the day after?' she asked.

'I should think I have!' He unbuttoned his overcoat and took out his bulging pocket-book. 'Here we are! I reserved a first-class carriage to Cooktown. There it is – "Mr and Mrs John Hammond". I thought we might as well do ourselves comfortably, and we don't want other people butting in, do we? But if you'd like to stop here a bit longer – ?'

'Oh, no!' said Janey quickly. 'Not for the world! The day after tomorrow, then. And the children –'

But they had reached the hotel. The manager was standing in the broad, brilliantly-lighted porch. He came down to greet them. A porter ran from the hall for their boxes.

'Well, Mr Arnold, here's Mrs Hammond at last!'

The manager led them through the hall himself and pressed the elevator-bell. Hammond knew there were business pals of his sitting at the little hall tables having a drink before dinner. But he wasn't going to risk interruption; he looked neither to the right nor the left. They could think what they pleased. If they didn't understand, the more fools they – and he stepped out of the lift, unlocked the door of their room, and shepherded Janey in. The door shut. Now, at last, they were alone together. He turned up the light.

The curtains were drawn; the fire blazed. He flung his hat on to the huge bed and went towards her.

But – would you believe it! – again they were interrupted. This time it was the porter with the luggage. He made two journeys of it, leaving the door open in between, taking his time, whistling through his teeth in the corridor. Hammond paced up and down the room, tearing off his gloves, tearing off his scarf. Finally he flung his overcoat on to the bedside.

At last the fool was gone. The door clicked. Now they were alone. Said Hammond: 'I feel I'll never have you to myself again. These cursed people! Janey' – and he bent his flushed, eager gaze upon her – 'let's have dinner up here. If we go down to the restaurant we'll be interrupted, and then there's the confounded music' (the music he'd praised so highly, applauded so loudly last night!). 'We shan't be able to hear each other speak. Let's have something up here in front of the fire. It's too late for tea. I'll order a little supper, shall I? How does that idea strike you?'

'Do, darling!' said Janey. 'And while you're away – the children's letters –'

'Oh, later on will do!' said Hammond.

'But then we'd get it over,' said Janey. 'And I'd first have time to –'

'Oh, I needn't go down!' explained Hammond. 'I'll just ring and give the order ... you don't want to send me away, do you?'

Janey shook her head and smiled.

'But you're thinking of something else. You're worrying about something,' said Hammond. 'What is it? Come and sit here – come and sit on my knee before the fire.'

'I'll just unpin my hat,' said Janey, and she went over to the dressing-table. 'A-ah!' She gave a little cry.

'What is it?'

'Nothing, darling. I've just found the children's letters. That's all right! They will keep. No hurry now!' She turned to him, clasping them. She tucked them into her frilled blouse. She cried quickly, gaily: 'Oh, how typical this dressing-table is of you!'

'Why? What's the matter with it?' said Hammond.

'If it were floating in eternity I should say "John!"' laughed Janey, staring at the big bottle of hair tonic, the wicker bottle of eau-de-Cologne, the two hair-brushes, and a dozen new collars tied with pink tape. 'Is this all your luggage?'

'Hang my luggage!' said Hammond; but all the same he liked being laughed at by Janey. 'Let's talk. Let's get down to things. Tell me' – and as Janey perched on his knees he leaned back and drew her into the deep, ugly chair – 'tell me you're really glad to be back, Janey.'

'Yes, darling, I am glad,' she said.

But just as when he embraced her he felt she would fly away, so Hammond never knew – never knew for dead certain that she was as glad as he was. How could he know? Would he ever know? Would he always have this craving – this pang like hunger, somehow, to make Janey so much part of him that there wasn't any of her to escape? He wanted to blot out everybody, everything. He wished now he'd turned off the light. That might have brought her nearer. And now those letters from the children rustled in her blouse. He could have chucked them into the fire.

'Janey,' he whispered.

'Yes, dear?' She lay on his breast, but so lightly, so remotely. Their breathing rose and fell together.

'Janey!'

'What is it?'

'Turn to me,' he whispered. A slow, deep flush flowed into his forehead. 'Kiss me, Janey! You kiss me!'

It seemed to him there was a tiny pause – but long enough for him to suffer torture – before her lips touched his, firmly, lightly – kissing them as she always kissed him, as though the kiss – how could he describe it? – confirmed what they were saying, signed the contract. But that wasn't what he wanted; that wasn't at all what he thirsted for. He felt suddenly, horribly tired.

'If you knew,' he said, opening his eyes, 'what it's been like – waiting today. I thought the boat never would come in. There we were, hanging about. What kept you so long?'

She made no answer. She was looking away from him at the fire. The flames hurried – hurried over the coals, flickered, fell.

'Not asleep, are you?' said Hammond, and he jumped her up and down.

'No,' she said. And then: 'Don't do that, dear. No, I was thinking. As a matter of fact,' she said, 'one of the passengers died last night – a man. That's what held us up. We brought him in – I mean, he wasn't buried at sea. So, of course, the ship's doctor and the shore doctor –'

'What was it?' asked Hammond uneasily. He hated to hear of death. He hated this to have happened. It was, in some queer way, as though he and Janey had met a funeral on their way to the hotel.

'Oh, it wasn't anything in the least infectious!' said Janey. She was speaking scarcely above her breath. 'It was heart.' A pause. 'Poor fellow!' she said. 'Quite young.' And she watched the fire flicker and fall. 'He died in my arms,' said Janey.

The blow was so sudden that Hammond thought he would faint. He couldn't move; he couldn't breathe. He felt all his strength flowing – flowing into the big dark chair, and the big dark chair held him fast, gripped him, forced him to bear it.

'What?' he said dully. 'What's that you say?'

'The end was quite peaceful,' said the small voice. 'He just' – and Hammond saw her lift her gentle hand – 'breathed his life away at the end.' And her hand fell.

'Who – else was there?' Hammond managed to ask.

'Nobody. I was alone with him.'

Ah, my God, what was she saying! What was she doing to him! This would kill him! And all the while she spoke: 'I saw the change coming and I sent the steward for the doctor, but the doctor was too late. He couldn't have done anything, anyway.'

'But – why you, why you?' moaned Hammond.

At that Janey turned quickly, quickly searched his face.

'You don't mind, John, do you?' she asked. 'You don't – It's nothing to do with you and me.'

Somehow or other he managed to shake some sort of smile at her. Somehow or other he stammered: 'No – go – on, go on! I want you to tell me.'

'But, John darling –'

'Tell me, Janey!'

'There's nothing to tell,' she said, wondering. 'He was one of the first-class passengers. I saw he was very ill when he came on board . . . But he seemed to be so much better until yesterday. He had a severe attack in the afternoon – excitement – nervousness, I think, about arriving. And after that he never recovered.'

'But why didn't the stewardess –'

'Oh, my dear – the stewardess!' said Janey. 'What would he have felt? And besides . . . he might have wanted to leave a message . . . to –'

'Didn't he?' muttered Hammond. 'Didn't he say anything?'

'No, darling, not a word!' She shook her head softly. 'All the time I was with him he was too weak...he was too weak even to move a finger...'

Janey was silent. But her words, so light, so soft, so chill, seemed to hover in the air, to rain into his breast like snow.

The fire had gone red. Now it fell in with a sharp sound and the room was colder. Cold crept up his arms. The room was huge, immense, glittering. It filled his whole world. There was the great blind bed, with his coat flung across it like some headless man saying his prayers. There was the luggage, ready to be carried away again, anywhere, tossed into trains, carted on to boats.

...'He was too weak. He was too weak to move a finger.' And yet he died in Janey's arms. She – who'd never – never once in all these years – never on one single solitary occasion –

No; he mustn't think of it. Madness lay in thinking of it. No, he wouldn't face it. He couldn't stand it. It was too much to bear!

And now Janey touched his tie with her fingers. She pinched the edges of the tie together.

'You're not – sorry I told you, John darling? It hasn't made you sad? It hasn't spoilt our evening – our being alone together?'

But at that he had to hide his face. He put his face into her bosom and his arms enfolded her.

Spoilt their evening! Spoilt their being alone together! They would never be alone together again.

TOBIAS WOLFF

LADY'S DREAM

LADY'S SUFFOCATING. Robert can't stand to have the windows down because the air blowing into the car bothers his eyes. The fan is on but only at the lowest speed, as the sound annoys him. Lady's head is getting heavy, and when she blinks she has to raise her eyelids by an effort of will. The heat and dampness of her skin give her the sensation of a fever. She's beginning to see things in the lengthening moments when her eyes are closed, things more distinct and familiar than the dipping wires and blur of trees and the silent, staring man she sees when they're open.

'Lady?' Robert's voice calls her back, but she keeps her eyes closed.

That's him to the life. Can't stand her sleeping when he's not. He'd have some good reason to wake her, though. Never a mean motive. Never. When he's going to ask somebody for a favor he always calls first and just passes the time, then calls back the next day and says how great it was talking to them, he enjoyed it so much he forgot to ask if they'd mind doing something for him. Has no idea he does this. She's never heard him tell a lie, not even to make a story better. Tells the most boring stories. Just lethal. Considers every word. Considers everything. Early January he buys twelve vacuum-cleaner bags and writes a different month on each one so she'll remember to change them. Of course she goes as long as she can on every bag and throws away the extras at the end of the year, because otherwise he'd find them and know. Not say anything – just know. Once she threw seven away. Sneaked them outside through the snow and stuffed them in the garbage can.

Considerate. Everything a matter of principle. Justice for all; yellow, brown, black, or white, all are precious in his sight. Can't say no to any charity but always forgets to send the money. Asks her questions about his own self. *Who's that actress I like so much? What's my favorite fish?* Is calm in every circumstance. Polishes his glasses all the time. They gleam so you can hardly see his eyes. Has to sleep on the right side of the bed. The sheets have to be white. Any other color gives him nightmares, and forget about patterns. Patterns would kill him. Wears a hard hat when he works around the house. Says her name a hundred times a day. Always has. Any excuse.

He loves her name. Lady. Married her name. Shut her up in her name. Shut her up.

'Lady?'

Sorry, sir. Lady's gone.

She knows where she is. She's back home. Her father's away but her mother's home and her sister Jo. Lady hears their voices. She's in the kitchen running water into a glass, letting it overflow and pour down her fingers until it's good and cold. She lifts the glass and drinks her fill and sets the glass down, then walks slow as a cat across the kitchen and down the hall to the bright doorway that opens onto the porch where her mother and sister are sitting. Her mother straightens up and settles back again as Lady goes to the railing and leans on her elbows and looks down the street and then out to the fields beyond.

'Lordalmighty it's hot.'

'Isn't it hot, though.'

Jo is slouched in her chair, rolling a bottle of Coke on her forehead. 'I could just die.'

'Late again, Lady?'

He'll be here.'

'Must have missed his bus again.'

'I suppose.'

'I bet those stupid cornpones were messing with him like they do,' Jo says. 'I wouldn't be a soldier.'

'He'll be here. Else he'd call.'

'No sir, I wouldn't be a soldier.'

'Nobody asked you.'

'Now, girls.'

'I'd like to see you a soldier anyway, sleeping all day and laying in bed eating candy. Mooning around. Oh, General, don't make me march, that just wears me out. Oh, do I have to wear that old green thing, green just makes me look sick, haven't you got one of those in red? Why, I can't eat lima beans, don't you know about me and lima beans?'

'Now, Lady...' But her mother's laughing and so is Jo, in spite of herself.

Oh, the goodness of that sound. And of her own voice. Just like singing. 'General, honey, you know I can't shoot that nasty thing, how about you ask one of those old boys to shoot it for me, they just love to shoot off their guns for Jo Kay.'

'Lady!'

The three of them on the porch, waiting but not waiting. Sufficient unto themselves. Nobody has to come.

But Robert is on his way. He's leaning his head against the window of the bus and trying to catch his breath. He missed the first bus and had to run to catch this one because his sergeant found fault with him during inspection and stuck him on a clean-up detail. The sergeant hates his guts.

He's an ignorant cracker and Robert is an educated man from Vermont, an engineer just out of college, quit Shell Oil in Louisiana to enlist the day North Korea crossed the parallel. The only Yankee in his company. Robert says when they get overseas there won't be any more Yankees and Southerners, just Americans. Lady likes him for believing that, but she gives him the needle because she knows it isn't true.

He changed uniforms in a hurry and didn't check the mirror before he left the barracks. There's a smudge on his right cheek. Shoe polish. His face is flushed and sweaty, his shirt soaked through. He's watching out the window and reciting a poem to himself. He's a great one for poems, this Robert. He has poems for running and poems for drill, poems for going to sleep and poems for when the rednecks start getting him down.

> Out of the night that covers me,
> Black as the Pit from pole to pole,
> I thank whatever Gods may be
> For my unconquerable soul.

That's the poem he uses to fortify himself. He thinks it over and over even when they're yelling in his face. It keeps him strong. Lady laughs when he tells her things like this, and he always looks at her a little surprised and then he laughs too, to show he likes her sass, though he doesn't. He thinks it's just her being young and spoiled and that it'll go away if he can get her out of that house and away from her family and among sensible people who don't think everything's a joke. In time it'll wear off and leave her quiet and dignified and respectful of life's seriousness – leave her pure Lady.

That's what he thinks some days. Most days he sees no

hope at all. He thinks of taking her home, into the house of his father, and when he imagines what she might say to his father he starts hearing his own excuses and apologies. Then he knows it's impossible. Robert has picked up some psychology here and there and believes he understands how he got himself into this mess. It's rebellion. Subconscious, of course. A subconscious rebellion against his father, falling in love with a girl like Lady. Because you don't fall in love. No. Life isn't a song. You choose to fall in love. And there are reasons for that choice, just as there's a reason for every choice, if you get to the bottom of it. Once you figure out your reasons, you master your choices. It's as simple as that.

Robert is looking out the window without really seeing anything.

It's impossible. Lady is just a kid, she doesn't know anything about life. There's a rawness to her that will take years to correct. She's spoiled and willful and half wild, except for her tongue, which is all wild. And she's Southern, not that there's anything wrong with that per se, but a particular kind of Southern. Not trash, as she would put it, but too proud of not being trash. Irrational. Superstitious. Clannish.

And what a clan it is, clan Cobb. Mr Cobb a suspender-snapping paint salesman always on the road, full of drummer's banter and jokes about nigras and watermelon. Mrs Cobb a morning-tonight gossip, weepily religious, content to live on her daughters' terms rather than raise them to woman's estate with discipline and right example. And the sister, Jo Kay. You can write that sad story before it happens.

All in all, Robert can't imagine a better family than the Cobbs to beat his father over the head with. That must be why he's chosen them, and why he has to undo that choice. He's made up his mind. He meant to tell her last time, but there was no chance. Today, no matter what. She won't understand. She'll cry. He will be gentle about it. He'll say she's a fine girl but too young. He'll say that it isn't fair to ask her to wait for him when who knows what might happen, and then to follow him to a place she's never been, far from family and friends.

He'll tell Lady anything except the truth, which is that he's ashamed to have picked her to use against his father. That's his own fight. He's been running from it for as long as he can remember, and he knows he has to stop. He has to face the man.

He will, too. Right after he gets home from Korea. His father will have to listen to him then. Robert will make him listen. He will tell him, he will face his father and tell him . . .

Robert's throat tightens and he sits up straight. He hears his breath coming so fast it sounds more like a gasp, and he wonders if anyone else has noticed. His heart is kicking. His mouth is dry. He closes his eyes and forces himself to breathe more slowly and deeply, imitating calm until it becomes almost real.

They pass the power company and the Greyhound station. Heat-flushed soldiers in shiny shoes stand around out front smoking. The bus stops on a street lined with bars, and the other men get off, hooting and pushing one another. There's just Robert and four women left on board. They turn off Jackson and bump across the railroad tracks and head east past the lumberyard. Black men are throwing planks into a truck, their shirts off, skin gleaming in the hazy light. Then they're gone behind a fence. Robert pulls the cord for his stop, waiting behind a wide woman in a flowered dress. The flesh swings like hammocks under her arms. She takes forever going down the steps.

The sun dazzles his eyes. He pulls down the visor of his cap and walks to the corner and turns right. This is Arsenal

Street. Lady lives two blocks down where the street runs into fields. There was no plan to how it ends – it just gives out. From here on there's nothing but farms for miles. At night Lady and Jo Kay steal strawberries from the field behind their house, then dish them up with thick fresh cream and grated chocolate. The strawberries have been stewing in the heat all day and burst open at the first pressure of the teeth. Robert disapproves of reaping another man's harvest, though he eats his share and then some. The season's about over. He'll be lucky if he gets any tonight.

He's thinking about strawberries when he sees Lady on the porch, and in this moment the sweetness of that taste fills his mouth. He stops as if he's just remembered something, then comes toward her again. Her lips are moving but he can't hear her, he's aware only of the taste in his mouth, and the closer he comes the stronger it gets. His pace quickens; his hand goes out for the railing. He takes the steps as if he means to devour her.

No, she's saying, no. She's talking to him and to the girl whose life he seeks. She knows what will befall her if she lets him have it. Stay here on this porch with your mother and your sister, they will soon have need of you. Gladden your father's eye yet awhile. This man is not for you. He will patiently school you half to death. He will kindly take you among unbending strangers to watch him fail to be brave. To suffer his carefulness, and to see your children writhe under it and fight it off with every kind of self-hurting reck-lessness. To be changed. To hear yourself and not know who is speaking. Wait, young Lady. Bide your time.

'Lady?'

It's no good. The girl won't hear. Even now she's bending toward him as he comes up the steps. She reaches for his cheek, to brush away the smudge he doesn't know is there.

He thinks it's something else that makes her do it, and his fine, lean face confesses everything, asks everything. There's no turning back from this touch. She can't be stopped. She has a mind of her own, and she knows something Lady doesn't. She knows how to love him.

Lady hears her name again.

Wait, sir.

She blesses the girl. Then she turns to the far-rolling fields she used to dream an ocean, this house the ship that ruled it. She takes a last good look, and opens her eyes.

MARGARET ATWOOD

BLUEBEARD'S EGG

SALLY STANDS AT the kitchen window, waiting for the sauce she's reducing to come to a simmer, looking out. Past the garage the lot sweeps downwards, into the ravine; it's a wilderness there, of bushes and branches and what Sally thinks of as vines. It was her idea to have a kind of terrace, built of old railroad ties, with wild flowers growing between them, but Edward says he likes it the way it is. There's a playhouse down at the bottom, near the fence; from here she can just see the roof. It has nothing to do with Edward's kids, in their earlier incarnations, before Sally's time; it's more ancient than that, and falling apart. Sally would like it cleared away. She thinks drunks sleep in it, the men who live under the bridges down there, who occasionally wander over the fence (which is broken down, from where they step on it) and up the hill, to emerge squinting like moles into the light of Sally's well-kept back lawn.

Off to the left is Ed, in his windbreaker; it's officially spring, Sally's blue scilla is in flower, but it's chilly for this time of year. Ed's windbreaker is an old one he won't throw out; it still says WILDCATS, relic of some team he was on in high school, an era so prehistoric Sally can barely imagine it; though picturing Ed at high school is not all that difficult. Girls would have had crushes on him, he would have been unconscious of it; things like that don't change. He's putter-ing around the rock garden now; some of the rocks stick out too far and are in danger of grazing the side of Sally's Peugeot, on its way to the garage, and he's moving them around. He likes doing things like that, puttering, humming to himself. He won't wear work gloves, though she keeps telling him he could squash his fingers.

Watching his bent back with its frayed, poignant lettering, Sally dissolves; which is not infrequent with her. *My darling Edward*, she thinks. *Edward Bear, of little brain. How I love you.* At times like this she feels very protective of him.

Sally knows for a fact that dumb blondes were loved, not because they were blondes, but because they were dumb. It was their helplessness and confusion that were so sexually attractive, once; not their hair. It wasn't false, the rush of tenderness men must have felt for such women. Sally understands it.

For it must be admitted: Sally is in love with Ed because of his stupidity, his monumental and almost energetic stupidity: energetic, because Ed's stupidity is not passive. He's no mere blockhead; you'd have to be working at it to be that stupid. Does it make Sally feel smug, or smarter than he is, or even smarter than she really is herself? No; on the contrary, it makes her humble. It fills her with wonder that the world can contain such marvels as Ed's colossal and endearing thickness. He is just so *stupid*. Every time he gives her another piece of evidence, another tile that she can glue into place in the vast mosaic of his stupidity she's continually piecing together, she wants to hug him, and often does; and he is so stupid he can never figure out what for.

Because Ed is so stupid he doesn't even know he's stupid. He's a child of luck, a third son who, armed with nothing but a certain feeble-minded amiability, manages to make it through the forest with all its witches and traps and pitfalls and end up with the princess, who is Sally, of course. It helps that he's handsome.

On good days she sees his stupidity as innocence, lamb-like, shining with the light of (for instance) green daisied meadows in the sun. (When Sally starts thinking this way about Ed, in terms of the calendar art from the service-station washrooms of her childhood, dredging up images of a boy with curly golden hair, his arm thrown around the neck of an Irish setter – a notorious brainless beast, she reminds herself – she knows she is sliding over the edge, into a ghastly kind of sentimentality, and that she must stop at once, or Ed will vanish, to be replaced by a stuffed facsimile, useful for little else but an umbrella stand. Ed is a real person, with a lot more to him than these simplistic renditions allow for; which sometimes worries her.) On bad days though, she sees his stupidity as willfulness, a stubborn determination to shut things out. His obtuseness is a wall, within which he can go about his business, humming to himself, while Sally, locked outside, must hack her way through the brambles with hardly so much as a transparent raincoat between them and her skin.

Why did she choose him (or, to be precise, as she tries to be with herself and sometimes is even out loud, *hunt him down*), when it's clear to everyone she had other options? To Marylynn, who is her best though most recent friend, she's explained it by saying she was spoiled when young by read-ing too many Agatha Christie murder mysteries, of the kind in which the clever and witty heroine passes over the equally clever and witty first-lead male, who's helped solve the crime, in order to marry the second-lead male, the stupid one, the one who would have been arrested and condemned and executed if it hadn't been for her cleverness. Maybe this is how she sees Ed: if it weren't for her, his blundering too-many-thumbs kindness would get him into all sorts of quagmires, all sorts of sink-holes he'd never be able to get himself out of, and then he'd be done for.

'Sink-hole' and 'quagmire' are not flattering ways of speaking about other women, but this is what is at the back of Sally's mind; specifically, Ed's two previous wives. Sally didn't exactly extricate him from their clutches. She's never even met the first one, who moved to the west coast fourteen years ago and sends Christmas cards, and the second one was middle-aged and already in the act of severing herself from Ed before Sally came along. (For Sally, 'middle-aged' means anyone five years older than she is. It has always meant this. She applies it only to women, however. She doesn't think of Ed as middle-aged, although the gap between them is considerably more than five years.)

Ed doesn't know what happened with these marriages, what went wrong. His protestations of ignorance, his refusal to discuss the finer points, is frustrating to Sally, because she would like to hear the whole story. But it's also cause for anxiety: if he doesn't know what happened with the other two, maybe the same thing could be happening with her and he doesn't know about that, either. Stupidity like Ed's can be a health hazard, for other people. What if he wakes up one day and decides that she isn't the true bride after all, but the false one? Then she will be put into a barrel stuck full of nails and rolled downhill, endlessly, while he is sitting in yet another bridal bed, drinking champagne. She remembers the brand name, because she bought it herself. Champagne isn't the sort of finishing touch that would occur to Ed, though he enjoyed it enough at the time.

But outwardly Sally makes a joke of all this. 'He doesn't *know*,' she says to Marylynn, laughing a little, and they shake their heads. If it were them, they'd know, all right. Marylynn is in fact divorced, and she can list every single thing that went wrong, item by item. After doing this, she adds that her divorce was one of the best things that ever happened to her. 'I was just a nothing before,' she says. 'It made me pull myself together.'

Sally, looking across the kitchen table at Marylynn, has to agree that she is far from being a nothing now. She started out re-doing people's closets, and has worked that up into her own interior-design firm. She does the houses of the newly rich, those who lack ancestral furniture and the confidence to be shabby, and who wish their interiors to reflect a personal taste they do not in reality possess.

'What they want are mausoleums,' Marylynn says, 'or hotels,' and she cheerfully supplies them. 'Right down to the ash-trays. Imagine having someone else pick out your ash-trays for you.'

By saying this, Marylynn lets Sally know that she's not including her in that category, though Sally did in fact hire her, at the very first, to help with a few details around the house. It was Marylynn who redesigned the wall of closets in the master bedroom and who found Sally's massive Chinese mahogany table, which cost her another seven hundred dollars to have stripped. But it turned out to be perfect, as Marylynn said it would. Now she's dug up a nineteenth-century keyhole desk, which both she and Sally know will be exactly right for the bay-windowed alcove off the living room. 'Why do you need it?' Ed said in his puzzled way. 'I thought you worked in your study.' Sally admitted this, but said they could keep the telephone bills in it, which appeared to satisfy him. She knows exactly what she needs it for: she needs it to sit at, in something flowing, backlit by the morning sunlight, gracefully dashing off notes. She saw a 1940's advertisement for coffee like this once; and the husband was standing behind the chair, leaning over, with a worshipful expression on his face.

Marylynn is the kind of friend Sally does not have to explain any of this to, because it's assumed between them. Her intelligence is the kind Sally respects.

Marylynn is tall and elegant, and makes anything she is wearing seem fashionable. Her hair is prematurely grey and she leaves it that way. She goes in for loose blouses in cream-coloured silk, and eccentric scarves gathered from interesting shops and odd corners of the world, thrown carelessly around her neck and over one shoulder. (Sally has tried this toss in the mirror, but it doesn't work.) Marylynn has a large collection of unusual shoes; she says they're unusual because her feet are so big, but Sally knows better. Sally, who used to think of herself as pretty enough and now thinks of herself as doing quite well for her age, envies Marylynn her bone structure, which will serve her well when the inevitable happens.

Whenever Marylynn is coming to dinner, as she is today – she's bringing the desk, too – Sally takes especial care with her clothes and make-up. Marylynn, she knows, is her real audience for such things, since no changes she effects in herself seem to affect Ed one way or the other, or even to register with him. 'You look fine to me,' is all he says, no matter how she really looks. (But does she want him to see her more clearly, or not? Most likely not. If he did he would notice the incipient wrinkles, the small pouches of flesh that are not quite there yet, the network forming beneath her eyes. It's better as it is.)

Sally has repeated this remark of Ed's to Marylynn, adding that he said it the day the Jacuzzi overflowed because the smoke alarm went off, because an English muffin she was heating to eat in the bathtub got stuck in the toaster, and she had to spend an hour putting down newspaper and mopping up, and only had half an hour to dress for a dinner they were going to. 'Really I looked like the wrath of God,' said Sally. These days she finds herself repeating to Marylynn many of the things Ed says: the stupid things. Marylynn is the only one of Sally's friends she has confided in to this extent.

'Ed is cute as a button,' Marylynn said. 'In fact, he's just like a button: he's so bright and shiny. If he were mine, I'd get him bronzed and keep him on the mantelpiece.'

Marylynn is even better than Sally at concocting formulations for Ed's particular brand of stupidity, which can irritate Sally: coming from herself, this sort of comment appears to her indulgent and loving, but from Marylynn it borders on the patronizing. So then she sticks up for Ed, who is by no means stupid about everything. When you narrow it down, there's only one area of life he's hopeless about. The rest of the time he's intelligent enough, some even say brilliant: otherwise, how could he be so successful?

Ed is a heart man, one of the best, and the irony of this is not lost on Sally: who could possibly know less about the workings of hearts, the kind symbolized by red satin surrounded by lace and topped by pink bows, than Ed? Hearts with arrows in them. At the same time, the fact that he's a heart man is a large part of his allure. Women corner him on sofas, trap him in bay-windows at cocktail parties, mutter to him in confidential voices at dinner parties. They behave this way right in front of Sally, under her very nose, as if she's invisible, and Ed lets them do it. This would never happen if he were in banking or construction.

As it is, everywhere he goes he is beset by sirens. They want him to fix their hearts. Each of them seems to have a little something wrong – a murmur, a whisper. Or they faint a lot and want him to tell them why. This is always what the conversations are about, according to Ed, and Sally believes it. Once she'd wanted it herself, that mirage. What had she invented for him, in the beginning? A heavy heart, that beat too hard after meals. And he'd been so sweet, looking at her with those stunned brown eyes of his, as if her heart were the genuine topic, listening to her gravely as if he'd never heard any of this twaddle before, advising her to drink less coffee. And she'd felt such triumph, to have carried off her imposture, pried out of him that minuscule token of concern.

Thinking back on this incident makes her uneasy, now that she's seen her own performance repeated so many times, including the hand placed lightly on the heart, to call attention of course to the breasts. Some of these women have been within inches of getting Ed to put his head down on their chests, right there in Sally's living room. Watching all this out of the corners of her eyes while serving the liqueurs, Sally feels the Aztec rise within her. *Trouble with your heart? Get it removed*, she thinks. *Then you'll have no more problems.*

Sometimes Sally worries that she's a nothing, the way Mary-lynn was before she got a divorce and a job. But Sally isn't a nothing; therefore, she doesn't need a divorce to stop being one. And she's always had a job of some sort; in fact she has one now. Luckily Ed has no objection; he doesn't have much of an objection to anything she does.

Her job is supposed to be full-time, but in effect it's part-time, because Sally can take a lot of the work away and do it at home, and, as she says, with one arm tied behind her back. When Sally is being ornery, when she's playing the dull wife of a fascinating heart man – she does this with people she can't be bothered with – she says she works in a

244

bank, nothing important. Then she watches their eyes dismiss her. When, on the other hand, she's trying to impress, she says she's in P.R. In reality she runs the in-house organ for a trust company, a medium-sized one. This is a thin magazine, nicely printed, which is supposed to make the employees feel that some of the boys are doing worthwhile things out there and are human beings as well. It's still the boys, though the few women in anything resembling key positions are wheeled out regularly, bloused and suited and smiling brightly, with what they hope will come across as confidence rather than aggression.

This is the latest in a string of such jobs Sally has held over the years: comfortable enough jobs that engage only half of her cogs and wheels, and that end up leading nowhere. Technically she's second-in-command: over her is a man who wasn't working out in management, but who couldn't be fired because his wife was related to the chairman of the board. He goes out for long alcoholic lunches and plays a lot of golf, and Sally runs the show. This man gets the official credit for everything Sally does right, but the senior executives in the company take Sally aside when no one is looking and tell her what a great gal she is and what a whiz she is at holding up her end.

The real pay-off for Sally, though, is that her boss provides her with an endless supply of anecdotes. She dines out on stories about his dim-wittedness and pomposity, his lobotomized suggestions about what the two of them should cook up for the magazine; *the organ*, as she says he always calls it. 'He says we need some fresh blood to perk up the organ,' Sally says, and the heart men grin at her. 'He actually said that?' Talking like this about her boss would be reckless – you never know what might get back to him, with the world as small as it is – if Sally were afraid of losing her job, but she isn't. There's an unspoken agreement between her and this man: they both know that if she goes, he goes, because who else would put up with him? Sally might angle for his job, if she were stupid enough to disregard his family connections, if she coveted the trappings of power. But she's just fine where she is. Jokingly, she says she's reached her level of incompetence. She says she suffers from fear of success.

Her boss is white-haired, slender, and tanned, and looks like an English gin ad. Despite his vapidity he's outwardly distinguished, she allows him that. In truth she pampers him outrageously, indulges him, covers up for him at every turn, though she stops short of behaving like a secretary: she doesn't bring him coffee. They both have a secretary who does that anyway. The one time he made a pass at her, when he came in from lunch visibly reeling, Sally was kind about it.

Occasionally, though not often, Sally has to travel in connection with her job. She's sent off to places like Edmonton, where they have a branch. She interviews the boys at the middle and senior levels; they have lunch, and the boys talk about ups and downs in oil or the slump in the real-estate market. Then she gets taken on tours of shopping plazas under construction. It's always windy, and grit blows into her face. She comes back to home base and writes a piece on the youthfulness and vitality of the West.

She teases Ed, while she packs, saying she's going off for a rendezvous with a dashing financier or two. Ed isn't threatened; he tells her to enjoy herself, and she hugs him and tells him how much she will miss him. He's so dumb it doesn't occur to him she might not be joking. In point of fact, it would have been quite possible for Sally to have had an affair, or at least a one- or two-night stand, on several of these occasions: she knows when those chalk lines are being drawn, when she's being dared to step over them. But she isn't interested in having an affair with anyone but Ed.

She doesn't eat much on the planes; she doesn't like the food. But on the return trip, she invariably saves the pre-packaged parts of the meal, the cheese in its plastic wrap, the miniature chocolate bar, the bag of pretzels. She ferrets them away in her purse. She thinks of them as supplies, that she may need if she gets stuck in a strange airport, if they have to change course because of snow or fog, for instance. All kinds of things could happen, although they never have. When she gets home she takes the things from her purse and throws them out.

Outside the window Ed straightens up and wipes his earth-smeared hands down the sides of his pants. He begins to turn, and Sally moves back from the window so he won't see that she's watching. She doesn't like it to be too obvious. She shifts her attention to the sauce: it's in the second stage of a *sauce suprême*, which will make all the difference to the chicken. When Sally was learning this sauce, her cooking instructor quoted one of the great chefs, to the effect that the chicken was merely a canvas. He meant as in painting, but Sally, in an undertone to the woman next to her, turned it around. 'Mine's canvas anyway, sauce or no sauce,' or words to that effect.

Gourmet cooking was the third night course Sally has taken. At the moment she's on her fifth, which is called *Forms of Narrative Fiction*. It's half reading and half writing assignments – the instructor doesn't believe you can under-stand an art form without at least trying it yourself – and Sally purports to be enjoying it. She tells her friends she takes night courses to keep her brain from atrophying, and her friends find this amusing: whatever else may become of Sally's brain, they say, they don't see atrophying as an option. Sally knows better, but in any case there's always room for improvement. She may have begun taking the courses in the belief that this would make her more interesting to Ed, but she soon gave up on that idea: she appears to be neither more nor less interesting to Ed now than she was before.

Most of the food for tonight is already made. Sally tries to be well organized: the overflowing Jacuzzi was an aberration. The cold watercress soup with walnuts is chilling in the refrigerator, the chocolate mousse ditto. Ed, being Ed, prefers meatloaf to sweetbreads with pine nuts, butterscotch pudding made from a package to chestnut purée topped with whipped cream. (Sally burnt her fingers peeling the chestnuts. She couldn't do it the easy way and buy it tinned.) Sally says Ed's preference for this type of food comes from being pre-programmed by hospital cafeterias when he was younger: show him a burned sausage and a scoop of instant mashed potatoes and he salivates. So it's only for company that she can unfurl her *boeuf en daube* and her salmon *en papillote*, spread them forth to be savoured and praised.

What she likes best about these dinners though is setting the table, deciding who will sit where and, when she's feeling mischievous, even what they are likely to say. Then she can sit and listen to them say it. Occasionally she prompts a little.

Tonight will not be very challenging, since it's only the heart men and their wives, and Marylynn, who Sally hopes will dilute them. The heart men are forbidden to talk shop at Sally's dinner table, but they do it anyway. 'Not what you really want to listen to while you're eating,' says Sally. 'All those tubes and valves.' Privately she thinks they're a conceited lot, all except Ed. She can't resist needling them from time to time.

'I mean,' she said to one of the leading surgeons, 'basically it's just an exalted form of dress-making, don't you think?'

'Come again?' said the surgeon, smiling. The heart men think Sally is one hell of a tease.

'It's really just cutting and sewing, isn't it?' Sally murmured. The surgeon laughed.

'There's more to it than that,' Ed said, unexpectedly, solemnly.

'What more, Ed?' said the surgeon. 'You could say there's a lot of embroidery, but that's in the billing.' He chuckled at himself.

Sally held her breath. She could hear Ed's verbal thought processes lurching into gear. He was delectable.

'Good judgement,' Ed said. His earnestness hit the table like a wet fish. The surgeon hastily downed his wine.

Sally smiled. This was supposed to be a reprimand to her, she knew, for not taking things seriously enough. *Oh, come on, Ed*, she could say. But she knows also, most of the time, when to keep her trap shut. She should have a light-up JOKE sign on her forehead, so Ed would be able to tell the difference.

The heart men do well. Most of them appear to be doing better than Ed, but that's only because they have, on the whole, more expensive tastes and fewer wives. Sally can calculate these things and she figures Ed is about par.

These days there's much talk about advanced technologies, which Sally tries to keep up on, since they interest Ed. A few years ago the heart men got themselves a new facility. Ed was so revved up that he told Sally about it, which was unusual for him. A week later Sally said she would drop by

249

the hospital at the end of the day and pick Ed up and take him out for dinner; she didn't feel like cooking, she said. Really she wanted to check out the facility; she likes to check out anything that causes the line on Ed's excitement chart to move above level.

At first Ed said he was tired, that when the day came to an end he didn't want to prolong it. But Sally wheedled and was respectful, and finally Ed took her to see his new gizmo. It was in a cramped, darkened room with an examining table in it. The thing itself looked like a television screen hooked up to some complicated hardware. Ed said that they could wire a patient up and bounce sound waves off the heart and pick up the echoes, and they would get a picture on the screen, an actual picture, of the heart in motion. It was a thousand times better than an electrocardiogram, he said: they could see the faults, the thickenings and cloggings, much more clearly.

'Colour?' said Sally.

'Black and white,' said Ed.

Then Sally was possessed by a desire to see her own heart, in motion, in black and white, on the screen. At the dentist's she always wants to see the X-rays of her teeth, too, solid and glittering in her cloudy head. 'Do it,' she said, 'I want to see how it works,' and though this was the kind of thing Ed would ordinarily evade or tell her she was being silly about, he didn't need much persuading. He was fascinated by the thing himself, and he wanted to show it off.

He checked to make sure there was nobody real booked for the room. Then he told Sally to slip out of her clothes, the top half, brassière and all. He gave her a paper gown and turned his back modestly while she slipped it on, as if he didn't see her body every night of the week. He attached electrodes to her, the ankles and one wrist, and turned a switch and fiddled with the dials. Really a technician was supposed to do this, he told her, but he knew how to run the machine himself. He was good with small appliances.

Sally lay prone on the table, feeling strangely naked. 'What do I do?' she said.

'Just lie there,' said Ed. He came over to her and tore a hole in the paper gown, above her left breast. Then he started running a probe over her skin. It was wet and slippery and cold, and felt like the roller on a roll-on deodorant.

'There,' he said, and Sally turned her head. On the screen was a large grey object, like a giant fig, paler in the middle, a dark line running down the centre. The sides moved in and out; two wings fluttered in it, like an uncertain moth's.

'That's it?' said Sally dubiously. Her heart looked so insubstantial, like a bag of gelatin, something that would melt, fade, disintegrate, if you squeezed it even a little.

Ed moved the probe, and they looked at the heart from the bottom, then the top. Then he stopped the frame, then changed it from a positive to a negative image. Sally began to shiver.

'That's wonderful,' she said. He seemed so distant, absorbed in his machine, taking the measure of her heart, which was beating over there all by itself, detached from her, exposed and under his control.

Ed unwired her and she put on her clothes again, neutrally, as if he were actually a doctor. Nevertheless this transaction, this whole room, was sexual in a way she didn't quite understand; it was clearly a dangerous place. It was like a massage parlour, only for women. Put a batch of women in there with Ed and they would never want to come out. They'd want to stay in there while he ran his probe over their wet skins and pointed out to them the defects of their beating hearts.

'Thank you,' said Sally.

251

Sally hears the back door open and close. She feels Ed approaching, coming through the passages of the house towards her, like a small wind or a ball of static electricity. The hair stands up on her arms. Sometimes he makes her so happy she thinks she's about to burst; other times she thinks she's about to burst anyway.

He comes into the kitchen, and she pretends not to notice. He puts his arms around her from behind, kisses her on the neck. She leans back, pressing herself into him. What they should do now is go into the bedroom (or even the living room, even the den) and make love, but it wouldn't occur to Ed to make love in the middle of the day. Sally often comes across articles in magazines about how to improve your sex life, which leave her feeling disappointed, or reminiscent: Ed is not Sally's first and only man. But she knows she shouldn't expect too much of Ed. If Ed were more experimental, more interested in variety, he would be a different kind of man altogether: slyer, more devious, more observant, harder to deal with.

As it is, Ed makes love in the same way, time after time, each movement following the others in an exact order. But it seems to satisfy him. Of course it satisfies him: you can always tell when men are satisfied. It's Sally who lies awake, afterwards, watching the pictures unroll across her closed eyes.

Sally steps away from Ed, smiles at him. 'How did you make out with the women today?' she says.

'What women?' says Ed absently, going towards the sink. He knows what women.

'The ones out there, hiding in the forsythia,' says Sally. 'I counted at least ten. They were just waiting for a chance.'

She teases him frequently about these troops of women,

which follow him around everywhere, which are invisible to Ed but which she can see as plain as day.

'I bet they hang around outside the front door of the hospital,' she will say, 'just waiting till you come out. I bet they hide in the linen closets and jump out at you from behind, and then pretend to be lost so you'll take them by the short cut. It's the white coat that does it. None of those women can resist the white coats. They've been conditioned by Young Doctor Kildare.'

'Don't be silly,' says Ed today, with equanimity. Is he blushing, is he embarrassed? Sally examines his face closely, like a geologist with an aerial photograph, looking for tell-tale signs of mineral treasure: markings, bumps, hollows. Everything about Ed means something, though it's difficult at times to say what.

Now he's washing his hands at the sink, to get the earth off. In a minute he'll wipe them on the dish towel instead of using the hand towel the way he's supposed to. Is that complacency, in the back turned to her? Maybe there really are these hordes of women, even though she's made them up. Maybe they really do behave that way. His shoulders are slightly drawn up: is he shutting her out?

'I know what they want,' she goes on. 'They want to get into that little dark room of yours and climb up onto your table. They think you're delicious. They'll gobble you up. They'll chew you into tiny pieces. There won't be anything left of you at all, only a stethoscope and a couple of shoelaces.'

Once Ed would have laughed at this, but today he doesn't. Maybe she's said it, or something like it, a few times too often. He smiles though, wipes his hands on the dish towel, peers into the fridge. He likes to snack.

'There's some cold roast beef,' Sally says, baffled.

*

Sally takes the sauce off the stove and sets it aside for later: she'll do the last steps just before serving. It's only two-thirty. Ed has disappeared into the cellar, where Sally knows he will be safe for a while. She goes into her study, which used to be one of the kids' bedrooms, and sits down at her desk. The room has never been completely redecorated: there's still a bed in it, and a dressing table with a blue flowered flounce Sally helped pick out, long before the kids went off to university: 'flew the coop', as Ed puts it.

Sally doesn't comment on the expression, though she would like to say that it wasn't the first coop they flew. Her house isn't even the real coop, since neither of the kids is hers. She'd hoped for a baby of her own when she married Ed, but she didn't want to force the issue. Ed didn't object to the idea, exactly, but he was neutral about it, and Sally got the feeling he'd had enough babies already. Anyway, the other two wives had babies, and look what happened to them. Since their actual fates have always been vague to Sally, she's free to imagine all kinds of things, from drug addiction to madness. Whatever it was resulted in Sally having to bring up their kids, at least from puberty onwards. The way it was presented by the first wife was that it was Ed's turn now. The second wife was more oblique: she said that the child wanted to spend some time with her father. Sally was left out of both these equations, as if the house wasn't a place she lived in, not really, so she couldn't be expected to have any opinion.

Considering everything, she hasn't done badly. She likes the kids and tries to be a friend to them, since she can hardly pretend to be a mother. She describes the three of them as having an easy relationship. Ed wasn't around much for the kids, but it's him they want approval from, not Sally; it's

254

him they respect. Sally is more like a confederate, helping them get what they want from Ed.

When the kids were younger, Sally used to play Monopoly with them, up at the summer place in Muskoka Ed owned then but has since sold. Ed would play too, on his vacations and on the weekends when he could make it up. These games would all proceed along the same lines. Sally would have an initial run of luck and would buy up everything she had a chance at. She didn't care whether it was classy real estate, like Boardwalk or Park Place, or those dingy little houses on the other side of the tracks; she would even buy train stations, which the kids would pass over, preferring to save their cash reserves for better investments. Ed, on the other hand, would plod along, getting a little here, a little there. Then, when Sally was feeling flush, she would blow her money on next-to-useless luxuries such as the electric light company; and when the kids started to lose, as they invariably did, Sally would lend them money at cheap rates or trade them things of her own, at a loss. Why not? She could afford it.

Ed meanwhile would be hedging his bets, building up blocks of property, sticking houses and hotels on them. He preferred the middle range, respectable streets but not flashy. Sally would land on his spaces and have to shell out hard cash. Ed never offered deals, and never accepted them. He played a lone game, and won more often than not. Then Sally would feel thwarted. She would say she guessed she lacked the killer instinct; or she would say that for herself she didn't care, because after all it was only a game, but he ought to allow the kids to win, once in a while. Ed couldn't grasp the concept of allowing other people to win. He said it would be condescending towards the children, and anyway you couldn't arrange to have a dice game turn out the way you wanted it to, since it was partly a matter of chance. If it was chance, Sally would think, why were the games so similar to one another? At the end, there would be Ed, counting up his paper cash, sorting it out into piles of bills of varying denominations, and Sally, her vast holdings dwindled to a few shoddy blocks on Baltic Avenue, doomed to foreclosure: extravagant, generous, bankrupt.

On these nights, after the kids were asleep, Sally would have two or three more rye-and-gingers than were good for her. Ed would go to bed early – winning made him satisfied and drowsy – and Sally would ramble about the house or read the endings of murder mysteries she had already read once before, and finally she would slip into bed and wake Ed up and stroke him into arousal, seeking comfort.

Sally has almost forgotten these games. Right now the kids are receding, fading like old ink; Ed on the contrary looms larger and larger, the outlines around him darkening. He's constantly developing, like a Polaroid print, new colours emerging, but the result remains the same: Ed is a surface, one she has trouble getting beneath.

'Explore your inner world,' said Sally's instructor in *Forms of Narrative Fiction*, a middle-aged woman of scant fame who goes in for astrology and the Tarot pack and writes short stories, which are not published in any of the magazines Sally reads. 'Then there's your outer one,' Sally said afterwards, to her friends. 'For instance, she should really get something done about her hair.' She made this trivial and mean remark because she's fed up with her inner world; she doesn't need to explore it. In her inner world is Ed, like a doll within a Russian wooden doll, and in Ed is Ed's inner world, which she can't get at.

She takes a crack at it anyway: Ed's inner world is a forest, which looks something like the bottom part of their ravine lot, but without the fence. He wanders around in there, among the trees, not heading in any special direction. Every once in a while he comes upon a strange-looking plant, a sickly plant choked with weeds and briars. Ed kneels, clears a space around it, does some pruning, a little skilful snipping and cutting, props it up. The plant revives, flushes with health, sends out a grateful red blossom. Ed continues on his way. Or it may be a conked-out squirrel, which he restores with a drop from his flask of magic elixir. At set intervals an angel appears, bringing him food. It's always meatloaf. That's fine with Ed, who hardly notices what he eats, but the angel is getting tired of being an angel. Now Sally begins thinking about the angel: why are its wings frayed and dingy grey around the edges, why is it looking so withered and frantic? This is where all Sally's attempts to explore Ed's inner world end up.

She knows she thinks about Ed too much. She knows she should stop. She knows she shouldn't ask, 'Do you still love me?' in the plaintive tone that sets even her own teeth on edge. All it achieves is that Ed shakes his head, as if not understanding why she would ask this, and pats her hand. 'Sally, Sally,' he says, and everything proceeds as usual; except for the dread that seeps into things, the most ordinary things, such as rearranging the chairs and changing the burnt-out lightbulbs. But what is it she's afraid of? She has what they call everything: Ed, their wonderful house on a ravine lot, something she's always wanted. (But the hill is jungly, and the house is made of ice. It's held together only by Sally, who sits in the middle of it, working on a puzzle. The puzzle is Ed. If she should ever solve it, if she should ever fit the last cold splinter into place, the house will melt and flow away down the hill, and then. . . .) It's a bad habit, fooling around with her head this way. It does no good. She knows that if she could quit she'd be happier. She ought to be able to: she's given up smoking.

She needs to concentrate her attention on other things. This is the real reason for the night courses, which she picks almost at random, to coincide with the evenings Ed isn't in. He has meetings, he's on the boards of charities, he has trouble saying no. She runs the courses past herself, medi-aeval history, cooking, anthropology, hoping her mind will snag on something; she's even taken a course in geology, which was fascinating, she told her friends, all that magma. That's just it: everything is fascinating, but nothing enters her. She's always a star pupil, she does well on the exams and impresses the teachers, for which she despises them. She is familiar with her brightness, her techniques; she's surprised other people are still taken in by them.

Forms of Narrative Fiction started out the same way. Sally was full of good ideas, brimming with helpful suggestions. The workshop part of it was anyway just like a committee meeting, and Sally knew how to run those, from behind, without seeming to run them: she'd done it lots of times at work. Bertha, the instructor, told Sally she had a vivid imagination and a lot of untapped creative energy. 'No wonder she never gets anywhere, with a name like Bertha,' Sally said, while having coffee afterwards with two of the other night-coursers. 'It goes with her outfits, though.' (Bertha sports the macramé look, with health-food sandals and bulky-knit sweaters and hand-weave skirts that don't do a thing for her square figure, and too many Mexican rings on her hands, which she doesn't wash often enough.) Bertha goes in for assignments, which she calls learning by doing. Sally likes assignments: she likes things that can be com-pleted and then discarded, and for which she gets marks.

The first thing Bertha assigned was The Epic. They read *The Odyssey* (selected passages, in translation, with a plot summary of the rest); then they poked around in James Joyce's *Ulysses*, to see how Joyce had adapted the epic form to the modern-day novel. Bertha had them keep a Toronto notebook, in which they had to pick out various spots around town as the ports of call in *The Odyssey*, and say why they had chosen them. The notebooks were read out loud in class, and it was a scream to see who had chosen what for Hades. (The Mount Pleasant Cemetery, McDonald's, where, if you eat the forbidden food, you never get back to the land of the living, the University Club with its dead ancestral souls, and so forth.) Sally's was the hospital, of course; she had no difficulty with the trench filled with blood, and she put the ghosts in wheelchairs.

After that they did The Ballad, and read gruesome accounts of murders and betrayed love. Bertha played them tapes of wheezy old men singing traditionally, in the Doric mode, and assigned a newspaper scrapbook, in which you had to clip and paste up-to-the-minute equivalents. The *Sun* was the best newspaper for these. The fiction that turned out to go with this kind of plot was the kind Sally liked anyway, and she had no difficulty concocting a five-page murder mystery, complete with revenge.

But now they are on Folk Tales and the Oral Tradition, and Sally is having trouble. This time, Bertha wouldn't let them read anything. Instead she read to them, in a voice, Sally said, that was like a gravel truck and was not conducive to reverie. Since it was the Oral Tradition, they weren't even allowed to take notes; Bertha said the original hearers of these stories couldn't read, so the stories were memorized. 'To re-create the atmosphere,' said Bertha, 'I should turn out the lights. These stories were always told at night.' 'To make them creepier?' someone offered. 'No,' said Bertha. 'In the days, they worked.' She didn't do that, though she did make them sit in a circle.

'You should have seen us,' Sally said afterwards to Ed, 'sitting in a circle, listening to fairy stories. It was just like kindergarten. Some of them even had their mouths open. I kept expecting her to say, "If you need to go, put up your hand." ' She was meaning to be funny, to amuse Ed with this account of Bertha's eccentricity and the foolish appearance of the students, most of them middle-aged, sitting in a circle as if they had never grown up at all. She was also intending to belittle the course, just slightly. She always did this with her night courses, so Ed wouldn't get the idea there was anything in her life that was even remotely as important as he was. But Ed didn't seem to need this amusement or this belittlement. He took her information earnestly, gravely, as if Bertha's behaviour was, after all, only the procedure of a specialist. No one knew better than he did that the procedures of specialists often looked bizarre or incomprehensible to onlookers. 'She probably has her reasons,' was all he would say.

The first stories Bertha read them, for warm-ups ('No memorizing for *her*,' said Sally), were about princes who got amnesia and forgot about their true loves and married girls their mothers had picked out for them. Then they had to be rescued, with the aid of magic. The stories didn't say what happened to the women the princes had already married, though Sally wondered about it. Then Bertha read them another story, and this time they were supposed to remember the features that stood out for them and write a five-page transposition, set in the present and cast in the realistic mode. ('In other words,' said Bertha, 'no real magic.') They couldn't use the Universal Narrator, however: they had done

260

that in their Ballad assignment. This time they had to choose a point of view. It could be the point of view of anyone or anything in the story, but they were limited to one only. The story she was about to read, she said, was a variant of the Bluebeard motif, much earlier than Perrault's sentimental rewriting of it. In Perrault, said Bertha, the girl has to be rescued by her brothers; but in the earlier version things were quite otherwise.

This is what Bertha read, as far as Sally can remember:

There were once three young sisters. One day a beggar with a large basket on his back came to the door and asked for some bread. The eldest sister brought him some, but no sooner had she touched him than she was compelled to jump into his basket, for the beggar was really a wizard in disguise. ('So much for United Appeal,' Sally murmured. 'She should have said, "I gave at the office." ') The wizard carried her away to his house in the forest, which was large and richly furnished. 'Here you will be happy with me, my darling,' said the wizard, 'for you will have everything your heart could desire.'

This lasted for a few days. Then the wizard gave the girl an egg and a bunch of keys. 'I must go away on a journey,' he said, 'and I am leaving the house in your charge. Preserve this egg for me, and carry it about with you everywhere; for a great misfortune will follow from its loss. The keys open every room in the house. You may go into each of them and enjoy what you find there, but do not go into the small room at the top of the house, on pain of death.' The girl promised, and the wizard disappeared.

At first the girl contented herself with exploring the rooms, which contained many treasures. But finally her curiosity would not let her alone. She sought out the smallest key, and, with beating heart, opened the little door at the top of the house. Inside it was a large basin full of blood, within which were the bodies of many women, which had been cut to pieces; nearby were a chopping block and an axe. In her horror, she let go of the egg, which fell into the basin of blood. In vain did she try to wipe away the stain: every time she succeeded in removing it, back it would come.

The wizard returned, and in a stern voice asked for the egg and the keys. When he saw the egg, he knew at once she had disobeyed him and gone into the forbidden room. 'Since you have gone into the room against my will,' he said, 'you shall go back into it against your own.' Despite her pleas he threw her down, dragged her by the hair into the little room, hacked her into pieces and threw her body into the basin with the others.

Then he went for the second girl, who fared no better than her sister. But the third was clever and wily. As soon as the wizard had gone, she set the egg on a shelf, out of harm's way, and then went immediately and opened the forbidden door. Imagine her distress when she saw the cut-up bodies of her two beloved sisters; but she set the parts in order, and they joined together and her sisters stood up and moved, and were living and well. They embraced each other, and the third sister hid the other two in a cupboard.

When the wizard returned he at once asked for the egg. This time it was spotless. 'You have passed the test,' he said to the third sister. 'You shall be my bride.' ('And second prize,' said Sally, to herself this time, 'is *two* weeks in Niagara Falls.') The wizard no longer had any power over her, and had to do whatever she asked. There was more, about how the wizard met his come-uppance and was burned to death, but Sally already knew which features stood out for her.

*

At first she thought the most important thing in the story was the forbidden room. What would she put in the forbidden room, in her present-day realistic version? Certainly not chopped-up women. It wasn't that they were too unrealistic, but they were certainly too sick, as well as being too obvious. She wanted to do something more clever. She thought it might be a good idea to have the curious woman open the door and find nothing there at all, but after mulling it over she set this notion aside. It would leave her with the problem of why the wizard would have a forbidden room in which he kept nothing.

That was the way she was thinking right after she got the assignment, which was a full two weeks ago. So far she's written nothing. The great temptation is to cast herself in the role of the cunning heroine, but again it's too predictable. And Ed certainly isn't the wizard; he's nowhere near sinister enough. If Ed were the wizard, the room would contain a forest, some ailing plants and feeble squirrels, and Ed himself, fixing them up; but then, if it were Ed the room wouldn't even be locked, and there would be no story.

Now, as she sits at her desk, fiddling with her felt-tip pen, it comes to Sally that the intriguing thing about the story, the thing she should fasten on, is the egg. Why an egg? From the night course in Comparative Folklore she took four years ago, she remembers that the egg can be a fertility symbol, or a necessary object in African spells, or something the world hatched out of. Maybe in this story it's a symbol of virginity, and that is why the wizard requires it unbloodied. Women with dirty eggs get murdered, those with clean ones get married.

But this isn't useful either. The concept is so outmoded. Sally doesn't see how she can transpose it into real life without making it ridiculous, unless she sets the story in, for

263

instance, an immigrant Portuguese family, and what would she know about that?

Sally opens the drawer of her desk and hunts around in it for her nail file. As she's doing this, she gets the brilliant idea of writing the story from the point of view of the egg. Other people will do the other things: the clever girl, the wizard, the two blundering sisters, who weren't smart enough to lie, and who will have problems afterwards, because of the thin red lines running all over their bodies, from where their parts joined together. But no one will think of the egg. How does it feel, to be the innocent and passive cause of so much misfortune?

(Ed isn't the Bluebeard: Ed is the egg. Ed Egg, blank and pristine and lovely. Stupid, too. Boiled, probably. Sally smiles fondly.)

But how can there be a story from the egg's point of view, if the egg is so closed and unaware? Sally ponders this, doodling on her pad of lined paper. Then she resumes the search for her nail file. Already it's time to begin getting ready for her dinner party. She can sleep on the problem of the egg and finish the assignment tomorrow, which is Sunday. It's due on Monday, but Sally's mother used to say she was a whiz at getting things done at the last minute.

After painting her nails with *Nuit Magique*, Sally takes a bath, eating her habitual toasted English muffin while she lies in the tub. She begins to dress, dawdling; she has plenty of time. She hears Ed coming up out of the cellar; then she hears him in the bathroom, which he has entered from the hall door. Sally goes in through the other door, still in her slip. Ed is standing at the sink with his shirt off, shaving. On the weekends he leaves it until necessary, or until Sally tells him he's too scratchy.

Sally slides her hands around his waist, nuzzling against

264

his naked back. He has very smooth skin, for a man. Sally smiles to herself: she can't stop thinking of him as an egg.

'Mmm,' says Ed. It could be appreciation, or the answer to a question Sally hasn't asked and he hasn't heard, or just an acknowledgement that she's there.

'Don't you ever wonder what I think about?' Sally says. She's said this more than once, in bed or at the dinner table, after dessert. She stands behind him, watching the swaths the razor cuts in the white of his face, looking at her own face reflected in the mirror, just the eyes visible above his naked shoulder. Ed, lathered, is Assyrian, sterner than usual; or a frost-covered Arctic explorer; or demi-human, a white-bearded forest mutant. He scrapes away at himself, methodically destroying the illusion.

'But I already know what you think about,' says Ed.

'How?' Sally says, taken aback.

'You're always telling me,' Ed says, with what might be resignation or sadness; or maybe this is only a simple statement of fact.

Sally is relieved. If that's all he's going on, she's safe.

Marylynn arrives half an hour early, her pearl-coloured Porsche leading two men in a delivery truck up the driveway. The men install the keyhole desk, while Marylynn supervises: it looks, in the alcove, exactly as Marylynn has said it would, and Sally is delighted. She sits at it to write the cheque. Then she and Marylynn go into the kitchen, where Sally is finishing up her sauce, and Sally pours them each a Kir. She's glad Marylynn is here: it will keep her from dithering, as she tends to do just before people arrive. Though it's only the heart men, she's still a bit nervous. Ed is more likely to notice when things are wrong than when they're exactly right.

Marylynn sits at the kitchen table, one arm draped over the

265

chairback, her chin on the other hand; she's in soft grey, which makes her hair look silver, and Sally feels once again how banal it is to have ordinary dark hair like her own, however well-cut, however shiny. It's the confidence she envies, the negligence. Marylynn doesn't seem to be trying at all, ever.

'Guess what Ed said today?' Sally says.

Marylynn leans further forward. 'What?' she says, with the eagerness of one joining in a familiar game.

'He said, "Some of these femininists go too far," ' Sally reports. ' "*Femininists.*" Isn't that sweet?'

Marylynn holds the pause too long, and Sally has a sudden awful thought: maybe Marylynn thinks she's showing off, about Ed. Marylynn has always said she's not ready for another marriage yet; still, Sally should watch herself, not rub her nose in it. But then Marylynn laughs indulgently, and Sally, relieved, joins in.

'Ed is unbelievable,' says Marylynn. 'You should pin his mittens to his sleeves when he goes out in the morning.'

'He shouldn't be let out alone,' says Sally.

'You should get him a seeing-eye dog,' says Marylynn, 'to bark at women.'

'Why?' says Sally, still laughing but alert now, the cold beginning at the ends of her fingers. Maybe Marylynn knows something she doesn't; maybe the house is beginning to crumble, after all.

'Because he can't see them coming,' says Marylynn. 'That's what you're always telling me.'

She sips her Kir; Sally stirs the sauce. 'I bet he thinks I'm a feminist,' says Marylynn.

'You?' says Sally. 'Never.' She would like to add that Ed has given no indication of thinking anything at all about Marylynn, but she doesn't. She doesn't want to take the risk of hurting her feelings.

The wives of the heart men admire Sally's sauce; the heart men talk shop, all except Walter Morly, who is good at bypasses. He's sitting beside Marylynn, and paying far too much attention to her for Sally's comfort. Mrs Morly is at the other end of the table, not saying much of anything, which Marylynn appears not to notice. She keeps on talking to Walter about St Lucia, where they've both been.

So after dinner, when Sally has herded them all into the living room for coffee and liqueurs, she takes Marylynn by the elbow. 'Ed hasn't seen our desk yet,' she says, 'not up close. Take him away and give him your lecture on nine-teenth-century antiques. Show him all the pigeon-holes. Ed loves pigeon-holes.' Ed appears not to get this.

Marylynn knows exactly what Sally is up to. 'Don't worry,' she says, 'I won't rape Dr Morly; the poor creature would never survive the shock,' but she allows herself to be shunted off to the side with Ed.

Sally moves from guest to guest, smiling, making sure everything is in order. Although she never looks directly, she's always conscious of Ed's presence in the room, any room; she perceives him as a shadow, a shape seen dimly at the edge of her field of vision, recognizable by the outline. She likes to know where he is, that's all. Some people are on their second cup of coffee. She walks towards the alcove: they must have finished with the desk by now.

But they haven't, they're still in there. Marylynn is bend-ing forward, one hand on the veneer. Ed is standing too close to her, and as Sally comes up behind them she sees his left arm, held close to his side, the back of it pressed against Marylynn, her shimmering upper thigh, her ass to be exact. Marylynn does not move away.

It's a split second, and then Ed sees Sally and the hand is

gone; there it is, on top of the desk, reaching for a liqueur glass.

'Marylynn needs more Tia Maria,' he says. 'I just told her that people who drink a little now and again live longer.' His voice is even, his face is as level as ever, a flat plain with no signposts.

Marylynn laughs. 'I once had a dentist who I swear drilled tiny holes in my teeth, so he could fix them later,' she says.

Sally sees Ed's hand outstretched towards her, holding the empty glass. She takes it, smiling, and turns away. There's a roaring sound at the back of her head; blackness appears around the edges of the picture she is seeing, like a television screen going dead. She walks into the kitchen and puts her cheek against the refrigerator and her arms around it, as far as they will go. She remains that way, hugging it; it hums steadily, with a sound like comfort. After a while she lets go of it and touches her hair, and walks back into the living room with the filled glass.

Marylynn is over by the french doors, talking with Walter Morly. Ed is standing by himself, in front of the fireplace, one arm on the mantelpiece, his left hand out of sight in his pocket.

Sally goes to Marylynn, hands her the glass. 'Is that enough?' she says.

Marylynn is unchanged. 'Thanks, Sally,' she says, and goes on listening to Walter, who has dragged out his usual piece of mischief: some day, when they've perfected it, he says, all hearts will be plastic, and this will be a vast improvement on the current model. It's an obscure form of flirtation. Marylynn winks at Sally, to show that she knows he's tedious. Sally, after a pause, winks back.

She looks over at Ed, who is staring off into space, like a robot which has been parked and switched off. Now she isn't sure whether she really saw what she thought she saw. Even if she did, what does it mean? Maybe it's just that Ed, in a wayward intoxicated moment, put his hand on the nearest buttock, and Marylynn refrained from a shriek or a flinch out of good breeding or the desire not to offend him. Things like this have happened to Sally.

Or it could mean something more sinister: a familiarity between them, an understanding. If this is it, Sally has been wrong about Ed, for years, forever. Her version of Ed is not something she's perceived but something that's been perpetrated on her, by Ed himself, for reasons of his own. Possibly Ed is not stupid. Possibly he's enormously clever. She thinks of moment after moment when this cleverness, this cunning, would have shown itself if it were there, but didn't. She has watched him so carefully. She remembers playing Pick Up Sticks, with the kids, Ed's kids, years ago: how if you moved one stick in the tangle, even slightly, everything else moved also.

She won't say anything to him. She can't say anything: she can't afford to be wrong, or to be right either. She goes back into the kitchen and begins to scrape the plates. This is unlike her – usually she sticks right with the party until it's over – and after a while Ed wanders out. He stands silently, watching her. Sally concentrates on the scraping: dollops of *sauce suprême* slide into the plastic bag, shreds of lettuce, rice, congealed and lumpy. What is left of her afternoon.

'What are you doing out here?' Ed asks at last.

'Scraping the plates,' Sally says, cheerful, neutral. 'I just thought I'd get a head start on tidying up.'

'Leave it,' says Ed. 'The woman can do that in the morning.' That's how he refers to Mrs Rudge, although she's been with them for three years now: *the woman*. And Mrs Bird before her, as though they are interchangeable. This has never bothered Sally before. 'Go on out there and have a good time.'

Sally puts down the spatula, wipes her hands on the hand towel, puts her arms around him, holds on tighter than she should. Ed pats her shoulder. 'What's up?' he says; then, 'Sally, Sally.' If she looks up, she will see him shaking his head a little, as if he doesn't know what to do about her. She doesn't look up.

Ed has gone to bed. Sally roams the house, fidgeting with the debris left by the party. She collects empty glasses, picks up peanuts from the rug. After a while she realizes that she's down on her knees, looking under a chair, and she's forgotten what for. She goes upstairs, creams off her make-up, does her teeth, undresses in the darkened bedroom and slides into bed beside Ed, who is breathing deeply as if asleep. *As if.*

Sally lies in bed with her eyes closed. What she sees is her own heart, in black and white, beating with that insubstantial moth-like flutter, a ghostly heart, torn out of her and floating in space, an animated valentine with no colour. It will go on and on forever; she has no control over it. But now she's seeing the egg, which is not small and cold and white and inert but larger than a real egg and golden pink, resting in a nest of brambles, glowing softly as though there's something red and hot inside it. It's almost pulsing; Sally is afraid of it. As she looks it darkens: rose-red, crimson. This is something the story left out, Sally thinks: the egg is alive, and one day it will hatch. But what will come out of it?

VLADIMIR NABOKOV

'THAT IN ALEPPO ONCE...'

DEAR V. – Among other things, this is to tell you that at last I am here, in the country whither so many sunsets have led. One of the first persons I saw was our good old Gleb Alexandrovich Gekko gloomily crossing Columbus Avenue in quest of the *petit café du coin* which none of us three will ever visit again. He seemed to think that somehow or other you were betraying our national literature, and he gave me your address with a deprecatory shake of his grey head, as if you did not deserve the treat of hearing from me.

I have a story for you. Which reminds me – I mean putting it like this reminds me – of the days when we wrote our first udder-warm bubbling verse, and all things, a rose, a puddle, a lighted window, cried out to us: 'I'm a rhyme!' Yes, this is a most useful universe. We play, we die: *ig-rhyme, umi-rhyme*. And the sonorous souls of Russian verbs lend a meaning to the wild gesticulation of trees or to some discarded newspaper sliding and pausing, and shuffling again, with abortive flaps and apterous jerks along an endless windswept embankment. But just now I am not a poet. I come to you like that gushing lady in Chekhov who was dying to be described.

I married, let me see, about a month after you left France and a few weeks before the gentle Germans roared into Paris. Although I can produce documentary proofs of matrimony, I am positive now that my wife never existed. You may know her name from some other source, but that does not matter:

273

it is the name of an illusion. Therefore, I am able to speak of her with as much detachment as I would of a character in a story (one of your stories, to be precise).

It was love at first touch rather than at first sight, for I had met her several times before without experiencing any special emotions; but one night, as I was seeing her home, something quaint she had said made me stoop with a laugh and lightly kiss her on the hair – and of course we all know of that blinding blast which is caused by merely picking up a small doll from the floor of a carefully abandoned house: the soldier involved hears nothing; for him it is but an ecstatic soundless and boundless expansion of what had been during his life a pin-point of light in the dark center of his being. And really, the reason we think of death in celestial terms is that the visible firmament, especially at night (above our blacked-out Paris with the gaunt arches of its boulevard Exelmans and the ceaseless alpine gurgle of desolate latrines), is the most adequate and ever-present symbol of that vast silent explosion.

But I cannot discern her. She remains as nebulous as my best poem – the one you made such gruesome fun of in the *Literaturnïe Zapiski*. When I want to imagine her, I have to cling mentally to a tiny brown birthmark on her downy forearm, as one concentrates upon a punctuation mark in an illegible sentence. Perhaps, had she used a greater amount of make-up or used it more constantly, I might have visualized her face today, or at least the delicate transverse furrows of dry, hot rouged lips; but I fail, I fail – although I still feel their elusive touch now and then in the blindman's buff of my senses, in that sobbing sort of dream when she and I clumsily clutch at each other through a heartbreaking mist and I cannot see the color of her eyes for the blank luster of brimming tears drowning their irises.

She was much younger than I – not as much younger as was Nathalie of the lovely bare shoulders and long earrings in relation to swarthy Pushkin; but still there was a sufficient margin for that kind of retrospective romanticism which finds pleasure in imitating the destiny of a unique genius (down to the jealousy, down to the filth, down to the stab of seeing her almond-shaped eyes turn to her blond Cassio behind her peacock-feathered fan) even if one cannot imitate his verse. She liked mine though, and would scarcely have yawned as the other was wont to do every time her husband's poem happened to exceed the length of a sonnet. If she has remained a phantom to me, I may have been one to her: I suppose she had been solely attracted by the obscurity of my poetry; then tore a hole through its veil and saw a stranger's unlovable face.

As you know, I had been for some time planning to follow the example of your fortunate flight. She described to me an uncle of hers who lived, she said, in New York: he had taught riding at a southern college and had wound up by marrying a wealthy American woman; they had a little daughter born deaf. She said she had lost their address long ago, but a few days later it miraculously turned up, and we wrote a dramatic letter to which we never received any reply. This did not much matter, as I had already obtained a sound affidavit from Professor Lomchenko of Chicago; but little else had been done in the way of getting the necessary papers, when the invasion began, whereas I foresaw that if we stayed on in Paris some helpful compatriot of mine would sooner or later point out to the interested party sundry passages in one of my books where I argued that, with all her many black sins, Germany was still bound to remain forever and ever the laughing-stock of the world.

So we started upon our disastrous honeymoon. Crushed

and jolted amid the apocalyptic exodus, waiting for un-scheduled trains that were bound for unknown destinations, walking through the stale stage setting of abstract towns, living in a permanent twilight of physical exhaustion, we fled; and the farther we fled, the clearer it became that what was driving us on was something more than a booted and buckled fool with his assortment of variously propelled junk – something of which he was a mere symbol, something monstrous and impalpable, a timeless and faceless mass of immemorial horror that still keeps coming at me from behind even here, in the green vacuum of Central Park.

Oh, she bore it gamely enough – with a kind of dazed cheerfulness. Once, however, quite suddenly she started to sob in a sympathetic railway carriage. 'The dog,' she said, 'the dog we left. I cannot forget the poor dog.' The honesty of her grief shocked me, as we had never had any dog. 'I know,' she said, 'but I tried to imagine we had actually bought that setter. And just think, he would be now whining behind a locked door.' There had never been any talk of buying a setter.

I should also not like to forget a certain stretch of high-road and the sight of a family of refugees (two women, a child) whose old father, or grandfather, had died on the way. The sky was a chaos of black and flesh-colored clouds with an ugly sunburst beyond a hooded hill, and the dead man was lying on his back under a dusty plane tree. With a stick and their hands the women had tried to dig a roadside grave, but the soil was too hard; they had given it up and were sitting side by side, among the anemic poppies, a little apart from the corpse and its upturned beard. But the little boy was still scratching and scraping and tugging until he tumbled a flat stone and forgot the object of his solemn exertions as he crouched on his haunches, his thin, eloquent neck showing all its vertebrae to the headsman, and watched with surprise and delight thousands of minute brown ants seething, zigzagging, dispersing, heading for places of safety in the Gard, and the Aude, and the Drôme, and the Var, and the Basses-Pyrénées – we two paused only in Pau.

Spain proved too difficult and we decided to move on to Nice. At a place called Faugères (a ten-minute stop) I squeezed out of the train to buy some food. When a couple of minutes later I came back, the train was gone, and the muddled old man responsible for the atrocious void that faced me (coal dust glittering in the heat between naked indifferent rails, and a lone piece of orange peel) brutally told me that, anyway, I had had no right to get out.

In a better world I could have had my wife located and told what to do (I had both tickets and most of the money); as it was, my nightmare struggle with the telephone proved futile, so I dismissed the whole series of diminutive voices barking at me from afar, sent two or three telegrams which are probably on their way only now, and late in the evening took the next local to Montpellier, farther than which her train would not stumble. Not finding her there, I had to choose between two alternatives: going on because she might have boarded the Marseilles train which I had just missed, or going back because she might have returned to Faugères. I forget now what tangle of reasoning led me to Marseilles and Nice.

Beyond such routine action as forwarding false data to a few unlikely places, the police did nothing to help: one man bellowed at me for being a nuisance; another sidetracked the question by doubting the authenticity of my marriage certificate because it was stamped on what he contended to be the wrong side; a third, a fat *commissaire* with liquid brown eyes, confessed that he wrote poetry in his spare time.

I looked up various acquaintances among the numerous Russians domiciled or stranded in Nice. I heard those among them who chanced to have Jewish blood talk of their doomed kinsmen crammed into hell-bound trains; and my own plight, by contrast, acquired a commonplace air of irreality while I sat in some crowded café with the milky blue sea in front of me and a shell-hollow murmur behind telling and retelling the tale of massacre and misery, and the grey paradise beyond the ocean, and the ways and whims of harsh consuls.

A week after my arrival an indolent plainclothesman called upon me and took me down a crooked and smelly street to a black-stained house with the word 'hotel' almost erased by dirt and time; there, he said, my wife had been found. The girl he produced was an absolute stranger, of course; but my friend Holmes kept on trying for some time to make her and me confess we were married, while her taciturn and muscular bedfellow stood by and listened, his bare arms crossed on his striped chest.

When at length I got rid of those people and had wandered back to my neighborhood, I happened to pass by a compact queue waiting at the entrance of a food store; and there, at the very end, was my wife, straining on tiptoe to catch a glimpse of what exactly was being sold. I think the first thing she said to me was that she hoped it was oranges.

Her tale seemed a trifle hazy, but perfectly banal. She had returned to Faugères and gone straight to the Commissariat instead of making inquiries at the station, where I had left a message for her. A party of refugees suggested that she join them; she spent the night in a bicycle shop with no bicycles, on the floor, together with three elderly women who lay, she said, like three logs in a row. Next day she realized that she had not enough money to reach Nice. Eventually she borrowed some from one of the log-women. She got into the wrong train, however, and traveled to a town the name of which she could not remember. She had arrived at Nice two days ago and had found some friends at the Russian church. They had told her I was somewhere around, looking for her, and would surely turn up soon.

Sometime later, as I sat on the edge of the only chair in my garret and held her by her slender young hips (she was combing her soft hair and tossing her head back with every stroke), her dim smile changed all at once into an odd quiver and she placed one hand on my shoulder, staring down at me as if I were a reflection in a pool, which she had noticed for the first time.

'I've been lying to you, dear,' she said. '*Ya lgunia.* I stayed for several nights in Montpellier with a brute of a man I met on the train. I did not want it at all. He sold hair lotions.'

The time, the place, the torture. Her fan, her gloves, her mask. I spent that night and many others getting it out of her bit by bit, but not getting it all. I was under the strange delusion that first I must find out every detail, reconstruct every minute, and only then decide whether I could bear it. But the limit of desired knowledge was unattainable, nor could I ever foretell the approximate point after which I might imagine myself satiated, because of course the denominator of every fraction of knowledge was potentially as infinite as the number of intervals between the fractions themselves.

Oh, the first time she had been too tired to mind, and the next had not minded because she was sure I had deserted her; and she apparently considered that such explanations ought to be a kind of consolation prize for me instead of the nonsense and agony they really were. It went on like that for eons, she breaking down every now and then, but soon rallying again, answering my unprintable questions in a breathless whisper or trying with a pitiful smile to wriggle into the semisecurity of irrelevant commentaries, and I crushing and crushing the mad molar till my jaw almost burst with pain, a flaming pain which seemed somehow preferable to the dull, humming ache of humble endurance.

And mark, in between the periods of this inquest, we were trying to get from reluctant authorities certain papers which in their turn would make it lawful to apply for a third kind which would serve as a stepping-stone toward a permit enabling the holder to apply for yet other papers which might or might not give him the means of discovering how and why it had happened. For even if I could imagine the accursed recurrent scene, I failed to link up its sharp-angled grotesque shadows with the dim limbs of my wife as she shook and rattled and dissolved in my violent grasp.

So nothing remained but to torture each other, to wait for hours on end in the Prefecture, filling forms, conferring with friends who had already probed the innermost viscera of all visas, pleading with secretaries, and filling forms again, with the result that her lusty and versatile traveling salesman became blended in a ghastly mix-up with rat-whiskered snarling officials, rotting bundles of obsolete records, the reek of violet ink, bribes slipped under gangrenous blotting paper, fat flies tickling moist necks with their rapid cold padded feet, new-laid clumsy concave photographs of your six subhuman doubles, the tragic eyes and patient politeness of petitioners born in Slutzk, Starodub, or Bobruisk, the funnels and pulleys of the Holy Inquisition, the awful smile of the bald man with the glasses, who had been told that his passport could not be found.

I confess that one evening, after a particularly abominable day, I sank down on a stone bench weeping and cursing a mock world where millions of lives were being juggled by the clammy hands of consuls and *commissaires*. I noticed she was crying too, and then I told her that nothing would really have mattered the way it mattered now, had she not gone and done what she did.

'You will think me crazy,' she said with a vehemence that, for a second, almost made a real person of her, 'but I didn't – I swear that I didn't. Perhaps I live several lives at once. Perhaps I wanted to test you. Perhaps this bench is a dream and we are in Saratov or on some star.'

It would be tedious to niggle the different stages through which I passed before accepting finally the first version of her delay. I did not talk to her and was a good deal alone. She would glimmer and fade, and reappear with some trifle she thought I would appreciate – a handful of cherries, three precious cigarettes, or the like – treating me with the unruffled mute sweetness of a nurse that trips from and to a gruff convalescent. I ceased visiting most of our mutual friends because they had lost all interest in my passport affairs and seemed to have turned vaguely inimical. I composed several poems. I drank all the wine I could get. I clasped her one day to my groaning breast, and we went for a week to Caboule and lay on the round pink pebbles of the narrow beach. Strange to say, the happier our new relations seemed, the stronger I felt an undercurrent of poignant sadness, but I kept telling myself that this was an intrinsic feature of all true bliss.

In the meantime, something had shifted in the moving pattern of our fates and at last I emerged from a dark and hot office with a couple of plump *visas de sortie* cupped in my trembling hands. Into these the USA serum was duly injected, and I dashed to Marseilles and managed to get tickets for the very next boat. I returned and tramped up the stairs. I saw a rose in a glass on the table – the sugar pink of its obvious beauty, the parasitic air bubbles clinging to its stem. Her two spare dresses were gone, her comb was gone, her checkered coat was gone, and so was the mauve hairband with a mauve bow that had been her hat. There was no note pinned to the pillow, nothing at all in the room to enlighten me, for of course the rose was merely what French rhymesters call *une cheville*.

I went to the Veretennikovs, who could tell me nothing; to the Hellmans, who refused to say anything; and to the Elagins, who were not sure whether to tell me or not. Finally the old lady – and you know what Anna Vladimirovna is like at crucial moments – asked for her rubber-tipped cane, heavily but energetically dislodged her bulk from her favourite armchair, and took me into the garden. There she informed me that, being twice my age, she had the right to say I was a bully and a cad.

You must imagine the scene: the tiny graveled garden with its blue Arabian Nights jar and solitary cypress; the cracked terrace where the old lady's father had dozed with a rug on his knees when he retired from his Novgorod governorship to spend a few last evenings in Nice; the pale-green sky; a whiff of vanilla in the deepening dusk; the crickets emitting their metallic trill pitched at two octaves above middle C; and Anna Vladimirovna, the folds of her cheeks jerkily dangling as she flung at me a motherly but quite undeserved insult.

During several preceding weeks, my dear V., every time she had visited by herself the three or four families we both knew, my ghostly wife had filled the eager ears of all those kind people with an extraordinary story. To wit: that she had madly fallen in love with a young Frenchman who could give her a turreted home and a crested name; that she had implored me for a divorce and I had refused; that in fact I had said I would rather shoot her and myself than sail to New York alone; that she had said her father in a similar case had acted like a gentleman; that I had answered I did not give a hoot for her *cocu de père.*

There were loads of other preposterous details of the kind – but they all hung together in such a remarkable fashion that no wonder the old lady made me swear I would not seek to pursue the lovers with a cocked pistol. They had gone, she said, to a château in Lozère. I inquired whether she had ever set eyes upon the man. No, but she had been shown his picture. As I was about to leave, Anna Vladimirovna, who had slightly relaxed and had even given me her five fingers to kiss, suddenly flared up again, struck the gravel with her cane, and said in her deep strong voice: 'But one thing I shall never forgive you – her dog, that poor beast which you hanged with your own hands before leaving Paris.'

Whether the gentleman of leisure had changed into a traveling salesman, or whether the metamorphosis had been reversed, or whether again he was neither the one nor the other, but the nondescript Russian who had courted her before our marriage – all this was absolutely inessential. She had gone. That was the end. I should have been a fool had I begun the nightmare business of searching and waiting for her all over again.

On the fourth morning of a long and dismal sea voyage, I met on the deck a solemn but pleasant old doctor with whom I had played chess in Paris. He asked me whether my wife was very much incommoded by the rough seas. I answered that I had sailed alone; whereupon he looked taken aback and then said he had seen her a couple of days before going on board, namely in Marseilles, walking, rather aimlessly he thought, along the embankment. She said that I would presently join her with bag and tickets.

This is, I gather, the point of the whole story – although if you write it, you had better not make him a doctor, as that kind of thing has been overdone. It was at that moment that I suddenly knew for certain that she had never existed at all. I shall tell you another thing. When I arrived I hastened to satisfy a certain morbid curiosity: I went to the address she had given me once; it proved to be an anonymous gap between two office buildings; I looked for her uncle's name in the directory; it was not there; I made some inquiries, and Gekko, who knows everything, informed me that the man and his horsey wife existed all right, but had moved to San Francisco after their deaf little girl had died.

Viewing the past graphically, I see our mangled romance engulfed in a deep valley of mist between the crags of two matter-of-fact mountains: life had been real before, life will be real from now on, I hope. Not tomorrow, though. Perhaps after tomorrow. You, happy mortal, with your lovely family (how is Ines? how are the twins?) and your diversified work (how are the lichens?), can hardly be expected to puzzle out my misfortune in terms of human communion, but you may clarify things for me through the prism of your art.

Yet the pity of it. Curse your art, I am hideously unhappy. She keeps on walking to and fro where the brown nets are spread to dry on the hot stone slabs and the dappled light of the water plays on the side of a moored fishing boat. Somewhere, somehow, I have made some fatal mistake. There are tiny pale bits of broken fish scales glistening here and there in the brown meshes. It may all end in *Aleppo* if I am not careful. Spare me, V.: you would load your dice with an unbearable implication if you took that for a title.

284

WILLIAM TREVOR

THE ROOM

'DO YOU KNOW why you are doing this?' he asked, and Katherine hesitated, then shook her head, although she did know.

Nine years had almost healed a soreness, each day made a little easier, until the balm of work was taken from her and in her scratchy idleness the healing ceased. She was here because of that, there was no other reason she could think of, but she didn't say it.

'And you?' she asked instead.

He was at once forthcoming. He said he'd been attracted by her at a time when he'd brought loneliness upon himself by quarrelling once too often with the wife who had borne his children and had cared for him.

'I'm sorry about the room,' he said.

His belongings were piled up, books and cardboard boxes, suitcases open, not yet unpacked. A word processor had not been plugged in, its cables trailing on the floor. Clothes on hangers cluttered the back of the door; an anatomical study of an elephant decorated one of the walls, with arrows indicating where certain organs were beneath the leathery skin. This grey picture wasn't his, he'd said when Katherine asked; it came with the room, which was all he had been able to find in a hurry. A sink was in the same corner as a washbasin, an electric kettle and a gas ring on a shelf, a green plastic curtain not drawn across.

'It's all a bit more special now that you're here,' he said, sounding as if he meant it.

When she got up to put on her clothes, Katherine could tell he didn't want her to go. Yet he, not she, was the one who had to; she could have stayed all afternoon. Buttoning a sleeve of her dress, she remarked that at least she knew now what it felt like to deceive.

'What it had felt like for Phair,' she said.

She pulled the edge of the curtain back a little more so that the light fell more directly on the room's single looking glass. She tidied her hair, still brown, no grey in it yet. Her mother's hadn't gone grey at all, and her grandmother's only when she was very old, which was something Katherine hoped she wouldn't have to be; she was forty-seven now. Her dark eyes gazed back at her from her reflection, her lipstick smudged, an emptiness in her features that had not to do with the need to renew her makeup. Her beauty was ebbing – but slowly, and there was beauty left.

'You were curious about that?' he asked, his own dressing complete. 'Deception?'

'Yes, I was curious.'

'And shall you be again?'

Still settling the disturbances in her face, Katherine didn't answer at once. Then she said, 'If you would like me to.'

Outside, the afternoon was warm, the street where the room was – above a betting shop – seemed brighter and more gracious than Katherine had noticed when she'd walked the length of it earlier. There was an afternoon tranquillity about it in spite of shops and cars. The tables were unoccupied outside the Prince and Dog, hanging baskets of petunias on either side of its regal figure, and a Dalmatian with a foot raised. There was a Costa Coffee next to a Pret a Manger and Katherine crossed to it. 'Latte,' she ordered from the girls who were operating the Gaggia machines and picked out a florentine from the glass case on the counter while she waited for it.

She hardly knew the man she'd slept with. He'd danced with her at a party she'd gone to alone, and then he'd danced with her again, holding her closer, asking her her name and giving his. Phair didn't accompany her to parties these days and she didn't go often herself. But she'd known what she intended, going to this one.

The few tables were all taken. She found a stool at the bar that ran along one of the walls. 'TEENAGER'S CURFEW!' a headline in someone else's evening paper protested, a note of indignation implied, and for a few moments she wondered what all that was about and then lost interest.

Phair would be quietly at his desk, in shirtsleeves, the blue-flecked shirt she'd ironed the day before yesterday, his crinkly, gingerish hair as it had been that morning when he left the house, his agreeable smile welcoming anyone who approached him. In spite of what had happened nine years ago, Phair had not been made redundant, that useful euphemism for being sacked. That he'd been kept on was a tribute to his success in the past, and of course it wasn't done to destroy a man when he was down. 'We should go away,' she'd said and remembered saying it now, but he hadn't wanted to, because running away was something that wasn't done, either. He would have called it running away; in fact, he had.

This evening, he would tell her about his day, and she would say about hers and would have to lie. And in turn they'd listen while she brought various dishes to the dining table, and he would pour her wine. None for himself because he didn't drink any more, unless someone pressed him, and then only in order not to seem ungracious. 'My

289

marriage is breaking up,' the man who'd made love to her in his temporary accommodation had confided when, as strangers, they had danced together. 'And yours?' he'd asked, and she'd hesitated and then said no, not breaking up. There'd never been talk of that. And when they danced the second time, after they'd had a drink together and then a few more, he asked her if she had children and she said she hadn't. That she was not able to had been known before the marriage and then became part of it – as her employment at the Charterhouse Institute had been until six weeks ago, when the institute had decided to close itself down.

'Idleness is upsetting,' she had said while they danced, and had asked her future lover if he had ever heard of Sharon Ritchie. People often thought they hadn't and then remembered. He shook his head and the name was still unfamiliar to him when she told him why he might have heard of it. 'Sharon Ritchie was murdered,' she'd said, and wouldn't have without the few drinks. 'My husband was accused.'

She blew on the surface of her coffee, but it was still too hot. She tipped sugar out of its paper spill into her teaspoon and watched the sugar darkening when the coffee soaked it. She loved the taste of that, as much a pleasure as anything there'd been this afternoon. 'Oh, suffocated,' she'd said when she'd been asked how the person called Sharon Ritchie had died. 'She was suffocated with a cushion.' Sharon Ritchie had had a squalid life, living grandly at a good address, visited by many men.

Katherine sat a while longer, staring at the crumbs of her florentine, her coffee drunk. 'We live with it,' she had said when they left the party together, he to return to the wife he didn't get on with, she to the husband whose deceiving of her had ended with a death. Fascinated by that, an hour ago in the room that was his temporary accommodation her afternoon lover had wanted to know everything.

On the Tube, she kept seeing the room: the picture of the elephant, the suitcases, the trailing cables, the clothes on the back of the door. Their echoed voices, his curiosity, her evasions and then telling a little more because, after all, she owed him something. 'He paid her with a cheque once – oh, ages ago. That was how they brought him into things. And when they talked to the old woman in the flat across the landing from Sharon Ritchie's she recognized him in the photograph she was shown. Oh, yes, we live with it.'

Her ticket wouldn't operate the turnstile when she tried to leave the Tube station, and she remembered that she had guessed how much the fare should be and must have got it wrong. The Indian who was there to deal with such errors was inclined to be severe. Her journey had been different earlier, she tried to explain; she'd got things muddled. 'Well, these things happen,' the Indian said, and she realized his severity had not been meant. When she smiled, he didn't notice. That is his way, too, she thought.

She bought two chicken breasts, free-range, organic; and courgettes and fruit. She hadn't made a list as she usually did, and wondered if this had to do with the kind of afternoon it had been and thought it probably had. She tried to remember which breakfast cereals needed to be replenished but couldn't. And then remembered Normandy butter and tomatoes. It was just before five o'clock when she let herself into the flat. The telephone was ringing and Phair said he'd be a bit late, not by much, maybe twenty minutes. She ran a bath.

The tips of his fingers stroked the arm that was close to him. He said he thought he loved her. Katherine shook her head.

'Tell me,' he said.

'I have, though.'

He didn't press it. They lay in silence for a while.

Then Katherine said, 'I love him more, now that I feel so sorry for him, too. He pitied me when I knew I was to be deprived of the children we both wanted. Love makes the most of pity, don't you think?'

'Yes. I do.'

She told him more, and realized she wanted to, which she hadn't known before. When the two policemen had come in the early morning, she had not been dressed. Phair was making coffee. 'Phair Alexander Warburton,' one of them had said. She'd heard him from the bedroom, her bathwater still gurgling out. She'd thought they'd come to report a death, as policemen sometimes have to: her mother or Phair's aunt, his next of kin. When she went downstairs, they were talking about the death of someone whose name she did not know. 'Who?' she asked, and the taller of the two policemen said Sharon Ritchie, and Phair said nothing. 'Your husband has explained,' the other man said, 'that you didn't know Miss Ritchie.' On a Thursday night, the eighth, two weeks ago, they said. What time – could she remember – had her husband come in?

She'd faltered, lost in all this. 'But who's this person? Why are you here?' And the taller policeman said there were a few loose ends. 'Sit down, Madam,' his colleague put in, and she was asked again what time her husband had come in. A worse delay than usual on the Underground, he'd said that night, the Thursday before last. He'd given up waiting and had gone away, as everyone else was doing. And then it wasn't easy to get a taxi because of the rain. 'You remember, Madam?' the taller policeman prompted, and something made her say Phair had come back at the usual time. She couldn't think; she couldn't because she was trying to remember if Phair had ever mentioned Sharon Ritchie. 'Your husband visited Miss Ritchie,' the same policeman said, and the other man's pager sounded and he took it to the window, turning his back to them. 'No, we're talking to him now,' he mumbled into it, keeping his voice low, but she could hear. 'Your husband has explained it was the day before,' his colleague said. 'And earlier – in his lunchtime – that his last visit to Miss Ritchie was.'

Remembering, Katherine wanted to stay here, in the room. She wanted to sleep, to be aware of the man she did not know well beside her, to have him waiting for her when she woke up. Because of the heat wave that had begun a week ago, he had turned the air-conditioning on, an old-fashioned contraption at the window.

'I have to go,' he said.

'Of course. I won't be long.'

Below them, another horse race had come to its exciting stage, the radio commentary faintly reaching them as they dressed. They went together down uncarpeted, narrow stairs, past the open door of the betting shop.

'Shall you come again?' he asked.

'Yes.'

And they arranged an afternoon, ten days away, because he could not always just walk out of the office where he worked.

'Don't let me talk about it,' she said before they parted. 'Don't ask, don't let me tell.'

'If you don't want to.'

'It's all so done with. And it's a bore for you, or will be soon.'

He began to say it wasn't, that was what the trouble was. She knew he began to say it because she could see it in his face before he changed his mind. And of course he was right; he wasn't a fool. Curiosity couldn't be just stifled.

They didn't embrace before he hurried off, for they had done all that. When she watched him go, it felt like a habit already, and she wondered as she crossed the street to the Costa café if, with repetition, her afternoons here would acquire some variation of the order and patterns of the work she missed so.

'Oh, none at all,' she'd said when she'd been asked if there were prospects yet of something else. And wondered now if she would ever again make her morning journey across London, skilful in the overcrowded Tube stations, squeezing on to trains that were crowded also. It was unlikely that there'd be, somewhere, her own small office again, her position of importance, and generous colleagues who made up for a bleakness and kept at bay its ghosts. She hadn't known until Phair said, not long ago, that routine, for him, often felt like an antidote to dementia.

She should not have told so much this afternoon, Katherine said to herself, sitting where she had sat before. She had never, to anyone else, told anything at all, or talked about what had happened to people who knew. I am unsettled, she thought, and, outside, rain came suddenly, with distant thunder, ending the heat that had become excessive.

When she'd finished her coffee, Katherine didn't leave the café because she didn't have an umbrella. There had been rain in London that night, too. Rain came into it because the elderly woman in the flat across the landing had looked out when it was just beginning, the six o'clock news on the radio just beginning, too. The woman had remembered that earlier she had passed the wide-open window half a flight down the communal stairway and went immediately to close it before, yet again, the carpet was drenched. It was while she was doing so that she heard the downstairs hall door opening and footsteps beginning on the stairs. When she reached her own door, the man had reached the landing. 'No, I never thought anything untoward,' she had later stated, apparently. Not anything untoward about the girl who occupied the flat across the landing, about the men who came visiting her. 'I didn't pry,' she said. She had turned round as she reached her own front door and had caught a glimpse of the man who'd come that night. She'd seen him before, the way he stood waiting for the girl to let him in, his clothes, his hair, even his footfall on the stairs: there was no doubt at all.

The café filled up, the doorway crowded with people sheltering, others queueing at the counter. Katherine heard the staccato summons of her mobile phone, a sound she hated, although originally she'd chosen it herself. A voice that might have been a child's said something she couldn't understand and then repeated it, and then the line went dead. So many voices were like a child's these days, she thought, returning the phone to her handbag. 'A fashion, that baby telephone voice,' Phair had said. 'Odd as it might seem.'

She nibbled the edge of her florentine, then opened the spill of sugar. The light outside had darkened and now was brightening again. The people in the doorway began to move away. It had rained all night the other time.

'Nothing again?' Phair always inquired when he came in. He was concerned about what had been so arbitrarily and unexpectedly imposed upon her, had once or twice brought back hearsay of vacancies. But even at his most solicitous, and his gentlest, he had himself to think about. It was worse for Phair and always would be, that stood to reason.

Her mobile telephone rang again and his voice said that in his lunch hour he'd bought asparagus because he'd noticed it on a stall, looking good and not expensive. They'd mentioned asparagus yesterday, realizing it was the season; she would have bought some if he hadn't rung. 'On the way out of the cinema,' she said, having already said that she'd just seen *La Strada* again. He'd tried for her an hour ago, he said, but her phone had been switched off. 'Well, yes, of course,' he said.

Six months was the length of an affair that took place because something else was wrong: the man she met in the afternoons said that, knowing more about affairs than Katherine did. And, as if he had always been aware that he would, when a little longer than six months had passed he returned to his wife. Since then, he had retained the room while this reunion settled – or perhaps in case it didn't – but his belongings were no longer there. To Katherine, the room looked bigger, yet dingier, without them.

'Why do you love your husband, Katherine? After all this – what he has put you through?'

'No one can answer that.'

'You hide from one another, you and he.'

'Yes.'

'Are you afraid, Katherine?'

'Yes. Both of us are afraid. We dream of her, we see her dead. And we know in the morning if the other one has. We know and do not say.'

'You shouldn't be afraid.'

They did not ever argue in the room, not even mildly, but disagreed without pursuing their disagreements. Or failed to understand and left that, too. Katherine did not ask if a marriage could be shored up while this room was still theirs for a purpose. Her casual lover did not press her to reveal what she still withheld.

'I can't imagine him,' he said, but Katherine did not attempt to describe her husband, only commented that his first name suited him. A family name, she said.

'You're fairly remarkable, you know. To love him so deeply still.'

'And yet I'm here.'

'Perhaps I mean that.'

'More often than not, people don't know why they do things.'

'I envy you your seriousness. It's that I'd love you for.'

Once, when again he had to go, she stayed behind. He was in a hurry that day; she wasn't quite ready. 'Just bang the door,' he said.

She listened to his footsteps clattering on the boards of the stairs and was reminded of the old woman saying she had recognized Phair's. Phair's lawyer would have asked in court if she was certain about that and would have wondered how she could be, since to have heard them on previous occasions she would each time have had to be on the landing, which surely was unlikely. He would have suggested that she appeared to spend more time on the communal landing than in her flat. He would have wondered that a passing stranger had left behind so clear an impression of his features, since any encounter there had been would have lasted hardly more than an instant.

Alone in the room, not wanting to leave it yet, Katherine crept back into the bed she'd left only minutes ago. She pulled the bedclothes up although it wasn't cold. The window curtains hadn't been drawn back and she was glad they hadn't. 'I didn't much care for that girl,' Phair said when the two policemen had gone. 'But I was fond of her in a different kind of way. I have to say that, Katherine. I'm sorry.' He had brought her coffee and made her sit there, where she was. Some men were like that, he said. 'We only talked. She told me things.' A girl like that took chances every time she answered her doorbell, he said; and when he cried Katherine knew it was for the girl, not for himself. 'Oh, yes, I understand,' she said. 'Of course I do.' A sleazy relationship with a classy tart was what she understood, as he had understood when she told him she could not have children, when he'd said it didn't matter, although she knew it did. 'I've risked what was precious,' her husband whispered in his shame, and then confessed that deceiving her had been an excitement, too. Risk came into it, Katherine realized then; risk was part of it, the secrecy of concealment, stealth. And risk had claimed its due.

The same policemen came back later. 'You're sure about that detail, Madam?' they asked, and afterwards, countless times, asked her that again, repeating the date and hearing her repeat that ten to seven was the usual time. Phair hadn't wanted to know – and didn't still – why she had answered as she had, why she continued to confirm that he'd returned ninety minutes sooner than he had. She couldn't have told anyone why, except to say that something like instinct came into it, and that she knew Phair as intimately as she knew herself, that it was impossible to imagine his taking the life of a girl no matter what his relationship with her had been. There was, of course – she would have said if she'd been asked – the pain of that relationship, of he and the girl being together, even if only for conversation. 'You quarrelled, sir?' the tall policeman inquired. You could see there'd been a quarrel, he insisted, no way you could say there hadn't been a disagreement that got out of hand. But Phair was not the quarrelling sort. He shook his head. In all his answers, he hadn't disputed much except responsibility for the death. He had not denied he'd been a visitor to the flat. He gave the details of his visits as he remembered them. He accepted that his fingerprints were there, while they accepted nothing. 'You're sure, Madam?' they asked again, and her instinct hardened, touched with apprehension, even though their implications were ridiculous. Yes, she was sure, she said. They said their spiel and then arrested him.

Katherine slept and when she woke did not know where she was. But only minutes had passed, less than ten. She washed at the basin in the corner, and slowly dressed. When he was taken from her, in custody until the trial's outcome, it was suggested at the institute that they could manage without her for a while. 'No, no,' she had insisted. 'I would rather come.' And in the hiatus that followed – long and silent – she had not known that doubt began to spread in the frail memory of the elderly woman, who in time would be called upon to testify to her statements on oath. She had not known that beneath the weight of importance the old woman was no longer certain that the man she'd seen on that wet evening – already shadowy – was a man she'd seen before. With coaching and encouragement, she would regain her confidence, it must have been believed by those for whom her evidence was essential: the prosecution case rested on identification, on little else. But the long delay had taken a toll, the witness had been wearied by preparation, and did not, in court, conceal her worries. When the first morning of the trial was about to end, the judge calmed his anger to declare that in his opinion there was no case to answer. In the afternoon, the jury was dismissed.

Katherine pulled back the curtains, settled her makeup, made the bed. Blame was there somewhere – in faulty recollection, in the carelessness of policemen, in a prosecution's ill-founded confidence – yet its attribution was hardly a source of satisfaction. Chance and circumstance had brought about a nightmare, and left it to a judge to deplore the bringing of a case that did not stand up. In dismissing it, his comments were stern, but neither that nor his perfect clarity was quite enough: too much was left behind. No other man was ever charged, although of course there was another man.

She banged the door behind her, as she'd been told to. They had not said goodbye, yet as she went downstairs, hearing again the muffled gabble of the racecourse commentator, she knew it was for the last time. The room was finished with. This afternoon, she had felt that, even if it had not been said.

She did not have coffee and walked by the Prince and Dog without noticing it. In her kitchen, she would cook the food she'd bought and they would sit together and talk about the day. She would look across the table at the husband she loved and see a shadow there. They would speak of little things.

She wandered, going nowhere, leaving the bustling street that was gracious also, walking by terraced houses, lace-curtained windows. Her afternoon lover would mend the marriage that had failed, would piece by piece repair the damage because damage was not destruction and was not meant to be. To quarrel often was not too terrible; nor, without love, to be unfaithful. They would agree that they were up to this, and friendly time would do the rest, not asked to do too much. 'And she?' his wife one day might wonder, and he would say his other woman was a footnote to what had happened in their marriage. Perhaps that, no more.

Katherine came to the canal, where there were seats along the water. This evening, she would lie, and they would speak again of little things. She would not say she was afraid, and nor would he. But fear was there, for her the nag of doubt, infecting him in ways she did not know about. She walked on past the seats, past children with a nurse. A barge with barrels went by, painted roses on its prow.

A wasteland, it seemed like where she walked, made so not by itself but by her mood. She felt an anonymity, a solitude here where she did not belong, and something came with that which she could not identify. Oh, but it's over, she told herself, as if in answer to this mild bewilderment, bewildering herself further and asking herself how she knew what she seemed to know. Thought was no good: all this was feeling. So, walking on, she did not think.

She sensed, without a reason, the dispersal of restraint. And yes, of course, for all nine years there'd been restraint. There'd been no asking to be told, no asking for promises that the truth was what she heard. There'd been no asking about the girl, how she'd dressed, her voice, her face, and if she only sat there talking, no more than that. There'd been no asking about a worse day than usual on the Underground and the waiting for a taxi in the rain. For all nine years, there had been silence in their ordinary exchanges, in conversation, in making love, in weekend walks and summer trips abroad. For all nine years, love had been there, and more than just a comforter, too intense for that. Was stealth an excitement still? That was not asked, and Katherine, pausing to watch another barge approaching, knew it never would be now. The flat was entered, and Sharon Ritchie lay suffocated on her sofa. Had she been the victim kind? That, too, was locked away.

Katherine turned to walk back the way she'd come. It wouldn't be a shock, nor even a surprise. He expected no more of her than what she'd given him, and she would choose her moment to say that she must go. He would understand; she would not have to tell him. The best that love could do was not enough, and he would know that also.

JHUMPA LAHIRI

A TEMPORARY
MATTER

THE NOTICE INFORMED them that it was a temporary matter: for five days their electricity would be cut off for one hour, beginning at eight P.M. A line had gone down in the last snowstorm, and the repairmen were going to take advantage of the milder evenings to set it right. The work would affect only the houses on the quiet tree-lined street, within walking distance of a row of brick-faced stores and a trolley stop, where Shoba and Shukumar had lived for three years.

'It's good of them to warn us,' Shoba conceded after reading the notice aloud, more for her own benefit than Shukumar's. She let the strap of her leather satchel, plump with files, slip from her shoulders, and left it in the hallway as she walked into the kitchen. She wore a navy blue poplin raincoat over grey sweatpants and white sneakers, looking, at thirty-three, like the type of woman she'd once claimed she would never resemble.

She'd come from the gym. Her cranberry lipstick was visible only on the outer reaches of her mouth, and her eyeliner had left charcoal patches beneath her lower lashes. She used to look this way sometimes, Shukumar thought, on mornings after a party or a night at a bar, when she'd been too lazy to wash her face, too eager to collapse into his arms. She dropped a sheaf of mail on the table without a glance. Her eyes were still fixed on the notice in her other hand. 'But they should do this sort of thing during the day.'

'When I'm here, you mean,' Shukumar said. He put a glass lid on a pot of lamb, adjusting it so only the slightest bit of steam could escape. Since January he'd been working at home, trying to complete the final chapters of his dissertation on agrarian revolts in India. 'When do the repairs start?'

'It says March nineteenth. Is today the nineteenth?' Shoba walked over to the framed corkboard that hung on the wall by the fridge, bare except for a calendar of William Morris wallpaper patterns. She looked at it as if for the first time, studying the wallpaper pattern carefully on the top half before allowing her eyes to fall to the numbered grid on the bottom. A friend had sent the calendar in the mail as a Christmas gift, even though Shoba and Shukumar hadn't celebrated Christmas that year.

'Today then,' Shoba announced. 'You have a dentist appointment next Friday, by the way.'

He ran his tongue over the tops of his teeth; he'd forgotten to brush them that morning. It wasn't the first time. He hadn't left the house at all that day, or the day before. The more Shoba stayed out, the more she began putting in extra hours at work and taking on additional projects, the more he wanted to stay in, not even leaving to get the mail, or to buy fruit or wine at the stores by the trolley stop.

Six months ago, in September, Shukumar was at an academic conference in Baltimore when Shoba went into labor, three weeks before her due date. He hadn't wanted to go to the conference, but she had insisted; it was important to make contacts, and he would be entering the job market next year. She told him that she had his number at the hotel, and a copy of his schedule and flight numbers, and she had arranged with her friend Gillian for a ride to the hospital in the event of an emergency. When the cab pulled away that morning for the airport, Shoba stood waving goodbye in her robe, with one arm resting on the mound of her belly as if it were a perfectly natural part of her body.

Each time he thought of that moment, the last moment he saw Shoba pregnant, it was the cab he remembered most, a station wagon, painted red with blue lettering. It was cavernous compared to their own car. Although Shukumar was six feet tall, with hands too big ever to rest comfortably in the pockets of his jeans, he felt dwarfed in the back seat. As the cab sped down Beacon Street, he imagined a day when he and Shoba might need to buy a station wagon of their own, to cart their children back and forth from music lessons and dentist appointments. He imagined himself gripping the wheel, as Shoba turned around to hand the children juice boxes. Once, these images of parenthood had troubled Shukumar, adding to his anxiety that he was still a student at thirty-five. But that early autumn morning, the trees still heavy with bronze leaves, he welcomed the image for the first time.

A member of the staff had found him somehow among the identical convention rooms and handed him a stiff square of stationery. It was only a telephone number, but Shukumar knew it was the hospital. When he returned to Boston it was over. The baby had been born dead. Shoba was lying on a bed, asleep, in a private room so small there was barely enough space to stand beside her, in a wing of the hospital they hadn't been to on the tour for expectant parents. Her placenta had weakened and she'd had a cesarean, though not quickly enough. The doctor explained that these things happen. He smiled in the kindest way it was possible to smile at people known only professionally. Shoba would be back on her feet in a few weeks. There was nothing to indicate that she would not be able to have children in the future.

These days Shoba was always gone by the time Shukumar woke up. He would open his eyes and see the long black hairs she shed on her pillow and think of her, dressed, sipping her third cup of coffee already, in her office downtown, where she searched for typographical errors in textbooks and marked them, in a code she had once explained to him, with an assortment of colored pencils. She would do the same for his dissertation, she promised, when it was ready. He envied her the specificity of her task, so unlike the elusive nature of his. He was a mediocre student who had a facility for absorbing details without curiosity. Until September he had been diligent if not dedicated, summarizing chapters, outlining arguments on pads of yellow lined paper. But now he would lie in their bed until he grew bored, gazing at his side of the closet which Shoba always left partly open, at the row of the tweed jackets and corduroy trousers he would not have to choose from to teach his classes that semester. After the baby died it was too late to withdraw from his teaching duties. But his adviser had arranged things so that he had the spring semester to himself. Shukumar was in his sixth year of graduate school. 'That and the summer should give you a good push,' his adviser had said. 'You should be able to wrap things up by next September.'

But nothing was pushing Shukumar. Instead he thought of how he and Shoba had become experts at avoiding each other in their three-bedroom house, spending as much time on separate floors as possible. He thought of how he no longer looked forward to weekends, when she sat for hours on the sofa with her colored pencils and her files, so that he feared that putting on a record in his own house might be rude. He thought of how long it had been since she looked into his eyes and smiled, or whispered his name on those rare occasions they still reached for each other's bodies before sleeping.

In the beginning he had believed that it would pass, that he and Shoba would get through it all somehow. She was only thirty-three. She was strong, on her feet again. But it wasn't a consolation. It was often nearly lunchtime when Shukumar would finally pull himself out of bed and head downstairs to the coffeepot, pouring out the extra bit Shoba left for him, along with an empty mug, on the countertop.

Shukumar gathered onion skins in his hands and let them drop into the garbage pail, on top of the ribbons of fat he'd trimmed from the lamb. He ran the water in the sink, soaking the knife and the cutting board, and rubbed a lemon half along his fingertips to get rid of the garlic smell, a trick he'd learned from Shoba. It was seven-thirty. Through the window he saw the sky, like soft black pitch. Uneven banks of snow still lined the sidewalks, though it was warm enough for people to walk about without hats or gloves. Nearly three feet had fallen in the last storm, so that for a week people had to walk single file, in narrow trenches. For a week that was Shukumar's excuse for not leaving the house. But now the trenches were widening, and water drained steadily into grates in the pavement.

'The lamb won't be done by eight,' Shukumar said. 'We may have to eat in the dark.'

'We can light candles,' Shoba suggested. She unclipped her hair, coiled neatly at her nape during the days, and pried the sneakers from her feet without untying them. 'I'm going to shower before the lights go,' she said, heading for the staircase. 'I'll be down.'

Shukumar moved her satchel and her sneakers to the side of the fridge. She wasn't this way before. She used to put her coat on a hanger, her sneakers in the closet, and she paid bills as soon as they came. But now she treated the house as if it were a hotel. The fact that the yellow chintz armchair in the living room clashed with the blue-and-maroon Turkish carpet no longer bothered her. On the enclosed porch at the back of the house, a crisp white bag still sat on the wicker chaise, filled with lace she had once planned to turn into curtains.

While Shoba showered, Shukumar went into the downstairs bathroom and found a new toothbrush in its box beneath the sink. The cheap, stiff bristles hurt his gums, and he spit some blood into the basin. The spare brush was one of many stored in a metal basket. Shoba had bought them once when they were on sale, in the event that a visitor decided, at the last minute, to spend the night.

It was typical of her. She was the type to prepare for surprises, good and bad. If she found a skirt or a purse she liked she bought two. She kept the bonuses from her job in a separate bank account in her name. It hadn't bothered him. His own mother had fallen to pieces when his father died, abandoning the house he grew up in and moving back to Calcutta, leaving Shukumar to settle it all. He liked that Shoba was different. It astonished him, her capacity to think ahead. When she used to do the shopping, the pantry was always stocked with extra bottles of olive and corn oil, depending on whether they were cooking Italian or Indian. There were endless boxes of pasta in all shapes and colors, zippered sacks of basmati rice, whole sides of lambs and goats from the Muslim butchers at Haymarket, chopped up and frozen in endless plastic bags. Every other Saturday they wound through the maze of stalls Shukumar eventually knew by heart. He watched in disbelief as she bought more food, trailing behind her with canvas bags as she pushed through the crowd, arguing under the morning sun with boys too young to shave but already missing teeth, who twisted up brown paper bags of artichokes, plums, ginger-root, and yams, and dropped them on their scales, and tossed them to Shoba one by one. She didn't mind being jostled, even when she was pregnant. She was tall, and broad-shouldered, with hips that her obstetrician assured her were made for childbearing. During the drive back home, as the car curved along the Charles, they invariably marveled at how much food they'd bought.

It never went to waste. When friends dropped by, Shoba would throw together meals that appeared to have taken half a day to prepare, from things she had frozen and bottled, not cheap things in tins but peppers she had marinated herself with rosemary; and chutneys that she cooked on Sundays, stirring boiling pots of tomatoes and prunes. Her labeled mason jars lined the shelves of the kitchen, in endless sealed pyramids, enough, they'd agreed, to last for their grand-children to taste. They'd eaten it all by now. Shukumar had been going through their supplies steadily, preparing meals for the two of them, measuring out cupfuls of rice, defrost-ing bags of meat day after day. He combed through her cookbooks every afternoon, following her penciled instruc-tions to use two teaspoons of ground coriander seeds instead of one, or red lentils instead of yellow. Each of the recipes was dated, telling the first time they had eaten the dish together. April 2, cauliflower with fennel. January 14, chicken with almonds and sultanas. He had no memory of eating those meals, and yet there they were, recorded in her neat proofreader's hand. Shukumar enjoyed cooking now. It was the one thing that made him feel productive. If it weren't for him, he knew, Shoba would eat a bowl of cereal for her dinner.

Tonight, with no lights, they would have to eat together. For months now they'd served themselves from the stove, and he'd taken his plate into his study, letting the meal grow cold on his desk before shoving it into his mouth without pause, while Shoba took her plate to the living room and watched game shows, or proofread files with her arsenal of colored pencils at hand.

At some point in the evening she visited him. When he heard her approach he would put away his novel and begin typing sentences. She would rest her hands on his shoulders and stare with him into the blue glow of the computer screen. 'Don't work too hard,' she would say after a minute or two, and head off to bed. It was the one time in the day she sought him out, and yet he'd come to dread it. He knew it was something she forced herself to do. She would look around the walls of the room, which they had decorated together last summer with a border of marching ducks and rabbits playing trumpets and drums. By the end of August there was a cherry crib under the window, a white changing table with mint-green knobs, and a rocking chair with checkered cushions. Shukumar had disassembled it all before bringing Shoba back from the hospital, scraping off the rabbits and ducks with a spatula. For some reason the room did not haunt him the way it haunted Shoba. In January, when he stopped working at his carrel in the library, he set up his desk there deliberately, partly because the room soothed him, and partly because it was a place Shoba avoided.

Shukumar returned to the kitchen and began to open drawers. He tried to locate a candle among the scissors, the eggbeaters and whisks, the mortar and pestle she'd bought in a bazaar in Calcutta, and used to pound garlic cloves and cardamom pods, back when she used to cook. He found a flashlight, but no batteries, and a half-empty box of birthday candles. Shoba had thrown him a surprise birthday party last May. One hundred and twenty people had crammed into the house – all the friends and the friends of friends they now systematically avoided. Bottles of vinho verde had nested in a bed of ice in the bathtub. Shoba was in her fifth month, drinking ginger ale from a martini glass. She had made a vanilla cream cake with custard and spun sugar. All night she kept Shukumar's long fingers linked with hers as they walked among the guests at the party.

Since September their only guest had been Shoba's mother. She came from Arizona and stayed with them for two months after Shoba returned from the hospital. She cooked dinner every night, drove herself to the supermarket, washed their clothes, put them away. She was a religious woman. She set up a small shrine, a framed picture of a lavender-faced goddess and a plate of marigold petals, on the bedside table in the guest room, and prayed twice a day for healthy grandchildren in the future. She was polite to Shukumar without being friendly. She folded his sweaters with an expertise she had learned from her job in a department store. She replaced a missing button on his winter coat and knit him a beige and brown scarf, presenting it to him without the least bit of ceremony, as if he had only dropped it and hadn't noticed. She never talked to him about Shoba; once, when he mentioned the baby's death, she looked up from her knitting, and said, 'But you weren't even there.'

It struck him as odd that there were no real candles in the house. That Shoba hadn't prepared for such an ordinary emergency. He looked now for something to put the birth-day candles in and settled on the soil of a potted ivy that normally sat on the windowsill over the sink. Even though the plant was inches from the tap, the soil was so dry that he had to water it first before the candles would stand straight. He pushed aside the things on the kitchen table, the piles of mail, the unread library books. He remembered their first meals there, when they were so thrilled to be married, to be living together in the same house at last, that they would just reach for each other foolishly, more eager to make love than to eat. He put down two embroidered place mats, a wedding gift from an uncle in Lucknow, and set out the plates and wineglasses they usually saved for guests. He put the ivy in the middle, the white-edged, star-shaped leaves girded by ten little candles. He switched on the digital clock radio and tuned it to a jazz station.

'What's all this?' Shoba said when she came downstairs. Her hair was wrapped in a thick white towel. She undid the towel and draped it over a chair, allowing her hair, damp and dark, to fall across her back. As she walked absently toward the stove she took out a few tangles with her fingers. She wore a clean pair of sweatpants, a T-shirt, an old flannel robe. Her stomach was flat again, her waist narrow before the flare of her hips, the belt of the robe tied in a floppy knot.

It was nearly eight. Shukumar put the rice on the table and the lentils from the night before into the microwave oven, punching the numbers on the timer.

'You made *rogan josh*,' Shoba observed, looking through the glass lid at the bright paprika stew.

Shukumar took out a piece of lamb, pinching it quickly between his fingers so as not to scald himself. He prodded a larger piece with a serving spoon to make sure the meat slipped easily from the bone. 'It's ready,' he announced.

The microwave had just beeped when the lights went out, and the music disappeared.

'Perfect timing,' Shoba said.

'All I could find were birthday candles.' He lit up the ivy, keeping the rest of the candles and a book of matches by his plate.

'It doesn't matter,' she said, running a finger along the stem of her wineglass. 'It looks lovely.'

In the dimness, he knew how she sat, a bit forward in her chair, ankles crossed against the lowest rung, left elbow on the table. During his search for the candles, Shukumar had found a bottle of wine in a crate he had thought was empty. He clamped the bottle between his knees while he turned in the corkscrew. He worried about spilling, and so he picked up the glasses and held them close to his lap while he filled them. They served themselves, stirring the rice with their forks, squinting as they extracted bay leaves and cloves from the stew. Every few minutes Shukumar lit a few more birthday candles and drove them into the soil of the pot.

'It's like India,' Shoba said, watching him tend his makeshift candelabra. 'Sometimes the current disappears for hours at a stretch. I once had to attend an entire rice ceremony in the dark. The baby just cried and cried. It must have been so hot.'

Their baby had never cried, Shukumar considered. Their baby would never have a rice ceremony, even though Shoba had already made the guest list, and decided on which of her three brothers she was going to ask to feed the child its first taste of solid food, at six months if it was a boy, seven if it was a girl.

'Are you hot?' he asked her. He pushed the blazing ivy pot to the other end of the table, closer to the piles of books and mail, making it even more difficult for them to see each other. He was suddenly irritated that he couldn't go upstairs and sit in front of the computer.

'No. It's delicious,' she said, tapping her plate with her fork. 'It really is.'

He refilled the wine in her glass. She thanked him.

They weren't like this before. Now he had to struggle to say something that interested her, something that made her look up from her plate, or from her proofreading files. Eventually he gave up trying to amuse her. He learned not to mind the silences.

'I remember during power failures at my grandmother's house, we all had to say something,' Shoba continued. He could barely see her face, but from her tone he knew her eyes were narrowed, as if trying to focus on a distant object. It was a habit of hers.

'Like what?'

'I don't know. A little poem. A joke. A fact about the world. For some reason my relatives always wanted me to tell them the names of my friends in America. I don't know why the information was so interesting to them. The last time I saw my aunt she asked after four girls I went to elementary school with in Tucson. I barely remember them now.'

Shukumar hadn't spent as much time in India as Shoba had. His parents, who settled in New Hampshire, used to go back without him. The first time he'd gone as an infant he'd nearly died of amoebic dysentery. His father, a nervous type, was afraid to take him again, in case something were to happen, and left him with his aunt and uncle in Concord. As a teenager he preferred sailing camp or scooping ice cream during the summers to going to Calcutta. It wasn't until after his father died, in his last year of college, that the country began to interest him, and he studied its history from course books as if it were any other subject. He wished now that he had his own childhood story of India.

'Let's do that,' she said suddenly.

'Do what?'

'Say something to each other in the dark.'

'Like what? I don't know any jokes.'

'No, no jokes.' She thought for a minute. 'How about telling each other something we've never told before.'

'I used to play this game in high school,' Shukumar recalled. 'When I got drunk.'

'You're thinking of truth or dare. This is different. Okay, I'll start.' She took a sip of wine. 'The first time I was alone in your apartment, I looked in your address book to see if you'd written me in. I think we'd known each other two weeks.'

'Where was I?'

'You went to answer the telephone in the other room. It was your mother, and I figured it would be a long call. I wanted to know if you'd promoted me from the margins of your newspaper.'

'Had I?'

'No. But I didn't give up on you. Now it's your turn.'

He couldn't think of anything, but Shoba was waiting for him to speak. She hadn't appeared so determined in months. What was there left to say to her? He thought back to their first meeting, four years earlier at a lecture hall in Cambridge, where a group of Bengali poets were giving a recital. They'd ended up side by side, on folding wooden chairs. Shukumar was soon bored; he was unable to decipher the literary diction, and couldn't join the rest of the audience as they sighed and nodded solemnly after certain phrases. Peering at the newspaper folded in his lap, he studied the temperatures of cities around the world. Ninety-one degrees in Singapore yesterday, fifty-one in Stockholm. When he turned his head to the left, he saw a woman next to him making a grocery list on the back of a folder, and was startled to find that she was beautiful.

'Okay,' he said, remembering. 'The first time we went out

to dinner, to the Portuguese place, I forgot to tip the waiter. I went back the next morning, found out his name, left money with the manager.'

'You went all the way back to Somerville just to tip a waiter?'

'I took a cab.'

'Why did you forget to tip the waiter?'

The birthday candles had burned out, but he pictured her face clearly in the dark, the wide tilting eyes, the full grape-toned lips, the fall at age two from her high chair still visible as a comma on her chin. Each day, Shukumar noticed, her beauty, which had once overwhelmed him, seemed to fade. The cosmetics that had seemed superfluous were necessary now, not to improve her but to define her somehow.

'By the end of the meal I had a funny feeling that I might marry you,' he said, admitting it to himself as well as to her for the first time. 'It must have distracted me.'

The next night Shoba came home earlier than usual. There was lamb left over from the evening before, and Shukumar heated it up so that they were able to eat by seven. He'd gone out that day, through the melting snow, and bought a packet of taper candles from the corner store, and batteries to fit the flashlight. He had the candles ready on the countertop, standing in brass holders shaped like lotuses, but they ate under the glow of the copper-shaded ceiling lamp that hung over the table.

When they had finished eating, Shukumar was surprised to see that Shoba was stacking her plate on top of his, and then carrying them over to the sink. He had assumed she would retreat to the living room, behind her barricade of files.

'Don't worry about the dishes,' he said, taking them from her hands.

318

'It seems silly not to,' she replied, pouring a drop of detergent onto a sponge. 'It's nearly eight o'clock.'

His heart quickened. All day Shukumar had looked forward to the lights going out. He thought about what Shoba had said the night before, about looking in his address book. It felt good to remember her as she was then, how bold yet nervous she'd been when they first met, how hopeful. They stood side by side at the sink, their reflections fitting together in the frame of the window. It made him shy, the way he felt the first time they stood together in a mirror. He couldn't recall the last time they'd been photographed. They had stopped attending parties, went nowhere together. The film in his camera still contained pictures of Shoba, in the yard, when she was pregnant.

After finishing the dishes, they leaned against the counter, drying their hands on either end of a towel. At eight o'clock the house went black. Shukumar lit the wicks of the candles, impressed by their long, steady flames.

'Let's sit outside,' Shoba said. 'I think it's warm still.'

They each took a candle and sat down on the steps. It seemed strange to be sitting outside with patches of snow still on the ground. But everyone was out of their houses tonight, the air fresh enough to make people restless. Screen doors opened and closed. A small parade of neighbors passed by with flashlights.

'We're going to the bookstore to browse,' a silver-haired man called out. He was walking with his wife, a thin woman in a windbreaker, and holding a dog on a leash. They were the Bradfords, and they had tucked a sympathy card into Shoba and Shukumar's mailbox back in September. 'I hear they've got their power.'

'They'd better,' Shukumar said. 'Or you'll be browsing in the dark.'

The woman laughed, slipping her arm through the crook of her husband's elbow. 'Want to join us?'

'No thanks,' Shoba and Shukumar called out together. It surprised Shukumar that his words matched hers.

He wondered what Shoba would tell him in the dark. The worst possibilities had already run through his head. That she'd had an affair. That she didn't respect him for being thirty-five and still a student. That she blamed him for being in Baltimore the way her mother did. But he knew those things weren't true. She'd been faithful, as had he. She believed in him. It was she who had insisted he go to Baltimore. What didn't they know about each other? He knew she curled her fingers tightly when she slept, that her body twitched during bad dreams. He knew it was honey-dew she favoured over cantaloupe. He knew that when they returned from the hospital the first thing she did when she walked into the house was pick out objects of theirs and toss them into a pile in the hallway: books from the shelves, plants from the windowsills, paintings from walls, photos from tables, pots and pans that hung from the hooks over the stove. Shukumar had stepped out of her way, watching as she moved methodically from room to room. When she was satisfied, she stood there staring at the pile she'd made, her lips drawn back in such distaste that Shukumar had thought she would spit. Then she'd started to cry.

He began to feel cold as he sat there on the steps. He felt that he needed her to talk first, in order to reciprocate.

'That time when your mother came to visit us,' she said finally. 'When I said one night that I had to stay late at work, I went out with Gillian and had a martini.'

He looked at her profile, the slender nose, the slightly masculine set of her jaw. He remembered that night well; eating with his mother, tired from teaching two classes back to back, wishing Shoba were there to say more of the right things because he came up with only the wrong ones. It had been twelve years since his father had died, and his mother had come to spend two weeks with him and Shoba, so they could honour his father's memory together. Each night his mother cooked something his father had liked, but she was too upset to eat the dishes herself; and her eyes would well up as Shoba stroked her hand. 'It's so touching,' Shoba had said to him at the time. Now he pictured Shoba with Gillian, in a bar with striped velvet sofas, the one they used to go to after the movies, making sure she got her extra olive, asking Gillian for a cigarette. He imagined her complaining, and Gillian sympathizing about visits from in-laws. It was Gillian who had driven Shoba to the hospital.

'Your turn,' she said, stopping his thoughts.

At the end of their street Shukumar heard sounds of a drill and the electricians shouting over it. He looked at the darkened façades of the houses lining the street. Candles glowed in the windows of one. In spite of the warmth, smoke rose from the chimney.

'I cheated on my Oriental Civilization exam in college,' he said. 'It was my last semester, my last set of exams. My father had died a few months before. I could see the blue book of the guy next to me. He was an American guy, a maniac. He knew Urdu and Sanskrit. I couldn't remember if the verse we had to identify was an example of a *ghazal* or not. I looked at his answer and copied it down.'

It had happened over fifteen years ago. He felt relief now, having told her.

She turned to him, looking not at his face, but at his shoes – old moccasins he wore as if they were slippers, the leather at the back permanently flattened. He wondered if it bothered her, what he'd said. She took his hand and pressed it. 'You didn't have to tell me why you did it,' she said, moving closer to him.

They sat together until nine o'clock, when the lights came on. They heard some people across the street clapping from their porch, and televisions being turned on. The Bradfords walked back down the street, eating ice-cream cones and waving. Shoba and Shukumar waved back. Then they stood up, his hand still in hers, and went inside.

Somehow, without saying anything, it had turned into this. Into an exchange of confessions – the little ways they'd hurt or disappointed each other, and themselves. The following day Shukumar thought for hours about what to say to her. He was torn between admitting that he once ripped out a photo of a woman in one of the fashion magazines she used to subscribe to and carried it in his books for a week, or saying that he really hadn't lost the sweater-vest she bought him for their third wedding anniversary but had exchanged it for cash at Filene's, and that he had gotten drunk alone in the middle of the day at a hotel bar. For their first anniversary, Shoba had cooked a ten-course dinner just for him. The vest depressed him. 'My wife gave me a sweater-vest for our anniversary,' he complained to the bartender, his head heavy with cognac. 'What do you expect?' the bartender had replied. 'You're married.'

As for the picture of the woman, he didn't know why he'd ripped it out. She wasn't as pretty as Shoba. She wore a white sequinned dress, and had a sullen face and lean, mannish legs. Her bare arms were raised, her fists around her head, as if she were about to punch herself in the ears. It was an advertisement for stockings. Shoba had been pregnant at the time, her stomach suddenly immense, to the point where Shukumar no longer wanted to touch her. The first time he saw the picture he was lying in bed next to her, watching her as she read. When he noticed the magazine in the recycling pile he found the woman and tore out the page as carefully as he could. For about a week he allowed himself a glimpse each day. He felt an intense desire for the woman, but it was a desire that turned to disgust after a minute or two. It was the closest he'd come to infidelity.

He told Shoba about the sweater on the third night, the picture on the fourth. She said nothing as he spoke, expressed no protest or reproach. She simply listened, and then she took his hand, pressing it as she had before. On the third night, she told him that once after a lecture they'd attended, she let him speak to the chairman of his department without telling him that he had a dab of pâté on his chin. She'd been irritated with him for some reason, and so she'd let him go on and on, about securing his fellowship for the following semester, without putting a finger to her own chin as a signal. The fourth night, she said that she never liked the one poem he'd ever published in his life, in a literary magazine in Utah. He'd written the poem after meeting Shoba. She added that she found the poem sentimental.

Something happened when the house was dark. They were able to talk to each other again. The third night after supper they'd sat together on the sofa, and once it was dark he began kissing her awkwardly on her forehead and her face, and though it was dark he closed his eyes, and knew that she did, too. The fourth night they walked carefully upstairs, to bed, feeling together for the final step with their feet before the landing, and making love with a desperation they had forgotten. She wept without sound, and whispered his name, and traced his eyebrows with her finger in the dark. As he made love to her he wondered what he would say to her the next night, and what she would say, the

323

thought of it exciting him. 'Hold me,' he said, 'hold me in your arms.' By the time the lights came back on downstairs, they'd fallen asleep.

The morning of the fifth night Shukumar found another notice from the electric company in the mailbox. The line had been repaired ahead of schedule, it said. He was disappointed. He had planned on making shrimp *malai* for Shoba, but when he arrived at the store he didn't feel like cooking anymore. It wasn't the same, he thought, knowing that the lights wouldn't go out. In the store the shrimp looked grey and thin. The coconut milk tin was dusty and overpriced. Still, he bought them, along with a beeswax candle and two bottles of wine.

She came home at seven-thirty. 'I suppose this is the end of our game,' he said when he saw her reading the notice.

She looked at him. 'You can still light candles if you want.' She hadn't been to the gym tonight. She wore a suit beneath the raincoat. Her makeup had been retouched recently.

When she went upstairs to change, Shukumar poured himself some wine and put on a record, a Thelonious Monk album he knew she liked.

When she came downstairs they ate together. She didn't thank him or compliment him. They simply ate in a darkened room, in the glow of a beeswax candle. They had survived a difficult time. They finished off the shrimp. They finished off the first bottle of wine and moved on to the second. They sat together until the candle had nearly burned away. She shifted in her chair, and Shukumar thought that she was about to say something. But instead she blew out the candle, stood up, turned on the light switch, and sat down again.

'Shouldn't we keep the lights off?' Shukumar asked.

She set her plate aside and clasped her hands on the table. 'I want you to see my face when I tell you this,' she said gently.

His heart began to pound. The day she told him she was pregnant, she had used the very same words, saying them in the same gentle way, turning off the basketball game he'd been watching on television. He hadn't been prepared then. Now he was.

Only he didn't want her to be pregnant again. He didn't want to have to pretend to be happy.

'I've been looking for an apartment and I've found one,' she said, narrowing her eyes on something, it seemed, behind his left shoulder. It was nobody's fault, she continued. They'd been through enough. She needed some time alone. She had money saved up for a security deposit. The apartment was on Beacon Hill, so she could walk to work. She had signed the lease that night before coming home.

She wouldn't look at him, but he stared at her. It was obvious that she'd rehearsed the lines. All this time she'd been looking for an apartment, testing the water pressure, asking a Realtor if heat and hot water were included in the rent. It sickened Shukumar, knowing that she had spent these past evenings preparing for a life without him. He was relieved and yet he was sickened. This was what she'd been trying to tell him for the past four evenings. This was the point of her game.

Now it was his turn to speak. There was something he'd sworn he would never tell her, and for six months he had done his best to block it from his mind. Before the ultrasound she had asked the doctor not to tell her the sex of their child, and Shukumar had agreed. She had wanted it to be a surprise.

Later, those few times they talked about what had happened, she said at least they'd been spared that knowledge.

325

In a way she almost took pride in her decision, for it enabled her to seek refuge in a mystery. He knew that she assumed it was a mystery for him, too. He'd arrived too late from Baltimore – when it was all over and she was lying on the hospital bed. But he hadn't. He'd arrived early enough to see their baby, and to hold him before they cremated him. At first he had recoiled at the suggestion, but the doctor said holding the baby might help him with the process of grieving. Shoba was asleep. The baby had been cleaned off, his bulbous lids shut tight to the world.

'Our baby was a boy,' he said. 'His skin was more red than brown. He had black hair on his head. He weighed almost five pounds. His fingers were curled shut, just like yours in the night.'

Shoba looked at him now, her face contorted with sorrow. He had cheated on a college exam, ripped a picture of a woman out of a magazine. He had returned a sweater and got drunk in the middle of the day instead. These were the things he had told her. He had held his son, who had known life only within her, against his chest in a darkened room in an unknown wing of the hospital. He had held him until a nurse knocked and took him away, and he promised himself that day that he would never tell Shoba, because he still loved her then, and it was the one thing in her life that she had wanted to be a surprise.

Shukumar stood up and stacked his plate on top of hers. He carried the plates to the sink, but instead of running the tap he looked out the window. Outside the evening was still warm, and the Bradfords were walking arm in arm. As he watched the couple the room went dark, and he spun around. Shoba had turned the lights off. She came back to the table and sat down, and after a moment Shukumar joined her. They wept together, for the things they now knew.

LORRIE MOORE

TERRIFIC MOTHER

ALTHOUGH SHE HAD been around them her whole life, it was when she reached thirty-five that, holding babies seemed to make her nervous – just at the beginning, a twinge of stage fright swinging up from the gut. 'Adrienne, would you like to hold the baby? Would you mind?' Always these words from a woman her age looking kind and beseeching – a former friend, she was losing her friends to babble and beseech – and Adrienne would force herself to breathe deep. Holding a baby was no longer natural – she was no longer natural – but a test of womanliness and earthly skills. She was being observed. People looked to see how she would do it. She had entered a puritanical decade, a demographic moment – whatever it was – when the best compliment you could get was, 'You would make a terrific mother.' The wolf whistle of the nineties.

So when she was at the Spearsons' Labor Day picnic, and when Sally Spearson handed her the baby, Adrienne had burbled at it as she would a pet, had jostled the child gently, made clicking noises with her tongue, affectionately cooing, 'Hello, punkinhead, hello, my little punkinhead,' had reached to shoo a fly away and, amid the smells of old grass and the fatty crackle of the barbecue, lost her balance when the picnic bench, the dowels rotting in the joints, wobbled and began to topple her – the bench, the wobbly picnic bench, was toppling her! And when she fell back-ward, wrenching her spine – in the slowed quickness of this

329

flipping world, she saw the clayey clouds, some frozen faces, one lone star like the nose of a jet – and when the baby's head hit the stone retaining wall of the Spearsons' newly terraced yard and bled fatally into the brain, Adrienne went home shortly thereafter, after the hospital and the police reports, and did not leave her attic apartment for seven months, and there were fears, deep fears for her, on the part of Martin Porter, the man she had been dating, and on the part of almost everyone, including Sally Spearson, who phoned tearfully to say that she forgave her, that Adrienne might never come out.

Martin Porter usually visited her bringing a pepper cheese or a Casbah couscous cup; he had become her only friend. He was divorced and worked as a research economist, though he looked more like a Scottish lumberjack – greying hair, red-flecked beard, a favourite flannel shirt in green and gold. He was getting ready to take a trip abroad. 'We could get married,' he suggested. That way, he said, Adrienne could accompany him to northern Italy, to a villa in the Alps set up for scholars and academic conferences. She could be a spouse. They gave spouses studios to work in. Some studios had pianos. Some had desks or potter's wheels. 'You can do whatever you want.' He was finishing the second draft of a study of First World imperialism's impact on Third World monetary systems. 'You could paint. Or not. You could not paint.'

She looked at him closely, hungrily, then turned away. She still felt clumsy and big, a beefy killer in a cage, in need of the thinning prison food. 'You love me, don't you,' she said. She had spent the better part of seven months napping in a leotard, an electric fan blowing at her, her left ear catching the wind, capturing it there in her head, like the sad sea

330

in a shell. She felt clammy and doomed. 'Or do you just feel sorry for me?' She swatted at a small swarm of gnats that had appeared suddenly out of an abandoned can of Coke.

'I don't feel sorry for you.'

'You don't?'

'I *feel for* you. I've grown to love you. We're grown-ups here. One grows to do things.' He was a practical man. He often referred to the annual departmental cocktail party as 'Standing Around Getting Paid'.

'I don't think, Martin, that we can get married.'

'Of course we can get married.' He unbuttoned his cuffs as if to roll up his sleeves.

'You don't understand,' she said. 'Normal life is no longer possible for me. I've stepped off all the normal paths and am living in the bushes. I'm a bushwoman now. I don't feel like I can have the normal things. Marriage is a normal thing. You need the normal courtship, the normal proposal.' She couldn't think what else. Water burned her eyes. She waved a hand dismissively, and it passed through her field of vision like something murderous and huge.

'Normal courtship, normal proposal,' Martin said. He took off his shirt and pants and shoes. He lay on the bed in just his socks and underwear and pressed the length of his body against her. 'I'm going to marry you, whether you like it or not.' He took her face into his hands and looked longingly at her mouth. 'I'm going to marry you till you puke.'

They were met at Malpensa by a driver who spoke little English but who held up a sign that said VILLA HIRSCH-BORN, and when Adrienne and Martin approached him, he nodded and said, 'Hello, *buongiorno*. Signor Porter?' The drive to the villa took two hours, uphill and down, through the countryside and several small villages, but it wasn't until the driver pulled up to the precipitous hill he called 'La Madre Vertiginoso', and the villa's iron gates somehow opened automatically, then closed behind them, it wasn't until then, winding up the drive past the spectacular gardens and the sunny vineyard and the terraces of the stucco outbuildings, that it occurred to Adrienne that Martin's being invited here was a great honour. He had won this *thing*, and he got to live here for a month.

'Does this feel like a honeymoon?' she asked him.

'A what? Oh, a honeymoon. Yes.' He turned and patted her thigh indifferently.

He was jet-lagged. That was it. She smoothed her skirt, which was wrinkled and damp. 'Yes, I can see us growing old together,' she said, squeezing his hand. 'In the next few weeks, in fact.' If she ever got married again, she would do it right: the awkward ceremony, the embarrassing relatives, the cumbersome, ecologically unsound gifts. She and Martin had simply gone to city hall, and then asked their family and friends not to send presents but to donate money to Greenpeace. Now, however, as they slowed before the squashed-nosed stone lions at the entrance of the villa, its perfect border of forget-me-nots and yews, its sparkling glass door, Adrienne gasped. Whales, she thought quickly. *Whales* got my crystal.

The upstairs 'Principessa' room, which they were ushered into by a graceful bilingual butler named Carlo, was elegant and huge – a piano, a large bed, dressers stenciled with festooning fruits. There was maid service twice a day, said Carlo. There were sugar wafers, towels, mineral water, and mints. There was dinner at eight, breakfast until nine. When Carlo bowed and departed, Martin kicked off his shoes and sank into the ancient tapestried chaise. 'I've heard these "fake" Quattrocento paintings on the wall are fake for tax purposes only,' he whispered. 'If you know what I mean.'

'Really,' said Adrienne. She felt like one of the workers taking over the Winter Palace. Her own voice sounded booming. 'You know, Mussolini was captured around here. Think about it.'

Martin looked puzzled. 'What do you mean?'

'That he was around here. That they captured him. I don't know. I was reading the little book on it. Leave me alone.' She flopped down on the bed. Martin was changing already. He'd been better when they were just dating, with the pepper cheese. She let her face fall deep into the pillow, her mouth hanging open like a dog's, and then she slept until six, dreaming that a baby was in her arms but that it turned into a stack of plates, which she had to juggle, tossing them into the air.

A loud sound awoke her – a falling suitcase. Everyone had to dress for dinner, and Martin was yanking things out, groaning his way into a jacket and tie. Adrienne got up, bathed, and put on panty hose, which, because it had been months since she had done so, twisted around her leg like the stripe on a barber pole.

'You're walking as if you'd torn a ligament,' said Martin, locking the door to their room as they were leaving.

Adrienne pulled at the knees of the hose but couldn't make them work. 'Tell me you like my skirt, Martin, or I'm going to have to go back in and never come out again.'

'I like your skirt. It's great. You're great. I'm great,' he said, like a conjugation. He took her arm and they limped their way down the curved staircase – Was it sweeping? Yes! It was sweeping! – to the dining room, where Carlo ushered them in to find their places at the table. The seating arrangement at the tables would change nightly, Carlo said in a

333

clipped Italian accent, 'to assist the cross-pollination of ideas'.

'Excuse me?' said Adrienne.

There were about thirty-five people, all of them middle-aged, with the academic's strange mixed expression of merriment and weariness. 'A cross between flirtation and a fender bender,' Martin had described it once. Adrienne's place was at the opposite side of the room from him, between a historian writing a book on a monk named Jaocim de Flore and a musicologist who had devoted his life to a quest for 'the earnest andante'. Everyone sat in elaborate wooden chairs, the backs of which were carved with gargoylish heads that poked up from behind either shoulder of the sitter, like a warning.

'De Flore,' said Adrienne, at a loss, turning from her carpaccio to the monk man. 'Doesn't that mean "of the flower"?' She had recently learned that *disaster* meant 'bad star', and she was looking for an opportunity to brandish and bronze this tidbit in conversation.

The monk man looked at her. 'Are you one of the spouses?'

'Yes,' she said. She looked down, then back up. 'But then, so is my husband.'

'You're not a screenwriter, are you?'

'No,' she said. 'I'm a painter. Actually, more of a print-maker. Actually, more of a – right now I'm in transition.'

He nodded and dug back into his food. 'I'm always afraid they're going to start letting *screenwriters* in here.'

There was an arugula salad, and osso buco for the main course. She turned now to the musicologist. 'So you usually find them insincere? The andantes?' She looked quickly out over the other heads to give Martin a fake and girlish wave.

'It's the use of the minor seventh,' muttered the musicologist. 'So fraudulent and replete.'

*

334

'If the food wasn't so good, I'd leave now,' she said to Martin. They were lying in bed, in their carpeted skating rink of a room. It could be weeks, she knew, before they'd have sex here. ' "*So fraudulent and replete,*" ' she said in a high nasal voice, the likes of which Martin had heard only once before, in a departmental meeting chaired by an embittered interim chair who did imitations of colleagues not in the room. 'Can you even use the word *replete* like that?'

'As soon as you get settled in your studio, you'll feel better,' said Martin, beginning to fade. He groped under the covers to find her hand and clasp it.

'I want a divorce,' whispered Adrienne.

'I'm not giving you one,' he said, bringing her hand up to his chest and placing it there, like a medallion, like a necklace of sleep, and then he began softly to snore, the quietest of radiators.

They were given bagged lunches and told to work well. Martin's studio was a modern glass cube in the middle of one of the gardens. Adrienne's was a musty stone hut twenty minutes farther up the hill and out onto the wooded headland, along a dirt path sunned on by small darting lizards. She unlocked the door with the key she had been given, went in, and immediately sat down and ate the entire bagged lunch – quickly, compulsively, though it was only 9:30 in the morning. Two apples, some cheese, and a jam sandwich. 'A jelly bread,' she said aloud, holding up the sandwich, scrutinizing it under the light.

She set her sketch pad on the worktable and began a morning full of killing spiders and drawing their squashed and tragic bodies. The spiders were starshaped, hairy, and scuttling like crabs. They were fallen stars. Bad stars. They were earth's animal try at heaven. Often she had to step on them twice – they were large and ran fast. Stepping on them once usually just made them run faster.

It was the careless universe's work she was performing, death itchy and about like a cop. Her personal fund of mercy for the living was going to get used up in dinner conversation at the villa. She had no compassion to spare, only a pencil and a shoe.

'Art *trouvé*?' said Martin, toweling himself dry from his shower as they dressed for the evening cocktail hour.

'Spider *trouvé*,' she said. 'A delicate, aboriginal dish.' Martin let out a howling laugh that alarmed her. She looked at him, then looked down at her shoes. He needed her. Tomorrow, she would have to go down into town and find a pair of sexy Italian sandals that showed the cleavage of her toes. She would have to take him dancing. They would have to hold each other and lead each other back to love or they'd go nuts here. They'd grow mocking and arch and violent. One of them would stick a foot out, and the other would trip. That sort of thing.

At dinner, she sat next to a medievalist who had just finished his sixth book on the *Canterbury Tales*.

'Sixth,' repeated Adrienne.

'There's a lot there,' he said defensively.

'I'm sure,' she said.

'I read deep,' he added. 'I read hard.'

'How nice for you.'

He looked at her narrowly. 'Of course, *you* probably think I should write a book about Cat Stevens.' She nodded neutrally. 'I see,' he said.

For dessert, Carlo was bringing in a white chocolate torte, and she decided to spend most of the coffee and dessert time talking about it. Desserts like these are born, not made, she would say. She was already practicing,

336

rehearsing for courses. 'I mean,' she said to the Swedish physicist on her left, 'until today, my feeling about white chocolate was why? What was the point? You might as well have been eating goddamn *wax*.' She had her elbow on the table, her hand up near her face, and she looked anxiously past the physicist to smile at Martin at the other end of the long table. She waved her fingers in the air like bug legs.

'Yes, of course,' said the physicist, frowning. 'You must be . . . well, are you one of the *spouses*?'

She began in the mornings to gather with some of the other spouses – they were going to have little tank tops printed up – in the music room for exercise. This way, she could avoid hearing words like *Heideggerian* and *ideological* at breakfast; it always felt too early in the morning for those words. The women pushed back the damask sofas and cleared a space on the rug where all of them could do little hip and thigh exercises, led by the wife of the Swedish physicist. Up, down, up down.

'I guess this relaxes you,' said the white-haired woman next to her.

'Bourbon relaxes you,' said Adrienne. 'This carves you.'

'Bourbon carves you,' said a redhead from Brazil.

'You have to go visit this person down in the village,' whispered the white-haired woman. She wore a Spalding sporting-goods T-shirt.

'What person?'

'Yes, what person?' asked the blonde.

The white-haired woman stopped and handed both of them a card from the pocket of her shorts. 'She's an American masseuse. A couple of us have started going. She takes lire or dollars, doesn't matter. You have to phone a couple days ahead.'

Adrienne stuck the card in her waistband. 'Thanks,' she said, and resumed moving her leg up and down like a tollgate.

For dinner, there was *tacchino alla scala*. 'I wonder how you make this?' Adrienne said aloud.

'My dear,' said the French historian on her left. 'You must never ask. Only wonder.' He then went on to disparage subaltered intellectualism, dormant tropes, genealogical contingencies.

'Yes,' said Adrienne, 'dishes like these do have about them a kind of omnihistorical reality. At least it seems like that to me.' She turned quickly.

To her right sat a cultural anthropologist who had just come back from China, where she had studied the infanticide.

'Yes,' said Adrienne. 'The infanticide.'

'They are on the edge of something horrific there. It is the whole future, our future as well, and something terrible is going to happen to them. One feels it.'

'How awful,' said Adrienne. She could not do the mechanical work of eating, of knife and fork, up and down. She let her knife and fork rest against each other on the plate.

'A woman has to apply for a license to have a baby. Everything is bribes and rations. We went for hikes up into the mountains, and we didn't see a single bird, a single animal. Everything, over the years, has been eaten.'

Adrienne felt a light weight on the inside of her arm vanish and return, vanish and return, like the history of something, like the story of all things. 'Where are you from ordinarily?' asked Adrienne. She couldn't place the accent.

'Munich,' said the woman. 'Land of Oktoberfest.' She dug into her food in an exasperated way, then turned back toward Adrienne to smile a little formally. 'I grew up watching all these grown people in green felt throw up in the street.'

338

Adrienne smiled back. This now was how she would learn about the world, in sentences at meals; other people's distillations amid her own vague pain, dumb with itself. This, for her, would be knowledge – a shifting to hear, an emptying of her arms, other people's experiences walking through the bare rooms of her brain, looking for a place to sit.

'Me?' she too often said, 'I'm just a dropout from Sue Bennet College.' And people would nod politely and ask, 'Where's that?'

The next morning in her room, she sat by the phone and stared. Martin had gone to his studio; his book was going fantastically well, he said, which gave Adrienne a sick, abandoned feeling – of being unhappy and unsupportive – which made her think she was not even one of the spouses. Who was she? The opposite of a mother. The opposite of a spouse.

She was Spider Woman.

She picked up the phone, got an outside line, dialed the number of the masseuse on the card.

'*Pronto!*' said the voice on the other end.

'Yes, hello, *per favore, parla inglese?*'

'Oh, yes,' said the voice. 'I'm from Minnesota.'

'No kidding,' said Adrienne. She lay back and searched the ceiling for talk. 'I once subscribed to a haunted-house newsletter published in Minnesota,' she said.

'Yes,' said the voice a little impatiently. 'Minnesota is full of haunted-house newsletters.'

'I once lived in a haunted house,' said Adrienne. 'In college. Me and five roommates.'

The masseuse cleared her throat confidentially. 'Yes. I was once called on to cast the demons from a haunted house. But how can I help you today?'

'You were?'

339

'Were? Oh, the house, yes. When I got there, all the place needed was to be cleaned. So I cleaned it. Washed the dishes and dusted.'

'Yup,' said Adrienne. 'Our house was haunted that way, too.'

There was a strange silence, in which Adrienne, feeling something tense and moist in the room, began to fiddle with the bagged lunch on the bed, nervously pulling open the sandwiches, sensing that if she turned, just then, the phone cradled in her neck, the child would be there, behind her, a little older now, a toddler, walked toward her in a ghostly way by her own dead parents, a Nativity scene corrupted by error and dream.

'How can I help you today?' the masseuse asked again, firmly.

Help? Adrienne wondered abstractly, and remembered how in certain countries, instead of a tooth fairy, there were such things as tooth spiders. How the tooth spider could steal your children, mix them up, bring you a changeling child, a child that was changed.

'I'd like to make an appointment for Thursday,' she said. 'If possible. Please.'

For dinner there was *vongole in umido*, the rubbery, wine-steamed meat prompting commentary about mollusk versus crustacean anatomy. Adrienne sighed and chewed. Over cocktails, there had been a long discussion of peptides and rabbit tests.

'Now lobsters, you know, have what is called a hemi-penis,' said the man next to her. He was a marine biologist, an epidemiologist, or an anthropologist. She'd forgotten.

'Hemipenis.' Adrienne scanned the room a little frantically.

'Yes.' He grinned. 'Not a term one particularly wants to hear in an intimate moment, of course.'

'No,' said Adrienne, smiling back. She paused. 'Are you one of the spouses?'

Someone on his right grabbed his arm, and he now turned in that direction to say why yes, he did know Professor so-and-so . . . and wasn't she in Brussels last year giving a paper at the hermeneutics conference?

There came *castagne al porto* and coffee. The woman to Adrienne's left finally turned to her, placing the cup down on the saucer with a sharp clink.

'You know, the chef has AIDS,' said the woman.

Adrienne froze a little in her chair. 'No, I didn't know.' Who was this woman?

'How does that make you feel?'

'Pardon me?'

'How does that make you feel?' She enunciated slowly, like a reading teacher.

'I'm not sure,' said Adrienne, scowling at her chestnuts. 'Certainly worried for us if we should lose him.'

The woman smiled. 'Very interesting.' She reached underneath the table for her purse and said, 'Actually, the chef doesn't have AIDS – at least not that I'm aware of. I'm just taking a kind of survey to test people's reactions to AIDS, homosexuality, and general notions of contagion. I'm a sociologist. It's part of my research. I just arrived this afternoon. My name is Marie-Claire.'

Adrienne turned back to the hemipenis man. 'Do you think the people here are mean?' she asked.

He smiled at her in a fatherly way. 'Of course,' he said. There was a long silence with some chewing in it. 'But the place *is* pretty as a postcard.'

'Yeah, well,' said Adrienne, 'I never send those kinds of

341

postcards. No matter where I am, I always send the kind with the little cat jokes on them.'

He placed his hand briefly on her shoulder. 'We'll find you some cat jokes.' He scanned the room in a bemused way and then looked at his watch.

She had bonded in a state of emergency, like an infant bird. But perhaps it would be soothing, this marriage. Perhaps it would be like a nice warm bath. A nice warm bath in a tub flying off a roof.

At night, she and Martin seemed almost like husband and wife, spooned against each other in a forgetful sort of love – a cold, still heaven through which a word or touch might explode like a moon, then disappear, unremembered. She moved her arms to place them around him and he felt so big there, huge, filling her arms.

The white-haired woman who had given her the masseuse card was named Kate Spalding, the wife of the monk man, and after breakfast she asked Adrienne to go jogging. They met by the lions, Kate once more sporting a Spalding T-shirt, and then they headed out over the gravel, toward the gardens. 'It's pretty as a postcard here, isn't it?' said Kate. Out across the lake, the mountains seemed to preside over the minutiae of the terracotta villages nestled below. It was May and the Alps were losing their snowy caps, nurses letting their hair down. The air was warming. Anything could happen.

Adrienne sighed. 'But do you think people have *sex* here?'

Kate smiled. 'You mean casual sex? Among the guests?'

Adrienne felt annoyed. '*Casual* sex? No, I don't mean *casual* sex. I'm talking about difficult, randomly profound Sears and Roebuck sex. I'm talking marital.'

Kate laughed in a sharp, barking sort of way, which for some reason hurt Adrienne's feelings.

Adrienne tugged on her socks. 'I don't believe in *casual* sex.' She paused. 'I believe in casual marriage.'

'Don't look at me,' said Kate. 'I married my husband because I was deeply in love with him.'

'Yeah, well,' said Adrienne, 'I married my husband because I thought it would be a great way to meet guys.'

Kate smiled now in a real way. Her white hair was grandmotherly, but her face was youthful and tan, and her teeth shone generous and wet, the creamy incisors curved as cashews.

'I'd tried the whole single thing, but it just wasn't working,' Adrienne added, running in place.

Kate stepped close and massaged Adrienne's neck. Her skin was lined and papery. 'You haven't been to see Ilke from Minnesota yet, have you?'

Adrienne feigned perturbance. 'Do I seem that tense, that lost, that . . .' And here she let her arms splay spastically. 'I'm going tomorrow.'

He was a beautiful child, didn't you think? In bed, Martin held her until he rolled away, clasped her hand and fell asleep. At least there was that: a husband sleeping next to a wife, a nice husband sleeping close. It meant something to her. She could see how through the years marriage would gather power, its socially sanctioned animal comfort, its night life a dreamy dance about love. She lay awake and remembered when her father had at last grown so senile and ill that her mother could no longer sleep in the same bed with him – the mess, the smell – and had had to move him, diapered and rank, to the guest room next door. Her mother had cried, to say this farewell to a husband. To at last lose

343

him like this, banished and set aside like a dead man, never to sleep with him again: she had wept like a baby. His actual death, she took less hard. At the funeral, she was grim and dry and invited everyone over for a quiet, elegant tea. By the time two years had passed, and she herself was diagnosed with cancer, her sense of humor had returned a little. 'The silent killer,' she would say, with a wink. 'The *Silent Killer.*' She got a kick out of repeating it, though no one knew what to say in response, and at the very end, she kept clutching the nurses' hems to ask, 'Why is no one visiting me?' No one lived that close, explained Adrienne. No one lived that close to anyone.

Adrienne set her spoon down. 'Isn't this soup *interesting?*' she said to no one in particular. '*Zup-pa mari-ta-ta!*' Marriage soup. She decided it was perhaps a little like marriage itself: a good idea that, like all ideas, lived awkwardly on earth.

'You're not a poetess, I hope,' said the English geologist next to her. 'We had a poetess here last month, and things got a bit dodgy here for the rest of us.'

'Really.' After the soup, there was risotto with squid ink.

'Yes. She kept referring to insects as "God's typos" and then she kept us all after dinner one evening so she could read from her poems, which seemed to consist primarily of the repeating line "the hairy kiwi of his balls".'

'Hairy kiwi,' repeated Adrienne, searching the phrase for a sincere andante. She had written a poem once herself. It had been called 'Garbage Night in the Fog' and was about a long, sad walk she'd taken once on garbage night.

The geologist smirked a little at the risotto, waiting for Adrienne to say something more, but she was now watching Martin at the other table. He was sitting next to the sociologist she'd sat next to the previous night, and as Adrienne watched, she saw Martin glance, in a sickened way, from the sociologist, back to his plate, then back to the sociologist. 'The *cook*?' he said loudly, then dropped his fork and pushed his chair from the table.

The sociologist was frowning. 'You flunk,' she said.

'I'm going to see a masseuse tomorrow.' Martin was on his back on the bed, and Adrienne was straddling his hips, usually one of their favourite ways to converse. One of the Mandy Patinkin tapes she'd brought was playing on the cassette player.

'The masseuse. Yes, I've heard.'

'You have?'

'Sure, they were talking about it at dinner last night.'

'Who was?' She was already feeling possessive, alone.

'Oh, one of them,' said Martin, smiling and waving his hand dismissively.

'Them,' said Adrienne coldly. 'You mean one of the spouses, don't you? Why are all the spouses here women? Why don't the women scholars have spouses?'

'Some of them do, I think. They're just not here.'

'Where are they?'

'Could you move?' he said irritably. 'You're sitting on my groin.'

'Fine,' she said, and climbed off.

The next morning, she made her way down past the conical evergreens of the terraced hill – so like the grounds of a palace, the palace of a moody princess named Sophia or Giovanna – ten minutes down the winding path to the locked gate to the village. It had rained in the night, and snails, golden and mauve, decorated the stone steps, sometimes dead center, causing Adrienne an occasional quick turn of the ankle. A dance step, she thought. Modern and bent-kneed. Very Martha Graham. *Don't kill us. We'll kill you.* At the top of the final stairs to the gate, she pressed the buzzer that opened it electronically, and then dashed down to get out in time. YOU HAVE THIRTY SECONDS said the sign. TRENTA SECONDI USCIRE. PRESTO! One needed a key to get back in from the village, and she clutched it like a charm.

She had to follow the Via San Carlo to Corso Magenta, past a gelato shop and a bakery with wreaths of braided bread and muffins cut like birds. She pressed herself up against the buildings to let the cars pass. She looked at her card. The masseuse was above a *farmacìa*, she'd been told, and she saw it now, a little sign that said MASSAGGIO DELLA VITA. She pushed on the outer door and went up.

Upstairs, through an open doorway, she entered a room lined with books: books on vegetarianism, books on healing, books on juice. A cockatiel, white, with a red dot like a Hindu wife's, was perched atop a picture frame. The picture was of Lake Como or Garda, though when you blinked, it could also be a skull, a fissure through the centre like a reef.

'Adrienne,' said a smiling woman in a purple peasant dress. She had big frosted hair and a wide, happy face that contained many shades of pink. She stepped forward and shook Adrienne's hand. 'I'm Ilke.'

'Yes,' said Adrienne.

The cockatiel suddenly flew from its perch to land on Ilke's shoulder. It pecked at her big hair, then stared at Adrienne accusingly.

Ilke's eyes moved quickly between Adrienne's own, a quick read, a radar scan. She then looked at her watch. 'You can go into the back room now, and I'll be with you shortly. You can take off all your clothes, also any jewellery – watches, or rings. But if you want, you can leave your underwear on. Whatever you prefer.'

'What do most people do?' Adrienne swallowed in a difficult, conspicuous way.

Ilke smiled. 'Some do it one way, some the other.'

'All right,' Adrienne said, and clutched her pocketbook. She stared at the cockatiel. 'I just wouldn't want to rock the boat.'

She stepped carefully toward the back room Ilke had indicated, and pushed past the heavy curtain. Inside was a large alcove – windowless and dark, with one small bluish light coming from the corner. In the centre was a table with a newly creased flannel sheet. Speakers were built into the bottom of the table, and out of them came the sound of eerie choral music, wordless oohs and aahs in minor tones, with a percussive sibilant chant beneath it that sounded to Adrienne like 'Jesus is best, Jesus is best,' though perhaps it was 'Cheese, I suspect.' Overhead hung a mobile of white stars, crescent moons, and doves. On the blue walls were more clouds and snowflakes. It was a child's room, a baby's room, everything trying hard to be harmless and sweet.

Adrienne removed all her clothes, her earrings, her watch, her rings. She had already grown used to the ring Martin had given her, and so it saddened and exhilarated her to take it off, a quick glimpse into the landscape of adultery. Her other ring was a smoky quartz, which a palm reader in Milwaukee – a man dressed like a gym teacher and set up at a card table in a German restaurant – had told her to buy and wear on her right index finger for power.

'What kind of power?' she had asked.

'The kind that's real,' he said. 'What you've got here,' he said, waving around her left hand, pointing at the thin silver and turquoise she was wearing, 'is squat.'

347

'I like a palm reader who dresses you,' she said later to Martin in the car on their way home. This was before the incident at the Spearson picnic, and things seemed not impossible then; she had wanted Martin to fall in love with her. 'A guy who looks like Mike Ditka, but who picks out jewellery for you.'

'A guy who tells you you're sensitive and that you will soon receive cash from someone wearing glasses. Where does he come up with this stuff?'

'You don't think I'm sensitive.'

'I mean the money and glasses thing,' he said. 'And that gloomy bit about how they'll think you're a goner, but you're going to come through and live to see the world go through a radical physical change.'

'That was gloomy,' she agreed. There was a lot of silence as they looked out at the night-lit highway lines, the fireflies hitting the windshield and smearing, all phosphorescent gold, as if the car were flying through stars. 'It must be hard,' she said, 'for someone like you to go out on a date with someone like me.'

'Why do you say that?' he'd asked.

She climbed up on the table, stripped of ornament and the power of ornament, and slipped between the flannel sheets. For a second, she felt numb and scared, naked in a strange room, more naked even than in a doctor's office, where you kept your jewellery on, like an odalisque. But it felt new to do this, to lead the body to this, the body with its dog's obedience, its dog's desire to please. She lay there waiting, watching the mobile moons turn slowly, half revolutions, while from the speakers beneath the table came a new sound, an electronic, synthesized version of Brahms's lullaby. An infant. She was to become an infant again. Perhaps she would become the Spearson boy. He had been a beautiful baby.

Ilke came in quietly, and appeared so suddenly behind Adrienne's head, it gave her a start.

'Move back toward me,' whispered Ilke. *Move back toward me*, and Adrienne shifted until she could feel the crown of her head grazing Ilke's belly. The cockatiel whooshed in and perched on a nearby chair.

'Are you a little tense?' she said. She pressed both her thumbs at the centre of Adrienne's forehead. Ilke's hands were strong, small, bony. Leathered claws. The harder she pressed, the better it felt to Adrienne, all of her difficult thoughts unknotting and traveling out, up into Ilke's thumbs.

'Breathe deeply,' said Ilke. 'You cannot breathe deeply without it relaxing you.'

Adrienne pushed her stomach in and out.

'You are from the Villa Hirschborn, aren't you?' Ilke's voice was a knowing smile.

'Ehuh.'

'I thought so,' said Ilke. 'People are very tense up there. Rigid as boards.' Ilke's hands moved down off Adrienne's forehead, along her eyebrows to her cheeks, which she squeezed repeatedly; in little circles, as if to break the weaker capillaries. She took hold of Adrienne's head and pulled. There was a dull cracking sound. Then she pressed her knuckles along Adrienne's neck. 'Do you know why?'

Adrienne grunted.

'It is because they are over-educated and can no longer converse with their own mothers. It makes them a little crazy. They have literally lost their mother tongue. So they come to me. I am their mother, and they don't have to speak at all.'

'Of course they *pay* you.'

'Of course.'

Adrienne suddenly fell into a long falling – of pleasure, of

349

surrender, of glazed-eyed dying, a piece of heat set free in a room. Ilke rubbed Adrienne's earlobes, knuckled her scalp like a hairdresser, pulled at her neck and fingers and arms, as if they were jammed things. Adrienne would become a baby, join all the babies, in heaven, where they lived.

Ilke began to massage sandalwood oil into Adrienne's arms, pressing down, polishing, ironing, looking, at a quick glimpse, like one of Degas's laundresses. Adrienne shut her eyes again and listened to the music, which had switched from synthetic lullabies to the contrapuntal sounds of a flute and a thunderstorm. With these hands upon her, she felt a little forgiven, and began to think generally of forgiveness, how much of it was required in life: to forgive everyone, yourself, the people you loved, and then wait to be forgiven by them. Where was all this forgiveness supposed to come from? Where was this great inexhaustible supply?

'Where are you?' whispered Ilke. 'You are somewhere very far.'

Adrienne wasn't sure. Where was she? In her own head, like a dream; in the bellows of her lungs. What was she? Perhaps a child. Perhaps a corpse. Perhaps a fern in the forest in the storm; a singing bird. The sheets were folded back. The hands were all over her now. Perhaps she was under the table with the music, or in a musty corner of her own hip. She felt Ilke rub oil into her chest, between her breasts, out along the ribs, and circularly on the abdomen. 'There is something stuck here,' Ilke said. 'Something not working.' Then she pulled the covers back up. 'Are you cold?' she asked, and though Adrienne didn't answer, Ilke brought another blanket, mysteriously heated, and laid it across Adrienne. 'There,' said Ilke. She lifted the blanket so that only Adrienne's feet were exposed. She rubbed oil into her soles, the toes; something squeezed out of Adrienne, like an

350

olive. She felt as if she would cry. She felt like the baby Jesus. The grown Jesus. *The poor will always be with us.* The dead Jesus. Cheese is the best. Cheese is the best.

At her desk in the outer room, Ilke wanted money. Thirty-five thousand lire. 'I can give it to you for thirty thousand, if you decide to come on a regular basis. Would you like to come on a regular basis?' asked Ilke.

Adrienne was fumbling with her wallet. She sat down in the wicker rocker near the desk. 'Yes,' she said. 'Of course.'

Ilke had put on reading glasses and now opened up her appointment book to survey the upcoming weeks. She flipped a page, then flipped it back. She looked out over her glasses at Adrienne. 'How often would you like to come?'

'Every day,' said Adrienne.

'*Every day?*'

Ilke's hoot worried Adrienne. 'Every *other* day?' Adrienne peeped hopefully. Perhaps the massage had bewitched her, ruined her. Perhaps she had fallen in love.

Ilke looked back at her book and shrugged. 'Every other day,' she repeated slowly, as a way of holding the conversation still while she checked her schedule. 'How about at two o'clock?'

'Monday, Wednesday, and Friday?'

'Perhaps we can occasionally arrange a Saturday.'

'Okay. Fine.' Adrienne placed the money on the desk and stood up. Ilke walked her to the door and thrust her hand out formally. Her face had changed from its earlier pinks to a strange and shiny orange.

'Thank you,' said Adrienne. She shook Ilke's hand, but then leaned forward and kissed her cheek; she would kiss the business out of this. 'Goodbye,' she said. She stepped gingerly down the stairs; she had not entirely returned to her body yet. She had to go slowly. She felt a little like she had just seen God, but also a little like she had just seen a hooker. Outside, she walked carefully back toward the villa, but first stopped at the gelato shop for a small dish of hazelnut ice cream. It was smooth, toasty, buttery, like a beautiful liqueur, and she thought how different it was from America, where so much of the ice cream now looked like babies had attacked it with their cookies.

'Well, Martin, it's been nice knowing you,' Adrienne said, smiling. She reached out to shake his hand with one of hers, and pat him on the back with the other. 'You've been a good sport. I hope there will be no hard feelings.'

'You've just come back from your massage,' he said a little numbly. 'How was it?'

'As you would say, "Relaxing". As I would say . . . well, I wouldn't say.'

Martin led her to the bed. 'Kiss and tell,' he said.

'I'll just kiss,' she said, kissing.

'I'll settle,' he said. But then she stopped, and went into the bathroom to shower for dinner.

At dinner, there was *zuppa alla paesana* and then *salsiccia alla griglia con spinaci*. For the first time since they'd arrived, she was seated near Martin, who was kitty-corner to her left. He was seated next to another economist and was speaking heatedly with him about a book on labour division and economic policy. 'But Wilkander ripped that theory off from Boyer!' Martin let his spoon splash violently into his *zuppa* before a waiter came and removed the bowl.

'Let us just say,' said the other man calmly, 'that it was a sort of homage.'

'If that's "homage",' said Martin, fidgeting with his fork,

'I'd like to perform a little "homage" on the Chase Manhattan Bank.'

'I think it was felt that there was sufficient looseness there to warrant further explication.'

'Right. And one's twin sibling is simply an explication of the text.'

'Why not?' The other economist smiled. He was calm, probably a supply-sider.

Poor Martin, thought Adrienne. Poor Keynesian Martin, poor Marxist Martin, perspiring and red. '*Left of Lenin?*' she had heard him exclaiming the other day to an agriculturalist. 'Left of *Lenin*? Left of the Lennon Sisters, you mean!' Poor godless, raised-an-atheist-in-Ohio Martin. 'On Christmas,' he'd said to her once, 'we used to go down to the Science Store and worship the Bunsen burners.'

She would have to find just the right blouse, just the right perfume, greet him on the chaise longue with a bare shoulder and a purring '*Hello, Mr Man.*' Take him down by the lake near the Sfondrata chapel and get him laid. Hire somebody. She turned to the scholar next to her, who had just arrived that morning.

'Did you have a good flight?' she asked. Her own small talk at dinner no longer shamed her.

'*Flight* is the word,' he said. 'I needed to flee my department, my bills, my ailing car. Come to a place that would take care of me.'

'This is it, I guess,' she said. 'Though they won't fix your car. Won't even discuss it, I've found.'

'I'm on a Guggenheim,' he said.

'How nice!' She thought of the museum in New York, and of a pair of earrings she had bought in the gift shop there but had never worn because they always looked broken, even though that was the way they were supposed to look.

'But I neglected to ask the foundation for enough money. I didn't realize what you could ask for. I didn't ask for the same amount everyone else did, and so I received substantially less.'

Adrienne was sympathetic. 'So instead of a regular Guggenheim, you got a little Guggenheim.'

'Yes,' he said.

'A Guggenheimy,' she said.

He smiled in a troubled sort of way. 'Right.'

'So now you have to live in Guggenheimy town.'

He stopped pushing at a sausage with his fork. 'Yes. I heard there would be wit here.'

She tried to make her lips curl, like his.

'Sorry,' he said. 'I was just kidding.'

'Jet lag,' she said.

'Yes.'

'Jetty-laggy.' She smiled at him. 'Baby talk. We love it.' She paused. 'Last week, of course, we weren't like this. You've arrived a little late.'

He was a beautiful baby. In the dark, there was thumping, like tom-toms, and a piccolo high above it. She couldn't look, because when she looked, it shocked her, another woman's hands all over her. She just kept her eyes closed, and concentrated on surrender, on the restful invalidity of it. Sometimes she concentrated on being where Ilke's hands were – at her feet, at the small of her back.

'Your parents are no longer living, are they?' Ilke said in the dark.

'No.'

'Did they die young?'

'Medium. They died medium. I was a menopausal, afterthought child.'

'Do you want to know what I feel in you?'

'All right.'

'I feel a great and deep gentleness. But I also feel that you have been dishonored.'

'Dishonored?' So Japanese. Adrienne liked the sound of it.

'Yes. You have a deeply held fear. Right here.' Ilke's hand went just under Adrienne's rib cage.

Adrienne breathed deeply, in and out. 'I killed a baby,' she whispered.

'Yes, we have all killed a baby – there is a baby in all of us. That is why people come to me, to be reunited with it.'

'No, I've killed a real one.'

Ilke was very quiet and then she said, 'You can do the side lying now. You can put this pillow under your head, this other one between your knees.' Adrienne rolled awkwardly onto her side. Finally, Ilke said, 'This country, its Pope, its church, makes murderers of women. You must not let it do that to you. Move back toward me. That's it.'

That's *not* it, thought Adrienne, in this temporary dissolve, seeing death and birth, seeing the beginning and then the end, how they were the same quiet black, same nothing ever after: everyone's life appeared in the world like a movie in a room. First dark, then light, then dark again. But it was all staggered, so that somewhere there was always light.

That's not it. That's not it, she thought. But thank you.

When she left that afternoon, seeking sugar in one of the shops, she moved slowly, blinded by the angle of the afternoon light but also believing she saw Martin coming toward her in the narrow street, approaching like the lumbering logger he sometimes seemed to be. Her squinted gaze, however, failed to catch his, and he veered suddenly left into a *calle*. By the time she reached the corner, he had disappeared entirely. How strange, she thought. She had felt close to something, to him, and then suddenly not. She climbed the path back up toward the villa, and went and knocked on the door of his studio, but he wasn't there.

'You smell good,' she greeted Martin. It was some time later and she had just returned to the room, to find him there. 'Did you just take a bath?'

'A little while ago,' he said.

She curled up to him, teasingly. 'Not a shower? A bath? Did you put some scented bath salts in it?'

'I took a very masculine bath,' said Martin.

She sniffed him again. 'What scent did you use?'

'A manly scent,' he said. 'Rock. I took a rock-scented bath.'

'Did you take a bubble bath?' She cocked her head to one side.

He smiled. 'Yes, but I, uh, made my own bubbles.'

'You did?' She squeezed his bicep.

'Yeah. I hammered the water with my fist.'

She walked over to the cassette player and put a cassette in. She looked over at Martin, who looked suddenly un-happy. 'This music annoys you, doesn't it?'

Martin squirmed. 'It's just – why can't he sing any one song all the way through?'

She thought about this. 'Because he's Mr Medleyhead?'

'You didn't bring anything else?'

'No.'

She went back and sat next to Martin, in silence, smelling the scent of him, as if it were odd.

For dinner there was *vitello alla salvia*, baby peas, and a pasta made with caviar. 'Nipping it in the bud.' Adrienne sighed. 'An early frost.' A fat elderly man, arriving late, pulled his chair out onto her foot, then sat down on it. She shrieked.

'Oh, dear, I'm sorry,' said the man, lifting himself up as best he could.

'It's okay,' said Adrienne. 'I'm sure it's okay.'

But the next morning, at exercises, Adrienne studied her foot closely during the leg lifts. The big toe was swollen and blue, and the nail had been loosened and set back at an odd and unhinged angle. 'You're going to lose your toenail,' said Kate.

'Great,' said Adrienne.

'That happened to me once, during my first marriage. My husband dropped a dictionary on my foot. One of those subconscious things. Rage as very large book.'

'You were married before?'

'Oh, yes.' She sighed. 'I had one of those rehearsal marriages, you know, where you're a feminist and train a guy, and then some *other* feminist comes along and gets the guy.'

'I don't know.' Adrienne scowled. 'I think there's something wrong with the words *feminist* and *gets the guy* being in the same sentence.'

'Yes, well –'

'Were you upset?'

'Of course. But then, I'd been doing everything. I'd insisted on separate finances, on being totally self-supporting. I was working. I was doing the child care. I paid for the house; I cooked; I cleaned. I found myself shouting, "This is feminism? Thank you, Gloria and Betty!"'

'But now you're with someone else.'

'Pretaught. Self-cleaning. Batteries included.'

'Someone else trained him, and you stole him.'

Kate smiled. 'Of course. What, am I crazy?'

'What happened to the toe?'

'The nail came off. And the one that grew back was wavy and dark and used to scare the children.'

'Oh,' said Adrienne.

'Why would someone publish six books on Chaucer?' Adrienne was watching Martin dress. She was also smoking a cigarette. One of the strange things about the villa was that the smokers had all quit smoking, and the non-smokers had taken it up. People were getting in touch with their alternative selves. Bequeathed cigarettes abounded. Cartons were appearing outside people's doors.

'You have to understand academic publishing,' said Martin. 'No one reads these books. Everyone just agrees to publish everyone else's. It's one big circle jerk. It's a giant economic agreement. When you think about it, it probably violates the Sherman Act.'

'A circle jerk?' she said uncertainly. The cigarette was making her dizzy.

'Yeah,' said Martin, reknotting his tie.

'But six books on Chaucer? Why not, say, a Cat Stevens book?'

'Don't look at me,' he said. 'I'm in the circle.'

She sighed. 'Then I shall sing to you. Mood music.' She made up a romantic Asian-sounding tune, and danced around the room with her cigarette, in a floating, wing-limbed way. 'This is my Hopi dance,' she said. 'So full of hope.'

Then it was time to go to dinner.

The cockatiel now seemed used to Adrienne and would whistle twice, then fly into the back room, perch quickly on the picture frame, and wait with her for Ilke. Adrienne closed her eyes and breathed deeply, the flannel sheet pulled up under her arms, tightly, like a sarong.

Ilke's face appeared overhead in the dark, as if she were a mother just checking, peering into a crib. 'How are you today?'

Adrienne opened her eyes, to see that Ilke was wearing a T-shirt that said SAY A PRAYER. PET A ROCK.

Say a prayer. 'Good,' said Adrienne. 'I'm good.' *Pet a rock.*

Ilke ran her fingers through Adrienne's hair, humming faintly.

'What is this music today?' Adrienne asked. Like Martin, she, too, had grown weary of the Mandy Patinkin tapes, all that unshackled exuberance.

'Crickets and elk,' Ilke whispered.

'Crickets and elk.'

'Crickets and elk and a little harp.'

Ilke began to move around the table, pulling on Adrienne's limbs and pressing deep into her tendons. 'I'm doing choreographed massage today,' Ilke said. 'That's why I'm wearing this dress.'

Adrienne hadn't noticed the dress. Instead, with the lights now low, except for the illuminated clouds on the side wall, she felt herself sinking into the pools of death deep in her bones, the dark wells of loneliness, failure, blame. 'You may turn over now,' she heard Ilke say. And she struggled a little in the flannel sheets to do so, twisting in them, until Ilke helped her, as if she were a nurse and Adrienne someone old and sick – a stroke victim, that's what she was. She had become a stroke victim. Then lowering her face into the toweled cheek plates the table brace offered up to her ('the cradle', Ilke called it), Adrienne began quietly to cry, the deep touching of her body melting her down to some equation of animal sadness, shoe leather, and brine. She began to understand why people would want to live in these dusky nether zones, the meltdown brought on by sleep or drink or this. It seemed truer, more familiar to the soul than was the busy, complicated flash that was normal life. Ilke's arms leaned into her, her breasts brushing softly against Adrienne's head, which now felt connected to the rest of her only by filaments and strands. The body suddenly seemed a tumour on the brain, a mere means of conveyance, a wagon; the mind's go-kart now taken apart, laid in pieces on this table. 'You have a knot here in your trapezius,' Ilke said, kneading Adrienne's shoulder. 'I can feel the belly of the knot right here,' she added, pressing hard, bruising her shoulder a little, and then easing up. 'Let go,' she said. 'Let go all the way, of everything.'

'I might die,' said Adrienne. Something surged in the music and she missed what Ilke said in reply, though it sounded a little like 'Changes are good.' Though perhaps it was 'Chances aren't good.' Ilke pulled Adrienne's toes, milking even the injured one, with its loose nail and leaky underskin, and then she left Adrienne there in the dark, in the music, though Adrienne felt it was she who was leaving, like a person dying, like a train pulling away. She felt the rage loosened from her back, floating aimlessly around in her, the rage that did not know at what or whom to rage, though it continued to rage.

She awoke to Ilke's rocking her gently. 'Adrienne, get up. I have another client soon.'

'I must have fallen asleep,' said Adrienne. 'I'm sorry.'

She got up slowly, got dressed, and went out into the outer room; the cockatiel whooshed out with her, grazing her head.

'I feel like I've just been strafed,' she said, clutching her hair.

Ilke frowned.

'Your bird. I mean by your bird. In *there*' – she pointed back toward the massage room – '*that* was great.' She

360

reached into her purse to pay. Ilke had moved the wicker chair to the other side of the room, so that there was no longer any place to sit down or linger. 'You want lire or dollars?' she asked, and was a little taken aback when Ilke said rather firmly, 'I'd prefer lire.'

Ilke was bored with her. That was it. Adrienne was having a religious experience, but Ilke – Ilke was just being social. Adrienne held out the money and Ilke plucked it from her hand, then opened the outside door and leaned to give Adrienne the rushed bum's kiss – left, right – and then closed the door behind her.

Adrienne was in a fog, her legs noodly, her eyes unaccustomed to the light. Outside, in front of the *farmacìa*, if she wasn't careful, she was going to get hit by a car. How could Ilke just send people out into the busy street like that, all loose and dazed? Adrienne's body felt doughy, muddy. This was good, she supposed. Decomposition. She stepped slowly, carefully, her Martha Graham step, along the narrow walk between the street and the stores. And when she turned the corner to head back up toward the path to the Villa Hirschborn, there stood Martin, her husband, rounding a corner and heading her way.

'Hi!' she said, so pleased suddenly to meet him like this, away from what she now referred to as 'the compound'. 'Are you going to the *farmacìa?*' she asked.

'Uh, yes,' said Martin. He leaned to kiss her cheek.

'Want some company?'

He looked a little blank, as if he needed to be alone. Perhaps he was going to buy condoms.

'Oh, never mind,' she said gaily. 'I'll see you later, up at the compound, before dinner.'

'Great,' he said, and took her hand, took two steps away, and then let her hand go, gently, midair.

She walked away, toward a small park – il Giardino Leonardo – out past the station for the vaporetti. Near a particularly exuberant rhododendron sat a short, dark woman with a bright turquoise bandanna knotted around her neck. She had set up a table with a sign: CHIROMANTE: TAROT E FACCIA. Adrienne sat down opposite her in the empty chair. 'Americano,' she said.

'I do faces, palms, or cards,' the woman with the blue scarf said.

Adrienne looked at her own hands. She didn't want to have her face read. She lived like that already. It happened all the time at the villa, people trying to read your face – freezing your brain with stony looks and remarks made malicious with obscurity, so that you couldn't read *their* face, while they were busy reading yours. It all made her feel creepy, like a lonely head on a poster somewhere.

'The cards are the best,' said the woman. 'Ten thousand lire.'

'Okay,' said Adrienne. She was still looking at the netting of her open hands, the dried riverbed of life just sitting there. 'The cards.'

The woman swept up the cards, and dealt half of them out, every which way in a kind of swastika. Then, without glancing at them, she leaned forward boldly and said to Adrienne, 'You are sexually unsatisfied. Am I right?'

'Is that what the cards say?'

'In a general way. You have to take the whole deck and interpret.'

'What does this card say?' asked Adrienne, pointing to one with some naked corpses leaping from coffins.

'Any one card doesn't say anything. It's the whole feeling of them.' She quickly dealt out the remainder of the deck on top of the other cards. 'You are looking for a guide, some kind of guide, because the man you are with does not make you happy. Am I right?'

'Maybe,' said Adrienne, who was already reaching for her purse to pay the ten thousand lire so that she could leave.

'I am right,' said the woman, taking the money and handing Adrienne a small smudged business card. 'Stop by tomorrow. Come to my shop. I have a powder.'

Adrienne wandered back out of the park, past a group of tourists climbing out of a bus, back toward the Villa Hirschborn – through the gate, which she opened with her key, and up the long stone staircase to the top of the promontory. Instead of going back to the villa, she headed out through the woods toward her studio, toward the dead tufts of spiders she had memorialized in her grief. She decided to take a different path, not the one toward the studio, but one that led farther up the hill, a steeper grade, toward an open meadow at the top, with a small Roman ruin at its edge – a corner of the hill's original fortress still stood there. But in the middle of the meadow, something came over her – a balmy wind, or the heat from the uphill hike, and she took off all her clothes, lay down in the grass, and stared around at the dusky sky. To either side of her, the spokes of tree branches crisscrossed upward in a kind of cat's cradle. More directly overhead she studied the silver speck of a jet, the metallic head of its white stream like the tip of a thermometer. There were a hundred people inside this head of a pin, thought Adrienne. Or was it, perhaps, just the head of a pin? When was something truly small, and when was it a matter of distance? The branches of the trees seemed to encroach inward and rotate a little to the left, a little to the right, like something mechanical, and as she began to drift off, she saw the beautiful Spearson baby, cooing in a clown hat; she saw Martin furiously swimming in a pool;

363

she saw the strewn beads of her own fertility, all the eggs within her, leap away like a box of tapioca off a cliff. It seemed to her that everything she had ever needed to know in her life she had known at one time or another, but she just hadn't known all those things at once, at the same time, at a single moment. They were scattered through and she had had to leave and forget one in order to get to another. A shadow fell across her, inside her, and she could feel herself retreat to that place in her bones where death was and you greeted it like an acquaintance in a room; you said hello and were then ready for whatever was next – which might be a guide, the guide that might be sent to you, the guide to lead you back out into your life again.

Someone was shaking her gently. She flickered slightly awake, to see the pale, ethereal face of a strange older woman peering down at her as if Adrienne were something odd in the bottom of a teacup. The woman was dressed all in white – white shorts, white cardigan, white scarf around her head. The guide.

'Are you . . . the *guide*?' whispered Adrienne.

'Yes, my dear,' the woman said in a faintly English voice that sounded like the Good Witch of the North.

'You are?' Adrienne asked.

'Yes,' said the woman. 'And I've brought the group up here to view the old fort, but I was a little worried that you might not like all of us traipsing past here while you were, well – are you all right?'

Adrienne was more awake now and sat up, to see at the end of the meadow the group of tourists she'd previously seen below in the town, getting off the bus.

'Yes, thank you,' mumbled Adrienne. She lay back down to think about this, hiding herself in the walls of grass, like a child hoping to trick the facts. 'Oh my God,' she finally said, and groped about to her left to find her clothes and clutch them, panicked, to her belly. She breathed deeply, then put them on, lying as flat to the ground as she could, hard to glimpse, a snake getting back inside its skin, a change, perhaps, of reptilian heart. Then she stood, zipped her pants, secured her belt buckle, and waved, squaring her shoulders and walking bravely past the bus and the tourists, who, though they tried not to stare at her, did stare.

By this time, everyone at the villa was privately doing imitations of everyone else. 'Martin, you should announce who you're doing before you do it,' said Adrienne, dressing for dinner. 'I can't really tell.'

'Cube-steak Yuppies!' Martin ranted at the ceiling. 'Legends in their own mind! Rumours in their own room!'

'Yourself. You're doing yourself.' She straightened his collar and tried to be wifely.

For dinner, there was *cioppino* and *insalata mista* and *pesce con pignoli*, a thin piece of fish like a leaf. From everywhere around the dining room, scraps of dialogue – rhetorical barbed wire, indignant and arcane – floated over toward her. 'As an aesthetician, you can't not be interested in the sublime!' Or 'Why, that's the most facile thing I've ever heard!' Or 'Good grief, tell him about the Peasants' Revolt, would you?' But no one spoke to her directly. She had no subject, not really, not one she liked, except perhaps movies and movie stars. Martin was at a far table, his back toward her, listening to the monk man. At times like these, she thought, it was probably a good idea to carry a small hand puppet.

She made her fingers flap in her lap.

Finally, one of the people next to her turned and introduced himself. His face was poppy-seeded with whiskers, and he seemed to be looking down, watching his own mouth move. When she asked him how he liked it here so far, she received a fairly brief history of the Ottoman Empire. She nodded and smiled, and at the end, he rubbed his dark beard, looked at her compassionately, and said, 'We are not good advertisements for this life. Are we?'

'There *are* a lot of dingdongs here,' she admitted. He looked a little hurt, so she added, 'But I like that about a place. I do.'

When after dinner she went for an evening walk with Martin, she tried to strike up a conversation about celebrities and movie stars. 'I keep thinking about Princess Caroline's husband being killed,' she said.

Martin was silent.

'That poor family,' said Adrienne. 'There's been so much tragedy.'

Martin glared at her. 'Yes,' he said facetiously. 'That poor, cursed family. I keep thinking, What can I do to help? What can I do? And I think and I think, and I think so much, I'm helpless. I throw up my hands and end up doing nothing. I'm helpless!' He began to walk faster, ahead of her, down into the village. Adrienne began to run to keep up. She felt insane. Marriage, she thought, it's an institution all right.

Near the main piazza, under a streetlamp, the woman had set up her table again under the CHIROMANTE: TAROT E FACCIA sign. When she saw Adrienne, she called out, 'Give me your birthday, signora, and your husband's birthday, and I will do your charts to tell you whether the two of you are compatible! Or –' She paused to study Martin sceptically as he rushed past. 'Or I can just tell you right now.'

'Have you been to this woman before?' Martin asked, slowing down. Adrienne grabbed his arm and started to lead him away.

'I needed a change of scenery.'

Now he stopped. 'Well,' he said sympathetically, calmer after some exercise, 'who could blame you.' Adrienne took his hand, feeling a grateful, marital love – alone, in Italy, at night, in May. Was there any love that wasn't at bottom a grateful one? The moonlight glittered off the lake like electric fish, like a school of ice.

'What are you doing?' Adrienne asked Ilke the next afternoon. The lamps were particularly low, though there was a spotlight directed onto a picture of Ilke's mother, which she had placed on an end table, for the month, in honour of Mother's Day. The mother looked ghostly, like a sacrifice. What if Ilke were truly a witch? What if fluids and hairs and nails were being collected as offerings in memory of her mother?

'I'm fluffing your aura,' she said. 'It is very dark today, burned down to a shadowy rim.' She was manipulating Adrienne's toes, and Adrienne suddenly had a horror-movie vision of Ilke with jars of collected toe juice in a closet for Satan, who, it would be revealed, *was* Ilke's mother. Perhaps Ilke would lean over suddenly and bite Adrienne's shoulder, drink her blood. How could Adrienne control these thoughts? She felt her aura fluff like the fur of a screeching cat. She imagined herself, for the first time, never coming here again. *Goodbye. Farewell.* It would be a brief affair, a little nothing; a chat on the porch at a party.

Fortunately, there were other things to keep Adrienne busy.

She had begun spray-painting the spiders, and the results were interesting. She could see herself explaining to a dealer back home that the work represented the spider web of solitude – a vibration at the periphery reverberates inward (experiential, deafening) and the spider rushes out from the centre to devour the gonger and the gong. Gone. She could see the dealer taking her phone number and writing it down on an extremely loose scrap of paper.

And there was the occasional after-dinner singsong, scholars and spouses gathered around the piano in various states of inebriation and forgetfulness. 'Okay, that may be how you learned it, Harold, but that's *not* how it goes.'

There was also the Asparagus Festival, which, at Carlo's suggestion, she and Kate Spalding, in one of her T-shirts – *all right, already with the T-shirts, Kate* – decided to attend. They took a hydrofoil across the lake and climbed a steep road up toward a church square. The road was long and tiring and Adrienne began to refer to it as the 'Asparagus Death Walk'.

'Maybe there isn't really a festival,' she suggested, gasping for breath, but Kate kept walking, ahead of her.

'Go for the burn!' said Kate, who liked exercise too much.

Adrienne sighed. Up until last year, she had always thought people were saying 'Go for the *bird*.' Now off in the trees was the ratchety cheep of some, along with the competing hourly chimes of two churches, followed later by the single off-tone of the half hour. When she and Kate finally reached the Asparagus Festival, it turned out to be only a little ceremony where a few people bid very high prices for clutches of asparagus described as '*bello, bello*', the proceeds from which went to the local church.

'I used to grow asparagus,' said Kate on their walk back down. They were taking a different route this time, and the lake and its ocher villages spread out before them, peaceful and far away. Along the road, wildflowers grew in a pallet of pastels, like soaps.

'I could never grow asparagus,' said Adrienne. As a child,

her favourite food had been 'asparagus with holiday sauce'. 'I did grow a carrot once, though. But it was so small, I just put it in a scrapbook.'

'Are you still seeing Ilke?'

'This week, at any rate. How about you?'

'She's booked solid. I couldn't get another appointment. All the scholars, you know, are paying her regular visits.'

'Really?'

'Oh, yes,' said Kate very knowingly. 'They're tense as dimes.' Already Adrienne could smell the fumes of the Fiats and the ferries and delivery vans, the Asparagus Festival far away.

'Tense as dimes?'

Back at the villa, Adrienne waited for Martin, and when he came in, smelling of sandalwood, all the little deaths in her bones told her this: he was seeing the masseuse.

She sniffed the sweet parabola of his neck and stepped back. 'I want to know how long you've been getting massages. Don't lie to me,' she said slowly, her voice hard as a spike. Anxiety shrank his face: his mouth caved in, his eyes grew beady and scared.

'What makes you think I've been getting –' he started to say. 'Well, just once or twice.'

She leapt away from him and began pacing furiously about the room, touching the furniture, not looking at him. 'How could you?' she asked. 'You know what my going there has meant to me! How could you not tell me?' She picked up a book on the dressing table – *Industrial Relations Systems* – and slammed it back down. 'How could you horn in on this experience? How could you be so furtive and untruthful?'

'I am terribly sorry,' he said.

'Yeah, well, so am I,' said Adrienne. 'And when we get home, I want a divorce.' She could see it now, the empty apartment, the bad eggplant parmigiana, all the Halloweens she would answer the doorbell, a boozy divorcée frightening the little children with too much enthusiasm for their costumes. 'I feel so fucking *dishonoured*!' Nothing around her seemed able to hold steady; nothing held.

Martin was silent and she was silent and then he began to speak, in a beseeching way, there it was the beseech again, rumbling at the edge of her life like a truck. 'We are both so lonely here,' he said. 'But I have only been waiting for you. That is all I have done for the last eight months. To try not to let things intrude, to let you take your time, to make sure you ate something, to buy the goddamn Spearsons a new picnic bench, to bring you to a place where anything at all might happen, where you might even leave me, but at least come back into life at last –'

'You did?'

'Did what?'

'You bought the Spearsons a new *picnic bench*?'

'Yes, I did.'

She thought about this. 'Didn't they think you were being hostile?'

'Oh . . . I think, yes, they probably thought it was hostile.'

And the more Adrienne thought about it, about the poor bereaved Spearsons, and about Martin and all the ways he tried to show her he was on her side, whatever that meant, how it was both the hope and shame of him that he was always doing his best, the more she felt foolish, deprived of reasons. Her rage flapped awkwardly away like a duck. She felt as she had when her cold, fierce parents had at last grown sick and old, stick-boned and saggy, protected by infirmity the way cuteness protected a baby, or should, it should protect a baby, and she had been left with her rage – vestigial girlhood rage – inappropriate and intact. She would hug her parents goodbye, the gentle, emptied sacks of them, and think *Where did you go?*

Time, Adrienne thought. What a racket.

Martin had suddenly begun to cry. He sat at the bed's edge and curled inward, his soft, furry face in his great hard hands, his head falling downward into the bright plaid of his shirt.

She felt dizzy and turned away, toward the window. A fog had drifted in, and in the evening light the sky and the lake seemed a singular blue, like a Monet. 'I've never seen you cry,' she said.

'Well, I cry,' he said. 'I can even cry at the sports page if the games are too close. Look at me, Adrienne. You never really look at me.'

But she could only continue to stare out the window, touching her fingers to the shutters and frame. She felt far away, as if she were back home, walking through the neighbourhood at dinner-time: when the cats sounded like babies and the babies sounded like birds, and the fathers were home from work, their children in their arms gumming the language, air shaping their flowery throats into a park of singing. Through the windows wafted the smell of cooking food.

'We are with each other now,' Martin was saying. 'And in the different ways it means, we must try to make a life.'

Out over the Sfondrata chapel tower, where the fog had broken, she thought she saw a single star, like the distant nose of a jet; there were people in the clayey clouds. She turned, and for a moment it seemed they were all there in Martin's eyes, all the absolving dead in residence in his face, the angel of the dead baby shining like a blazing creature, and she went to him, to protect and encircle him, seeking the heart's best trick, *oh, terrific heart*. 'Please, forgive me,' she said.

And he whispered, 'Of course. It is the only thing. Of course.'

ALI SMITH

MAY

I TELL YOU. I fell in love with a tree. I couldn't not. It was in blossom.

It was a day like all the other days and I was on my way to work, walking the same way as usual between our house and the town. I wasn't even very far from home, just round the corner. I was looking at the pavement and wondering as I walked whether the local council paid someone money to go walking around looking at the ground all day for places where people might trip. What would a job like that be advertised as in the paper, under what title? Inspector of Pavements and Roads. Kerb Auditor. Local Walkways Erosion Consultant. I wondered what qualifications you would need to be one. On a TV quiz show the host would say, or at a party a smiling stranger would ask, and what do you do? and whoever it was would reply, actually I'm an Asphalt Observance Manager, it's very good money, takes a great deal of expertise, a job for life with excellent career prospects.

Or maybe the council didn't do this job any more. Probably there was a privatized company who sent people out to check on the roads and then report back the findings to a relevant council committee. That was more likely. I walked along like that, I remember, noting to myself in my head all the places I would report which needed sorting, until the moment the ground ahead of me wasn't there any more. It had disappeared. At my feet the pavement was covered with what looked like blown silk. It was petals. The petals were a beautiful white. I glanced up to see where they'd come from, and saw where they'd come from.

A woman came out of a house. She told me to get out of her garden. She asked was I on drugs. I explained I wasn't. She said she'd call the police if I wasn't gone the next time she looked out of her window and she went back inside the house, slamming her door. I hadn't even realized I was in someone's garden, never mind that I'd been there for a long enough time for it to be alarming to anybody. I left her garden; I stood by the gate and looked at the tree from the pavement outside it instead. She called the police anyway; a woman and a man came in a patrol car. They were polite but firm. They talked about trespassing and loitering, took my name and address and gave me a warning and a lift home. They waited to see that I did have a key for our house, that I wasn't just making it up; they waited in their car until I'd unlocked the door and gone inside and shut it behind me; they sat outside the house not moving, with their engine going, for about ten minutes before I heard them rev up and drive away.

I had had no idea that staring up at a tree for more than the allotted proper amount of time could be considered wrong. When the police car stopped outside our house and I tried to get out, I couldn't – I had never been in a police car before and there are no handles on the insides of the doors in the back – you can't get out unless someone lets you out. I thought at first I wasn't able to find the handle because of what had happened to my eyes. They were full of white. All I could see was white. The thing with the woman and the police had taken place to me through a gauze of dazed white with everyone and everything like radio-voice ghosts, a drama happening to someone else somewhere at the back of me. Even while I was standing in the hall listening for them to drive away I still couldn't see anything except through a kind of shifting, folding, blazing white; and after they'd gone, after quite a while of sitting on the carpet feeling the surprising hugeness of the little bumps and shrugs of its material under my hands, I could only just make out, through the white, the blurs which meant the edges of the pictures on our walls, the pile of junk mail on the hall table and the black curl of the flex of the phone on the floor beside me.

I thought about phoning you. Then I thought about the tree. It was the most beautiful tree I had ever seen. It was the most beautiful thing I have ever seen. Its blossom was high summer blossom, not the cold early spring blossom of so many trees and bushes that comes in March and means more snow and cold. This was blue-sky white, heat-haze white, the white of the sheets that you bring in from the line in the garden dry after hardly any time because the air is so warm. It was the white of sun, the white that's behind all the colours there are, it was open-mouthed white on open-mouthed white, swathes of sweet-smelling outheld white lifting and falling and nodding, saying the one word yes over and over, white spilling over itself. It was a white that longed for bees, that wanted you inside it, dusted, pollen-smudged; it was all the more beautiful for being so brief, so on the point of gone, about to be nudged off by the wind and the coming leaves. It was the white before green, and the green of this tree, I knew, would be even more beautiful than the white; I knew that if I were to see it in leaf I would smell and hear nothing but green. My whole head – never mind just my eyes – all my senses, my whole self from head to foot, would fill and change with the chlorophyll of it. I was changed already. Look at me. I knew, as I sat there blinking absurdly in the hall, trying to simply look, holding my hand up in front of my eyes and watching it moving as if it belonged to someone else, that I would never again in my whole life see or feel or taste anything as beautiful as the tree I'd finally seen.

I got to my feet by leaning against the wall. I fumbled through thin air across to the stairs and reached out for the banister. I got to the top, crawled from the landing into our bedroom and made myself lie down on the bed and shut my eyes, but the white was still there, even behind the shut lids. It pulsed like a blood-beat; dimmer and lighter, lighter and dimmer. How many times had I passed that tree already in my life, just walked past it and not seen it? I must have walked down that street a thousand times, more than a thousand. How could I not have seen it? How many other things had I missed? How many other loves? It didn't matter. Nothing else mattered any more. The buds were like the pointed hooves of a herd of tiny deer. The blossom was like – no, it was like nothing but blossom. The leaves, when they came, would be like nothing but leaves. I had never seen a tree more like a tree. It was a relief. I thought of the roots and the trunk. I thrilled to the very idea that the roots and the trunk sent water up through the branches to the buds or blossom or leaves and then when it rained water came back through the leaves to be distributed round the tree again. It was so clever. I breathed because of it. I blessed the bark that protected the spine and the sap of the tree. I thought of its slender grooves. I imagined the fingering of them. I thought of inside, the rings going endlessly round, one for every year of its life and all its different seasons, and I burst into tears like a teenager. I lay on my back in the bed and cried, laughing, like I was seventeen again. It was me who was like something other than myself. I should have been at work, and instead I was lying in bed, hugging a pillow, with my heart, or my soul, or my mind or my lungs or whatever it was that was making me feel like this, high and light; whatever it was had snapped its string and blown away and now there it was above me, out of my reach, caught in the branches at the top of a tree.

I fell asleep. I dreamed of trees. In my dream I had climbed to a room which was also an orchard; it was at the very top of a massive old house whose downstairs was dilapidated and peeling and whose upstairs was all trees. I had climbed the broken dangerous stairs past all the other floors and got to the door of the room; the trees in it were waiting for me, small and unmoving under the roof. When I woke up I could see a lot more clearly. I washed my face in the bathroom, straightened my clothes. I looked all right. I went down to the kitchen and rooted through the cupboard under the sink until I found your father's old binoculars in their leather case. I couldn't make it out from the bathroom window or from either of the back bedroom windows but from up in the loft through the small window, if I leaned out at an angle so the eaves weren't in the way, I could easily see the white of the crown of it shimmering between the houses. If I leaned right out I could see almost the whole of it. But it was tricky to lean out at the same time as balancing myself between the separate roof struts so I fetched the old board we'd used under the mattress in the first bed from the back of the shed, sawed it into two pieces so I could get it through the loft hatch, then went back down to the shed, found the hammer and some nails and nailed the pieces of board back together up in the loft.

Birds visited the tree. They would fly in, settle for a moment, sometimes for as long as a minute, and they would fly off again. They came in ones and twos, a flutter of dark in the white. Or they would disappear into the blossom. Insects, which are excellent food for birds, tend to live on the trunks and the branches of trees. Ants can use trees as the ideal landscape for ant-farms, where they breed and corral and fatten up insects like aphids and use them for milk. (I found these things out later that evening on the internet.) Traffic drove unnoticing past the tree. People passed back and fore behind it. Mothers went past it to fetch children from school, brought them home from school past it the other way. People came home from work all round it. The sun moved round it in the sky. Its branches lifted and fell in the light wind. Petals spun off it and settled on a car or a lawn or fell maddeningly out of range where I couldn't see them land. Time flew. It really did. I must have watched for hours, all afternoon, until you were suddenly home from work yourself and shouting at me for being up in the loft. I came down, went online and typed in the word *tree*. There was a lot of stuff. I came off when you called me for supper, then went back on again after supper and came off again when you told me that if I didn't come to bed immediately so you could get some sleep then you would seriously consider leaving me.

I woke up in the middle of the night furious at that woman who thought she owned the tree. I sat straight up in the bed. I couldn't believe how angry I was. How could someone think they had ownership of something as unownable as a tree? Just because it was in her garden didn't mean it was hers. How could it be her tree? It was so clearly my tree.

I decided I would do something; I would go round now in the dark and anonymously throw stones at her house, break a window or two then run away. That would show her what she didn't own. That would serve her right. It was quarter to two on the alarm. You were asleep; you turned and mumbled something in your sleep. I got out carefully so as not to disturb you and took my clothes to the bathroom so my putting them on wouldn't wake you.

It was raining quite heavily when I went out. I scouted about in our back garden under our trees for some good-sized stones to throw. (It wasn't that our own trees were any less important than the tree I'd seen; they were nice and fine and everything; it was simply that they weren't it.) I found some smooth beach stones we'd brought back from somewhere and put them in my jacket pocket and I went out the back way so you wouldn't hear anything at the front. On my way round to the woman's house there was a skip at the side of the road; someone was putting in a driveway, digging up a front porch. There were lots of pieces of brick and half-brick in the skip and a lot of smashed-up thrown-away paving slab. Nobody saw me. There was nobody at all on the street, on any of the streets, and only the very occasional light in a window.

When I got to the woman's house it was completely in darkness. I was soaked from the rain and there were the petals plastered wet all over the pavement outside her garden gate. I tucked my piece of slab under my arm, soundlessly opened the gate. I could have been a perfect burglar. I crossed her lawn soundlessly and I stood under the tree.

The rain was knocking the petals off; they dropped, water-weighted and skimpy, into a circle of white on the dark of the grass round the edge of the dripping tree. The loaded branches magnified the noise; the rain was a steady hum above me through which I could hear the individual raindrops colliding with the individual flowers. I had my breath back now. I sat down on the wet grass by the roots; petals were all over my boots and when I ran my hand through my hair petals stuck to my fingers. I arranged my stones and half-bricks and my slab in a neat line, ready in case I needed them. Petals stuck to them too. I peeled a couple off. They were like something after a wedding. I was shivering now, though it wasn't cold. It was humid. It was lovely. I leaned back against its trunk, felt the ridges of it press through my jacket into my back and watched the blossom shredding as the rain brought it down.

You sit opposite me at the table in the kitchen and tell me you've fallen in love. When I ask you to tell me about who-ever it is, you look at me, reproachful.

Not with *someone*, you say.

Then you tell me you're in love with a tree.

You don't look at all well. You are pale. I think maybe you have a fever or are incubating a cold. You toy with the matting under the toaster. I pretend calm. I don't look angry or upset at all. I scan the line of old crumbs beneath the matting, still there from god knows how many of our break-fasts. I think to myself that you must be lying for a good reason because you never usually lie, it's very unlike you to. But then recently, it's true, you have been very unlike your-self. You have been defiant-looking, worried-looking and clear-faced as a child by turns; you have been sneaking out of bed and leaving the house as soon as you think I'm asleep, and you keep telling me odd facts about seed dispersal and reforestation. Last night you told me how it takes the energy of fifty leaves for a tree to make one apple, how one tree can produce millions of leaves, how there are two kinds of wood in the trunk of a tree, heartwood and sapwood, and that heartwood is where the tree packs away its waste products, and how trees in woods or groves that get less sunlight because they grow beneath other trees are called under-story trees.

I fell in love with a tree. I couldn't not. I am perfectly within my right to be angry. Instead, I keep things smooth. There's a way to do this. I try to think of the right thing to say.

Like in the myth? I say.

It's not a myth, you say. What myth? It's really real.

Okay, I say. I say it soothingly. I nod.

Do you believe me? you say.

I do, I say. I sound as if I mean it.

It takes a little while before I do actually believe that it's all about a tree and of course, when I do allow myself to, I'm relieved. More, I'm delighted. All these years we've been together and my only real rival in all this time doesn't even have genitals. I go around for quite a while smiling at my good luck. A tree, for goodness' sake, I laugh to myself as I pay for a bag of apples in the supermarket or pull the stick out of a cherry, flick the stick away, toss the cherry in the air and catch it in my mouth, pleased with myself, hoping someone saw.

I am such an innocent. I have no idea.

This is what it takes to make me believe it. I come home from work a couple of days later and find you gouging up the laminate in the middle of the front room with a hammer and a screwdriver. The laminate cost us a fortune to put down. We both know it did. I sit on the couch. I put my head in my hands. You look up brightly. Then you see my face.

I just want to see what's underneath, you say.

Concrete, I say. Remember when we moved in and before there was a floor there was the concrete, and it was horrible, and that's why we put the flooring down?

Yes, but I wanted to know what was under the concrete, you say. I needed to check.

And how are you going to get through the concrete? I say. You'll never do it with a screwdriver.

I'm going to get a drill from Homebase, you say. We need a drill anyway.

You sit beside me on the couch and you tell me you are planning to move the tree into our house.

You can't keep a tree in a house, I say.

Yes, you can, you say. I've looked into it. All you have to do is make sure that you give it enough water and that bees can pollinate it. We would need to keep some bees as well. Would that be okay?

What about light? I say. Trees need light. And what about its roots? That's why people cut trees down, because the roots of them get under the foundations of houses and are dangerous and pull them up. It's crazy to actually go out of your way to pull up the foundations of the house you're living in. No?

You scowl beside me.

And what kind of a tree is it? I ask.

Don't what kind of tree me, you say. I've told you, it's irrelevant.

I haven't actually been permitted to see this famous tree yet; you are keeping it a secret, close to your heart. I know it's situated somewhere over the back since that's the way the loft window faces and you are spending all the daylight hours that you're home in the loft. I know it's just come into leaf and that before, when you first saw it, it was blossoming, all that stuff about it being white, I've heard it several times now, how you were going to phone me but you couldn't see anything but it, etc. Every night in bed before I pretend to go to sleep it's been you telling me more and more things about trees as if desperate to convince me; on the first night I asked you what kind it was and you went into a huff (probably, I thought myself, because in your subterfuge, your attempt to screen your affair or whatever it is from me, you'd simply forgotten to pick a kind and I'd caught you out); because what kind it is, you said, waving your arms about in a pure show of panic, is just a random label given by people who need to categorize things, people are far too hung up on categorization, the point about this is that it can't be categorized, it's the most beautiful tree I've ever seen, that's all I know and all I need to know, I don't need to give it a name, that's the whole point, you said, don't you see?

No, I say, sitting calm and reasonable in front of the wreckage of our room. Listen, what I mean is. Some trees can be kept inside and others can't. It'd stunt them. They would die. And it sounds to me from your description and everything, though I haven't seen it myself as you know, but it does sound to me as if your tree is too big for the inside of a house already.

I know, you say. You drop the screwdriver on the un-damaged bit of floor at our feet and you lean into me, miserable. I can sense triumph. You are warm under my arm. I shake my head. I keep my sad face on as if I understand.

And probably its roots are too settled now to move it without doing damage, I say.

I know, you say, defeated. I was wondering about that.

And anyway, I go on, but gently, because I know the effect it will have. The thing about your tree is, it belongs to someone else. It's not your tree to take. Is it?

Probably I shouldn't have said that, though it was worth it to find myself holding you so close later that night, a night you didn't leave me, weren't cold and wooden to me. Certainly it is one of the reasons I have to go and fetch you out of the police station the next day where you are being questioned about wilful damage to someone else's property. I've done nothing wrong, you keep telling me all the way home. You say it over and over, and you tell me it's what you repeatedly told the man recording you saying it in the interview room. I notice that you want to go the long way home, that you're keen not to take the shortcut. Once I've settled you in the house, up in the dangerous loft again with a cup of tea I've made you, I sneak out. I head for the streets you didn't want us to walk down. At first nothing is out of place. Then outside a house on a well-to-do street I know I've found it when I look down and see that someone has written, quite large, on the pavement in bright green paint, the words: PROPERTY IS THEFT.

There is a tree in the garden. I look hard at it. But it is just a tree; it's nothing more than a tree, it looks like any old tree, with its early-evening mayflies hovering near it in the shafts of low sun, its leaves pinched and new and the grass beneath it patchy and shadowed. I can feel myself getting angry. I try to think of other things. I tell myself that the correct term for mayflies is ephemeroptera; I remember from university, though I can't think why or how I ever learned such a fact, especially I can't think why I would have retained it until now. There they are regardless, whatever they're called, annoyingly in the air. For an instant I hate them. I fantasize about spraying them all with something that would get rid of them. I think about taking an axe to the tree. I think about the teeth of saws and of the sawdust the different kinds of wood behind its bark would make.

I wonder if an anonymous letter to the person who owns this house about its dangers to the foundations (though it is nowhere near the foundations) might make him or her consider removing it. Dear Sir, I imagine myself typing, before I shake my head at myself and turn to go and as I do I see the words again on the pavement. The way they're scrawled, how fast and sloping and green their letters are,

386

reminds me of you when we first knew each other, when we were still not far past adolescence ourselves, still knew we'd alter the world.

A woman comes out of the front door of the house. She clearly wants me to stop laughing outside her house. She shouts at me to go away. She says if I don't she'll call the police.

I go home. You're up in the loft. I worry about you up there. It has no floor and you're balancing, passionate, on nothing but thin wood. I imagine you seeing the tree through the thick circles of magnifying glass in the binoculars I used to play with when I was a child; inside your head the tree is close-up, silent, there but untouchable, moving, like super-8 film. I know you; you never compromise; there's no point in calling you down. But you've left me some Greek salad on a plate covered by another plate in the kitchen, a fork neatly beside it. I sit on the couch in front of the dug-up laminate and while I'm eating I remember the story about the old couple who are turned into two trees; they let the strangers who knock at the door into their house then find that the gods have visited, and their favour is granted them. I search around in the books until I find the book, but I can't find the story about the old couple in it. I find the one about the grieving youth who becomes a tree, and the jealous girl who inadvertently causes the death of her rival and is turned into a shrub, and the boy who plays such beautiful music in the open air that the trees and bushes pick their roots up and move closer, making a shady place for him to play, and the god who falls in love with the girl who doesn't want him, who's happy without him, and who, when he chases her, is an exceptionally fast runner, being such a good huntress, that she almost outruns him. But since he's a god and she's a mortal she can't, and as soon as she knows her strength is waning and he's going to catch her up and have her, she prays to her father, the river, to help her. He helps her by turning her into a tree. All of a sudden her feet take root. Her stomach hardens into bark. Her mouth seals up and her face mosses over; her eyes seal shut behind lichen. Her arms above her head grow shoots and hundreds of leaves spring out of each finger.

I fold down the page at this story. I get some work things ready for tomorrow and call you, tell you as usual that I'm off to bed, that if you don't come now so I can put the lights out and get some sleep I'm going to leave you.

When we're in bed I hand you the book, open at the story. You read it. You look pleased. You read it again, leaning over me to catch the light. I read my favourite bit over your shoulder, the bit about the shining loveliness of the tree, and the god, powerless, adorning himself with its branches. You fold the page down again, close the book and put it on the bedside cabinet. I switch the light off.

As soon as you think I'm asleep, when I'm breathing regularly to let you believe I am, you get up. After I hear the gentle shutting of the door, I slide myself out of bed and into my clothes and I go downstairs and out the back door too. This first night I wish I'd pulled on a thicker jacket; in future I will know to.

When I get to the house with the tree I see you there in the dark under it. You are lying on your back on the ground. You look like you're asleep.

I lie down next to you under the tree.

ACKNOWLEDGMENTS

MARGARET ATWOOD: 'Bluebeard's Egg' from *Bluebeard's Egg and Other Stories* by Margaret Atwood. Copyright © 1983, 1986 by O. W. Toad, Ltd. Reprinted by permission of Houghton Mifflin Harcourt Publishing Company. All rights reserved.

'Bluebeard's Egg' from *Bluebeard's Egg* by Margaret Atwood, published by Jonathan Cape. Reprinted by permission of The Random House Group Ltd.

ELIZABETH BOWEN: 'Dead Mabelle' from *The Collected Stories of Elizabeth Bowen* by Elizabeth Bowen, copyright © 1981 by Curtis Brown Limited, Literary Executors of the Estate of Elizabeth Bowen. Used by permission of Alfred A. Knopf, a division of Random House, Inc.

'Dead Mabelle' by Elizabeth Bowen. Reproduced with permission of Curtis Brown Group Limited, London, on behalf of the Estate of Elizabeth Bowen. Copyright © Elizabeth Bowen 1929.

T. C. BOYLE: 'Swept Away' from *Tooth and Claw* by T. Coraghessan Boyle, copyright © 2005 by T. Coraghessan Boyle. Used by permission of Viking Penguin, a division of Penguin Group (USA) Inc.

'Swept Away' from *Tooth and Claw* by T. Coraghessan Boyle, Copyright © 2004 by T. Coraghessan Boyle, is reproduced by permission of Sheil Land Associates.

ITALO CALVINO: 'Blood Sea' from *T Zero* by Italo Calvino, copyright © 1967 by Giulio Einaudi Editore, s.p.a., English